INTERSECTING DESTINIES

A Novel of Mystery, Romance, and Resolution

Linda Edmister

ISBN 979-8-9863138-6-3 (Paperback)
ISBN 979-8-9863138-7-0 (Digital)

where fiction meets fun and faith

www.misteredbooks.com

Books in the *Intersections* Series
Intersecting Lives
Intersecting Dreams
Intersecting Beliefs
Intersecting Destinies

Author's Note:

The final volume of this book series finds our characters facing life-changing decisions brought about by the upheaval and uncertainty of our modern, fallen world. Substantial cross-cultural differences highlight the challenge of maintaining spiritual convictions while offering friendship and compassion to our neighbors.

I trust no offense will be taken at the sparing use of very mild, colorful language in keeping with our equally colorful characters. The Scripture passages, which begin each chapter, are intended to be read as poetic pointers rather than taken contextually. All other passages relate to the storyline.

*For my children, Megan and Larry.
You continue to inspire me
with your wit, knowledge, and support.*

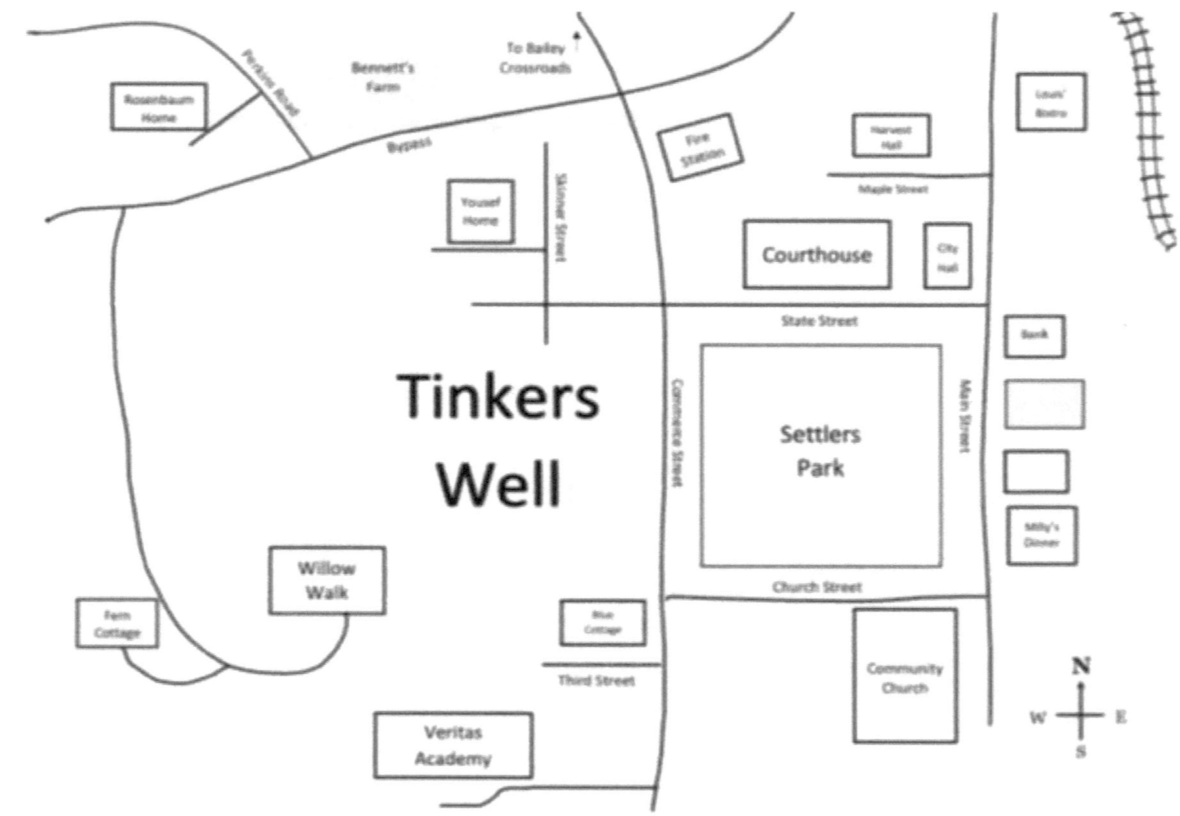
Tinkers Well
Perkins Road
Bennett's Farm
To Bailey Crossroads
Rosenbaum Home
Bypass
Fire Station
Harvest Hall
Louis' Bistro
Skinner Street
Yousef Home
Maple Street
Courthouse
City Hall
State Street
Bank
Settlers Park
Commerce Street
Main Street
Milly's Diner
Willow Walk
Church Street
Fern Cottage
Blue Cottage
Community Church
Third Street
Veritas Academy
N
W
E
S

PROLOGUE

Thus saith the Lord God: In that day projects shall enter into thy heart, and thou shalt conceive a mischievous design.

Ezekiel 38:10 (DRA)

Thousands of milling locals and tourists filled the *Nepomuk Terrasse* and the Philosopher's Walk and overflowed to line the banks of the Neckar, where the *Alte Brücke* spans the river in the heart of Old Town. Thunder from a passing summer storm could be heard still rumbling in the distance, and the occasional flash of heat lightning illuminated a dusky sky quickly succumbing to velvety darkness. Pale stars began to appear here and there, but their luster soon faded into insignificance when a collective expression of awe rose to greet the slow spread of eerie light from a well-stocked arsenal of flares. The wavering, red glow flooded the massive ruins of Heidelberg Castle, transforming the ancient stone into molten lava.

Held to commemorate the burning of the castle at the hands of Louis XIV in the late 17th century, the impressive spectacle was repeated each summer and never failed to grab the viewer's imagination, bringing history into stark relief in a way that dry textbooks never could. The visual senses eventually returned to something approaching normal as the glow died to an ember at the base of the brooding edifice. But those same senses, and their auditory partners, were assaulted once again, this time by millions of shimmering lights exploding in the night sky. As each dimmed and fell toward earth, they were followed by another round of fireworks bursting with brilliant color and light. Each barrage eclipsed the one before until wonder filled the hearts of all present, inviting them to step back effortlessly into childhood – all, save one.

An old man, stooped and infirm, made slow progress behind the mesmerized crowds, finally entering a *Wirtshaus* on the *Nepomuk*. Exposed half-timbered exterior construction was echoed inside where decorative plates and medals lined the interior walls. The colorful hardware provided evidence of years of *Volksmarsch* participation by the proprietor and the regulars of the *Stammtisch* crowd. Beer *Steine* from local breweries and those farther afield topped an oversized bar. The cozy ambience hardly registered with the man who seized on an empty table in a lonely corner. He sought a place of refuge in the small bar-restaurant anticipating the clamorous mobs who would surely demand sustenance following the sound and light show currently still in full swing outside. A shock of white hair framed a face whose formerly smooth black surface was pock-marked and lined with age. Tinted lenses hinted at a sensitivity to light – even in the dim recess of the corner.

"Guten Abend, mein Herr. Was möchten Sie trinken?" inquired a roving waiter.

"Hauswein, bitte." The answer came in a rich voice quite at odds with the overall weary essence of the speaker. At a soft level, it still hinted of strength and power.

"Rot oder weiss?"

"Rot, bitte. Danke sehr."

When presented with his order, the man threw a bill on the table and muttered *"Stimmt so."* The ring of his voice, though he continued to speak at a lowered level, struck an incongruent note when compared to his outward appearance.

He sat sipping the deep red liquid, enjoying the leisure of old age and the peace of languor. Occasionally, he lifted his head to study those who came rushing into the building as the last sounds of explosions faded away.

Young couples, boisterous groups of university students, retired couples on long-anticipated holidays all flocked in until the room was nearly filled to overflowing. Presently, a nondescript middle-aged gentleman wearing slacks and a casual sport coat approached the table occupied by the elderly man.

"Ist hier noch frei?" At the old man's affirmative nod, the newcomer claimed the only empty seat remaining in the bar. The practice of sharing a table with a perfect stranger was a common practice in Germany. Neither showed any signs of unease. The obliging waiter appeared once more and provided the gentleman with his requested *Bock Bier*, but in the act of collecting payment, he was jostled by a passing *Fräulein* on her way to greet friends. Metal serving tray and coins fell to the floor with a crash. Cursing under his breath while simultaneously apologizing for his clumsiness, the harassed young man squatted to recover the fallen objects. He bowed stiffly to the two men at the table and turned to be swallowed up by one of the large university groups nearby.

The men sat in silence until the din in the room grew to such proportions there was little chance of anyone listening to their conversation. It seemed unlikely that they would be able to hear each other! But when the older man eventually lifted his gaze from the dregs in his wine glass to look aimlessly around the room, he spoke in clarion tones, giving full scope to the subdued resonance that had only been implied earlier. The voice could be heard distinctly by his tablemate. So remarkable was its rich vocal timbre that it had been described over the years – mostly by women – as deeper than the throbbing depths of the ocean, and smoother than waves washing up on a pristine beach. The utterance of such accolades never occurred to the other man. He merely showed himself alert and ready to converse, albeit ostensibly as strangers.

"Guten Abend, Herr Richter."

"Nein, nein! Auf Englisch, bitte." The gentleman in the sport coat spoke with agitation and a pronounced German accent. "Despite being in the center of what is apparently the destination for every international tourist

in Europe at the moment, I feel safer steering clear of *Deutsch*. I am convinced that, even here, native speakers outnumber those of other tongues, and discretion is essential for the success of our plans. And even though I don't feel compelled to hide behind a silly disguise, as you do, I am in agreement that the exchange of information in person, while rather a dated technique, is perhaps the safer option now when computers can be hacked by school children and cell phones cloned at will." In a quarrelsome manner, he added, "Such intrusions make our jobs damnably difficult."

"As you say." The man of the white hair pulled a wry smile and bowed his head again, but he continued to speak in deep, lyrical tones that would have brought glory to any Wagnerian opera. "My contact has informed me that a convention will be held in Kansas City in the United States some time next summer. Those attending will be introduced to the latest in industrial security technology."

"Kansas City? I do not believe I am familiar with this city."

"Precisely. The generally prevailing belief amongst practitioners in the field is that, while able to boast of the amenities of a cosmopolitan metropolis, Kansas City can only do so on a reduced scale. Its relative obscurity is its greatest asset."

"I see." Taking a final swig of his beer, the other man wiped his mouth and sighed. "'Tis a pity, but so it must be, I suppose. I would have enjoyed an excuse to visit Las Vegas, or New York, or Los Angeles." Putting his disappointment aside, he asked, "But the jewels – they will be there. Yah? You are sure of this?"

"Jewels, Euros, gold. Oh yes, my friend. How better to sell a failsafe system than to test it with something of value at stake."

"And you are sure of your contact?" There was an edginess to the question.

"He is beyond reproach. I have been in this business long enough, I should know whom I can trust," the other replied rather sharply, then sat brooding for a few moments. "Despite enjoying a lifetime of risks and subsequent lavish rewards, I find that I grow weary of this game. This will be my final score, Richter, after which I shall retire to the islands – Caribbean, Polynesian, Greek – who knows, but I *will* live in style. This I have promised myself."

"But you haven't yet told me where specifically I am to meet you in this nondescript city of no importance. I will not be double-crossed, not at this juncture. I have plans of my own."

The clearing of the deep voice caused the table to vibrate. "Do not push me, *Herr* Richter. If you have no faith in 'honor among thieves,' we will never succeed." An address was passed between the two men on a crumpled piece of torn paper. "The hotel is scheduled for a grand opening in July. I will be present at the soft opening in June. I mean to thoroughly acquaint myself with the facility before the conference. I suggest you do the same, but we must have no open contact until the appointed time. Now, much as I have enjoyed this delightful interlude" he said, lowering his voice to a quiet rumble, "I think it best that we part company. You will, of course, leave first. An old man cannot move quickly."

He bowed his head lower until his chin rested on his chest. When he heard the other chair scrape back accompanied by a soft-spoken "*Tschüss,*" he waited five minutes and appeared to wake himself with a jerk. After making a show of rising with an effort, he shuffled to the door.

A busboy in jeans and t-shirt seemed to materialize out of nowhere. If he bore a marked resemblance to the waiter, the similarity went unnoticed. Wearing latex gloves, he picked up the wine glass and beer *Stein* at their bases and lowered each carefully into a greasy canvas bag slung across his upper body. Intentionally dropping a spoon on the floor, he bent down to pick it up with one hand, while reaching under the table with the other to remove a small device attached there. It followed the other objects into the bag, and, leaving a basin of dirty dishes on the table, the youth disappeared into the night.

Chapter 1

That is why a man leaves his father and mother and unites with his wife, and they become one family.

Genesis 2:24 (NET)

Nine months later – June 2022.

Weeds.

Weeds in her garden, weeds in her relationships, and weeds in her thoughts.

Rose Ludlow found herself pondering God's rationale in allowing the tiresome creepers to spoil *any* aspect of his beautiful creation, let alone allowing them to run amuck everywhere!

"But they probably only began to grow after the fall," she reasoned aloud and compared the parallel phenomenon in her own life. Everything was wonderful and solid as a rock one minute, and the next, illogically unsettled.

Reaching for her husband's pillow, she held it tightly and wished she could close her eyes and open them to find him, once more, lying next to her. But Tim wouldn't be home for two more days. A longer-than-usual annual training had taken army reserve Captain Ludlow overseas into a European theater of operations rife with unrest. Communication had been restricted to short calls or messages with limited content on Facepage. At least the occurrence of one or the other every few days let her know he was alive and well.

Thoughts of Tim brought with them a mixed bag of emotions. Rose looked over at his side of the bed and bade her fancy conjure up his intense blue eyes under a thatch of thick, blond hair. Her lips curled in response to his imaginary teasing smile, outlined by a sturdy jaw. She could almost hear the deep sound of his laughter as they enjoyed a shared moment of perfect harmony. Closing her eyes, she invited the sense of his strong embrace into her consciousness, but her eyes were jarred open when she rested her head on his broad, comforting shoulder, only to be greeted by the reality of its absence. Chastising herself for being a "pea brain" instead of a mature, married woman, Rose forced her mind to focus instead on the words she had spoken to Tim, assuring him of her own well-being. During those precious shared moments, she had sought to hide from him the inexplicable depression and worry that haunted her. Unbidden tears put her thoughts on hold, forcing her to pluck another tissue from the nightstand and wipe her eyes.

A visit to her grandmother earlier that day had left her feeling even more unsure of herself. Granny Gert, who was spending the summer with her college friend, Aletha Mason, was usually a reliable source of comfort and practical advice for Rose. Advice she had provided in spades on that occasion, though whether Rose found it comforting was debatable.

Gert's robust voice, like her short, squat frame, was substantial and not easily ignored. Snorting through her beak-like nose, she had regarded her granddaughter with affectionate mockery.

"Now, Rosie, you know how you can make a mountain out of a molehill with your wild imagination. It's probably just a bad case of PMS, what with missing Tim and all. Is it time for your monthly visitor?" Her grandmother's quaint euphemism usually made Rose smile, but even Granny Gert's old-fashioned words failed to pierce her enforced gloom that day.

"Who knows? You remember how irregular my cycles are. I had a weird, really short one about a month ago. But since they can be anywhere from five to seven weeks apart, I can hardly blame that."

Rose sighed and dabbed her eyes while her grandmother patted her tumbled curls. Granny Gert's eyes narrowed speculatively, and she asked in a curiously casual way, "You haven't been feeling poorly lately, have you? Maybe a little... tummy trouble?"

Aletha, Tim's grandmother, and someone Rose had come to treasure for her own soft-spoken wisdom and kindness, didn't miss much, despite her blindness. She perked up at the question but said nothing, choosing to follow the conversation with her ears. Though still a clear, china blue, her eyes had failed her years before.

Like Gert, Aletha's stature was diminutive, though it was fragile rather than sturdy and her porcelain-like features delicate instead of hawkish. While her soft, white hair might be described as fluffy, Gert's looked as if it had suffered the effects of electrocution. The mismatched pair couldn't have appeared more dissimilar – or been more devoted to one another's interests, which, in this instance, ran parallel. Smiling in silent appreciation of her friend's expert interrogation technique, Aletha remained unusually reticent for the rest of the visit.

"Well, maybe a little... in the mornings," Rose replied. She sat quietly contemplating the question, then looked up suddenly with a worried frown. "Do you think it's something serious? Maybe I have an ulcer!" Not content with one dramatic self-diagnosis, she added, "Or cancer!" Looking into a dismal future, she failed to see Granny Gert shake her head in exasperation. "Oh, why did Tim have to be gone now when I need him so much? What am I going to do?" Rose wailed and began a fresh bout of tears.

"Oh, for heaven's sake, young lady! You can start by drying your eyes and stop acting like a goose! Cancer, indeed! I expect you're just a little out of sorts. And I don't know why you're asking me instead of your sister, the midwife. Maybe Violet can diagnose what ails you over the phone. I'm not the one wearing a stethoscope!"

Embarrassed by what she was finally forced to recognize as overreaction, Rose replied, a little shamefaced, "I may be a goose, but I won't ruin everyone's excitement over Lily's announcement just because my imagination is working overtime again. Violet is already planning to deliver Lily's baby in early December, and Mother and Daddy are thrilled with the prospect of a second grandchild." She sighed deeply and added, "I won't have them worrying over my silly troubles."

All Granny Gert would say was, "You just take yourself to that clinic tomorrow morning, and I'm sure everything will be sorted out." With that limited encouragement, Rose soon took her leave. The instant she was out of sight, Gert patted Aletha's hand.

Aletha responded with a knowing smile, "Won't Tim be surprised when he gets home!" Her helper dog – a golden retriever named Scout – contributed a decisive bark, providing a fitting final word on the subject.

Rose had then spent the afternoon listlessly pulling early weeds from her otherwise immaculate planting beds. While she plied the soil with her spade, she replayed the conversation in her mind and drew little reassurance from it. Mental weeds seemed to infest her bleak reflections for the rest of the day.

Now, lying alone in the darkness, she spoke aloud as if to fill the emptiness of the room. "Granny Gert is disgusted with me, Aletha will hardly speak to me, and I'm probably dying. Maybe I'll feel better when the doctor confirms the worst." On that lowering thought, Rose rolled over and willed herself to sleep.

The next morning, having successfully secured a same-day appointment, Rose parked in front of the new outpatient clinic recently opened in Tinkers Well. With heavy footsteps, she approached the front door, wishing Tim could have been there to hold her hand and support her shrinking spirits; his solid physical and spiritual strength never failed to bolster hers.

An hour later, a very different Rose almost skipped to her car. Her face glowed with such joy that the absence of makeup was barely noticeable. She was actually glad that Tim wasn't due home until the following day. His prolonged absence would allow her to prepare a very special welcome – one that he would not soon forget!

After returning his weapon to the company arms room and ensuring that all his troops had rides home, Tim Ludlow headed for Tinkers Well on autopilot. Rose was emitting a homing signal with all the force of a 200-foot transmitting tower. Though the two had only been married seven months, she had become his rock, his shelter in the storm. And storm clouds were building to such heights around him, he desperately needed to hear her wise counsel and tender words of assurance. The fact that the need to unburden his heart claimed precedence in his thoughts over the fulfillment of more obvious desires, spoke of the strain Tim had been living under for some time. While only encountering a watered-down version of concerning protocol trends during his regular two-day reserve training cycles, he had been able to mentally compartmentalize them. But after three weeks of living with the implementation of these policies in real time, and witnessing their demoralizing repercussions, he could no longer ignore them or trust in a positive outcome through wishful thinking. Unfortunately, the effects of cultural upheaval were not restricted to his military service. The passage of harmful federal legislation threatened his very livelihood, as well.

Though he and Rose both wanted children, he had been content to claim all his wife's attention and love in the relatively short time they had been married. Now, for the first time since their wedding, he felt genuinely thankful that they had no kids on the way; this was not the time. It was difficult enough to contemplate a future in which he had only himself and Rose to provide for. The thought of bringing another innocent life into the turbulence and uncertainty of the next few years added substantial weight to his worries. Seeking solace, he focused once more on Rose. Although, in recent months, she had often changed the subject when he had attempted to open discussions on troubling topics, his need of her presence blinded him to those memories. Instead, he thought only of the wise counsel she had given him on other occasions. He convinced himself that she would know what to say. She would diffuse his worry and gently remind him to have a little faith. Tim's foot fell with increased purpose on the accelerator as he sped west toward home and Rose and their island of serenity.

Rose had indeed outdone herself. *Willow Walk*, the whimsical name she had bestowed on the Ludlows' beautifully restored Victorian home, gleamed from floor to ceiling. Fresh-cut flowers brought summer indoors; a tantalizing aroma pervaded the large farmhouse kitchen; and freshly aired sheets adorned the bed in their third-floor retreat. A long, sustained honk on the horn heralded Tim's arrival and beckoned Rose outside to greet him.

When Tim, still clad in ACUs[1], stepped from his truck, all thoughts of her big news were momentarily set aside. Rose saw only her beloved husband who had come home to her. Though difficult to say when the title "honeymooner" expires, for that brief shining moment Rose felt like a bride again. Tim held out his arms and she ran into them as if pulled by the irresistible force of a powerful magnet. Without saying a word, they clung to one another, savoring the knowledge that each had reached safe harbor.

Tim pulled away first to revel in his wife's beauty. Though lacking in inches, her compact form curved in all the right places and stood up to his six feet, two inches quite nicely. Soft, round eyes glowed with happiness, and shining auburn curls framed a smile that fascinated, teased, and enticed him all at the same time. Tim answered its invitation with a kiss that left them both a little breathless and desirous of a more substantial greeting later.

It said much for her powers of restraint that Rose chatted only of everyday nothings while Tim unloaded his gear in the garage before turning toward the house. After digging out a bulging canvas bag from an

---

[1] ACU – Army Combat Uniform

overstuffed duffel bag, he donned his backpack and held out the smaller bag to his wife. "I brought you something – my dirty laundry." With a laugh, she reached for it, but Tim insisted on carrying it for her. "It's the least I can do."

"The absolute *very* least," Rose said, and waited for his laughing concession. Instead, his grin faded, and a frown gathered between his eyes.

"Rose, there are some things I'd like to talk to you about… after dinner… things that have been on my mind for several months." Earlier in the year, he had unintentionally left Rose out of the discussion of a new business venture that involved their home. Her understandable hurt and resentment had left him disgusted with himself and resolved never to make that mistake again. She might have shown unwillingness to enter conversations aimed at introducing unsavory topics during the interim, but he still put his faith in her.

Recalling her own recent, misplaced fears, she let anxiety momentarily override her happiness and asked in some concern, "Tim, are you okay? Is something wrong?"

Not wanting to cause her needless worry on what should be an evening of celebration, Tim decided that such discussions would be better postponed for a few days and replied quickly, "No, no, of course not. There are just a few ideas I need to run by you." Goaded by her continued fearful expression, he added, "I feel great…truly – especially now that I'm home. What, don't I look like the perfect male specimen?"

After surveying him critically from head to toe, Rose leaned closer to sniff strategically. "You look – and smell – like you haven't bathed in a while," she said, effectively breaking down any restraint between them. Once inside, she took charge of the laundry and shooed Tim off to shower while she completed dinner. She wanted everything to be perfect.

The old farm table, an homage to the past in an otherwise fully modernized kitchen, had been transformed into an elegant dining surface covered in lace and fine china. A simple vase of baby's breath served as both a centerpiece and a stand for the menu Rose had printed that afternoon. Taking his place at the head of the table, Tim remarked that he was underdressed for the occasion, though he appeared more himself in cargo shorts and a polo shirt.

"Everything looks great, honey, but you didn't have to do all this for me. I'd have been happy with a burger and fries on a paper plate."

"Not for my conquering hero!" Rose said. She missed his fleeting frown while she took her seat on his right. "Will you ask the blessing?"

Tim looked down at his empty plate. "What exactly am I asking a blessing for?" It was the opening she had been waiting for. Handing him the menu, she asked him to read it out loud. Eyeing her with open curiosity, he obeyed. "Let's see. For appetizers we have *BLT Egglets* and *Piglets in a Blanket.*" A quick glance at her innocent expression, where a smile hovered despite her best efforts to conceal it, inspired him to continue somewhat suspiciously. "Okay… though I have no idea what an egglet is." Looking again at the menu, he took up where he had left off. "Then we'll have…hot dog! – *Baby Back Ribs!*"

Rose finally let her smile shine and insisted he go on.

"That's good enough for me! But apparently, we will also be enjoying *Tater Tots, Glazed Baby Carrots,* and *Baby Peas with Pearl Onions.*" A little confused, Tim looked again at Rose, who couldn't have hidden her glow with a black bag pulled over her head. "I don't get it. Did the grocery store run out of full-sized food while I was gone?"

"Keep reading."

"And for dessert, *Petite Baby Ruth® Cupcakes.*" Even more puzzled, Tim looked at Rose for illumination. Without a word, she handed him a gift bag. Slowly, with a growing sense of unease, he reached in to pull out a miniature football, then a small wooden workbench (complete with a tiny hammer), and finally an individually wrapped box. Tim took his time unwrapping it; he needed that time to compose his thoughts and his expression. This was the last thing he was prepared for, but he would not disappoint Rose – never again! Gingerly lifting the lid, he spied a pair of baby sneakers.

Forcing himself to smile, he asked hesitantly, "Are you telling me…?"

Rose jumped to her feet and began joyously spinning around in circles, declaring, "We're having a baby! We're having a baby! Wee!"

When she collapsed in a dizzy, deliriously happy heap in his lap, Tim buried his head against her shoulder. He resolved not to let her see the struggle of competing emotions fighting for supremacy in his spirit: wonder and dread, certainty and insecurity, joy and fear. It was legitimate shock that won in the end; he just sat there in bewilderment.

"Were we expecting this?" he asked in a dazed voice.

"Well, we weren't *not* expecting it. We did agree to trust in God's timing and let nature take its course. Remember?"

Looking into her tender, teasing eyes, he asked, "But how did it happen *so soon?*"

Rose giggled and leaned her forehead against his. "If you have to ask that question, big man, you haven't been paying attention."

"Fair enough," Tim replied with a sheepish grin.

The perpetual glow that illuminated Rose from the inside out was momentarily damped when her face clouded over. "You are happy about the baby, aren't you, sweetheart?"

How does a man tell the woman he loves above all else that he can be happy about the prospect of imminent parenthood and apprehensive at the same time? Tim settled on an evasive response. "Of course, I'm happy, but if I'm going to be a father, I'll need sustenance to keep up my strength." He helped Rose to her feet, then lightly swatted her bottom. "Now, how about some of that 'baby' food, woman?" Worry melted into a saucy smile as she sashayed to the stove.

Dinner was the success Rose had hoped it would be. If she did most of the talking, she didn't notice; she was too engrossed in nursery plans, and in speculation as to whether they would have a boy or a girl. Adding urgency to surprise, Rose disclosed that, owing to her misinterpretation of pregnancy symptoms, the baby would join them sometime in December. "We'll have a better pinpoint due date after my ultrasound on Monday." Receiving Tim's assurance that he would accompany her for that all-important appointment, she sat for a while in rapt contemplation of a glowing future.

Though Tim may have digested her words with more effort than her delicious cooking, he schooled his features to reflect contentment. When Rose disclosed her foolish fears over her unexplained, tumultuous emotions, he momentarily wondered if she could sense his own inner turmoil; she knew him so well. But his fears on that score were apparently misplaced. Finally sorting out the delightful source of her hormonal mood swings, her emotions seemed to have swung to the top and nested there. Tim had never known Rose to look more radiant. Swept along on the wave of her infectious joy, his contentment became real.

Hours later, when the moon had taken prominent residence in the night sky, and stars twinkled through the skylight over their bed, Tim absently stroked Rose's silken curls. Her head lay on his chest, her breath warm on his skin. The shallow, even breathing helped settle him, though sleep would not come. In its place, the concerns and worry that had been held at bay by the euphoria of their ultimate reunion slowly crept back into his psyche.

Tim was no coward. While both his physical and moral courage were unquestioned, he now faced a different kind of enemy – one with infinitely more scope and power. A clash of light versus darkness, truth versus delusion, and good versus evil had invaded the American and world cultures to such an extent that his own government had fallen prey to its insidious advance. Tim shuddered when he contemplated the outcome. Soon, he must discuss his concerns with Rose, because there were decisions to be made that would affect them both, and now, a growing family as well.

If only I didn't have to burden her with this right now, he thought. *If only I could bounce this off someone else first.*

Suddenly, Tim knew what he desperately needed – his dad's advice. But Peter Ludlow had been gone for over two years. Tim could no longer go to him for wise council or ask him to bring common-sense clarity to any situation. Peter's guiding hand had seen Tim through many youthful follies and challenges and had set him on a course to success with his steadfast love and support. His death had left a profound void in Tim's life. But just as the younger Ludlow had come to grips with that tragedy through the help of friends and a new work focus, Tim's biological father had burst onto the scene, on the heels of a tornado, and sent his world spinning once more off its axis. This time, it was Rose who gently encouraged and steadied Tim, urging him to give Timothy Miles Hawthorne a chance.

Navigating the treacherous path between mistrust and forgiveness had ultimately ended in success. Father and son began a tenuous relationship that gradually evolved into friendship. Much as Tim had loved and respected Peter Ludlow, it was his newfound connection with Miles that helped him better understand his own natural strengths and innate giftings. Friendship and comradery had grown into trust and sincere affection. Tim had never actually put the thought into words, but in the quiet of the moment, when his heart sought comfort and guidance, he came face to face with the reality that he loved his father, his real father – the man who had shaped him from conception without any knowledge of his existence. Tim found the notion oddly disquieting, as if caring for Miles somehow diminished his deep attachment to Peter. Despite knowing such reasoning to be irrational, Tim felt inexplicably torn, as if this season of uncertainty demanded that all happiness be tempered with doubt.

Tim was not the only Ludlow Miles had reconnected with. Marilyn Hawthorne Ludlow, Tim's mother, had also been on a journey of emotional discovery. That journey would ultimately lead his parents, once more, to the altar. Their engagement party, slated for the following day, fell, ironically, on the same weekend as Father's Day.

With everything coming at him at once, Tim wondered if God was testing him for some reason. *How will I get through this? Am I strong enough and wise enough to make the right decisions – to be a good husband, a good father? Will I know if I'm following God's will?* Anxiety began to smother him in the darkness, and his breathing became more labored. Without any cognitive awareness of his response, Tim's hold on Rose tightened until she stirred in his arms and pulled away to lean on her forearm. Reaching out with her other hand, she tousled his hair.

"I guess you really did miss me," she teased. "Did I not convince you that I missed you too?" She had, of course – thoroughly. "If you need more evidence, I think I might be able to dig some up – if the verdict is still out, that is."

It was an offer Tim had no intention of refusing, though her generosity brought him far more than passing pleasure. It reminded him that no matter what the future might hold, they would face it together. Whether he was worthy of the gift or not, God had blessed him with Rose. With her at his side, Tim could take on an army of demons.

CHAPTER 2

Gather yourselves together, yea, gather together...

Zephaniah 2:1a (ASV)

Roused by sunlight peering through the overhead skylight, Tim rubbed his eyes and opened them to see his wife lying on her side watching him. With a tender smile of greeting on her lips, Rose said playfully, "Good morning... Daddy."

A phrase from an ancient psalm floated through his sluggish brain. "*...joy comes in the morning.*" The pressures and concerns that had been building in intensity for the past several months were no less pressing or impactful, but the doubts and fears of the night had flown. Tim returned a slow smile. "Good morning... Mommy," he replied, and gathered Rose in his arms. Three hours later, he awoke again to find her gone, and a note pinned to her pillow.

"I know you're a little jet-lagged, so I left you to catch up on your sleep. But we can't spend *all* day in bed!"

Though Tim might have argued the point, his stomach was growling loud enough to overrule any other consideration. A substantial breakfast, which Rose had kept warm until nearly lunchtime, fueled them for a quick tour of projects under contract with his building renovation business. The late start, however, also made them late for his parents' engagement party that afternoon. They arrived at the designated destination – a gleaming new hotel in Kansas City – shortly after 2:00.

The *Prairie Gateway*, a soaring twelve-story structure near the heart of the metropolitan area, stood as a shining testament to modern architectural innovation and style. Built by Miles' former business associate – a fellow developer from New York City – the hotel offered both sumptuous accommodation and easy access to nearby points of interest. Its expansive, split lobby provided intimate guest registration, while allowing for gracious formal entertaining in the adjacent open area. Lit by sunlight filtered through 50 feet of glass, the hall looked out on a small green space next to the building. Trailing vines and tropical plants added a splash of color to a soothing water wall cascading over a sheet of stone between sizeable bi-level planters on an interior wall opposite the windows.

Because Miles had provided the out-of-state builder with some crucial insider information on local codes and resources, the hotel's grateful owner had offered Miles' use of the *Plains Oasis Room* for any occasion of his choosing. Miles, with Marilyn's blessing, chose it for their engagement party. The soft opening, a week earlier, broke the ice for the new facility and ensured any bugs were worked out before the Hawthorne/Ludlow gathering.

On the lookout for his son and daughter-in-law, Miles only granted the young couple time to deposit their gift bag on a nearby sideboard before steering them toward their seats at the head table. A reunion of sorts followed as Tim's closest friends greeted him with handshakes and derisive comments regarding his tardy appearance.

"You got home yesterday – *yesterday* – and you *still* couldn't get enough of that marital bliss stuff to make it here on time," Derek Warner pointed out. "You'd better not be late for *my* engagement party," he added and crossed his muscular arms with customary attitude. A sly wink led slowly to a wide grin that split his smooth, dark face from side to side. Rose kissed his cheek soundly and promised they would never miss a minute of such an important event.

"Rose, you are definitely his better half," Derek said, nodding his head at Tim, who grinned in agreement.

"Though the possibility seems extremely unlikely, I will ask the obvious question. Have you then succeeded in securing a fiancée during the three weeks of Tim's deployment?" Abraham Yousef inquired with interest. His bride, Amy, couldn't help laughing as the two combatants squared off once more in what had been a running, verbal fencing match for the past two years. Towering above his much shorter friend, Abe maintained his perpetual manner of polite deference while daring Derek to answer him.

"For your information, Slim, Miss America is bound to slide into my orbit any day now," Derek replied smartly, executing a smooth, fluid motion. "So, keep your calendar open. That's all I'm saying."

Any calculated response was forestalled when Amy took Abe's arm and propelled him to their seats. The Yousefs, both tall and slim, made a striking couple. She never tired of admiring his arresting profile with its angled bone structure, prominent nose, and hooded eyes. Neatly cropped black hair and a goatee softened the edges of his face and gave him an air of distinction. A coaxing smile from Amy's generous mouth accompanied by a melting look from her wide, expressive eyes, successfully recaptured her husband's attention. In an unthinking, intimate gesture, Abe brushed a stray strand of soft brown hair from her cheek and was again her slave.

Aiding Amy to maintain order, Angelica Warner told Derek to "keep all 'o that nonsense to yourself and save your boastin' for the day you've a right to it." Her warm Caribbean accent robbed the words of any sting, as did her indulgent contemplation of her only child. Fine facial features under a bright floral scarf, combined with rich mocha-colored skin, masked her age, which could have been judged at anything from 45 to 55. In truth, it was much closer to the latter, but her noble bearing and gently swaying carriage usually inspired skepticism in anyone considering such a notion. Order being restored, Miles, with Marilyn at his side, welcomed everyone and invited all present to continue to enjoy the *hors d' oeuvres* provided on high bar tables scattered throughout the large space. The engaged couple presently left their table to "work" the room. It was an occasion neither had dreamed of, and they wanted to express their gratitude to all who had come to share it with them.

The miracle of God's perfect timing brought Miles back into Marilyn's life 30-plus years after the couple divorced. At the time of their stormy separation, Miles had no knowledge of the unborn child he had fathered. It wasn't until the two former spouses met again under extraordinary circumstances that he learned of Tim's existence. Marilyn was then a widow and hesitant to allow Miles back into her life and her heart. She continued to catch glimpses of the ambitious, driven young husband she had called "Timothy." His redemption, however, ultimately proved to be genuine. Humility and forbearance now guided his ambition, presenting to her a vulnerability and selflessness she never thought to witness. His soul and his priorities had all been redeemed and renewed on a day fraught with life-changing revelations for everyone. It was nine months, however, before Marilyn found herself unable to withstand any longer the evidence of her eyes, the reasoning of her mind, and the urging of her heart. The ruthless, unfeeling Timothy she had divorced truly was a new man. His respectful, but relentless, pursuit of her love had culminated in their engagement on Easter Sunday, two months earlier.

Now middle-aged, with fine lines etched across each countenance, they, nonetheless, presented a picture of youthful exuberance fortified by the substance of maturity and life experience. Watching his father's face, Tim had a unique glimpse into his own future. The same prominent jawline and cleft chin still spoke of strength and determination, while the deep-set blue eyes gleamed with humor. Graying temples in otherwise dark hair were more pronounced than Tim might expect in the blond coloring he shared with his mother. Hers might be artificially enhanced now, but her innate poise and grace had grown with each passing year, and her dreamy, slightly downturned eyes still held the power to pierce Miles' soul.

The person most gratified by the present turn of events was Miles' mother, Aletha Mason. She and her old school chum, "Trudy" Gunn – known to all others as Rose's Granny Gert – remained at the table when everyone else went in search of the promised appetizers. Rose thoughtfully brought each lady a plate of savories, then joined Tim to greet other friends from church. The family matriarchs were perfectly content to enjoy the delicious fare while speculating as to whether Tim and Rose would make a special announcement that day or leave it for the next. It soon became apparent that it was to be saved for Father's Day, which was just as well, they decided. It was news best shared first in an intimate family setting. The milling crowds around them hardly qualified.

The event room, filled almost to capacity, easily facilitated the mingling of Miles' business contacts with a number of fellow teachers from Marilyn's school, in addition to members of their Community Church family. No one present knew everyone. In this intersection of such diverse lives, anyone might fit in and appear at home.

With their plates sufficiently loaded, the younger occupants of the head table returned to enjoy the spoils of their foraging. Between mouthfuls, the "old married couples" began to tease Derek with their favorite pastime: *"What will the future Mrs. Warner look like?"* Though Derek put on a lively show of indignation, as was expected, his blistering verbal reprisals and comical posturing had become such a part of his personality that he was able to continue his schtick while allowing his mind to wander. He contemplated the five friends gathered there and the circuitous route each had taken to come together at such a place and time.

Derek had called Chicago home all his life until joining the army after completing a bachelor's degree in physical education. He was never really attracted to the idea of teaching, but he *was* attracted to a discipline that focused on muscle development over mental development. Unfortunately, he failed to think through the process fully. Having spent his final semester doing student teaching at a city high school, he couldn't get away fast enough from the concept of wrangling undisciplined students for the rest of his life. One semester of that had felt like an eternity. For a brief period, Derek had considered following in his father's footsteps as a police officer, but he was still dealing with the residual effects of losing his father at just 16 when the elder Warner was killed in the line of duty. Instead, he decided to shake the dust of Chicago from his cross trainers and enlist in the army while he figured out his other options.

It was during a posting to Louisiana that Derek ran – literally – into an old acquaintance from his high school days in Chicago when the two had participated in area meetings of the Fellowship of Christian Athletes™. Tim Ludlow, then a newly promoted captain, had just arrived at Ft. Polk, and was checking out local churches. The old friends nearly collided as Tim was leaving the early service and Derek was arriving for the second. Never a fan of rising early if he didn't have to, Derek reasoned that God would be happy to see him whenever he showed up.

Because they had no official interaction, the difference in rank wasn't an issue, and they naturally reconnected. Both appreciated the opportunity to share their past, and their faith walk. It was Tim who had urged Derek to apply for Officer Candidate School, and Tim who had been there to cheer for his buddy following completion of an intense 12-week course. A cocky Second Lieutenant named Warner finally sported gold bars on the shoulder boards of his dress blue uniform, with an attitude to match.

After completing his basic leadership course, Derek believed that he had found his calling as a platoon leader. It was a unique job that recognized and rewarded his top physical condition and one, moreover, that simultaneously afforded him the opportunity to tell upwards of 40 people what to do. Some troops were almost as unruly as those students from his teaching days, but he was the boss. Derek even considered making the military a career. A final deployment to Afghanistan, however, changed his plans in ways he could never have foreseen. In the desolate reaches of a wildly uncivilized region loosely owing allegiance to a country where horses were often more highly prized for transportation than mechanized vehicles, Derek forged an unlikely bond with one of the soldiers in his platoon.

The friendship never would have been birthed in a regular garrison setting at a base in the States, but God used the singular location to work out his grand plan. Ordinarily, officers and enlisted soldiers in the same unit do not mix on a social level other than for official functions. But when all ranks live, work, and interact 24/7, there is a natural tendency to cross those hazy lines, especially during long hours of lonely observation at remote sites. Beyond being platoon leader and subordinate squad leader, First Lieutenant Derek Warner and Staff Sergeant Ahmad Yousef should never have become friends by all the modern social dictates that teach us to look for barriers between ourselves and others rather than commonalities.

Derek was an African American with the rich flavoring of Jamaica added on his mother's side. Staff Sergeant Yousef was Lebanese by birth. Derek was the only child of working-class parents and had grown up in a large Midwestern city. Ahmad Yousef's family members were all well-educated. His parents had immigrated to the United States when he was seven, with four children born in their native country and one added on American soil. Both young men had college degrees, but Ahmad had much the stronger intellect, which had allowed him to pursue a technically difficult academic discipline. Any of those socio-economic factors might have forced the two to maintain the distance dictated by their military ranks and positions, but it was their respective faiths that should have been the final sticking point. Derek was a deeply committed Christian, and Ahmad a devout follower of Islam. Ironically, it was that would-be insurmountable difference that ultimately brought them together.

Over the course of nearly a year in country, 1LT Warner and SSG Yousef shared their faiths. Because of Derek's respectful willingness to hear what Ahmad had to say about Islam, he was able to raise speculation and curiosity about Christianity in the other's mind. Ultimately, the young Muslim was led to a saving relationship with Jesus Christ. That glorious moment was followed almost immediately by a life-changing event that sent them in very different directions.

During a night patrol, the platoon took on heavy fire. SSG Yousef's left knee and tibia were shattered, another soldier was killed, and Derek began a tortuous journey of dealing with the ensuing guilt. That the guilt was self-imposed and underserved removed little from its weightiness. It led him out of the army at the same time Tim Ludlow was struggling with the recent loss of his own father. Reluctantly, Tim made the decision to join the ranks of the civilian population of a small town in Kansas where his widowed mother lived. Putting to use his expert carpentry skills, he started a one-man renovation business but quickly realized he needed another set of hands, even if they were unskilled. Having kept up with Derek through social media, Tim knew his friend could use some help, too. Thankful for Tim's timely intervention, Derek had accepted the hand of mercy, packed up his mother and all their earthly belongings, and moved to Kansas. Within a few months, the plight of Ahmad Yousef came to Derek's attention on Facepage. The combat amputee had been cut off from his family because of his rejection of Islam, so Tim and Derek offered the new believer a home and a place in their business, though Tim had never actually met the man. Two friends became three, and *Three Brother's Construction, Inc.* was born.

Reflecting on all that had passed in seemingly impossible ways, Derek shook his head at the miracle of those five people sharing the celebration of a couple none of them had even been aware of a few years earlier. He felt humbled by the blessings of a Divine Providence who had brought them all together – brought them together and caused them to flourish. The renovation business had become so successful that they had taken on four more crew members, all veterans like themselves.

"Ahmad" became "Abraham" to honor the true story of that patriarch's son of promise. Abe was always ready and eager to explain it was through Isaac, and not Ishmael, that God had brought about his plan of salvation for mankind by the birth, death, and resurrection of Isaac's descendant, Jesus, the Jewish Messiah who was both fully man *and* wholly God.

Rose's infectious laughter momentarily penetrated Derek's reflections, causing him to shift his attention to consideration of the other additions to Three Brothers – two sisters.

Tim had been bowled over by the petite, kind-hearted Rose Thompson when she came to Kansas the year before in the company of her spirited grandmother. Refreshingly pretty, rather than classically beautiful, Rose's natural openness and lively imagination lent a whimsical loveliness to her features that drew Tim like a bee to honey. The couple had had a rough start, marked by misadventure and a few emotional stumbles. But thanks to Tim's buddies, and everyone else in Tinkers Well who believed the two belonged together, they were now seasoned spouses.

Amy Walker was the only native Kansan of the five, but she was also a recent transplant to Tinkers Well. At about the time Abe joined Three Brothers, Amy took a job in Tinkers Well as a music teacher at the local middle school. The two had met routinely at church social events but both had been too insecure to approach the other despite a mutual attraction. Fate intervened in the form of Rose Thompson's visit to Kansas. She and Amy struck up an immediate friendship, and with Derek's help, Rose conspired to get the hesitant lovebirds together. A thoroughly gratifying success was followed two months later by devastating disappointment. Abe had been called home when his distant father offered the olive branch of reconciliation.

Not knowing what the future would hold, but wanting to respect his father's gesture, Abe had taken heartbreaking leave of Amy with no prospect of ever seeing her again. An unforeseen opportunity to lead a newfound Muslim friend to faith in Jesus, followed by a heated final exchange between father and son, found Abe back in Tinkers Well. Wondering if Amy would ever speak to him again, let alone forgive him and allow him a second chance, Abe humbly approached her on the eve of the Thompson/Ludlow wedding. Their verbal exchange had also been heated, but with a far more satisfactory outcome. The rehearsal dinner, intended to celebrate the impending marriage of Tim and Rose, had also signaled a new beginning for Abraham and Amy, who now had almost three months of marriage under their belts.

Derek loved, respected, and teased Rose and Amy like sisters even as he saw how their advent had changed the dynamic between the three men. They could no longer be the three lone musketeers as they had been. The loyalties and responsibilities of the other two had broadened in scope and shifted in focus, and Derek wouldn't have had it any other way. But it's not easy to be the odd man out. Though he appreciated the knowledge that he would always be welcome in their homes and in their lives, Derek had accepted the reality that things would never be quite the same.

His musings were again interrupted when he caught Abe making a derogatory prediction.

"While I am sure she will be a paragon of virtue, I feel certain that Derek's soulmate must have some flaw – perhaps a spitting gap in her teeth."

Patent indignation of Abe's comment instantly replaced Derek's expression of patient longsuffering.

"*Spitting gap?* For your information, my man, the future Mrs. Warner will be one fine woman. She'll have fine teeth, a fine figure, and most importantly, one *fine* husband. You can take that to the bank, suckers."

As he knew it would, Derek's comprehensive comeback set off a competition among the others to hit upon the mythical shortcomings of his equally mythical bride. He couldn't help laughing as each imperfection became more outrageous: a twitching eye, a unibrow, a high, squeaky voice, even a propensity to belch publicly. The would-be bridegroom answered with his own description of female perfection until four of them declared a truce in favor of tackling the *hors d'oeuvres* table again; Tim had business with his father.

When the young people departed, Angelica sat idly listening to the other conversations around her: Aletha remarking on the delectable food; Gert commenting on the impracticality of soaring three-story windows, wondering who on earth would clean them; Tim threatening to have Miles drawn and quartered if he failed to take good care of his mother; and Miles assuring Tim that the treasure of his life, his "Mari," would be treated like a queen.

While listening in quiet amusement to the nonsense shared by her son and his friends, Angelica had, nevertheless, been aware of a niggling tug at her subconscious. Though all five young people had returned to the table, she focused instead on the crowd milling about the spacious lobby, searching for any faces or voices that might have registered in her mind without any real recognition on her part. But she saw only those she already knew to be present.

What, then, is pullin' so insistently at my ear? she wondered.

Closing her eyes to block out any extraneous distractions, Angelica let her mind process the sounds around her. She heard the chink of empty glasses as they were cleared from random surfaces. She tuned in to the colorful strains of a woodwind quintet playing on a raised dais in one corner. She listened to the sounds of laughter, the garble of Abe trying to argue with Derek around a mouthful of shrimp puff, and someone regaling a group with tales of far-flung travel and adventure. Something about that voice, in particular, resonated with her. Angelica focused her ear more intently until a chance phrase caused her to sit bolt upright with her eyes suddenly opened wide in shock. She looked around wildly, attempting to pinpoint the source of the voice even as the thudding of her heart blotted out every sound but its own racing rhythm. While striving, unsuccessfully, to pin down the face she sought so frantically, Angelica tried to convince herself of the impossibility that such a long-buried memory had surfaced again in this unlikeliest of places.

When Miles stood to talk shop with a colleague, Marilyn glanced at Angelica sitting on her other side and became instantly alarmed. Her friend's face appeared as white as such a richly hued complexion could.

"Angelica, what on earth is the matter? You look like you've seen a ghost!"

Clinging to the reassuring pressure of Marilyn's fingers, she whispered, "He's here."

"*Who* is here?"

"I don't expect you to believe it. *I* don't believe it. But I would know that voice anywhere."

Still completely in the dark, Marilyn could only frown her incomprehension.

"Do you remember me tellin' you about my childhood friend, Sabryna?" Angelica waited while Marilyn searched her memory.

"Do you mean the young girl who got mixed up with a…a jewel thief, was it, when you were still living in Jamaica?" At Angelica's nod, Marilyn continued doubtfully, "But you can't mean…"

"Oh, but I do. Samuel Jamison[2] is *in this room!*"

---

[2] *Intersecting Lives*

CHAPTER 3

As is sometimes the case, a day of festive observance can inadvertently recall a tragedy. It wasn't that Tim resented the happiness shared by his parents as they reveled in Miles' first Father's Day together or that he begrudged them the joy they would surely share at the unexpected news of a grandchild arriving in the not-too-distant future. He was even prepared to endure with grace any subsequent teasing about forthcoming sleepless nights and dirty diapers. For Tim, though, the combined celebratory events also recalled the memory of the man who had raised him, and the pleasure denied Peter Ludlow of welcoming grandchildren to carry on his name. He and Marilyn had never been blessed with any children of their own. The word "bittersweet" came forcibly to mind when Tim considered the full import of the day. Knowing it was what Peter would have wanted, Tim deliberately favored the more positive end of that spectrum.

Little did Tim know that he was not alone in experiencing conflicting emotions. A first Father's Day carries great meaning for any dad, but when it occurs for a man in his mid-50s, the recognition bestowed upon him holds substantially more worth than any tribute paid to a king. More than 30 Father's Days had come and gone with Miles Hawthorne none the wiser of their significance in his life. In the present, observing those gathered to celebrate the event in his honor, he felt the same wave of humility that often washed over him when he considered the impossible gifts God had showered on him during the past year. Finally listening to the call of his Savior in a moment of complete brokenness, Miles had surrendered all the trappings of wealth and power that had hardened his heart and soul for so long. In exchange, he had found peace, divine purpose, and love. He was part of a family again.

Miles looked at his mother, so frail and aged, who, nonetheless, displayed the courage of giants and the kindness of angels; at his Mari, who gazed at him with pride and tenderness; and at his son, whose birth, and ultimate forgiveness and friendship, had made this day possible. Excitement and humility vied for honors within him. He intentionally chose to embrace the first emotion while fully cognizant of the second.

With the nucleus of the family settled comfortably in Marilyn's creatively eclectic living room, following the departure of the regular Sunday potluck brunch guests, the festivities had begun.

All the usual Father's Day offerings made an appearance. Tastefully colorful socks – which Miles had taken to wearing – two matching ties, and the cologne most appealing to Marilyn made up the bulk of gifts piled up around him. Aletha gave Miles a three-part frame, the first section displaying a photo of his father, James Hawthorne, holding him as a baby. The middle section framed an exultant Tim on his wedding day, with Miles standing next to him smiling proudly. The remaining panel was left empty.

"Now you have something to remind you of your legacy – where it started, how far it has come, and hopefully, where it is going. Bless you, Timothy," Aletha said with a catch in her voice. That was more than enough sentiment for Granny Gert, who presented Miles with a stout pair of work gloves.

"I reckon we're related now, somehow, and I expect Rosie or Marilyn will want to put you to work outside just when you're ready to take a nap or watch a ballgame on a Saturday afternoon."

With his lips twitching at the corners, Miles thanked her cordially, then turned to look at his son, whose face gave nothing away. But when he looked from Tim to Rose, his instinct told him to beware; Rose couldn't hide a broad grin, and she fairly bounced off the floor where she had been sitting next to Tim's chair. Pulling her husband to his feet, she handed him one of the gift bags she was holding and offered a brief explanation.

"I know this is Father's Day, but we decided," (meaning Rose had decided), "that you both deserve a special present today." Miles and Marilyn eyed the pair standing before them with speculative interest.

"Okay, open them, open them, open them!" Rose cried impatiently. Pulling out a t-shirt, Miles turned his to the front first and a smile of wonder spread across his face as he read the colorful words: "World's Greatest Grandpa." He jumped up to engulf his son in a comprehensive hug, then slapped him on the back before leaning over to salute Rose's blooming cheek.

Though father and son had both chosen uninhibited celebration over introspection that day, the words accompanying Miles' spontaneous reaction nearly derailed Tim's resolve. Caught off guard by the stunning announcement, Miles shook his head in disbelief and said, "I'm Peter all over again!" In his bemusement, he looked into a regrettable past and failed to see the grin freeze on Tim's face.

I can't believe Miles would dare to make such an outrageous comment. How could he possibly compare himself to Peter Ludlow! thought Tim, deeply wounded by the man he had come to respect and admire. His father's next words, however, dispelled any anger or resentment, turning them to shame. Miles spoke almost to himself.

"The apostle Peter denied Jesus three times out of fear and was left in despair and bitter regret. In my case, it was blind ambition and a hardened heart that caused me to forfeit three decades of fatherhood. But Jesus gave Peter a second chance that restored their relationship, just as he has given me a second chance – again." Looking once more at his son, he said, "I might not be able to give you any parenting advice, but maybe, after *you* figure it out, you can give me some tips on changing diapers." Tim laughed in relief, though he maintained some skepticism as to whether he would ever actually witness Miles Hawthorne perform such a menial task. He was gradually learning, however, not to underestimate the depth of his father's character. "I think I can speak for your mother," Miles said, turning to confirm Marilyn's smiling agreement, "you can call us any time you need a babysitter."

His words performed a twofold task. They assured the parents-to-be of reliable babysitting for future date nights and, unwittingly, freed Tim to love and honor each man who had been, and always would be, his father. In that moment, the load of care weighing on Tim seemed to, if not lift, at least to shift a little, allowing him to breathe a bit easier and to enjoy the rest of the day. This included listening to prophecies about the manifold perfections of their mutual great-grandchild by the only two present who showed no sign of surprise at the news. Granny Gert and Aletha only smiled and nodded their heads knowingly. Tim had long since stopped being astounded by anything they said or did.

"Letha, you'll probably say I'm imagining things, but there seemed to be something 'off' with Tim today."

The two old friends had been dropped off at *Fern Cottage*, Aletha Mason's quaint Victorian home, by the young Ludlows on their way to *Willow Walk*. The sun had already sailed past the top of the surrounding oak trees, and the gazebo at the back of the house was once again in shade. They sat there sipping cups of tea while indulging in their most cherished pursuit – other people's business. Scout snoozed at their feet, content to leave them to their devices.

"Well, you know I can't watch how people *appear*, but I'm a keen listener. Do you mean that he would often go from laughing one minute to quiet and reserved the next?"

"Exactly! Instead of giving Rosie a hard time over her fantastic plans for redecorating the entire house to suit the nursery and one tiny little baby, he just frowned or smiled half-heartedly."

"Yes, and when Timothy made that comment about being Peter again, I heard a quick intake of breath by Tim. I had the feeling that he misunderstood the reference at first and was angered by it – you know, thinking that Timothy was referring to Peter Ludlow, and that he had taken the poor man's place. Fortunately, everything was clarified quickly, and no harm done. I don't think Timothy even noticed the confused reaction."

Impressed once again by her old chum's powers of observation, Gert remarked, "You don't miss much, do you, Letha? There was that, yes. But also, later, Miles was asking Tim, in a joking sort of way, if he had any apprehension about fatherhood. Tim laughed off the question and started talking about sports, or fishing or something else." She paused for a few moments, frowning into her teacup. Always one to favor the direct approach, Gert asked abruptly, "You don't think Tim is having misgivings about this baby, do you?"

"Nonsense! I've known Tim his whole life, and I can't think of anyone better suited to being a husband and a father. There's surely no question about his love for Rose…"

"Course not! He's nutty on her – has been since day one. No, I'd say there's something else worrying him. The problem is that Rosie is so taken up with all things baby, she might not see the signs. Ever since she was a little girl, whenever she was keen on something, she thought about nothing else."

"Oh, dear. And Tim is just the sort of man to try to carry everything on his shoulders and not bother her with anything that might spoil her happiness. I'm afraid those two could be headed for a big fall."

Collecting their empty cups, Gert rose and directed Aletha to lead the way to the kitchen. "Then I reckon we'll have to intervene before they get themselves into a rare pickle. It's a good thing we're still around. If you'll hold the door, Letha, I'll just deposit these in the dishwasher," she said, eyeing the tea service resting on a tarnished silver tray. "Do you think you could fix us some microwave popcorn?"

"Oh, are we going to have a movie night?" Aletha asked with happy anticipation as she reached for the popcorn bags in a handy cabinet.

"What do you say to 'Father of the Bride?'"

After depositing a bag in the microwave, Aletha pushed the appropriate buttons, covered in Braille symbols, and suggested, "Perhaps the more appropriate choice would be 'Father's Little Dividend' – with Spencer Tracy, of course."

"That's the ticket! I'll go get the TV and DVD player set up while you finish that. Now remember, just leave the hot bag in a bowl. We can empty it when it cools a little," she added, ever mindful of respecting her friend's independence and capabilities, all the while wanting to protect her.

Popcorn and TV duly made ready, the pair sat down to an enjoyable evening that allowed them to escape the cares of the present and to delight in simpler times of days long passed.

Returning to *Willow Walk* later than anticipated, Tim was, nonetheless, determined to open a discussion with Rose over all that had been worrying him for the past several months. He needed to get things out in the open, to hear her input, to make decisions. But when he led her into the family room, she excused herself to run upstairs, promising to return in a few minutes. She did, and with her reappearance, Tim's brain went blank.

Every coherent thought suffered acute mental paralysis. He may have planned to share his concerns, but Rose's captivating change of raiment suggested that she was just as determined to blot them out entirely in favor of continuing their celebration and welcoming him home all over again. After all, he had been gone three weeks! As he surrendered himself to her superior claims, Tim mumbled, "It'll keep till tomorrow."

Never had two lovers been more content.

The Great Plains OB/GYN clinic on the western outskirts of Kansas City bustled with customers. Young women in various stages of pregnancy populated the waiting room, while older women, inured to the indignity of yearly check-ups, read a book or watched repetitious healthcare tips on a TV screen. No sign of ailment attached to Rose who floated into the lobby with an irrepressible smile lighting her face. Tim began to catch some of her eagerness until she was asked by the receptionist to provide her proof of medical insurance. He flinched almost imperceptibly and caught himself withdrawing by slow degrees from the proceedings. Rose was so excited, she saw and heard nothing until her name was called. Pasting a smile on his face, Tim accompanied her to the ultrasound suite and waited with a growing sense of unease. That he recognized such feelings as being completely illogical helped little. When Rose, now clothed in the proper gown, lay on the exam table as directed by the radiology technician, he had to force himself to watch the screen.

The room was pleasantly cool and dark. Tim felt warm, almost hot. The tech, who identified herself as Keisha, spoke in calm, low tones as she methodically moved the scanning device over Rose's abdomen; Tim grew incrementally more agitated. Still, he watched. When the scanner zeroed in on an image, the tech smiled and pointed to the screen. "Meet your baby." The miracle he beheld momentarily replaced Tim's anxiety with excitement and wonder. He felt Rose's hand clasp his tighter and glanced at her face to see silent tears of happiness run onto her brilliant smile. He moved his lips in mute prayer.

This is our baby! Dear God, thank you! With your help, I know it will all work out.

The scanner moved again, then it began moving back and forth between two different points. Keisha continued to speak in soothing tones, but Tim could hear uncertainty in her voice. She laid the scanner aside, lowered Rose's robe, and spoke directly to the young mother. "Now, I don't want you to worry. Everything is perfectly normal. I'll just see if the doctor can pop in for a minute to confirm my readings."

Telling Rose not to worry during the first ultrasound of her first baby was like asking the earth to stop revolving around the sun! The need to calm her obvious qualms helped Tim forget his own…for a while. When Keisha returned with Dr. Hardesty, an agreeably frumpy individual with an oversized lab coat, Tim's misgivings shrunk even further. The doctor's manner was that of a kindly aunt stepping in to encourage a novice in the art of knitting. She immediately put Rose at ease.

"Now, now, young lady, what have we here?" Dr. Hardesty asked, as if expecting to behold a new species of human. "Yes, yes, I see," she murmured as Keisha moved the scanner to the curious images. "You're having quite a day. Yes, quite a day."

With each comment, Tim's internal warning system began clanging again. *If she repeats herself one more time, I'm out of here!* Tim waited in mute agony for the doctor's next utterance.

Still smiling, Dr. Hardesty addressed both parents and held up two fingers. "Two! It seems you've won the jackpot! You'll be welcoming two babies before the year is out."

The walls began to close in. Tim's breath came in short, shallow gulps, which left him feeling light-headed, while his heart seemed bent on pounding out of his chest. The accompanying sensation of nausea sent him headlong for the door and an escape to fresh air. With sweat pouring down his face, Tim moved toward the emergency exit as if his life depended on it. Once outside he sank down on a bench and laid his head back against the brick wall. Though oblivious to the building's alarm sounding, he eventually became aware of someone sitting next to him. A firm hand forced his head between his knees and held it there while another hand placed a cold, wet compress on the back of his neck. All the while, a voice directed him to take deep breaths and relax.

Back in the exam room, Rose had looked on, horrified. Her strong, solid, dependable husband had just deserted her! Had she had any thought but that of betrayal, she might have spared a moment of concern for him. Or she might have marveled at the speed with which Dr. Hardesty directed someone from the staff to follow Tim, instructing her to follow "the usual steps" upon catching up with the agitated father. But all Rose could process was Tim's defection.

Turning her attention once more to her primary patient, the doctor patted Rose reassuringly on the foot and spoke in a soothing voice, "Dear, dear, such a commotion! You mustn't be too hard on him, Mrs. Ludlow. He is probably under a lot of stress from any number of sources, and the news of twins just tipped the scales. This happens to fathers from time to time, but they all survive."

Survive?! I need him to want these babies as much as I do! How could he have pretended to be excited about this pregnancy, when all the time, he clearly dreaded it! Oh, what are we going to do?

Twenty-plus years of practicing Obstetrics never quite prepared Dr. Hardesty for the sharp pang of sympathy she felt on a patient's behalf when the indisputable reality of parenthood hit the prospective father squarely between the eyes. She knew it would all work out in the end; it usually did – especially for two people who were obviously devoted to one another. But going into a pregnancy with emotional turmoil, no less the pregnancy of two babies, puts the mother at a health disadvantage. Dr. Hardesty silently vowed to "keep a close eye on this one." During Rose's initial office visit, immediately following the ultrasound, the doctor did her best to help the young mother focus on prenatal care and provided a more definite due date – New Year's Eve. Rose barely acknowledged the festive timing. And despite Tim's personal first responder popping her head in to report, "Mr. Ludlow is just fine now," Rose walked outside with a cloud hanging over her. Tim was waiting for her on a bench next to the main entrance.

Guilt and shame engulfed him in silent misery. But if ever there was a time for him to man up, it was now. Tim stood, and reaching out to his wife, began a humble apology. "Rose, I am *so* sorry. I don't know what came over me. The nurse told me it was probably a panic attack. Can you believe it? A *panic attack*! I've never had a panic attack in my life! Not on dangerous jobs, not when my dad died, not even in combat. I realize my stupid reaction not only humiliated me; it hurt you, too. *Please* forgive me." Without thinking, she laid her hand in his, knowing only a desire to wipe the pain of remorse from his eyes.

Then something snapped.

The same pregnancy hormones that, up to that point, had further tenderized an already tender heart, now surged into a source of merciless resentment. Snatching her hand away, Rose thought, *He feels humiliated? What about me!* Aloud, she began a diatribe that mortified her as much as it shocked her, but she couldn't stop.

"I knew you didn't really want this baby; I mean b-babies. You've been pretending the whole time! Why didn't you *tell* me instead of letting me b-be embarrassed like that?" Unbidden tears flowed down her cheeks. Tim, aware that other people were watching them, attempted to steer Rose toward the car, but she shook off his hand. "You ran out on me, on our children, with everyone watching! Do you have any idea how crushed and disappointed I feel right now?"

This was not the time or place to talk it out. On impulse, Tim sought to protect his wife, if only from herself. He grabbed her arm and forcibly escorted her toward the parking lot. In an undervoice, he said compellingly, "Rose, not here, not now. Let's just go home and work through this."

Again, she pulled away from him, but at least she willingly walked to the truck – in silence. Waiting only until Tim had closed her door and climbed behind the wheel, she uttered the dramatic cry, "*I'm* the one who has never been so humiliated!" Tim was spared the necessity of replying to such a dire claim when her tears turned into sobs. When he attempted to begin another apology, Rose stopped crying long enough to say, "I don't want to talk about it now." She then spent the entire journey home casting periodic animadversions on his character and his conduct until she had worked herself into such a state that she almost jumped from Tim's truck before it came to a halt near their kitchen door.

Slamming first the truck door, then the back door, Rose disappeared into the house on a fresh wave of despair. Her performance was wasted on Tim, however, who headed back down the long drive the instant she hopped from the truck, leaving enough rubber on the cement to warrant a new set of tires.

Never had two lovers been more miserable!

CHAPTER 4

> *"What have I done wrong to make you chase after me as though I were a criminal?"*
>
> *Genesis 31:36b (NLT)*

"Ya must be *jokin'*!" In moments of agitation, Angelica Warner's Jamaican accent became pronounced. So outraged was she by the detective's suggestion, she nearly slipped into her native *patois.* Surrounded by a room of strangers, whose names and titles were mostly a verbal blur, Angelica sought denial on any of the faces gazing purposely at her. The appeal failed.

"But, Mrs. Warner, you are a gift from heaven, from *le bon Dieu!* An unlooked-for opportunity like this rarely occurs in the course of an investigation, and when it falls into our lap at just the crucial moment, it must be exploited. You can see that, no?"

"Young man –"

"Inspector François Dulac, at your service, madame," the detective reminded her, bowing slightly. He might have been a spokesman for tanning beds, so rich was his skin tone. Jet black hair and expressive eyes with delicately arched brows gave him a devilishly charming look.

"Excuse me. Inspector Dulac, what you're really sayin' is that *I* must be exploited," Angelica replied with uncharacteristic asperity.

"No, no, not a' 'tall." Dulac's calm, well-modulated voice sought to reassure her. Had Angelica not been so upset, she might have appreciated his elegant French accent. "We are not asking you to do anything that would put you in any kind of danger. No, madame, *certainement pas!* It is simply a question of identifying him. You see, over the years this man who calls himself Samuel Jamison – though he was christened Samuel Jameson MacDougal – has become something of a human chameleon. The man speaks at least six languages fluently, can pass himself off as twenty years younger or older than his actual age because of his great physicality, and is a master of assessing his environment and determining what or who he can use to his advantage. He has impersonated a diplomat from Niger, a prince from the United Arab Emirates, and a merchant from Mumbai, to name but a few.

"His one defining feature is his voice, which is truly *magnifique!* We – meaning the police forces of at least half a dozen countries – have been chasing him about the world for nearly 40 years – long before my time with the Sûreté. When we believe to have information about a possible target, he appears somewhere a thousand miles away. And even when we are certain to have him within our grasp, security films have proven to be useless without any sound. He is a master at transforming his face, and as such, has become virtually invisible."

"Aye, bu' we ha' been fer-r-ther hindered by his damnable her-r-itage." An older man, tailored suit notwithstanding, spoke in a raspy, colorful voice proclaiming his Scottish roots with a brogue thick enough to cut with a chainsaw. Speaking courteously to Angelica, Chief Inspector Fergusson recounted Jamison's amazing story.

Samuel's grandfather, Hamish MacDougal, had fled to the French controlled sector of the Caribbean at the behest of his own father, who threatened to disinherit the wayward youth if he remained in Scotland. Relieved to be rid of such a troublesome child, the old man had settled a large enough sum on the boy to allow him to purchase a modest sugar cane plantation on St. Honoré, one of the region's more obscure islands. Old MacDougal's hope that word of any further escapades by his son would be less likely to reach him from a French-held territory rather than a British one proved to be true, and Hamish was all but forgotten by the MacDougal clan.

True to his nature, Hamish had taken for his bride the reigning beauty of the island, a mulatto enchantress named Monique. She presented him with one son, Morgan, whose mixed ethnicity leant a pleasant cast to his skin and underscored, rather than obscured, much of his European ancestry. His wild streak and Scottish name proclaimed him to be Hamish's son, and the two rebellious spirits fought together for the island's freedom from French control. National sovereignty finally being granted, Hamish lived only long enough to see Morgan made president of the fledgling country.

In addition to teaching Morgan to appreciate beauty, especially in women, Hamish had passed on his ruggedly handsome facial features. When the exigencies of diplomacy demanded that he take a wife, Morgan had no difficulty in seducing and marrying a not-too-distant cousin. On a small island, where the gene pool holds little variation, such liaisons were not uncommon. Désirée, with her lovely face and figure, succeeded in capturing Morgan's previously roving eye long enough to bear him four sons in six years. The boys favored one another so much they were often mistaken for twins when encountered in pairs. With all their similarities, one telltale feature set them apart – the voice. Jean-Pierre, Claude, and André all had pleasant, baritone voices quite similar in tone and timbre. Samuel alone possessed a voice that could almost shake the ground with the force of a volcanic eruption. As he matured, and realized the instrument's full potential, he learned to control it enough to fool people into thinking he was one of his brothers. But in unguarded moments, he allowed his voice its full power and scope, enjoying the impact on his audience.

More than a mere dutiful wife and mother, Désirée boasted a sharp intellect and a shrewd mind. It was she who determined that her sons would be raised multilingual by insisting both English and French be spoken in the home and by employing a native Indian nanny from Delhi. French,

English, and Hindi could be heard at any given time in the MacDougal household. As young children do, the boys picked up the nuances of the vastly different tongues quickly and maintained their use when sent to exclusive boarding schools in Europe for their education. Such beginnings produced a renowned plastic surgeon, a judge in the French appellate court, a successful international businessman, and Samuel Jamison, professor of linguistics and international thief. By the time he fully spread his wings and launched himself on the world, Samuel had dropped the MacDougal and changed the 'e' of Jameson to an 'i,' thus providing himself with a new surname.

As she listened to a detailed history of the man Angelica had thought only a garden-variety scoundrel at the time of their initial interaction, she quickly realized that she had underrated him in comparing him to the late, unlamented Simon Atherton.[3] Though the British private investigator also had manipulated anyone susceptible enough to fall under his spell, Simon had lacked the advantage Samuel Jamison had in his parentage. Where Simon had grown up on the rough streets of London, clawing and improvising to get ahead, Jamison had been born with a silver spoon in his mouth. Angelica found herself fascinated by the story even as she experienced shocked disapproval at the wanton misuse of such origins.

Observing Angelica's struggle to wade through Inspector Fergusson's accent, Monsieur Dulac thoughtfully took up the account of Samuel Jamison's career, which grew more fantastic with each added layer. "Oh, it is as he says, Madame Warner, I assure you. The good Fergusson is a man of truth. But perhaps you will allow me to continue. It is a tale most bizarre, *n'est-ce pas?*"

According to Dulac and verified by Fergusson, who produced a guttural snort of agreement at appropriate intervals, Jamison took to burglary on a whim. Born with a formidable intellect, Jamison grew bored with merely

---

[3] *Intersecting Lives, Intersecting Dreams*

adding academic credentials to his name. During his undergraduate years, he traveled the islands with his parents while home on holiday from the University of Edinburgh. His father, by then an elder statesman, moved in the first circles. He and his wife added elegance and class to any gathering, and the list of elevated company in the islands being somewhat limited, they were often sought as welcome guests. Young Samuel proved to be as personable as his outward appearance had promised, so whenever the youngest MacDougal was available, he was naturally included in any invitation, as his brothers had been before him.

With a desire to add a little spice to the otherwise dull social routine of such visits, Samuel created a diversion to challenge his wits; he set out to learn of and steal the valuables in whatever home they visited. How he came by the information varied. Gullible chambermaids, careless valets who enjoyed gossiping with the upper crust, and giggling debutants alike were happy to share any details they could provide, not realizing Samuel's interest was less in them than in the jewels and cash they spoke of. Initially, it was enough to steal the items and return them before he departed without being caught. While he had little care for any grief he might cause the home's owners, he wanted no hint of blame to attach to his parents. The MacDougals were all ruthless in as much as they made the most of the skills and talents each possessed, determined to reach whatever heights were open to them. But they were also fiercely loyal. The sons were devoted to their parents and to one another, and heaven help the man who threatened any of them!

The steal-and-replace pastime entertained young Samuel until he completed undergraduate studies with honors. With an eye to the future, he had kept his hand in during the school year while visiting the estates of Europe's aristocracy and their wealthy merchant neighbors. The offspring of many of that class populated the student body of the university, and Samuel ensured his popularity among the more socially elite by entertaining those peers with imitations of international characters of renown, complete with mannerisms and dialects. Quickly becoming the draw for every social gathering held on the school's hallowed grounds, Samuel cemented his place in UK society. Following graduation, having determined that he had exhausted the list of potential connections in the land of his forefathers, he chose Heidelberg University for postgraduate work. The location afforded him easy access to Europe and the opportunity to perfect his already firm grasp of German. To German, French, English, and Hindi he added Arabic and numerous African dialects.

"The man possesses a mind like a computer. For we poor policemen, attempting to capture and bring to justice such a one has been a task most formidable." Angelica began to think it a task most impossible! However, she found herself caught up in the unfolding story, wondering how it could get any more fantastic. Inspector Dulac provided the details.

A PhD in Linguistics followed almost effortlessly. When not mastering the intricacies of yet another language with relative ease, Samuel turned his attention to the science of locks and security measures, and a new vista opened before him. While Jamison had no desire to be saddled with a permanent teaching post, the title of professor added respectability to elitism. With strategic precision he pursued a few adjunct professorships in various locations in order to build his reputation and to establish numerous operating bases. With such a pedigree, no door was closed to him.

Midway through his doctoral studies, Samuel began to experiment with his methods of larceny based on his newly acquired knowledge of safes, locks, and rudimentary surveillance systems. On a visit to his home on St. Honoré to mourn his father's passing, the youngest MacDougal made the rounds of the islands – using his altered name – and left a chain of unaccountable hotel robberies in his wake.

"We believe this may have been the time period you encountered him, Madame Warner. Was it perhaps in 1986?" Dulac asked.

"Why, yes!" Angelica gasped. "June of 1986. I was just sixteen. But how did you know?"

"Several '*otels* on the island reported thefts during that period. Jamison was – 'ow do you say – flexing his muscles, so to speak," said the young inspector, flapping his arms in comical fashion.

"Flexing, oh aye, that's a fairr description. Bu' tell the guid leddy aboot those brrothers o' h'n." In typical fashion, Fergusson snorted, then nodded to indicate that Dulac should continue.

Jamison's presence could be traced, coincidentally, to other locations at the time they had been burgled, thus putting hotel security on the alert regionwide. However, Samuel was never caught with any stolen goods in his possession. Nor was there any movement of those goods among local fences, or detection of such property by airport or harbor customs officials. The jewels and other valuables simply disappeared. It was only in later years that authorities began to connect the travels of André MacDougal, a respected businessman, with those of his brother Samuel. Easily recognizable stones, artifacts, and precious metals disappeared from a stately home or prestigious university in one country only to reappear on the black market on the other side of the world while Jamison stayed put.

And though the youngest MacDougal's face had been captured on many closed-circuit cameras, leaving him recognizable to the naked eye, facial recognition software was still only in its developmental stages and not yet widely used during his most active years. His image might pop up on Scotland Yard's computer following inquiries into a grand theft in Devonshire, while at the same time be verified by a detective of the *Sûreté* as that of another man identifying himself as Samuel Jamison.

At precisely the same time as that of the robbery, the second man was giving a lecture in the presence of 300-plus people at the *Sorbonne*. No one questioned the authenticity of a man so closely resembling the expected guest lecturer. His voice was perhaps a little hoarse, with none of the rich tones remembered by some present, but a trifling sore throat easily explained any discrepancy. After all, the man spoke with great authority on Hindi and its influence on western languages. With the application of a little Botox® to fill out the lips and brow, and a vocal spray of his own concocting to alter the voice, Dr. MacDougal was invisible. Almost as fluent in Hindi as his brother, Jean-Pierre became Samuel with ease. It was a trick they had perpetrated many times. There was hardly any worry over prosecution if the fraud was unmasked. The case would be thrown out on the grounds of insufficient evidence by a judge known for his impatience with such a waste of the court's time. Samuel was not the only brother to have altered his name.

Though Claude kept the name change from his father out of respect, he recognized the advantage of playing up the French side of his ancestry. Given the old man's failing health and the distance separating them, the subterfuge posed no problem. Upon completing law school, it was not Claude MacDougal, but Claude Maximilian Dugal who joined a local bar association in France. Ruthlessly adhering to the rigid career path he set for himself, Max Dugal attained the rank of judge precisely on schedule. Once installed in that exalted position, he allowed Samuel free range within his judicial reach and any others he could influence. Dugal provided similar services for his other brothers, and the four operated with impunity throughout Europe.

"Are you tellin' me the whole *lot o' them* were thieves? A doctor, a businessman, a professor, *and* a judge? Ya must be jokin'!" Angelica wondered how many more times she would feel compelled to repeat herself.

Chief Inspector Fergusson grunted and replied with the cryptic utterance, " 'Struth!"

With a deferential glance at his superior, Dulac quickly clarified, "What, perhaps, the good chief inspector means to say is that any, or all, of his brothers may have aided or abetted Jamison from time to time, though no criminal charges could ever be laid against them. It was Jamison alone who was, that is to say, *is* the master criminal. Whether the others shared in the spoils of his ill-gotten gain, or merely took perverse pleasure in circumventing the law, as their grandfather Hamish might have done, is of a conjecture most speculative."

Here the young Frenchman was interrupted by a third man who had remained silent during the fascinating history. Angelica almost jumped when he spoke; the understated, nondescript office décor had enveloped him in an efficient, neutral sort of camouflage. Comfortable was the word that came to mind when she turned her attention to Mr. Dawson – *his* name she had remembered. Of medium height, he filled out his neat brown suit without appearing overweight, and a warm, open smile lit the rounded contours of an amiable face only a few shades darker than his clothing. Sporting a whimsical striped bow tie and matching vest, and with his round head covered in grizzled, woolly hair, Dawson gave Angelica the impression of a human teddy bear. A pleasant voice furthered the effect, infusing a note of ease in a room that had become charged with an undercurrent of tension.

"Mrs. Warner, I realize this has all been a bit overwhelming. I know it was to me when I first heard this incredible story," he added, disarming Angelica completely. She could feel herself relax and returned his smile in full measure, grateful for his kind consideration of her feelings. Such an approach had not only served Dawson well in the hospitality business; it proved to be more effective in gaining her trust than all Dulac's Gallic gestures or Fergusson's brusque explosions of commentary.

"But I still don't understand what would be expected o' me," Angelica said, though with far fewer misgivings than she had had minutes before.

"As these gentlemen explained it to me when they approached me and the hotel's owner before we ever began construction, they wanted to use this facility to set a trap for this Jamison fellow. You see, a convention of security specialists is to be held here at the end of next month at the behest of the combined white-collar crime divisions of several international agencies. The meeting will feature the newest technologies and…" Mr. Dawson paused to look at Chief Inspector Fergusson in inquiry, as if seeking permission to continue. Rightly understanding the latter's grunt and nod to be the granting of such a request, he added, "…and a collection of jewels, cash, and gold worth a king's ransom – the idea being to dangle enough bait to attract some big fish. And by what I can gather, this Samuel Jamison is one of the biggest."

As her pulse began to race, Angelica searched the faces of the other men and noted a reflection of her concern on Dulac's, while Fergusson's remained stoic, giving nothing away.

"But you mustn't say such things to me!" Angelica cried out in building agitation. "Why, I might accidentally repeat some or all o' what ya tellin' me to anyone!" Dulac's eyes nearly started from their sockets. Fergusson cleared his throat and glared at Angelica from under bushy eyebrows. Casually taking a seat in the chair next to hers, Dawson crossed his legs as if settling down for a pleasant chat with a friend.

"Oh, I doubt that. You've been vouched for by Miles Hawthorne and your pastor, and anyone can see that you are a woman of character."

Angelica would have a few choice words for Miles later! It was he who had convinced her to meet with Mr. Dawson and the others following her unbelievable disclosure to Marilyn, though he had been vague about details. He had told her only that they would appreciate any information she could give them about Samuel Jamison since she was probably the only person in all the Great Plains to have met him.

Bristling a little, Angelica demanded to know what they expected of her to have put her under the burden of such a confidence. It was Inspector Dulac who, somewhat reluctantly, outlined her part in their plan, though he wasn't crazy about what he considered the hotel manager's premature revelation of classified details. He was far less trusting than their genial host or the chief inspector.

"Madame Warner, as I mentioned earlier, we hoped you would consider acting as our ears to assist us to identify and follow Jamison. Though, I must say, the disclosures by Monsieur Dawson now rather make that request an imperative." Dulac frowned at Dawson who merely continued to beam with good humor. "None of us have actually seen this man because he abandoned the itinerant professor role early in his career. Perhaps its very respectability began to pall compared to the challenge and excitement of grand larceny. And, of course, as I explained earlier, he must have established numerous international working bases by then. Police agencies around the world have amassed countless images of his many aliases. He is an eccentric millionaire, an oil sheik, a Zulu chief – who can name them all? Unfortunately, impersonations by his brothers have rendered many of the images useless, and his ability to disguise himself has evolved into an art form most advanced. It is the voice, that so remarkable voice, the *caractéristique* among all others, which sets him apart, and you alone have recognized this, here, in this '*otel.* Such a stroke of luck confirms the information we received from a clever operative in Germany. It is of the good fortune most remarkable. So, you see, madame, you must 'elp us!"

While he addressed Angelica, the young Frenchman's whole being grew more French; his arms and hands swung wide in dramatic gestures, and his eyebrows danced as he leaned ever closer to her, oozing Gallic suavity. She nearly applauded after his final appeal but caught herself in time. Looking at each of the three men in turn, Angelica made a decision.

"I think before I agree to anythin', you must tell me precisely what your expectations are concernin' my part in this ridiculous plan."

An hour later, Angelica drove home with her head in a whirl, wishing she had never laid eyes on Samuel Jamison!

A formerly muddy field had dried to a hard-packed surface as the result of an early drought. Tim Ludlow negotiated the ruts with care and parked in front of a somewhat weary-looking farmhouse. It struck an incongruent note amid the heavy machinery moving to and from a metal framework structure 200 yards away. Merely an architectural rendering just two months earlier, a building outline had miraculously emerged from the repurposed farm fields like a ghost ship on the horizon. Scattered remnants of volunteer corn and wheat were all that remained to bear witness to the land's origins. The brainchild of Miles Hawthorne, *Veritas Academy* was also a labor of love.

Upon reentering her life the year before, Miles had reacted to Marilyn Ludlow's answer to what she thought a lighthearted conversational gambit in anything but lighthearted fashion. Her wistful statement that she would love to be able to offer families in the area an education alternative for their children, became a reality when Miles presented her, on Easter, with drawings of a proposed Christian school. Initially shocked by such a gesture, Marilyn finally recognized the unaffected generosity and devotion represented by Miles' actions and gladly accepted both the gift and his proposal of marriage.

With many projects underway elsewhere, Miles had handpicked contractors he could trust for both the school and the new housing development to be built around it. The farmhouse, alone, he turned over to the only man he believed capable of bringing the old building back to life. In forging a relationship with the son he had known for less than a year, Miles developed deep respect for Tim's expertise in architectural renovation. Where most builders saw hundred-year-old structures as impediments needing to be torn down to make way for modern construction, Tim saw beauty in the rare, dated craftsmanship found in buildings from bygone eras. It was to Tim that Miles turned over the old farmhouse, entrusting him with another project close to his heart.

By sheer chance, Miles happened to be on site that Monday. When he heard a car door slam violently, he glanced out the window to see his son approach the old house with an expression resembling brewing thunder. Fully aware that Rose had been scheduled for an ultrasound that morning, Miles' heart sank when he saw Tim's scowl. *Surely, only bad news could result in such a reaction,* thought the man so new to fatherhood. And while the old Miles might have avoided a meeting fraught with emotional outpouring, the new Miles walked purposely toward the door, desiring only to provide a listening ear.

The sight of Miles stepping onto the front porch momentarily stopped Tim in his tracks. After dropping off Rose, Tim's only thought had been a wish to find somewhere to be alone – somewhere to lick his wounds and fully take in the news he wanted desperately to be happy about. He had to think of a way to make up for embarrassing and disappointing the wife he adored. The last thing he needed was to put on a brave face for his father, but Miles' presence left him with no choice. Squaring his shoulders, Tim temporarily buried his inner turmoil and forced a smile onto his reluctant lips. The conspicuous effort caused Miles' heart to sink even further.

Miles loved his son but understood that the relational security necessary for sharing a deep wound is something developed over a lifetime. He was quite certain that, had it been Peter Ludlow who stood there waiting to receive his son, Tim would have instinctively unburdened his heavy spirit to the dad who had always been there for him. With no wish to do so, Miles knew his very presence was letting his son down, unintentionally or not. Likewise, despite initially thinking all he wanted from Miles was a hurried farewell, Tim suddenly knew an urge to pour out his troubles to his father – the father he had come to know and look up to. Then just as suddenly, he realized that Miles would probably feel acutely uncomfortable in such a situation. A man with essentially no experience in parenting would hardly welcome that kind of interaction. And being men, the two were unable to share their thoughts, leaving both woefully misguided and mute.

Shaking hands like near strangers, each retreated into the safe sphere of meaningless conversation. Rose's ultrasound appointment was general knowledge within the greater family, yet Miles never asked about the outcome, and Tim wondered at such evident unconcern about his future grandchild after such a show of excitement the day before. With a mental gag in place, Miles avoided asking the questions that were burning for answers, though Tim obviously had no desire to share with him any information about the baby. It was all Miles could do to maintain a nonchalant air. He soon drove off, hoping Marilyn would have a definite report.

Miles' departure inadvertently fueled a sense of resentment in Tim. Based on his father's behavior, *nobody* wanted to hear his side of the story, or *any* of the story, for that matter. Without thinking, Tim began aimlessly walking through the rooms of the old farmhouse. On previous visits, he had smiled in appreciation of the imposing solid oak mantlepieces, delicately arched doorways, and leaded glass transoms. All he saw on this tour were echoes of rejection, indifference, and guilt. Gradually, rejection turned to unfair accusation, indifference to lack of compassion, and guilt to resentment.

Yes, I hurt her feelings, but how can she blame me for my reaction? It's not like I planned to have a panic attack! And I tried to apologize, over and over, but she wouldn't let me! She treated me like some kind of criminal when all I tried to do was to be there for her and to support her. And Miles – he acted like he'd never heard that we were even having a baby! It was as if he changed overnight and didn't care at all. I thought I knew him better than that. I may have messed up – I know I messed up, but I don't deserve to be treated like that!

With emotions seething, Tim went about the rest of the day in a black humor that kept everyone on the Three Brothers crew at arms' length and in the dark.

During the drive back to Tinkers Well, Angelica pondered everything she had heard that day. *So, I am to help trap the illusive Samuel Jamison,* she thought. Out loud, she said again, "They must be jokin'!" And yet she had to admit to a certain interest in the impossible plan.

With the approval of young Dulac and the fierce Scotsman, Chief Inspector Fergusson, Mr. Dawson had asked that she consider coming to work at the hotel under a variety of guises: a front-desk clerk, a floating hostess or server for the hotel's restaurant and poolside grill, and a pseudo "assistant manager" overseeing housekeeping. Because Jamison could materialize at any time in any camouflage of his choosing, it was imperative that Angelica become well known, and her presence readily accepted anywhere in the hotel. If he established a recognizable pattern, her responsibilities could be shifted accordingly. The whole scheme seemed utterly fantastic to her.

Though she was quite adept at using a computer for social-media purposes or shopping online, she had never had occasion to delve into any more complicated software than that needed to register grades during the years she had worked as a teacher's assistant. With less trepidation, Angelica considered the roles of hostess and server. A lifetime of cooking for and entertaining people from all walks of life might stand her in good stead there, and no one kept a neater or cleaner house. But the thought of overseeing the housekeeping, if only on a superficial basis, of a house with over 200 rooms momentarily shook her courageous decision.

Then she thought of her childhood friend, Sabryna. She remembered how Samuel Jamison had shamelessly used her to help him in his crimes, then thoughtlessly seduced her, leaving her with child, and destroying her innocence. No one in Tinkers Well had a bigger heart or a more forgiving spirit than Angelica Warner. Nevertheless, as she pulled into her driveway, she vowed to do all within her power to bring that scoundrel to justice. Samuel Jamison would not be given the chance to take advantage of anyone ever again, if she had anything to say about it!

Hours spent weeping and chastising herself for being a fool brought Rose Ludlow to a full sense of the unforgivable way she had behaved after the ultrasound that morning. The anger she had felt toward Tim had finally dissolved into shame and remorse. It was not by Tim's actions that she was robbed of the joy she should have been reveling in over the news of twins. It was her reaction to his obvious distress that kept chipping away at her conscience. Rose had accused him of failing her. After hours of reflection, however, she came to realize it was her refusal to allow him to apologize and explain what had happened that was the greater failing.

Her husband was an honorable, godly man of integrity – the best man she had ever known – and she loved him more than she had thought it possible to love anyone. Yet when he needed her compassion and words of comfort, something he rarely asked of her, Rose had shut him down. Tears eventually gave way to resolution.

"I will not allow anything to come between us!" she announced fiercely to the ceramic roosters strutting across the top of her white Shaker cabinets. "I'll cook all his favorite foods," she said, more to herself than to her kitchen fowl, "and show him a wife who cares more about him than about what some radiology technician thinks!"

Rose set to work like a dynamo and was just walking down the back stairs, after putting the finishing touches on her makeup, when she heard Tim's truck coming down the drive. Her steps slowed and she was suddenly assailed by nervousness. She stood by the old farm table, now draped with a merry checkered tablecloth, unsure of what to say. Considering all her verbal missteps earlier that day, Rose thought it best to let Tim speak first. Smiling shyly, she waited for his entrance.

Determined all the way home not to let his ruffled ego get the better of him, Tim greeted his wife with a simple "Hi," and a cautious smile. No "Hi, sweetheart, you look gorgeous," or "Hi, honey, what smells so good?" Rose knew herself to be beyond forgiveness. Nonetheless, she attempted a light-hearted note.

"I thought you might be home a little earlier tonight," she began but faltered when she saw Tim's brows draw together. "Not that you weren't somewhere important… I mean I know you were probably working on something important because, of course, it would be… since all your work is important… you know what I mean."

Her obvious aim to make amends for her earlier hurtful comments was not lost on Tim. Nor was the delicious aroma coming from the stove, or her appearance in a dress that set off her changing curves in a most pleasing way. He opened his mouth to respond in the same vein when a little devil inside him goaded him to make one little comment in his defense. It would be his last for some time.

"Rose, I'll say it one more time. I am sorry for what happened this morning. I truly am, but I didn't appreciate being treated like a criminal. Like I said before, I didn't plan to react that –"

"– I didn't treat you like a criminal! How can you say such a thing?" Her well-intentioned plan to express regret and to ask forgiveness was momentarily forgotten. Quickly recovering, however, she tried again. "I know I could have been a little more understanding –"

"– a *little* more? You didn't give me a chance to explain what had happened, or to even ask me if I was all right. That's not the Rose *I* know."

It wasn't the Rose she knew either, but her own internal devil edged her further down a road she had resolved to avoid at all costs. "Well, the Tim *I* know would never have made the question necessary!" Before they continued an argument that no one could win, Tim lifted his hand and walked toward the door to the hallway.

"I can't do this right now. I'm afraid I'll say something I can never take back." As far as Rose was concerned, he had already crossed that line. "Besides, I have a lot of work to do tonight."

"You mean you won't eat any of this food I spent hours preparing especially for you?" Tears stung Rose's eyes.

"I'm sorry. I'm just not hungry," Tim replied on a weary note and walked to the library with shoulders hunched.

Left alone in the kitchen, Rose stared down the hallway for a full two minutes wondering how she had allowed all the contrite words and actions she had meant to convey to be drowned out by the ugly, unforgiving words that had come pouring out of her mouth. The dinner she had lovingly and thoughtfully prepared was left untouched on the stove. Desperately seeking distraction, Rose ran up to her hobby room and pretended to work on some window treatments for the nursery, but her preoccupied mind necessitated the ripping out of one wayward seam after another until she gave up altogether and went to bed early. Just before switching off her lamp, she reached for her Bible on the nightstand. In the excitement and anticipation of the morning, she had neglected her daily scripture reading and hoped that she might now find some solace in its pages. Flipping to Romans 7, the words of one verse leapt off the page and smote her with the power of a physical blow.

> *For the good that I want, I do not do, but I practice the very evil that I do not want.*
>
> *Romans 7:19 (NASB)*

Regret and shame returned tenfold. The mental oblivion of slumber eluded her, though she made a pretense of being asleep when she heard Tim climbing the stairs with heavy steps. He slipped into bed with his back to hers and tried, without success, to ignore the sound of his wife softly weeping into her pillow. Each lay enveloped in a shroud of misery and despair that neither knew how to penetrate.

What should have been the happiest day of their marriage turned out to be their worst nightmare.

CHAPTER 5

Silence between the reluctant domestic combatants was eventually exchanged for polite conversation whenever husband and wife happened to be at home together during their waking hours, which wasn't often. Tim left the house early on Tuesday and returned home late to find his dinner left on a plate in the microwave. Rose had taped a note on the back door saying she was attending a women's event at church. By Wednesday, Tim's conscience compelled him to face the error of his response to the situation. He arrived home with remorse and flowers in hand, only to be greeted by his wife with a wooden smile and a reminder that they were dining with his parents that evening to celebrate the big news with their friends. It was the last place either wanted to be. Their joint performance as seemingly overjoyed expectant parents, however, surprised them both. They convinced themselves that no one present could possibly have suspected anything was amiss.

Having witnessed Tim's stormy mood two days earlier, Abe Yousef wondered at his total change in demeanor. As a newlywed himself, he noted the uncharacteristic reserve between husband and wife in unguarded moments. Derek Warner speculated as to what might have caused such a rift when they should have been gushing over baby stuff, while Miles and Marilyn looked on helplessly. Neither parent had a clue about the results of the ultrasound, but the superficial show of excitement by their son and daughter-in-law failed in its object as far as they were concerned. The grandmothers were way ahead of everyone in their observations.

But it was Pastor Lindeman who watched the troubled couple with particular concern. He had coached them during their premarital counseling and frowned at their obvious rejection of one of the chief tenants he had attempted to instill in them. "Don't let the sun set on your anger," he whispered under his breath, always quick to commiserate with those experiencing a similar mistake from his own past. Making a mental note to call Tim the next day, he turned his attention to key lime pie and gave himself up to enjoying an evening out with his wife amid convivial company.

"I don't know why they didn't just hold up a banner that declared, 'We are terribly unhappy, and we don't know how to get out of the fix we're in!' I told you they'd get themselves into a pickle," Gert commented to Aletha as they sat on the front porch, swinging in a listless manner. With barely a word of farewell, the young Ludlows had deposited their grandmothers at *Fern Cottage* and gone on to their own home further down the drive. "Maybe we can figure out a way to help them without them realizing that's what we're doing."

"That may sound good in theory, Trudy, but I'm not sure how to go about it." Aletha sighed wistfully and added, "It was so much easier when we merely had to bring about a miracle to get them together in the first place. Helping people who seem bent on misery, however, is quite another thing."

Gert snorted in agreement. "You may be right, Letha, though I'm inclined to think we could come up with *something* if we just put our heads together."

After a few minutes of frowning silence, Aletha sighed again, this time conceding defeat. "I'm afraid I'm fresh out of ideas, Trudy. I hate to admit it, but this present trouble may be more difficult than we can, or should, attempt to handle."

"Nonsense! We simply haven't hit on the solution yet. And while I firmly believe that Tim and Rosie love each other deeply and that they'd find their way through whatever foolishness has them acting like ninnies, I don't intend to let them continue to make everyone around them equally unhappy until they do! Now, what might do the trick…"

In the end, the answer proved to be more delightfully inspired and satisfactory than either could have wished.

Of those intimates closest to Rose and Tim Ludlow, Derek Warner's opinion of the untenable situation marched exactly in sync with Granny Gert's. Looking on in disgust as two of his best friends walked around like lovesick zombies, he wished they would just sort out whatever undoubtedly frivolous problem currently absorbed their thoughts so that things could get back to normal. Even if he'd been in a humor to help by providing what he considered to be his superior wisdom and advice, Derek had seen Tim through enough tough times to know better than to try to drag anything out of him or get him to listen to reason unless he was ready to do so. Driving home after dinner, Derek muttered, "And they can't understand why I don't jump on the marriage band wagon. If this is an example of 'marital bliss,' count me out!" Leaving Tim and Rose to sort out their issues by themselves, Derek turned his attention to his own immediate future.

He and another Three Brothers crew member, José Nuñez, had recently completed work on a house flip in town. The two had worked on the project as itinerant residents, and with the house completed and its sale imminent, they had worked themselves out of a place to live. Prior to the remodeling endeavor, Derek had shared a home with his mother. With no other obvious options open to him, he packed up his personal things and planned to move back in. The old arrangement was the easy fallback, though Derek had made an unexpected discovery during his stint in the reno house.

Both he and José had returned from Afghanistan with varying degrees of PTSD. Derek's own struggle, rooted more in self-imposed guilt, rather than the shock that had held such a grip on José's mind and spirit, gradually lessened through counseling and the embrace of a new life and profession. At 31, he knew he had moved past the emotional crutch of his mother's care and was ready to stand on his own again. He recognized, however, that José's emotional scars still had a significant hold over that young veteran. Another consideration impacted José – the impending arrival of his cousin and her two-year-old daughter from California.

José had called his aunt and uncle's modest two-bedroom home his own since leaving the army. Located in a town near Tinkers Well, they had welcomed their nephew and encouraged him to join the Three Brothers construction crew, believing the work might potentially offer healing for José's troubles. When he agreed to sign on with Derek in the house flip, the extra space created in the Nuñez home prompted his aunt and uncle to invite the young mother and child to fill the void, knowing they needed a change of scenery and direction. José's temporary residence would soon be gone, however, and the idea of moving back into a small house overrun with two more people caused his stress level to skyrocket. Noting the signs of anxiety in his friend, Derek made another discovery. His mother's care and companionship were not the only crutches he had clung to.

When he joined Tim Ludlow in his remodeling work, Derek was happy to leave all the decision making and planning to the man who knew his profession best. When the two bachelors welcomed Abe to join them and form *Three Brothers Construction, Inc.*, Tim continued to bear the brunt of running the business. Though Derek picked up quite a bit of knowledge and skill in the world of renovation during the ensuing two years, it was Tim – not Derek – who purchased the house he and José had just finished renovating. Mentally squaring his shoulders, Derek decided it was high time he struck out on his own, so to speak.

Before José could withdraw again into a shell of stress-induced paralysis, Derek considered the ramifications of an alternate pursuit he had been thinking about for some time. The residents of Tinkers Well and the members of Community Church, in particular, had supported and encouraged him during the rough period of adjustment from combat vet to productive citizen. It was time to give something back. A return to the Warner home now would allow him the freedom to pursue a new part-time endeavor while removing the worry of where to hang his hat. And knowing his mother, he was sure she would happily open her door to José as well.

Training to be a volunteer firefighter was not a step Derek had ever anticipated taking. Since reentering the civilian world, he had been content to fall in with whatever opportunity came his way rather than planning for the future. Over the past year, while watching his friends pursue their sweethearts, get married, and provide homes for their families, Derek's conscience began nudging him to take more responsibility for his present and future.

Though always ready to decry the married state, Derek secretly longed to share his life with someone special. But drop-dead gorgeous women who were predisposed to recognize and fully value his magnificent physique, sparkling personality, and – above all – his outstanding humility, were few and far between in Tinkers Well. So, for the time being, he would help José by providing him a home and a place of security and help the community by adding an additional first responder to the ranks. At least the prospect of pursuing a new goal gave Derek a purposeful step forward while he waited for God to further direct his journey.

At first, dubious of Mark Lindeman's invitation to meet for lunch at *Milly's Diner* on Thursday, Tim finally conceded to the request when Mark explained that he wanted input from various parishioners on plans for young men's ministries within the church. Tim had great respect for his pastor and counted him a trusted friend. He was, therefore, a little surprised to find himself the only man providing the input. He had expected to find Abe or Derek, or any number of others present for the meeting. Tim's suspicions surfaced again, but Mark greeted him with the news that he was holding one-on-one sessions to gather information before hosting a collective exchange. Though the excuse might have sounded a bit thin, Tim always found it difficult to walk into *Milly's Diner* in anything but a softened mood. His crew had renovated the place a year earlier, bringing it up to date with a fresh interior that attracted younger customers, while honoring seasoned visitors by maintaining a vibe of the 1950s. Mellowed by Milly's personal attention and insistence that his money was no good there, Tim began to relax for the first time in days. He found himself caught up in the discussion and lowered his guard enough to ask if the pastor might consider a class for "husbands only" to offer advice on breaking down barriers with their wives.

"You know, in case one of us has to deal with a situation like that," he explained in an off-hand way. Tim almost hoped Mark might ask him for an example. He was certainly ready to unburden himself and find help from someone more neutral than his immediate family and friends. The answer was not what he expected.

Laughing a little, Mark replied, "I might have asked the same thing when Lisa and I were first married. I was a second-year seminary student at the time and ready to set the world on fire by modeling the perfect marriage, the perfect home life. But, as young couples often do, we had a stupid argument – I'm not sure I even remember what it was all about – that grew into a terrible breach between us."

In truth, he remembered every detail precisely, but there are elements of every marriage meant to be preserved in a sacred trust. The specific circumstances were less important than the object lesson anyway. Because

Tim had already rejected the answer to his dilemma provided during premarital counseling, Mark felt compelled to share from his own experience, hoping it might provide more pointed inspiration for his troubled friend.

"I was too proud to admit I needed help. And the fact that I was head over heels in love with her and unable to get through to her, or to get her to open up to me, made me feel even more like a failure."

Hearing a reflection of his own story recounted by someone else, Tim cringed and wondered fleetingly if he and Rose had been as convincing in their superficial portrayal of perfect happiness as they thought.

"And to top it off, I was taking a summer course in counseling. It was a case of 'physician heal thyself,' but all I seemed to do was make matters worse. I actually began to question my calling to the ministry all because of a quarrel with my wife!"

Tim couldn't decide if he was relieved or concerned that his spiritual mentor had fallen into the same pit he currently occupied. *What hope do I have?* he asked himself.

"Not coincidentally, I ultimately found advice in the place I should have looked first. The class was studying a very familiar text from 1 Peter 3. I know what you're thinking: why couldn't I figure out the solution from something I've read a hundred times? I think that's why the Bible is such a fascinating book. It speaks to us at different times in precisely the way we need to hear it. And though I trust and favor scholarly translations such as the *English Standard Version* or the *New American Standard Bible*, occasionally reading a text in more modern vernacular helps us to see the words in a new light. On a whim I checked out every other version I could find. It was a phrase in the *Good News Translation* that pulled me up short. I've never forgotten it.

In the same way, you husbands must live with your wives with the proper understanding that they are more delicate than you.

"You see, I wanted my wife to face a problem the way I did. I expected her to react the same way I did. If I could admit my fault and apologize, she should either accept the apology with grace or take responsibility for her own error and apologize. We would agree to forget it and move on. But women are gloriously, wonderfully, *maddeningly* different than we are. They tend to bury their hurt in their hearts and give lip service to being okay when what they really want is to share that hurt. And they expect men to understand that about them without having to spell it out for us. Lisa didn't say it in so many words, but she *wanted* me to drag the hurt out into the open – to *fight* for us, for our relationship and our marriage. That's why the phrase '*the proper understanding that they are more delicate than you,*' hit me between the eyes. I wanted her to react like a man, but she insisted on behaving like a woman – thank heavens! That's when I got a crazy idea."

Mark paused when Milly replaced his empty lunch plate with a slice of peach pie à la mode. Having finally perceived a flicker of hope, Tim grew impatient for more pastoral direction. The other man, however, appeared more interested in enjoying his dessert. Sensing of Tim's impatience, the pastor continued his narrative between mouthfuls while he polished off his pie.

"One of our professors owned a farm about an hour's drive from the seminary. He leased out the land for sharecropping and only went out there on the weekends. That's not important. But what *is* important is that he invited students to go there anytime we needed a place of solitude to study, or pray, or just think." A burgeoning idea was planted in Tim's brain. "So, when I picked her up at work the day after I read that passage, I didn't head right home. She didn't notice at first because we were sharing meaningless chitchat about our respective workdays, which was about the only conversation we could manage at the time."

Tim stared in astonishment at the other man. *Is it possible that he's making this up? Could he and Lisa have had such an eerily similar experience? It doesn't seem likely. Then again, pastors are human too…*

"We got to the edge of the city before she tuned in to the fact that the scenery was not what it should have been. And she wasn't too pleased about it either. But I kept driving toward the farm, even as she got more upset. I drove right past the farmhouse and onto a dirt road that led us into the middle of an endless cornfield. We couldn't see anything but corn: no trees, no animals – just corn. We might as well have been marooned on a desert island for all the signs of civilization apparent. We were well and truly alone: no distractions, no way of escape to avoid a confrontation, no excuses. There was nothing we could do but talk. And we talked for hours. We talked until we could laugh again. We talked until the sun set and the mosquitoes chased us out of there and back to our home – back to us." Mark stopped talking and a sweet smile softened his face as he gazed into a fond memory.

He was jerked out of his reverie when he heard Tim mumble, "Maybe not a cornfield, but…"

"Oh, good grief, I didn't mean to bore you with one of my long-winded stories," Mark said, watching Tim for any other positive signs of having heard his subtle suggestion. But the other man was already working out a nebulous plan, detached from his surroundings and his host. Mark wisely left him alone and rose to take his leave after depositing a generous tip on the table. The movement caught Tim's attention.

"What? I'm sorry, Mark. Did you say something?"

"Nothing of importance. I'll see you Sunday," he said. But Tim was already formulating details and missed the last words. *No matter,* thought Pastor Lindeman. *I think I've done a good day's work. Lord, please bless his efforts.*

Tim followed a few minutes later. As soon as he climbed into his truck, he called the two people he could count on to assist him in pulling off his plan.

Angelica greeted Derek's decision to move home with mixed feelings. While she was delighted to welcome him, the proposed move caused her to question her belief that he was again gaining emotional independence. Derek's suggestion that José join them, after explaining his friend's plight, relieved her worry on that score. Derek had now become the nurturer. The change in roles allowed her to pursue her own venture without concern for her son's well-being.

True to the perfection of God's timing, these intersecting life changes occurred almost simultaneously, smoothing the path for one transition after another. Derek learned of his mother's employment at the hotel a week before the closing date for his current residence. They were sharing a meal in her homey kitchen, fragrant with the spices of the islands. It was the night following the Ludlows' big announcement. And though both mother and son had noted the young parents' odd behavior at the festive event, they avoided the subject. Each had their own news to share.

Thankful for the occasion to have her son all to herself for an evening, Angelica planned a menu sure to please. Derek appreciated the gesture, believing it to be a token of all the great meals he and José would enjoy when they settled into the bungalow. He had not yet disclosed his plan to become a volunteer firefighter, but he chose to postpone his announcement until he had wrapped his mouth around a piece of mango cheesecake waiting on the sideboard. In the interim, his mother shared her unforeseen work engagement and the reasons behind it. Derek was surprised by the news, but he applauded her courage in stepping out of her comfort zone.

"I am so proud of you, Mama! For as long as I can remember, you've spent all your time taking care of others. First, it was me and Daddy. And when he died, you tried so hard to be both mother and father to me. When I finally left home, you started reaching out to anyone who needed help in our community, just like you do here. Don't try to deny it," he warned before she could argue the point, "I heard all about it when I went home to Chicago after I left the army." Pausing only long enough to exchange humility for cockiness, he added quietly, "And then you made a bigger sacrifice than I realized at the time. You left the only home you had known for nearly 30 years and moved with me to Tinkers Well so that I could have a new beginning."

"And I would walk away from this 'job' I've been roped into without a thought if I believed you still needed me. But you're not the same man who moved here two years ago. It's I who should be sayin' how proud I am o' *you*." With a brisk change of manner, Angelica said, "Now, before you have me weepin' for no good reason, have some more o' this jerk chicken. Otherwise, you'll have it for leftovers tomorrow."

Filling Derek's plate before he could protest, Angelica added a surprising twist to the situation. "I've been drivin' into Kansas City for work every day this week, which is not a big deal, but with you and José movin' in here, you've given me the perfect excuse for movin' out." Derek stared at her with a look of surprise mingled with alarm. "Now before you start worryin' needlessly or misunderstandin' the situation, just get back to your jerk chicken, and let me explain," she said, nodding at his temporarily neglected plate. "This job I've taken doesn't necessarily have regular hours, because I could be asked to work in a number o' different roles depending on the situation." Derek merely frowned. His mouth was already full. "My boss–"

"– Mr. Dawson," Derek mumbled from the corner of his mouth.

"Don't talk with your mouth full," Angelica chided.

Derek smiled and mumbled from the other corner, "Yes, Mama."

"Mr. Dawson has offered – well, actually asked me – to consider livin' in an apartment in the city while I'm workin' at the hotel. His daughter Veronica – he calls her Ronnie – is a civil engineer, and she'll be workin' on a project for her company somewhere in South America over the next four months, and she would feel better havin' someone to look after her place while she's gone. She wouldn't charge me anything to stay there. Mr. Dawson told me she would just be grateful to have someone to take care o' her cat and water all o' her plants."

"*Whoa-hoa,* wait just a minute!" A laden fork halted an inch from Derek's mouth. "You're telling me a man you hardly know is asking you to live in the apartment of someone you've never met while you're working 'irregular' hours? And you don't think that sounds a little shady?"

"Now before you go conjurin' up all manner o' nonsense, let me tell you that Mr. Dawson is a respectable gentleman. I'm sure of it. The cat is the real problem, you see; he – Mr. Dawson – is allergic to them so he can't take the poor thing in." If anything, Derek's suspicions grew.

Angelica reached for the mango cheesecake she had prepared for dessert and sliced a generous portion for Derek who quickly polished off his jerk chicken in anticipation of a rare treat. She continued calmly while Derek's look of skepticism grew.

"Derek, don't be so quick to judge. If after meetin' Ronnie tomorrow I have any reservations, I will politely decline, and you've given me the perfect excuse. I can always say I need to stay here and look after you." She patted his hand and added gently, "Which, strictly speakin', isn't really true anymore, is it?"

"What do you mean? Of course it's true! I mean, if you're living in the city, who's going to cook for José and me and make sure we don't drown under a pile of dirty laundry? Who's going to pick up after us and clean and…?" Derek looked into his mother's compassionate eyes – eyes that had never judged him – and was humbled anew. With a rueful smile, he answered himself. "The same two guys who've been taking care of themselves for the past three months, right?"

Angelica stood to wrap her arms around him and kiss the top of his head. "I *am* proud o' you, Derek Isaiah Warner. Your father would be proud o' you, too. And before you go all worst-case scenario, consider that I will still prepare a few meals for you, just as I have been doin' since you, Tim, and Abe lived together at *Willow Walk* before Tim's weddin'. And just like José's Aunt Lupe has been doin' from time to time." Derek grinned sheepishly and helped himself to another slice of cheesecake.

"I wouldn't be stayin' there the whole time anyway. Cats can go for several days by themselves if they have food and water and a fresh litter box. But on the days I'm workin' at the hotel, i' t'will be more convenient for me to be livin' just ten minutes away instead of drivin' 30 or 40 minutes from Tinkers Well. You must see that."

His doubts somewhat mollified, Derek mumbled his agreement. His mouth was full again.

Rather than feeling any indignation at her son's suspicions, Angelica was quite gratified by his concern – and by his assumption of responsibility for himself and José. Their respective altered living arrangements were quickly placed on the back burner, however, when Derek disclosed his plans to become a volunteer firefighter. His mother began to see him through a different lens. He *had* turned a corner – a corner she believed to be finally behind him, and she gave silent thanks.

Now if only he would show such enthusiasm over a girl, there might be hope for grandchildren after all! Angelica kept the thought to herself and spent the rest of the evening listening to a comprehensive outline of her son's training schedule.

A selection of lunch meats, sliced veggies, and spreads covered one end of the kitchen table while, on the other end, Granny Gert sliced and tossed two apples into a baggie, then deposited them in a shopping bag. She and Aletha carried on a flow of inconsequential chatter while Rose assembled the sandwich each had requested. The fact that Rose had never known her grandmother to eat banana on her peanut butter and jelly sandwich went unchallenged. In the back of her mind, Rose could think of only one person who did, and she would not think about him, so she turned her divided attention once more to the older ladies, who could have rivaled any auctioneer for the maximum number of words produced in the shortest space of time. The hope of forestalling any piercing questions by Rose came to naught when they finally had to pause to draw breath.

"I do appreciate you inviting me to join you for lunch, but you don't need me to help make a few sandwiches, so what are you two really up to?" Suspicion momentarily blinded Rose to the warm appeal of the quaint kitchen with its gingham curtains and reproduction enamel stove in a brick alcove. Nor did the guileless innocence Aletha had perfected to an art form succeed in redirecting Rose's thoughts.

"Why, whatever can you mean, dear? It is such a lovely day, and Trudy and I thought it could only improve with your presence," she responded sweetly. Rose immediately suspected a plot.

"Rosie, you know better than to be rude to your hostess." But Granny Gert's gruff rejoinder, which usually embarrassed her granddaughter into silence, misfired.

"Now I *know* you're up to something."

"Nonsense. I give you my word, we have no ulterior motive other than preparing a simple lunch. Though, if you must know, we did try to come up with an idea that would help you patch up things with Tim." Rose's quizzical smile faded to be replaced by a pained look. "But we just couldn't think of anything." As an afterthought, Gert mumbled in disgust, "We must be losing our touch!"

"Please don't interfere, Granny Gert," Rose pleaded. "I know you mean well, but really, everything's fine," she added on a forlorn note.

"Just as you say. Now hand me those sandwiches so I can wrap them for later, and go ahead and make a few more. No sense in getting all this out twice in one day." While the two were conversing, Aletha popped a few cookies into the shopping bag along with some bottles of water. Rose caught the action out of the corner of her eye and might have questioned it, but at that moment the doorbell rang.

"Rosie, you just run along and answer that, will you, while Letha and I finish up here."

In a freak moment of *déjà vu,* Rose had a flashback to her honeymoon in Belize. Upon opening the door, she found her husband standing before her clad in colorfully patterned swim trunks, a tank top, and flip-flops. Caught completely by surprise, Rose could only stare, while her brain thought, irrationally, *Oh golly! I'd almost forgotten how masculine he is…*

Instead of a frown or the polite, detached expression that had greeted her all week, a rakish smile warmed the solid contours of Tim's face and caused her heart to skip a beat. She didn't quite know what to make of the change.

"Good afternoon, ladies," Tim said, addressing the two who had followed Rose into the front hall. His lighthearted note buoyed everyone's spirits. Addressing himself to his wife, he asked politely, "Mrs. Ludlow, would you care to join me for a cruise around the lake? I see our lunch is ready." Gert held up the bag of goodies in triumph.

"*Our* lunch?" Rose protested and looked accusingly at her grandmother.

"Don't blame them. They were only following my orders."

"Your *orders?*" Mustering what indignation she could, Rose said, "Who are you to give everyone orders? And for that matter, why aren't you at work?"

"Work will keep. This won't." As he spoke Tim stepped through the doorway and closer to his wife who instinctively backed away.

"Wh-what do you m-mean?"

"I mean," he said, gazing at her upturned face with such tender longing that a kaleidoscope of butterflies took flight in Rose's stomach. "I'm tired of walking on emotional eggshells. I'm tired of pretending that we're happy. I'm tired of being married without a wife." Rose bowed her head, ashamed of her culpability in the truth he spoke. Reaching out to gently lift her chin, Tim added, "I mean, I'd like to spend a perfect Friday afternoon with you." When she looked away, unable to meet his eyes, he prodded, "Well?"

Rose stepped away again and began wringing her hands while she threw out lame excuses to decline his invitation. "I can't. I'm having lunch with Granny Gert and Aletha," she said, momentarily forgetting that the luncheon invitation had apparently only been a ruse. "And I have a lot to do at home this afternoon." Tim's quizzical smile challenged her to produce a better answer. Quickly looking past him at the boat hitched to his truck, Rose continued, "And there's laundry, and…and I want to practice decoupage for that little table I mean to put in the nursery." At the reference to their pending arrivals, her chin shot out in defiance, and she dared to glance at his face. His relentless smile was her undoing. Dropping her eyes once more, she added lamely, "I can't go to the lake. I don't have a swimsuit with me."

Tim advanced closer and took her hands, but Rose refused to meet his gaze. "You're in luck; I put one in the truck. You can change at the dock." In the face of her determined silence, he asked one more time. "Will you come with me?" When his wife clamped her lips firmly together, Tim grinned and shocked everyone by saying with unholy glee, "Excellent!" Turning to their grandmothers who had hung on every word of the exchange, he directed Aletha to bring along the lunch. "And Granny Gert, will you kindly hold the door?" To Rose, Tim said genially, "Have it your way," and bent down to clasp her around the knees before slinging her over his shoulder.

"Oooh!" she cried. "What do you think you're doing?! Tim…" Rose began wiggling and kicking her feet. "Put me down!"

"As you wish."

Having thoughtfully left the passenger door of his truck open, Tim complied with her demand by dumping her on the seat and fastening her seatbelt. Rose had lost all semblance of control. Curiously, the prospect did not worry her. As Tim had hoped, she found the situation fraught with unexpected romance. Being unceremoniously flung over her husband's shoulder and carried against her will to his truck was not quite the same as being whisked from peril and tossed across the saddle bow of a waiting steed, but Rose was quick to give her imagination its full scope in overriding such deficiencies. She was not about to let him maintain the upper hand, however, and instinctively put up the pretense, at least, of resentment.

"Tim, this is ridiculous! You can't just… kidnap me! I demand to be treated with some respect." She folded her arms and attempted to glare at him, but his gut-wrenching smile was quickly wearing down her defenses.

Leaning in so that only Rose could hear, Tim murmured, "I *am* showing you respect." His gaze never faltered, but his voice lost its teasing note. "This is me *fighting* for you – for us. If you don't feel up to graciously accepting my invitation, I can stow you in the boat with the rest of the gear. Now, which is it to be?" The smile that had pierced her emotional defenses had been replaced by a look of unyielding authority. The butterflies released earlier fled abruptly when Rose's stomach began doing full somersaults.

Folding her arms, Rose looked away again – this time to hide a betraying smile. Barely stifling an irritating impulse to giggle, she managed to say quietly, "I'll stay here."

Turning to his accomplices, Tim kissed the wrinkled cheek of first one, then the other. "Aletha, Granny Gert, I salute you. I don't think I could have pulled this off without your help." Passersby might easily have assumed he had just awarded each the Medal of Honor.

"Don't forget your lunch, Sonny," Gert said and handed him the stuffed bag, which he tossed into the backseat before driving off with boat in tow. She waved until they were out of sight.

"Well, it's a beginning," Aletha remarked hopefully, "now it's up to them."

Chapter 6

"Lord, how many times should I forgive my brother or sister who sins against me? Should I forgive as many as seven times?" Jesus said, "Not just seven times, but rather as many as seventy times seven."

Matthew 18:21b-22 (CEB)

Little was said after Tim launched the boat into Sunrise Lake though the air between husband and wife was charged with a host of chaotic emotions, among them trepidation, curiosity, and hope. Rose experienced an odd tingling sensation whenever she glanced at Tim, who had to exercise the patience of Job to hold his tongue until they reached their destination. Navigating a hidden passage almost obscured by overhanging trees, he maneuvered the boat into a surprisingly open cove tucked in between a screening jut of land on one side and open farmland on the opposite shore. A few disinterested cows looked up at the sound of uninvited guests. Determining the individuals in the boat to be non-threatening, the four-legged sisterhood continued to nibble their way across the field before ambling away, leaving Tim and Rose alone – completely and utterly alone

After setting the anchor and pulling the canvas sunshade into place, Tim looked at his wife. She had changed clothes at the dock and was now wearing the tankini she had first worn at a BBQ the year before. It had been a golden day when each had enjoyed the other's company without reservation and without the specter of a British P.I. coming between them. Tim had stowed that particular swimsuit in the boat, hoping it might remind Rose of happier times when the bond between them was only a veiled promise of what was to come. The plan worked.

With hesitant trust, she allowed her husband to lead her to the bench seat in the back of the boat where any space between them could be minimized into nonexistence. Sitting side by side, Rose gazed into his troubled eyes, and any desire to giggle fled. Indeed, she had no idea how to proceed. Tim did; he had thought of nothing else for days.

"Rose, before you say anything, let me say this. I am so, *so* sorry. I am more sorry about all that has happened this week than I have been about anything in my whole life. Without meaning to, I hurt the person I love most, and I couldn't figure out how to make it right. My crazy reaction to the news of twins robbed you of sharing with me what should have been a glorious, once-in-a-lifetime moment." Tim swallowed a lump in his throat before going on. "With the best will in the world, I can never give that moment back to you. It's lost forever. But I *can* give you a promise. I love you, and I love these babies," he said, gently placing one hand over her abdomen. "And from here on out, I vow to be – or at least *try* to be – the best husband and father possible." He lifted his hand to wipe the tears that had spilled onto Rose's cheeks. "*Please* forgive me."

Smiling shyly with lips that trembled slightly, she stroked his cheek until she had coaxed a tentative smile from his drooping mouth.

"You're not the only one who is sorry," she said. "You tried to explain what happened to you after the ultrasound, but I wouldn't let you, and then I continued to behave like the foolish, overly emotional women I despise. *I'm* the one who needs to apologize. Can you ever forgive *me?*"

"Well, if you can agree that we're both a couple of sorry people and forgive me for being an idiot, a fool, and a moron, then I can forgive you for being a tender woman with a tender heart – not that I ever want that to change." He was enormously encouraged by the uninhibited smile that lifted his heavy spirit and set it once more on solid ground.

"Now, before you get all mushy and try to convince me that I'm incredibly handsome, charming, *and* brilliant," he said, reveling in her answering gurgle of laughter, "let me tell you what I should have told you as soon as I got home. It's the conversation I should have been more insistent about having months ago. But I thought I could put off some decisions we'll have to make – soon. The news of one baby caught me off guard. The revelation of two babies moved up the timeline from soon to immediately."

Tim's voice had grown sober once more, and he lost the boyish grin that had given flight to the fickle butterflies in Rose's stomach. Pitched once more into uncertainty, she allowed her emotions to send the winged creatures careening in random directions until she felt ill. *What on earth is he talking about?* Rose wondered. Her hands returned his clasp, seeking enlightenment and reassurance.

"I'll soon hit my ten-year mark in the army and eligibility for a significant promotion. It's the point in a military career when everyone has to decide, 'Do I stay in, or do I get out?' I thought I would make the army a career, then my dad died. I thought I'd finish out my 20 years in the reserves, and then the collective sanity of the world died."

A bewildered expression greeted his words. He tried again.

"The military has always been a proving ground for social change. And in some cases, such as desegregation, it was a positive thing. But for at least the past 10 years, these changes have been more focused on political correctness than on mission readiness. Rather than continuing to recognize and applaud women for serving effectively and honorably in combat support and service support roles – which they've been doing for *decades*, by the way – a sweeping decision was made to allow women to serve in all combat arms specialties as well. The decision was not based on logic or practicality or because it served the best interests of the army. Oh, no. Political leaders – and sadly, some of those were senior military officers –

finally caved to pressure from special interest groups simply to advance their own careers.

"I know that women can be strong and tough – no one is disputing that. But the strongest, best athletes in the world – think of Olympians – compete only with other athletes of the same sex. That's not sexist, it's common sense. As a rule, and again, I recognize that there are exceptions, men have larger bone mass and skeletal strength than women because of the difference in respective hormone production. That difference also promotes greater muscle development in men. Any rational person recognizes that science. But with women now allowed to occupy every combat MOS[4], some idiot came up with a gender-neutral Army Combat Fitness Test to measure *every* soldier's physical readiness.

"Some bureaucrat decided that – overnight – female supply sergeants, communications officers, mechanics, and medical personnel were supposed to have the same physical capabilities as men in combat. Not only did that nimrod throw science out the window; he threw women under the bus as well. The test was an abysmal failure with barely half of enlisted women passing, while almost all of their male counterparts passed, especially since some of the male standards were *lowered* to sell the lie. It was then changed to a six-event test that had an even *higher* fail rate for female soldiers. Since then, it's been one unsuccessful experiment after another, with readiness being the ultimate victim.[5]

"Now it's across-the-board diversity that drives personnel regulations, not merit-based performance. The concept has been around a long time,

---

[4] Military Occupational Specialty

[5] *"Army Scraps Gender-Neutral Standards Pushed by Discredited Social Engineers."* Center for Military Readiness, posted April 19, 2022. https://www.cmrlink.org/issues/full/army-scraps-genderneutral-standards-pushed-by-discredited-social-engineers#:~:text=Now%20the%20Army%20has%20given,Army%20used%20for%2040%20years.

but it hasn't been pushed like it is now. With the ugly world players growing stronger and uglier, our military seems bent on getting weaker and more 'woke.' I *hate* making statements like that because I am *very* proud of the sacrifice and heroism displayed by our nation's army throughout its history. And I'm proud to have been a part of that, but I believe overall force readiness is declining. Almost all the service branches have recruiting shortfalls, with the exception of the super high-tech Space Force, and half of their 'ranks' are civilians. Now politicians are talking about requiring women to register for selective service. The idea that we can't find enough able-bodied men in a country this size who are willing to step up to defend its citizens just fries my bacon! Now we're supposed to draft our daughters and our mothers – the bedrock of our young families?"

"Oh, Tim, I had no idea! I mean, all these ideas are given such a positive spin in the news – not that I've ever watched much news. Maybe I should pay more attention," she added, a little shamefaced.

"Rose, I just don't know if I can function in this toxic environment anymore. I have to bite my tongue all the time and pretend to uphold command directives I am adamantly opposed to, especially standards regarding LGBT-whatever 'Alphabet' people – I can never get all those letters straight. I hadn't had to deal with any of this personally until this deployment when our battalion was collocated with a unit from New England. They had gay and transgender members, and we had to jump through hoops to accommodate these people while providing security and what little privacy we could for all the straight soldiers. It was total nonsense and detracted enormously from performing our mission.

"You know my heart on these social issues because we've talked about them as they relate to the perfection and beauty of creation and God's provision of grace for a fallen world. On the one hand, I feel great compassion for people who are so confused about who God made them to be they can't function normally in their own skin. On the other hand, this spreading psychotic behavior disturbs me deeply. It has *no* place in the army, especially on the battlefield. Besides, *no one* has the right to demand that I participate in his or her mental delusions." He concluded on such a dejected note, Rose stood and wrapped her arms around her husband, holding his head against her heart.

"Tim, I have never loved you more for being a caring, honorable man. If your spirit is so conflicted about these things, leave the army behind. You have served your country faithfully with distinction for many years. No one would judge you for resigning your commission."

Not wanting to move away from her affirming embrace, Tim, nonetheless, pulled back to add another consideration.

"I had almost decided to do just that, until you told me about the baby, and then two babies."

"What on earth has my pregnancy got to do with it?" she asked, confused.

"Because, sweetheart," he replied gently, "our medical insurance is tied to my reserve military service. We can find other health insurance, but even if the pre-existing condition of pregnancy is covered, the cost will be a small fortune compared to what we're paying now. I don't want you to think for a minute that we won't find the money somehow, whether that means taking out a mortgage on the house or selling this boat. We'll figure it out. If it had been just one baby, you could have gone to a midwife, someone like your sister Violet. But from what little research I've done since Monday, that's not a recommended course with twins. I think that's what pushed me over the edge when you had the ultrasound. All I could see were our options shrinking."

"Then why can't you just wait six months until after the twins are born?" For Rose that was the obvious solution. She wondered at his inability to see it.

Before answering, Tim pulled her down beside him again. "There are other variables I haven't told you about yet. The military has a program called 'Stop Loss' which, technically, isn't used anymore. But with our world in such a volatile state, and with the inability of the services to fill their ranks with an all-volunteer force, I wouldn't bet against it being instituted again. Quite simply, it means the army could make me stay as long as they need me. That probably won't happen, but there are no guarantees. And there is another consideration. I don't want you to be alarmed, but I must tell you everything, because I promised myself that if you ever forgave me and let me explain my inexplicable recent actions, I would hold nothing back."

Sitting in the comforting circle of her husband's arm, Rose listened to Tim's disclosures as if listening to the voice of a documentary narrator.

"You know our southern border doesn't exist anymore – or our northern border, for that matter. In addition to drug smugglers, human traffickers, and other undocumented undesirables passing into the U.S. undeterred, there are *thousands* of mainland Chinese coming into the States illegally, and they're being released into communities all over the country.[6] Estimates are that most are male of military age.[7] What could that mean for our national defense at home, when we have an increasing number of our military units deployed globally?

"I realize the world is in a mess. It has been almost from the beginning. And though the United States continues to use its strength and influence to defend freedom and provide aid for the oppressed, *we can't fix everything.* Only Jesus can put things right when he returns, and no one knows when that will be. What we do know is that centuries before the establishment of the nation promised to Abraham, he was told that those who bless that nation would be blessed. We honor that admonition, regardless of the merit

---

[6] America First Policy Institute, "*The Trojan Horse at the Southern Border: Malign CCP Infiltration,*" February 14, 2024. https://americafirstpolicy.com/issues/the-trojan-horse-at-the-southern-border-malign-ccp-infiltration

[7] Ozimek, Tom, *"Alarming Rise in Military-aged Chinese Men Entering US Illegally,"* Epoch Times, February 20, 2024.
https://www.myheraldreview.com/news/border/alarming-rise-in-military-aged-chinese-men-entering-us-illegally-border-patrol-union-chief-warns/article_00831fe0-d016-11ee-8f22-1fc3bc785d38.html

or failings of Abraham's descendants, because we honor Abraham's God – *our* God – whose plan was to use that nation to bless all people. And though we know that covenant promise to be fulfilled in the nation of Israel, some government leaders plot to have the U.S. turn her back on our strongest ally in the Middle East, while getting us entangled in one 'forever war' after another which last decades and gain us nothing. And the insanity just seems to escalate. Given the hidden threats within our own borders, I would go out of my mind if I thought you, and now our kids, were in any kind of danger with me potentially on the other side of the world."

Tim's embrace tightened with each dire statement, while a spark of resentment inspired Rose to say with rekindled heat, "Tim, you did it again!" As she turned to face him, he frowned at the anger in her voice. "These were all concerns you were aware of *before* you went to Romania, but you shared *none* of this with me."

Touched on the raw by her accusation, he responded with barely controlled frustration. "I *did* try to talk to you about this – several times. But whenever I attempted to open a discussion about anything besides work, or home decorating, or the latest potential dating opportunity for Derek, you quit listening or made it clear you didn't want to talk about whatever the distasteful subject was, so I finally gave up. But with everything I had to deal with during my deployment, I decided we would have to tackle these topics whether you wanted to discuss them or not. And then you told me about the baby, and I didn't want to ruin… it just seemed better at the time to wait…"

"I think you tried to tell me as soon as you got home, and repeatedly after that, didn't you?" Rose cringed a little at his rueful nod. "But I wouldn't let you. I'm ashamed to admit it."

A heavy silence fell between them. Rose spoke into it first, her voice laden with guilt. "It's me who has let *you* down. You've been unsuccessful in getting me to wake up to unpleasant reality because I'm a dreamer who wants to live in a fairytale. I always have been."

"And that's one of the things I love most about you," Tim said. But Rose would not let herself off the hook so easily.

"I know I keep saying I want you to tell me everything that's worrying you, but the truth is, I'm afraid to listen to disturbing news. I can't live every minute of my life in fear, so I just tune it out. That means that, by default, I've let you carry the weight alone. You deserve a better wife than that." She finished on a forlorn note, unable to look into her husband's tender eyes.

"Sweetheart, we don't have to live every moment in fear. The reality of our fallen world, which, admittedly, continues to fall at an alarming rate, is not where our hope lies. We *know* that ultimately God is in control. His plan for our country and our world is, and always has been, his to execute according to his perfect plan. But it's important to be aware of what's going on around us. And your honesty compels me, in turn, to say that I haven't forced the issue because I have mistakenly – I realize that now – tried to insulate you with the romantic version of life you crave. Now, after dumping the whole filthy mess on you, I feel like an enormous weight has been lifted from my heart and mind. I just wish that heaviness didn't have to shift to you and drag you down in the process."

"I can't deny that what you've told me hasn't been tough to hear, but, as Granny Gert would probably say, 'it's high time you grew up, young lady!'" Rose replied, in a fair imitation of her grandmother. Lifting her head at the sound of Tim's spontaneous laughter, she smiled and added in a decisive manner, "I can't very well be a good mother and protect my children from harm if I don't know where the potential danger comes from. Besides, this is what I signed up for – 'for better or for worse.' It's not that I *want* to hear unsettling truth, but being able to share our concerns, to know what the other is going through – that's the side of marriage that will long outlast the fairytale."

Tim gazed at her as pride and relief swelled within him. Slowly his lop-sided grin appeared and turned Rose's internal organs into melting wax. "Well, Mrs. Ludlow," he said, "It appears that we need to be more open in our communication. I mean, if we can't talk about little things like world insanity, financial crisis, and universal moral decay, what *can* we talk about?" Her responsive laughter was music to his heavy heart.

"We could talk about babies," Rose suggested with a smile. "Maybe float some ideas about possible names. What say you, kind sir?"

Encouraged by her lightened attitude, yet not ready to leave the world occupied by only the two of them, Tim proposed a timely alternative. "An excellent suggestion, but how about we first discuss whatever's in that lunch bag?"

The hurt, the anger, the insecurity that had haunted them both seemed to vaporize into thin air. Tim captured his beloved in an unyielding embrace and kissed her until her toes curled. The moment might have been prolonged, but an insistent gurgling erupted into mutual laughter when Rose's stomach demanded attention. She had been too depressed to eat much of anything for several days.

The lunch provided by Granny Gert and Aletha was ambrosia: mere peanut butter and jelly surpassed the succulence of a perfectly grilled steak; the apples were sweeter than any picked from a tree in God's pristine garden; and bottled water became the rarified flow from the fountain of youth. Not until Tim had polished off the last of the oatmeal cookies was his expression of supreme contentment jarred into a frown by a chance remark.

Reclining against float cushions on the sunken deck of the boat, Tim lay with his eyes closed and a smile on his face while Rose packed up what little was left of their midday meal. She abruptly broke off humming a lilting tune to announce, "We did it. We may not have solved all the world's problems, but at least we confronted them – together. We do make a pretty good team after all, Ludlow." She was a little surprised by his response to her teasing use of his last name.

"Not all, I'm afraid," he said and sat up abruptly. "I can't believe I forgot to mention one more thing – and it's a biggie."

Resolved not to let worry again cast its insistent shadow, Rose sat on a cushion next to her husband and waited.

"Rose, we need to think about the future of *Willow Walk Weddings*."

"What? *Why?* It's a big success! You said so yourself. You also said that if we keep up our current booking pace, we'll be able to pay back the investors in two years. Nothing has changed."

"It *is* a success, and that's due largely to your marketing blitz and your ability to make anyone see things your way." Rose was somewhat mollified by his praise though she sensed a big "but" coming.

"Remember I said there were some gay guys in a unit we trained with? One of them worked in his Battalion Ops Office, like me. I was talking with him one day, and I mentioned my construction business and our wedding chapel sideline. He made a point of telling me I'd better get in line with the provisions of the Respect for Marriage Act, or I could lose *Willow Walk Weddings.*"

"*What?*" Rose cried in dismay.

"Apparently, this guy – I'll call him 'Lieutenant Tentpeg' – and his partner filed a lawsuit against B&B owners who refused to host a same-sex wedding at their facility. He admitted the owners were pretty decent about it, but he and his future husband – *Ugh!* How can anyone say that and not hear how *wrong* it sounds! Anyway, they wouldn't let the owners off the hook even when the people explained that their religious beliefs prevented them from being a part of something they knew to be antithetical to biblical teaching."

"But that's terrible! I thought religious freedom was supposed to be protected by that legislation."

"It is – if the organization in question is a faith-based non-profit like a church or a college. But private businesses that provide wedding services such as photography, flowers, wedding cakes, and wedding *venues…*"

"*Willow Walk Weddings,*" Rose breathed in dismay.

"…are not specifically covered by the legislation.[8] We could go on for years without any problems, *or we* could get a call tomorrow asking us to host a 'Pride' gathering or a wedding for two women. If we don't go along with the request, we could be in legal hot water. And before you say it, yes, we should have thought of this before we launched a speculative enterprise. Miles mentioned it once or twice in passing, but I think we were all so wrapped up in the possibilities of the business – and getting everything just right for Abe and Amy's wedding – that we never considered a downside like this. I suppose the likelihood of any political pushback from future clients seemed almost impossible in a small town like Tinkers Well."

Tim was silent for a few minutes, but the strain of holding everything in for so long finally erupted in a frustrated tirade he could not stop. "Damnit all! Excuse my language, but it just infuriates me that such a small percentage of the population can control the thoughts and… and livelihoods of decent, law-abiding people. And let me make this clear: I am *not* saying that people with a tragically warped understanding of human intimacy can't be outwardly pleasant or highly productive, despite whatever negative personal experience or perverse philosophy contributed to their deviant behavior.

"Look, I know I'm as much of a sinner as anyone; I can never deny that. But at least I *recognize* my sin. I pray for forgiveness and seek to put it behind me. This 'alternative lifestyle,' which flies in the face of everything we know to be natural and healthy, is an affront to the Creator who set the world in order. Now this sad mockery of divinely inspired human purpose is not only celebrated by those who practice it, we, as a society, are expected to condone it *and* celebrate it. How is it that these poor souls, enslaved by something straight from the pit of hell, are protected by law and allowed to

---

[8] Center for Public Justice "*What Houses of Worship, Faith-based Organizations, and People of Faith Need to Know – and do – about the Respect for Marriage Act.*" December 13, 2022. Page 8. https://cpjustice.org/new-resource-what-you-need-to-know-about-the-respect-for-marriage-act/

dictate the conscience of a nation that, from its inception, was built on Judeo-Christian values? It isn't right! Oh, I know we still have the right to vote, and I am hopeful for a miracle this fall, but only God knows that outcome."

Tim sighed and looked at Rose. In defeated resignation, he concluded, "It's just that we've both worked so hard to make our wedding business a going concern, and we've done it with honor and integrity."

"And with great customer feedback, I might add!" Rose declared with spirit.

"You may indeed, Mrs. Ludlow!" Tim said with a sudden, boyish grin.

For months he had been taunted and tested by demons of despair. He should have known they were no match for Rose. Mentally kicking himself for the tenth time over not sharing his concerns with her earlier, Tim wondered how many years of marriage it would take for him to get things right the first time instead of having to learn everything the hard way.

He took her hands and looked into her lovely, trusting eyes. "Are we agreed that I resign my commission now – before the babies come?"

"Agreed. And just remember, even if you're not serving your country in the military anymore, there are other ways to serve."

"What do you mean?"

"You're a respected businessman and well-known in the community. You've hired several veterans and helped them to begin a new life. Maybe you should also consider running for public office. You could start off with the school board…"

"But I thought we agreed our kids would attend the new Christian school Miles is building."

"We did, and they will, but it can't accommodate every child in Tinker's Well or Harrington County. Tim, those other kids deserve a sound education too without all the harmful nonsense being forced into public school curriculums. And who knows how long it will be before parents are fighting for the right to educate their children at home or to send their kids to an alternate school of their choice. Someone has to speak for them."

"I can't argue that, but I don't see how managing a very full-time business and being father to two babies will allow time for that kind of commitment."

"Well, maybe not right away, but we'll see…" Rose answered with a sly smile. "First the school board, then mayor of Tinkers Well, then the governorship…"

"Whoa! Slow down, gorgeous!" Shaking his head, Tim added, "You have the wildest imagination…"

Rose ignored the interruption. "Anyway, we'll think of something to cover the medical piece. I can always ask Violet for advice. And we've been saving money to replace my old car. We could postpone that a while to cover the costs."

"We will *not* put off getting rid of that antique. Your safety, and now our children's, is too important," Tim replied in a voice that brooked no debate. "Shoot, we probably need to look at a van now anyway. At this rate, we'll probably have five or six kids before we know it!" A delighted giggle escaped Rose. The short bursts of laughter continued to bolster his spirit by ever increasing degrees.

"Maybe we need to book more events – but only if you feel comfortable still keeping that option open." She said, looking hopefully at Tim.

"I suppose it wouldn't hurt to have a little faith about all of this. I'm ashamed to admit it, but despite all I said earlier about God being in control, my gut reaction to every challenge is to try to solve the problem myself instead of leaving it in far better hands than mine. If God can create a universe out of nothing, he can protect us from any outrageous demands or at least show us how to handle them in a way that honors him, if, or when, they arise."

"Ti-im," Rose spoke his name in two syllables with a cajoling expression that should have warned him to expect the unexpected. He was too distracted by the beguiling smile he had missed so desperately.

"I had another thought." She had once again eliminated any space between them. "What if you moved your business office to the barn." She held up her hand before he could object. "I know you said it was too big for your needs, but… wait for it… what if we had our own *home renovation show?* We could film it there!"

"*What?* Are you *nuts?*" Tim found it difficult to look serious while shaking with laughter.

"We could have a show where I come up with all the ideas, and you figure out how to make them work. Of course, you'd have to act like you thought I was crazy…"

"Woman, you *are* crazy!"

"…but in the end, you would create something twice as brilliant, and I would take credit for it all being my idea. *Or* you could run your plans for a project by me, and I could change *everything.* Audiences love when couples argue. Maybe we could call the show *Hammer and Tongs.*"

"Rose Elizabeth…"

"Ooh, I just thought of something else! Audiences also love babies. When they're big enough, the twins could be a big draw wearing tiny tool belts and work boots…"

Delighting in one of his wife's flights of fancy as never before, Tim prompted, "*Or…*"

"*Or* we could include the whole Three Brothers crew. You know Derek would jump all over the opportunity to perform his routine, and maybe Abe could be in a few episodes in between seminary classes. Their dialogue alone could boost ratings, and we could go by…oh, I don't know…" Rose snapped her fingers. "How about *Renovation Masters of Disasters,* or…" Catching sight of Tim's comical dismay, she said, "Too long? What do you think of *Family Fix-it?* Or maybe…"

"Or maybe," Tim cut in before his bride could suggest any more delightfully absurd ideas; he knew her imagination to be boundless. "We could continue to host weddings and events in the truly estimable way you have perfected."

"Or that," Rose replied with a captivating smile that caused his heart to beat at warp speed.

Fueled by a glorious, uninhibited adrenaline rush, Tim jumped to his feet, picked up his wife who made only a pretense of protest, and tossed her into the water. When she surfaced, spluttering and laughing, he proposed the most welcome suggestion of the day. "Or, for now, we could pretend we're the only two people alive without a care in the world."

After throwing a few floats and foam noodles in her direction, Tim joined Rose. They spent the afternoon splashing and lazing around in their secluded retreat as they discovered anew the security and freedom of unconditional love.

Gratefully following Tim's suggestion that everyone knock off work early on Friday, Derek pointed his beat-up truck in the direction of the Warner home. After his conversation with his mom the night before, he and José decided to go ahead and move to their new residence after work that day, so they'd have the weekend to get settled in. As Derek approached the house, José showed signs of unusual animation.

"Hey, *ese*, you see that van parked in front of the house. My cousin must be here already! Man, you got to meet her. Sometimes, she scares me to death because she's so smart, but she's also pretty cool. Her daughter is a real c*hanguita.*"

"Say *what?*"

"Sorry - a li'l monkey. You know, really cute."

"Oh, so nothing like you," Derek responded and quickly exited the truck.

Just then two women and a little girl rounded the corner from the rear of the house. The older woman Derek recognized as José's Tia Lupe, whom he had met when invited to join the Aguilar family for dinner on numerous occasions. Short and compact like José, she beamed a smile of welcome – a smile *almost* as bright as José's; she lacked any gold-capped teeth. She had also, wisely, left the fascination with tattoos to her nephew.

"Derek! We did not expect you to be home so early, or we would have waited to come for a proper visit. But I wanted to show my niece Kavya, and little Anika, José's new home. Since your sweet mama was not at home either, we took a quick look around outside. Come, Ani, Kavya, meet José's friend Derek. He is practically a member of *la Familia* Aguilar."

At any other time, Derek would have responded to the simple statement with the warmth it deserved. At any other time, he would have teased José about being the runt of the family. At any other time, he would have made playful advances to the little girl hiding behind her mother's legs, her unruly curls stirred by a light breeze. But this was not any other time.

Catapulted in an instant into the realm of fantasy, Derek's reason was engulfed in a fog; glib words of greeting failed to make their way to his lips, and his broad grin sagged into a gaping hole of vacuous stupidity. Later, he couldn't say whether he had managed to extend his hand to shake that of the young woman whose every movement captivated him, or if it had hung lifeless at his side. Tim would have recognized the symptoms and the unlikelihood of a speedy recovery – if any recovery was to be expected at all.

In a dreamlike state, where motion is achieved only through great effort, and desired objects elude possession, Derek beheld a vision surely fashioned by God in one of his more inspired moments. Smooth brown skin, rich and creamy – as if it had poured from a chocolate fountain – wrapped a figure of celestial proportions. Luxuriant, wavy hair hung almost to her waist, framing a face dominated by translucent amber eyes, their luster partially veiled by thick lashes. A thin, proud nose hooked slightly at the end daring anyone to describe it as pert, and full, bronze lips merely hinted at an enigmatic smile, much like da Vinci's *Mona Lisa*. The embodiment of female perfection standing before him must have been as tall as he was, but Derek felt no threat from her commanding stature. His only thought was a clarion call of certainty that echoed through his fuzzy brain.

I don't know how. I don't know when. But this is the woman I'm going to marry!

Alas that few epiphanies are universally shared.

CHAPTER 7

Angelica's meeting with Mr. Dawson's daughter turned into a dinner for the three of them at Ronnie's apartment. The new "tenant" was warmly received and quickly became acquainted with the cat Bastet, who regarded herself as only marginally less exalted than her ancient Egyptian preceptress. Any hesitation about making the proposed move to the city quickly dissipated as Angelica found herself enjoying the evening and the company more than she had anticipated. Without really expecting to make it a late night, she had, nevertheless, left a note for Derek telling him not to wait up for her. She would properly welcome José on Saturday morning, promising a big breakfast.

By the time Derek had sufficiently recovered his wits after the disastrous meeting with Kavya, the ladies were long gone, and he and José were settling into their new digs. With his return to the Warner home, the absence of his mother left Derek feeling oddly out of place. Angelica had always been the heart of their home, especially after his dad died. Though absent in form, her presence could be felt everywhere – from the tropical décor in the living room to the colorful woven rug in the hallway leading to the kitchen, with its lingering hint of exotic island spices. For the first time in his life, Derek looked around at all that was familiar and comfortable and suddenly knew a desire for something else. The realization that the "something else" involved a certain new acquaintance he accepted without reservation. The path to that goal was less clear.

Derek shook off the disquieting sensation and scoured the fridge for leftovers. He had already rationalized his less than gallant reaction to Kavya as an aberration. All his friends knew he was the "King of Cool." The end of a bruising work week, the distraction of unrest in the Ludlow home, and the upheaval of another move gave him plentiful excuses for his unusual behavior. It was simply a question of learning more about her, Derek told himself. Believing that knowledge is power, Derek set out to learn more about Kavya from the one person both parties had in common. The sooner he could penetrate her inscrutable aura, the sooner she would succumb to his charms. As only Derek would, he considered it a certainty.

Taking a seat at the kitchen table, he glanced at José, who was nibbling the last microscopic piece of flesh off a chicken bone, and casually asked him about his extended family.

Not so easily taken in, José grinned and said, "Man, I never seen you look so stupid. Your mouth was like, hanging open to catch flies, and you couldn't even talk." He threw back his head and laughed gleefully. "Hey, *ese*, you don' want to know about my 'family.' You want to know about *Kav-ya*," he teased in a sing-song voice, and was not intimidated in the least by Derek's infuriated glare. "Didn' I tell you she was a li'l scary?"

"She wasn't scary," Derek snapped back. "It's just that, knowing you, I was a little surprised to see that she was taller than five foot nothing. And she was well… well-groomed. She had good teeth," he added lamely, avoiding José's eye."

"Good *teeth*? Ha! Man, you thought she was *hot*. Go ahead, you can admit it. I won' tell nobody… maybe." Rarely did José have the upper hand around Derek. He had it now and intended to make the most of it.

"Okay. She's pretty," Derek admitted grudgingly.

Without a word, José folded his arms and grinned at Derek.

"Okay, okay, so she's beautiful. In fact, she's gorgeous! Satisfied?"

"Oh, sure, *I'm* satisfied. But I'm not the fool who went *loco* over her."

"Derek Warner does not go *loco*, *estúpido*! Now shut up and hand me that pie."

"Hey, no' bad, *ese*. I may teach you to speak Spanish yet." José's persistent toothy grin began to drill down on Derek's last nerve until a curious thought took possession of his brain. His eyes narrowed as he leaned his arms on the table and looked suspiciously at the other man.

"Wait a minute. Kavya *is* beautiful. So tell me, my 'li'l friend,' how is it that she is *your* cousin? I mean, in what mythical realm could anyone so gorgeous be a relation of yours? She's a… a… *goddess*, and you're, well… you." Derek leaned back and waited for an answer.

His good humor unimpaired, José said simply, "Because we're really not related at all, or maybe I should say only sort of." Quick to take advantage of the confusion caused by his reply, he claimed the last slice of mango cheesecake without a fight.

"Wait. You told me she was your cousin. I heard you distinctly say the words 'my cousin.' And what does 'only sort of' mean? Are you messing with me, little man?" Derek demanded.

José, enjoying the cheesecake on so many levels, shoveled another piece in his mouth. "Dude, this is the most fun I've had in a long time!"

"You either level with me, brother, or I won't share this last slice of cheeseca…"

Realizing he had been outmaneuvered, Derek jumped up and started after José, who swallowed the last bite in one gulp and dashed into his bedroom, slamming the door behind him. His uncontrolled laughter almost drowned out the sound of Derek banging on the door. Accepting defeat, at least temporarily, Derek slumped to the floor and waited. Presently, still wiping his streaming eyes, José cautiously peered into the hall.

"Is it safe?"

"Depends on whether you want to see tomorrow or not," Derek answered through clenched teeth.

José, knowing Derek's threats to contain more sound and fury than actual bite, took compassion on his friend and sat next to him on the floor. He then began a somewhat disjointed tale.

Derek knew of José's teen years in California and why he had chosen not to return to his parents' home, but instead, had decided to live with his aunt and uncle in Kansas after leaving the army. To Derek, it seemed an odd way to recount his apparently not-so-familial relationship to Kavya, but as José peeled away layer after layer of their joint history, all became clear. The revelations shared gave Derek much to think about when he later lay on his bed in a bemused state. Possessing an almost superhuman ability to sleep anywhere, at any time, for an unspecified period, Derek soon dozed off dreaming of mysterious golden eyes and a smile impossible to interpret. He never heard his mom come into the room to turn off the lamp.

With little hope of ever encountering Samuel Jamison, despite the repeated assurances of Mr. Dawson that such a likelihood was inevitable, Angelica had agreed to start her foray into crime detection at the location where she was most likely to meet anyone staying at the hotel. In spite of its up-to-date amenities, the *Prairie Gateway* still required overnight guests to register at the desk. Angelica later learned that digital hotel keys could be issued through an app, but the one-on-one, personal contact with front-desk personnel ensured better visual tracking of each individual and provided a feel of Midwest hospitality. She wondered if the practice would change after the big security conference, but since it would no longer affect her, she decided it was of little importance.

So engrossed did she become in the inner workings of guest check-in, Angelica nearly forgot why she was there. Pleased with her own aptitude for mastering the hotel's registration software and guest protocol, she settled into her new routine with ease. Her friendly, open personality made her a hit with coworkers, as did her lilting accent and colorful head scarves. Her rapid assimilation into the team bolstered her confidence and left her feeling as if she had worked there for years.

A full week passed without incident until Angelica was caught off guard one day, causing her to stop abruptly in the middle of a transaction. The sound she had been dreading caught her ear. Quickly completing her task, she focused all her attention on that auditory clue. A mid-afternoon lull rested on the expansive lobby. Sounds of children laughing and splashing floated down the corridor from the pool, while a few small parties populated the tables in the lounge, their desultory conversations barely discernable.

The only other people in the immediate vicinity were an arriving guest exiting a taxi and the bellhop who ushered the gentleman's luggage inside. The large, vaulted foyer gave directly onto the front entrance where the doors were kept open to invite guests in, swept along by a stiff Missouri breeze. In truth, the gust of air was provided by large fans holding the midday heat at bay. As they approached the desk, Angelica again heard the voice. Impossible that it could come from the man wearing tailored shorts and a short-sleeved button-down shirt. He was too young – possibly 40 to 50 years old. Besides, as they drew closer, she detected a European accent and decided that such fair skin could not be achieved artificially. With genuine shock, she realized it must be the bellhop whose deep voice had penetrated her thoughts. A bellhop!

But surely, she thought in amazement, *Samuel Jamison could never pass himself off as a bellhop!*

Angelica had no opportunity to further process the possibility before the European approached the desk and declared himself to be a Mr. Klaus Richter from Bamberg, Germany. Thankful that she could go through the motions of welcoming him and getting him checked in without really thinking, Angelica barely acknowledged his cursory bow of thanks before he turned away to claim his luggage.

"No need to follow me upstairs," he said. "I can get the one suitcase and briefcase. I do thank you for your help," he added and passed to the bellhop what could have been anything from a monetary bill to a rodeo ticket; she couldn't be sure. But of one thing, Angelica was certain. Though the façade was the antithesis of what she had expected, she knew the other man to be Samuel Jamison. An individual of imposing presence – despite the anonymity of a service uniform – he dominated any space he occupied. Deftly pocketing the slip of paper, he nodded politely to the new arrival. It was his final comment that clinched the recognition for her.

"I thank you for your patronage of the *Prairie Gateway* and for your illuminating conversation. It has been a brief but delightful interlude in an otherwise dull afternoon." The voice may have been muted, but the resonance was unmistakable.

And those words, Angelica thought with loathing, *those disgustin' words – "delightful interlude."* She had never forgotten the parting note Jamison had left for her friend Sabryna when he abandoned her all those years before. Little could he have imagined that they would fuel Angelica's resolve to see this farce through.

While his mother pursued a thief, Derek Warner set his sights more firmly on his own quarry. That formidable mission coincided with the start of his firefighter training. Rather than being daunted by the competing demands on his time, Derek embraced the challenge. He was always open to any excuse to drive to the Aguilar home. Unfortunately, no opportunities presented themselves immediately following his first meeting with Kavya. Confident in the belief that all women have a soft spot for any man in uniform – particularly a firefighter's uniform – he focused first on passing his initial training course. It quickly became apparent that the first goal would prove to be more easily attainable than the second.

Derek responded almost effortlessly to the discipline and structure of the training so reminiscent of his years in the army. Where other candidates struggled to strap on a 100-pound pack and continue to work through required drills, Derek took the added stress in stride. The demanding Thursday evening instruction cycles made for rough Friday workdays, but Derek was nothing if not tough. After only two weeks of training, he was hooked. As much as he enjoyed working on the Three Brothers' crew, Derek felt drawn to this new occupation in an almost spiritual way.

He had lived half a lifetime without his father. Where consideration of following in his dad's footsteps as a police officer had never sat easily with Derek, working toward certification as a volunteer firefighter and fellow first responder came as naturally as breathing. He sometimes imagined his father's broad smile, so like his own, beaming at him with pride. Derek drew physical and mental strength from that vision. The same self-confidence that elevated him above his peers in one realm, however, ultimately brought about his undoing in another. He learned quickly that running into a burning building posed fewer hazards than running after his heart's desire.

Scornful of the idea that Derek Warner might have any more than a shallow interest in her existence, Kavya Jackson began to get reacquainted with her surroundings. The unincorporated wide spot in the road known as Bailey Crossroads – it could hardly be called a town – boasted a population of only 463, most of whom were farmers. Tinkers Well was the closest proper town of any size, besides being the county seat of Harrington County. The displaced California girls found the Aguilar home at once strange and restful; strange only in the sense that the wide-open spaces, fresh air, and lack of traffic were at such variance with their home in Santa Monica. Ani soaked up the attention showered on her by Tia Lupe and her husband Carlos, allowing Kavya time to reclaim her youth – and to begin again.

While the little girl succumbed to the call of slumber brought on by mornings spent running endlessly around the yard shooing chickens or playing with a litter of puppies, her mother drove into Tinkers Well to seek some form of temporary employment until her classes at UMKC began in the fall. She drove to Tinkers Well relying chiefly on her phone's GPS. It had been nine years since her last visit.

Unlike Rose Ludlow, who could observe such ordinary scenes as cornfields, farmhouses, and clumps of trees, and attribute fantastic tales to each one, Kavya Jackson had no interest in anything not directly related to the mission of the moment. Scudding clouds and picturesque homesteads were invisible to her. She looked only to the future. Blind to her surroundings, Kavya contemplated what might lie ahead for herself and little Ani. The effort failed when her mind drifted instead to the past – a safe, long-ago past when she and her sister, three years Kavya's junior, had enjoyed an idyllic childhood, a past when her parents had loved each other, and their children had been secure in that love.

As the daughter of a diplomat with the USDA's Foreign Agricultural Service, Kavya spent most of her first ten years in India. Her father, Dwayne Jackson, a tall, athletic black man with a quick mind and a lust for life, was still a PhD student at UC Davis when he was invited to present a paper to an important association of agribusinessmen from Uttar Pradesh. The event, hosted at the Indian Consulate in San Francisco, not only exposed Jackson to influential contacts, it was there he met Chandra Singh, daughter of the Consul General.

As reserved and serious as Jackson was outgoing, Chandra held a fascination for him. With her privileged lineage and roots in diplomacy, she moved among the distinguished company as one born to it. Jackson was charmed by the grace and poise that illuminated her grave countenance with subtle beauty. She was drawn to him by the liveliness she lacked. The two were married six months later.

Recollections of her earliest years in Mumbai were vague, but with her father's almost unprecedented follow-on posting within India to the US Embassy in New Delhi, young Kavya began to take in the world around her and to make memories she still recalled 20 years later. She was six at the time. Kavya remembered visiting her father's office at the embassy where US Marines in sharp uniforms greeted them formally at the main entrance before slipping each little girl a piece of candy and a solemn wink. She and Anika competed for honors as the first to spot the ambassador's dog, Molly, who had free range of the embassy grounds and might appear anywhere inside a building or out in the compound. And each year the family participated in an embassy-wide Fourth of July party to celebrate the birth of their parent country.

The Jackson girls were reminded repeatedly by their father that they were Americans. They learned of the United States from him and from teachers at their American international school, though the culturally diverse student body was hardly indicative of that citizenship. Kavya and her American friends thought nothing of playing alongside their Indian peers or with kids from any number of third-country nations. They shared a world of vibrant colors, pulsating music, and exotic flavors – a land where ancient history came alive through ornamental artwork and exquisitely intricate architecture. For young Kavya, that was her normal, and she believed that life for everyone must look essentially the same. That belief was one of few that Kavya and her sister shared.

The two could not have been more different, either physically or emotionally, each presenting a striking blend of their biracial heritage. Kavya owed her delicate features and soft, wavy hair to her mother, but her height – well above the average for Indian girls – was attributed to her father. In contrast, Anika's kinky hair and broad facial contours, together with her short frame, gave her a somewhat comical appearance, earning her the nickname "Monkey." Where Kavya's skin was a rich brown, Anika's was much lighter, almost sallow.

The Jackson sisters, though fond of one another, maintained a give-and-take relationship; Kavya surrendered all her parents' attention, while Anika claimed it. Both girls showed promising intellects at an early age, but it was Anika who craved adoration and praise for every accomplishment. Kavya, having also inherited from her mother a serious, introverted nature, knew her own value without being constantly reminded of it. Though she was by far the more attractive of the two, it was Anika who drew everyone's attention, Anika who was her parents' pet, Anika who could do no wrong. Any sibling might be excused for resenting such a command of the family limelight. Kavya, content in her sister's shadow, accepted life on her own terms. It was only in retrospect that she was able to discern a fissure in her placid existence.

The long sojourn abroad began to highlight fundamental differences in ideologies and priorities between her parents. Chandra was supremely content with their life in India as Jackson never was. The job intrigued him and satisfied him so long as he could see positive outcomes from interaction between their respective governments. When politics or religion got in the way of what he considered to be progress, however, he became increasingly impatient to move to some other region of the world where his talents might be put to better use. He tried to hide his restlessness, but Kavya sensed it. She noticed many things.

Though only a child, she was aware of her father's disapproval when Chandra began to subtly undermine American traditions in the home while encouraging the girls to embrace, more and more, their Indian roots. It puzzled young Kavya because she had heard her parents agree on a broad philosophy of introducing their children to many cultures and belief systems rather than pointing them toward any definitive religion. Their father believed it best to let each make her own decision regarding creeds of faith, even if that meant following no religious path at all. Unbeknownst to him, however, Chandra began to give the girls statues of various Hindu gods and goddesses. Kavya remembered her delight in the colorful images and the stories intertwined around each deity, though her mother's devotion to the practice of Hinduism seemed, to her, almost fanatical. The only practice Dwayne Jackson followed religiously was playing golf every Sunday.

Thinking back on those early years, Kavya recalled an almost indiscernible shift in family dynamics when the Jacksons returned to American soil for a required posting in Washington D.C. It was Chandra who then grew disenchanted with life. Her primary solace was found in immersing herself in the sizable Indian community there. But that distraction only became a possibility when Isabella Cruz entered their lives.

The young Mexican woman, then in her early thirties, had served as nanny to another State Department family for ten years. She had joined them when they were posted to Mexico City and had traveled with them as they moved about the world. With her former charges destined to attend a boarding school for their high-school years, she was on the brink of returning to Mexico when Chandra learned of her employment availability. Isabella's soothing presence helped ease growing tension in the Jackson home. She provided Anika with the attention she craved and gave Kavya a renewed sense of security and peace.

Unlike her younger sister, who was oblivious to anything beyond the limited scope of her own interests, ten-year-old Kavya looked beyond the dynamics of her family to embrace an unfamiliar new world. Though far less vibrant and chaotic than the streets of India, the broad avenues and formal layout of Washington D.C., appealed to Kavya. The stately buildings and memorials, shrouded in reverence, inspired her, as if the very structures themselves approved of her emotional restraint and quiet maturity. Her notion of school shifted only slightly; the international diplomatic community surrounding the nation's capital continued to fill her classroom with the children of the world. The charmed life of Kavya and Anika Jackson would last another four years.

During those years, Isabella became more of a mother to Kavya than Chandra had ever been. In addition to being confidant, encourager, disciplinarian, and role model, she filled the void in another significant area. Isabella had been raised to follow the Catholic faith, though her understanding of God's attributes and her knowledge of the Bible had been much expanded due to the influence of her former employers who were Protestant believers. In her nurturing role as nanny and surrogate mother, she passed on those beliefs to Kavya and her sister. Anika, truly her mothers' child, scorned the Bible stories and illustrations she found commonplace and unimaginative, and chose instead to follow Chandra in her various forms of worship.

In her serious fashion, Kavya gave considerable thought to the simple idea of a single God who rules over the world he created with righteousness and justice. It took her a while to wrap her mind around a Son of God, and the need for him to pay a penalty for her sins, or the notion that she was held accountable for her sins at all, wondering where Karma fit in. When it came to the Holy Spirit, Kavya attempted to equate the idea of God living within a believer to being a goddess herself. Isabella gently suggested the child ponder the questions for a while; understanding would come.

Kavya's disquiet over such matters echoed an uneasy truce that ruled the Jackson home. Each hoped that a new overseas posting to Canberra, Australia would foster family reconciliation and personal renewal.

They were never to find out.

In the present, driving along sunlit country roads under a bold blue sky, Kavya looked back on those dark days, wishing she could shut down her brain and fast forward through the next ten years. But once begun, she could not block the memories.

At 14 and 11, Kavya and Anika couldn't wait to see such curious animals as wallabies, echidnas, and bandicoots, or common, yet exotic, birds like rosellas and rainbow lorikeets. All the wheels were in motion. Everyone had visas, including Isabella; the sisters were both enrolled in Girls Grammar School for the spring semester – July through December; their embassy sponsor contacted them regularly with information updates; and their assigned house was being refurbished for their arrival.

Two weeks before departure, Chandra met with a neurologist recommended by her own physician who had noticed recurring symptoms she had tried to hide. A definitive diagnosis of ALS pitched everyone's life into chaos. With the uncertainty of the disease's progression, decisions had to be made quickly.

Reluctantly leaving the Foreign Service behind, Jackson was able to move within the USDA to a job in Santa Monica, California. Chandra pleaded with him to request a return assignment to India. Her husband's inability to make her see that such an option was an impossibility planted a seed of resentment between them that grew into a secondary illness. What had been her quiet, dignified poise became subtle emotional manipulation of her family. Chandra finally succeeded in convincing Jackson to take her to the Singh family home in Goa, India while she was still reasonably independent. Against her husband's wishes, she insisted that Anika accompany her. Within a month she acknowledged her inability to handle the child and sent her back to California in the company of a servant.

While the Jackson clan adjusted to a radically new normal, Isabella Cruz was caught up in her own family's drama. Her older sister begged that her only son be allowed to come to Tia Bella after school, and at any other time she could include him in the care of her own charges. José Nuñez, the heir apparent to all his parents' aspirations and dreams, was on his way to becoming a *cholo* in a local *Chicano* gang. Through nothing short of a miracle, the two sisters worked less than two miles apart, the eldest sister and her husband being employed as servants for a prominent local family. They believed their only hope of saving José from a disastrous future was to provide him with a safe haven away from negative influences. Knowing how patiently the Nuñez family had waited for work visas, then green cards, and how tirelessly they had strived to keep their immigration status respectable, Isabella felt a responsibility to help them just as the Jacksons had helped her.

She agreed to the request, wondering how she was to balance everything. José's crisis, however, turned out to be their salvation, at least for a while.

Her mother's rejection had nearly broken Anika. That emptiness, coupled with her insatiable need to be in the spotlight, led her into more and more mischief at school until the unimaginable happened. José showed up on their doorstep with a chip on his shoulder, and Anika immediately recognized a kindred spirit. José became her project. In her incorrigible, impish way, she drew him out by slow stages. She commiserated with him on being the runt and the misfit in alien surroundings. Surprising even herself, Anika tapped into a heretofore undiscovered well of patience that neither she, nor anyone else in the house, believed she possessed. Perhaps it was intuitive recognition of another hurting soul or simply acceptance of an answer to boredom. Whatever the reason, Anika threw herself into transforming José, which, in turn, allowed Isabella to temporarily suspend worry over him in favor of caring for the rest of the Jackson family. Despite Anika's best efforts, José's English, though greatly improved, remained heavy with ethnic slang. Being a true nonconformist herself, she decided it suited him. Her determination to prepare him for life in America, though a relative stranger to the country herself, seemed to be in no danger of waning.

Grateful for Anika's intervention, Isabella, nonetheless, recognized that both she and Kavya needed a break from the strain hanging over them all. With their father's approval – and financing – she sent the two girls, along with José, to her younger sister, Lupe Aguilar, in Kansas. Lupe and her husband Carlos were never able to have children. To fill the emptiness in their lives, they had worked at any and every job they could find to scrape together a nest egg. After receiving their green cards, they pooled all their resources to qualify for a farm loan. Their move to Kansas, though a blessing financially, had isolated them from their relatives, so they greeted Isabella's request with enthusiasm and welcomed the mismatched trio from California with open arms. The short respite turned into a summer visit, and the misfits became a family. The girls referred to José's aunt and uncle as their own, and the three youngsters called one another "cousin," though they interacted more like siblings. The Kansas homecoming was repeated each summer, and during fall and spring school holidays, until Kavya and José graduated from high school. The end of that summer signaled the end of an era as each moved on with their life choices. José enlisted in the army. Kavya followed a different path. Her mother had returned permanently to the Jackson home.

During her three-year stay in India, Chandra had held court for her visiting husband and children on their sporadic trips to see her. She had greeted them almost as if they were strangers, as indeed they had become. Jackson brought her home at last, a shell of the woman she had once been.

Completing high school a year early, Kavya enrolled that fall in a two-year nursing program and graduated 18 months later. For the next two years, she provided around-the-clock care for her invalid mother because Chandra couldn't bear to have anyone else attend to her. She prayed to her various Hindu gods but found no peace. Kavya prayed to the God she had learned of as a young girl, but she received no miracle. Isabella was left to keep the household and its master going. The man once so full of life was bewildered by the spectacle of looming death. Rather than turning his affection toward his daughters, Jackson began to withdraw from home life. He poured all his energy into his work because it allowed him to forget. Sadly, that meant he forgot his children, too.

When the end came, Kavya was spent. She had sacrificed her youth and had come through the experience much older than her 21 years. Anika lived in a world of her own, a world of excess and hollow entertainments. With José's departure, she lost her brother and her purpose. With her mother's death, she lost everything else.

Kavya could no longer bear the burden of responsibility for her family. She had given all she had to see her mother to her rest. No more worry; no more tears; no more regrets. She was done with the weight of emotion. Her head began to clear and with that clarity came direction. For the time being she would study microbiology – unemotional, calculable science – with an eye to medical research in the future. Kavya had done all she could for her mother; it was not enough. Others would continue to suffer unless a cure or long-term treatment could be found. Perhaps she would find it. Chandra's death became a new beginning for Kavya and her father, who gradually emerged from emotional solitude and began to see the world beyond crop estimates and agricultural export reports. For Anika, her mother's passing initiated a death spiral.

For a short period after José left for basic training, Anika had tried to think of a way to help Kavya, but it quickly became apparent that she was of no use in a sick room. She sought her father's comfort, but he had already moved beyond her reach. Even Isabella, who truly loved the difficult teenager, never really understood her. During the years of José's presence in the Jackson home, she had been so grateful for his intervention that, for a while after his departure, Isabella forgot that Anika had no one else to turn to. When the realization broke through her consciousness, it was too late. To Isabella's deep regret, Anika had discovered her own way of navigating the uncertainty of life alone.

She managed to hold herself together long enough to finish high school, but her wild nature soon took over, and she threw herself into every conceivable dissipation. One young man found a way to touch Anika's heart. She sobered up enough to regain a measure of physical wellbeing and to get a job. The future was just beginning to look hopeful when it was taken from her in an instant. She never saw the other car coming. That tragedy coincided with the breakup of Kavya's one and only love affair. Anika's namesake was born an hour before her death. A senseless accident became the sad epitaph for a life that had once been filled with promise.

Anika's funeral occurred a week after Kavya's college graduation. The fragile faith Kavya had placed in the hands of a just and loving God died with her mother. It was buried with her sister. Accepting the path of loneliness as inevitable, she put her life on hold yet again. Kavya withdrew her registration for grad school and stayed with her father to see him past the second tragedy while caring for the precious new life whose welfare ultimately became her all-consuming focus. Little Ani's father was never in the picture. So preoccupied did she become with the child, Kavya failed to see beauty rise from the ashes of despair in another quarter. She woke up one day to the knowledge that her father and Isabella had found comfort in one another and in a faith he had long spurned. A month after they returned from their honeymoon, Kavya packed the big van – purchased initially to accommodate her mother's wheelchair – strapped Ani in her car seat, and pointed her nose toward Kansas, the only other place she had ever felt loved.

Reaching the outskirts of Tinkers Well, Kavya shook her head as if to rid her thoughts of the past and its lingering horrors. It was time to look ahead. Almost as if by instinct, the van found its way to an empty parking spot in front of *Milly's Diner.* The future is always easier to discern over a piece of pie.

After the initial shock of coming face to face with a nemesis from her youth, Angelica accepted the reality of Samuel Jamison's presence and set out to keep an eye on him. The "bellhop" materialized a few more times, though never again in the company of Mr. Richter. The European was booked in for a five-week stay, ostensibly to negotiate some ticklish business dealings. His curt responses to Angelica's friendly greetings served to foster rather than to discourage scrutiny of any possible interactions between himself and Jamison. Faithfully following the instructions given to her at that first meeting with Mr. Dawson, and what she thought of as a mini contingent from Interpol, she immediately reported any suspicious observations which were gratefully received by her boss.

When Jamison disappeared for a few days, Angelica blamed herself for not being more attentive. Mr. Dawson sought to reassure her and disabuse her mind of such an errant thought. He invited her to join him for lunch in the hotel's restaurant where, to her amazement, her ears caught the sound of that unmistakable voice once again. It took her a while to pinpoint the source because the normally resonant instrument spat out guttural sounds and unintelligible words instead of the more fluid English she had been listening for. Quickly eliminating a group of businessmen in dark suits, and a gathering of local sports personalities, she honed in on a man in a full-length white robe speaking into a cell phone with great animation. Facial recognition was made more difficult due to a colorful headdress held in place by a rope-like band adorning the man's head. A full beard further blurred the features. Were it not for the voice floating across the room from his general direction, she would have discounted him altogether. Any visible skin, which was quite limited, was a light olive. With only a need to disguise the hands and small portions of the face not covered by a beard, Jamison had changed ethnicities with little more than theatrical make-up and costuming – that and another language. Recalling his personal history, as recounted by Inspector Dulac and Chief Inspector Fergusson, Angelica found herself reluctantly admiring Jamison's remarkable intelligence and adaptability. Ashamed of such treacherous thoughts, she brought her mind back to the task at hand.

With a mere nod of the head, she directed the eyes of her luncheon host to a table next to a large window looking onto the garden space adjacent to the pool. Dawson glanced casually in the direction indicated, then turned again to his tablemate whose obvious attempts to remain calmly nonchalant surprised a rumble of laughter out of him. The warmth of the sound was reflected in his smile. Both did much to assuage Angelica's guilty conscience. She found herself returning the smile without any self-consciousness or embarrassment.

From their first meeting, it was Dawson alone who had given Angelica the confidence to believe she could take on a host of daunting new jobs and thereby unmask a villain. It was his continued encouragement that convinced her to take a further leap of faith – to move into unfamiliar surroundings and make them her own. After only a few weeks, he had gone from hotel manager to casual supervisor to friend. The easy acceptance of their relaxed relationship helped Angelica to surrender the self-imposed load of care she had assumed as sole gatekeeper for the *Prairie Gateway*. From that day forward they became a team, and though they remained "Mr. Dawson" and "Mrs. Warner," the task of bringing down Samuel Jamison turned into an adventure to be shared.

CHAPTER 8

John 20:29b (HCSB)

June slipped into July almost unnoticed. For Rose Thompson, however, the subtle calendar adjustment signaled a new chapter for her marriage. Once again secure in her husband's love, though with eyes open more to the world outside her own romantic bubble, she began to take notice of a significant anomaly close to home which had previously escaped her scrutiny. Through the simple expedient of cornering Derek at Sunday brunch, she demanded an explanation for his unusual behavior of late.

"I don't know what you're talking about, missy." His overdone air of innocence was wasted on Rose.

"I'm talking about the way your mind seems to be somewhere else all the time. I'm talking about all the opportunities you had to hit Abe with a snappy comeback, and you let them slide. I'm talking about you spending the whole Sunday service constantly looking around the sanctuary. Who were you looking for?"

Derek had shared news of his love interest with Tim and Abe the week before and was a little surprised that they had managed to keep it from their wives. He almost wished they hadn't. Surrendering to the inevitable, he told Rose to grab Amy so that he only had to tell his story once. Derek's two "sisters" were thrilled that he had at last succumbed to the power of Cupid's arrow, though from what he told them, they both speculated – correctly –

that his pathway to happiness was liable to be strewn with more than a fair share of rocks and thorns. When he wandered back to the kitchen, the girls set to work, sure in the belief that their assistance in his amorous pursuit to be essential for its success.

They were sitting in Marilyn Ludlow's living room, surrounded by more inspired decorating ideas than either could hope to incorporate in their own homes in a lifetime. Looking around at the years of Ludlow family history represented there, Rose wondered, not for the first time, where Tim's parents would live after their wedding, whenever that might be. Assuming that occasion to be months, if not years away, she turned her attention once more to the project at hand.

"I wish we'd known about Kavya sooner. We could have made a big deal of the Fourth of July and had a picnic at our place instead of just driving into town to watch the fireworks. I know that was only three days ago, but surely, we don't need much of an excuse to invite a few guests to a BBQ," said Rose.

"We don't need *any* excuse, as far as I can see," Amy replied. "It's summer. It's hot. Who wouldn't want to sit in the shade and relax, or dip their toes in your new pool?"

The pool was an above-ground model added in May before Tim's deployment. He and Rose eventually planned on a much bigger inground pool, but their suddenly rising expenses, coupled with a drastic shift in priorities, pushed that dream to the unforeseeable future.

"Besides," said Amy, expanding on her theme, "there isn't a man on the Three Brothers crew who would turn down a free, home-cooked meal. And that includes Jada, though she doesn't usually participate in anything outside of work unless her brother comes with her."

"Maybe if we convince her she won't have to go near the pool, she'll show up." Jada Young's antipathy to water was common knowledge among her coworkers. "Jamal's out of town on business for a while, and I promised him we'd look after her while he's gone – at least as much as she'll let us,"

Rose said, not very hopeful on that front. But Jada's needs would have to wait. Rose and Amy had bigger fish to fry.

Before Rose could suggest limited additions to the invitation list, Granny Gert arrived, towing Aletha behind her. Settling her friend in a nearby wingback chair, she shoved her wide girth into the small open space at the end of the couch and announced that the younger women obviously needed the wisdom of their elders to "put together whatever you're putting together."

"What makes you think we're putting anything together?" Rose protested.

"Don't pretend you're a nitwit, Rosie! Letha and I overheard Derek talking to your husbands. Apparently, he's 'head over tea kettle' in love with José's sister, or cousin, or someone or other…"

"I believe he said 'cousin,' Trudy – José's cousin Kavya. Such a lovely name…"

"Aletha, did you just 'happen' to overhear the conversation, too?" Rose asked suspiciously.

"That's enough impertinence from you, young lady! Of course, she did. How else do you expect us to keep up with everything?" Granny Gert was in rare form. "From what we could gather, he's not making much headway with the girl, so we figured you and Amy would want to help things along, so here we are to help you help things along."

"I couldn't have said it better myself, Trudy," Aletha said, beaming in the general direction of the lively exchange.

Any scheme of Granny Gert's and Aletha's concocting was always well-intentioned and inevitably outrageous. Unable to withstand the temptation to find out what the two had cooked up between them, Amy said, "We had just decided to host a simple BBQ at *Willow Walk* and were discussing the invitation list. I don't suppose you have any suggestions besides the Three Brothers crew?" Intentionally blind to Rose frantically waving her hands in the negative and glaring at her friend, Amy managed to maintain a straight face while she waited with great anticipation for Granny Gert's reply.

"Now, let's see…" Any hope Rose cherished that her grandmother might limit her contributions died an early death. Once Gertrude Gunn got wound up, there was no stopping her. Aletha's gentle promptings served only to add fuel to a bonfire. "You'll want to include José's aunt and uncle so that Kavya's inclusion isn't so obvious. She can't very well decline if the whole family is invited."

"An excellent point, Trudy. And if her aunt and uncle attend the BBQ, she'll have to bring her little girl too. Won't that be fun!"

Gert snapped her fingers. "Perfect! Rosie, get your friends Landry and Karen to come. Their two young'uns can play with – what was her name, Letha?"

"I believe Derek called her Ani. But Trudy, surely Cookie's older brother won't want to play with two little girls…"

"I hadn't thought about that…" Before Rose could rein in the "Welcome Wagon" or point out that the Landrys had no ties to Kavya *or* Tim's coworkers, Granny Gert had come up with a solution. "Invite Reenie Fields and her nephew, Matt. His youngest son is K.C.'s best friend."

"Now isn't that clever of you! The entire family has had such a difficult time since that dreadful woman's arrest."

"A hussy, that's what she was!" Gert clarified with relish.

At the risk of applying bellows to the mounting flames of her grandmother's runaway hospitality, Rose couldn't help but agree on that point at least. "Brittany Murdock,"[9] she mumbled in disgust. Rose had never quite forgiven the would-be felon for nearly wrecking her Easter dinner. "And those two boys need to be reminded that they are loved and appreciated by this community. Now that their father is out of jail, and they're used to having him around again, they might start interacting like

---

[9] *Intersecting Beliefs*

they used to with Tim and Abe, and especially Derek," Rose pointed out. "You know how women admire men who are kind to children."

Despite the initial plan of keeping the gathering to an intimate number, the addition of more and more people threatened to qualify it as a county-wide event! Finding a pen and paper, Amy quickly began to scribble the names mentioned. She had just caught up when Aletha shared another inspired idea.

"Do you know who else needs to be reminded that they're loved and appreciated?" All eyes turned to her. "Isaac and Deborah Rosenbaum. With all the cruel anti-Semitism surfacing now, we need to assure them of our support and friendship. Why, without their help, we would never have apprehended Mrs. Murdock." Even though the actual arrest had been at the hands of airport security, Aletha and Granny Gert and their friends would always claim honors for bringing it about. "Would that be all right, Rose dear?"

"Well, I…"

"I love that idea!" Amy chimed in before her friend had time to consider an answer. "You all may not know that Abe is taking a summer seminar course to get a taste of what to expect in seminary this fall. It was kind of a last-minute decision, and the only class left open was Old Testament prophecy. He's been meeting with the Rosenbaums every week to get their Jewish take on the writings. In one way, it's kind of sad because they can't see the correlation between the prophecies and Jesus as their Messiah. On the other hand, they are willing to listen to Abe's understanding of the words and their fulfillment. Like Abe says, 'Where there's curiosity, there's hope.'"

Rose glanced at the growing list with misgiving. "If all these people are invited, we can't very well leave out Miles and Marilyn. And we've forgotten the most important guest of all."

Before she could enlighten them, Amy slapped her forehead and exclaimed, "Angelica, of course! How could we have forgotten her?"

"Good heavens!" Aletha cried in dismay. "An unforgivable oversight!" As an afterthought, she said, "I suppose it's because we've seen so little of her lately now that she's working in the security office at that nice new hotel in Kansas City. In fact, I believe she's working today, though I can't imagine what she finds to do."

Never without an answer, Gert said, "I hear she's on the trail of some international jewel smugglers!"

"Now Trudy, you know you're just making that up. What we heard when Timothy and Marilyn thought we weren't listening had more to do with apprehending someone attempting to steal a great deal of money. Or was it *counterfeit* money? I wonder if people actually steal cash anymore…"

"Whatever it is, I don't know why you and me, and the Rosenbaums and Reenie weren't brought in on the job. We've already proven ourselves to be ace crime solvers. And speaking of Deborah and Isaac, we should invite at least one other mature man," completely discounting the nine other men already mentioned. "Isaac won't want to spend all his time with a bunch of old hens. How about Bobby Taylor? They seem to have hit it off at Bingo. And they can both tell some humdinger stories! Besides, I think Bobby's a little sweet on Reenie Fields."

The others in the room had become so much background. "Bobby Taylor. Now there's someone who really should be included. His sister and brother-in-law are staying with him now, and we've never met them. Trudy, do you remember hearing that they had some medical limitations? A nice afternoon in the fresh air might do wonders for them."

The mild trepidation Rose experienced earlier began to wash over her like a towering tsunami. *How am I going to manage all this on short notice?* she asked herself, followed quickly by, *I'm not sure any newcomer would feel comfortable in such mixed company!*

Recognizing her friend's panic, Amy chided herself for contributing to letting things get out of hand. Marilyn Ludlow, looking on from the French doors leading to the backyard, judged it time to intervene.

"Are you ladies planning a party?" One glance at Rose's helpless expression told Marilyn she would not be overstepping to offer her input. Glancing at the extensive and eclectic list of invitees handed to her by Amy, she blinked several times before commenting brightly, "My, this is quite… comprehensive!" Gert nudged her granddaughter and smiled in a superior way. "Might I make a few suggestions?" Marilyn asked her sorely tried daughter-in-law.

Rose's eyes pleaded, "Yes, please!" which was all the encouragement Marilyn needed. Sitting on an ottoman next to Aletha, she calmly but efficiently took charge. Relief and admiration battled for primacy as Rose marveled at the ease with which Marilyn managed everything. After announcing that Sunday brunch at the Ludlow home would be put on hold for a while because of time demands associated with getting the new school staffed and students registered, she forestalled any expressions of disappointment by offering two welcome alternatives. Rose and Amy would co-host a BBQ at *Willow Walk* on the following Sunday afternoon around 5:00, while Aletha simultaneously opened her home to the seniors mentioned. Marilyn assured her that she and Miles would help with the meal at *Fernwood Cottage* and suggested that the others might appreciate being asked to contribute something, as well.

"Irene Murdock usually brings a dish for the Sunday potluck, and she won't have anyone to cook for next weekend; she mentioned that Matt and the boys will be away on a camping trip," Marilyn pointed out. Turning to her mother-in-law, she said, "Aletha, you've often mentioned the delicious kosher dishes Deborah brings on Bingo night. I'll bet if you asked her, she would be pleased to prepare something. And do you suppose Bobby Taylor would be willing to cook some meat in his outdoor oven?"

"You just leave that to me, Marilyn," Granny Gert declared, answering on behalf of her friend.

Marilyn smiled inwardly, believing with little effort in Gert's ability to induce Mr. Taylor to roast an entire side of beef, if necessary!

With everything settled satisfactorily, the afternoon crowd soon departed. Marilyn and Miles waved farewell from the front porch after speaking to everyone in turn. When the last guest drove out of sight, he put his arm around Marilyn's shoulders and murmured into her hair, "You handled that brilliantly, my dear."

She moved in the circle of his arm and returned his embrace, resting her head on his shoulder. "Events are working out better than we had hoped," she said and smiled in perfect contentment.

It had never been her intention to work on Sundays. That was a day to be set aside for worship, for fellowship, for rest. When Mr. Dawson asked Angelica Warner to come in on that particular Sunday, however, she found herself agreeing to the request despite her resolution to the contrary. He had mitigated her misgivings with the information that an important contact would be made that day without specifying who that might be. She reported to the front desk promptly at 8 a.m., only to be whisked away a few minutes later by her boss who had driven up to the front entrance to collect her.

"But I don't understand," Angelica said in some confusion while Mr. Dawson held the car door for her. As he climbed behind the wheel, she asked, "Is the contact you mentioned not here at the hotel?" His benign smile gave nothing away. Narrowing her eyes, she asked suspiciously, "You're up to somethin', aren't you?" A few weeks earlier, she would never have dreamed of addressing him in such a familiar fashion. Nor would she have imagined a gleam in his eye or a warm chuckle in response to her query. But such was the change in their relationship that friendly, open conversation came with ease.

"Why, Mrs. Warner, are you accusing me of deception?" he asked with a smile.

"Now you can just save your smooth-talkin' for someone who doesn't know you better," she replied primly, with one eyebrow lifted in challenge.

Dawson laughed again – a jolly laugh that fit his "Teddy Bear" persona to perfection. He was again sporting a striped bowtie, though he had forgone the matching vest and a suit coat in deference to the mid-summer heat. "I find your ability to see right through me a bit disconcerting, Mrs. Warner, though I have no wish to be other than honest with you." Before Angelica could decide what to make of such a statement, he went on. "You may not realize it, but during the short period of our acquaintance you have been an inspiration to me. You see, after my wife died, my regular attendance at church began to fall off. Oh, I could think of any number of excuses – none of them valid. Then you walked through the portals of the *Prairie Gateway* with, of all things, a passing knowledge of one of the most notorious professional thieves of our generation. That knowledge was the missing link in the plan to capture Samuel Jamison."

Now Angelica's head was truly in a whirl. She couldn't fathom what her knowledge of Samuel Jamison could possibly have to do with Mr. Dawson's church attendance! The passing comment about being an inspiration she chose to steer clear of.

"It was obvious to me, Dulac, and Fergusson, not to mention a conglomerate of security specialists you will probably never meet, that you must be a part of the plan. I admired your resolve to agree to our suggestion, despite your understandable hesitancy. But do you know what I admired the most?" Dawson glanced at Angelica, who wore a blank expression. "I admired your adamant objection to working on a Sunday, and your reasons for saying so.

"Like you, I used to honor the Lord's Day. My wife and I raised our children in the faith, though they have both been a bit hit-and-miss with their regular attendance since they set out on their own. I was hardly an example for them. I essentially forfeited my role as spiritual leader in the family to my wife, simply because it was easier. She died five years ago; still I failed to pick up that mantle of leadership. I blame myself for not being a better role model for my kids, especially my son. Your example was the inspiration I needed."

Angelica was about to offer a sarcastic retort along the lines of, "You were so inspired that you convinced me to set aside my principles and come to work today," when she suddenly noticed their surroundings. Dawson was pulling into the parking lot of a Baptist church.

"I know it was selfish of me to ask you to miss attendance at your own church, but I needed your further help, and believe it or not, this church is involved. Am I beyond forgiveness?"

Folding her arms, Angelica looked out her passenger window to hide a smile. "Your contrition might be a *little* more convincin'," she said, "if you could keep that twinkle out o' your eye!" She turned back when she heard him chuckle.

"I'll try to remember that," he replied meekly while negotiating a parking space.

Dawson ushered Angelica into a sanctuary built along traditional lines where rows of pews led from a center aisle. He indicated that she should precede him into a pew about midway down the aisle. The only other occupant of the pew was a young black man wearing a brightly colored shirt and khaki slacks. He smiled a welcome, and something clicked in her memory. Angelica tried to pin it down, but the thought remained elusive. The prelude eventually captured her attention, and she allowed the simple joy of worship to fill her mind and spirit. The music was lively and uninhibited without being irreverent and reminded her of worship as a child in Jamaica. Mr. Dawson's gravelly bass added a deeper layer of harmony to the warmth of Angelica's alto. Their duet complimented the mixed voices around them. The practices of singing and morning prayer, followed by corporate reading of Scripture, were hardly new to her, but with nothing else to do but participate, Angelica realized how she had allowed herself to miss out on much of the experience at her own church. When she wasn't greeting people at the door or helping the elderly or young mothers with children to their seats, she was volunteering in the infant room of the church nursery. Derek had not been wrong in pointing out that she tried to take care of everyone. There had been pride in his voice. There had also been the suggestion that it might be time to allow others to step up.

The thought brought a sweet smile to her lips just as Mr. Dawson glanced at her. Though she failed to catch his gratified look, Angelica missed nothing else that morning. The sermon was enlightening and convicting, and following the service, she experienced the novelty of being the newcomer who was warmly welcomed rather than the other way around. The young man in their pew had disappeared during the closing song without an introduction. When Dawson led her to the education wing of the church, Angelica assumed they would be attending an adult Bible study. A detour took them instead to the fellowship hall, where she was surprised to find that same young man evidently waiting for them. After greeting Mr. Dawson with a handshake, he turned to Angelica.

"Mrs. Warner, I apologize for these unusual tactics, but Mr. Dawson and I agreed that this would be the safest place to meet without raising any eyebrows." The smooth voice with its British accent caused another twinge of memory, though enlightenment would not come.

Once again completely in the dark, Angelica waited patiently for an explanation.

Her boss smiled his usual genial smile as if there was nothing untoward in the situation. Pulling out a chair, Dawson invited her to be seated at a table in the otherwise deserted room, then indicated that the men take a seat as well.

"Mrs. Warner, may I introduce you to Christopher Gordon, our new head of security at the *Prairie Gateway.*"

"Your new *what?*"

"I should also tell you that Mr. Gordon has been the other inspiration that has drawn me back to this place."

Though usually quite articulate, Angelica remained at a loss for words. She could do nothing but look from one man to the other for illumination.

"It was young Gordon here who asked me for church recommendations when he came to us three months ago, and it was he who asked that I accompany him on his first Sunday here. I was so ashamed that a stranger had to invite me to visit my own church, I could not refuse. For the past two months I have been finding my way home. Your faithful witness," he said, looking humbly from Gordon to Angelica, "helped me see what I had been missing, and I thank you both."

With the shock of such a revelation, Angelica grabbed hold of the one glaring inconsistency in his explanation. "While I'm very happy that the both o' you have found a fine church to call your home – I quite liked the service, by the way – I don't understand how Mr. Gordon has been here for *three months!* Why wasn't he present for that ridiculous meetin' with Inspector Dulac and that Fergusson fellow when I was railroaded into this charade?" She glared at Mr. Dawson who had the gall to allow a smile to ruin his expression of guilty humility. Christopher Gordon offered an explanation.

"You mustn't blame Mr. Dawson. I intentionally avoided that meeting for reasons I cannot go into now, but I beg of you not to acknowledge my existence as other than whatever cover I may be using at the time. In fact, you have probably seen me around the hotel as a handyman, or a busboy, or a…"

"That's it! I knew you looked familiar, but I couldn't place you." The pat explanation fit. Angelica scrutinized his face more carefully and frowned. For some inscrutable reason, she was still not content with that answer alone. Telling herself she was just being fanciful, she said, "That may explain one puzzle, but I don't understand why we are meetin' *here.*"

"Because we thought it the least likely place to be accidentally recognized by Jamison and his partners," Gordon explained.

"His *partners?* Ya must be jokin'!" Exasperation grew along with amazement and her accent broadened. "I suppose now ya be wantin' me to report on everyone that scoundrel talks to!"

The two men exchanged a quick glance before Dawson replied smoothly, "Only if you think it might be of interest. It is critical, however, that you not give any indication that you know of or recognize Christopher Gordon. Is that clear?"

"Nothin' is clear!" Angelica retorted, then added more calmly, "I don't understand any of it, but I believe you to be honorable men, so I will do as you ask. Though I suppose i' t'will be all right to speak o' you to Inspector Dulac when he arrives in a week?" she asked Mr. Gordon.

"No one," he replied quietly though with all the intensity of a fire alarm. "You have only been read in on my identity because our paths are likely to cross often – and because we can trust you."

None of it made sense to Angelica. The enormity of what she had become involved in, however, was clear. Having reached an agreement, the three went to class where the men were greeted as regulars. A discussion of the Sermon on the Mount did much to calm Angelica's inner turmoil.

An early evening breeze made a half-hearted attempt to bring the temperature down a few degrees though the humidity remained at sauna level. An arctic blast straight off the North Pole, however, would have failed to penetrate Derek's thoughts. Reclining on a patio lounge chair, he stared at the many potted plants scattered about without really seeing them. The sweet scents of gardenia and jasmine floated on the heavy air, while a flowering mandevilla vine competed with a neighboring hibiscus for "best in show." Whenever his mother looked at these tropical beauties, she was reminded of the Caribbean. Derek saw only amber eyes and a scornful smile mocking him.

Dinner at the Aguilar home earlier that week had left him with conflicting feelings. He had believed the evening would provide him the opportunity to show Kavya the real Derek Warner – a smooth talker who was self-confident, clever, and charming. Any impression, he thought, would be better than the initial one he had left her with – a gaping fool with half a brain. José had warned him not to take too much for granted. Kavya was different than other women, he had said. Having failed to clearly articulate that difference, Derek merely assumed his friend meant that few women could compete with Kavya's beauty and aura of mystery.

He had approached the visit with some level of confidence knowing Lupe Aguilar to be on his side. In her eyes, at least, Derek Warner could do no wrong. Anyone who took the time and patience to help José develop self-reliance and courage, not to mention coaching him to better understand the Bible, qualified for sainthood in her book. José's knowledge of Scripture had soon outstripped hers, and she did not fully comprehend everything he tried to explain to his aunt, but she knew Derek Warner to be an answer to prayer. When Lupe initially met him, she recognized him immediately – not his face, but his character. The idea of just such a man had been planted in her mind for some time, and unbeknownst to him, she had been praying fervently for his advent in their lives for over two years.

When Isabella Cruz had called her sister with the tragic news of Anika Jackson's death, Lupe had flown to California immediately. At Anika's funeral, Lupe grieved the passing of one who had been as a child to her, but it was Kavya's stricken, stoic silence that pierced her heart. It was as if all the love Kavya had poured out on the people she cared for – her mother, Anika, the fiancé who had deserted her – had been thrown back in her face, and she was no longer able to feel anything. She refused to even look at the tiny infant who cried out for her mother. Isabella had stepped in to fill the newborn's immediate needs, but it was Lupe who showed Kavya how to love again by teaching her to care for baby Anika. The emptiness of her own womb was offset by the overflow of love for a mother and child in crisis.

She taught Kavya to treasure the dark hours before dawn when rocking Ani was a priceless gift carved out of time. She helped Kavya discover the simple magic of counting ten tiny fingers and toes. She smiled sweetly while bathing the fragile life held in her gentle hands, allowing Kavya to glimpse the sacred intimacy of motherhood.

A month elapsed before Lupe returned to Kansas and Carlos and their perennial empty cradle. She believed herself to have fulfilled a mission ordained by the Father and gave thanks that she had been chosen for such an errand of mercy. Without realizing it, her selfless outpouring of love had softened Kavya's heart not only for Ani, but for Jackson and Isabella as well. Kavya's journey to true wholeness would be long and arduous, though, and Lupe knew the young woman would find it difficult to ever allow herself to be open to romantic love or to trust a man again.

It was then that Lupe began to pray for someone special to come into Kavya's life – a man of integrity who was physically and spiritually strong but gentle and tender enough to gain the confidence of a wounded soul. She believed Derek to be that man. His positive influence on José's life was all the proof she needed. But when Derek and Kavya met unexpectedly, and he reacted so foolishly to her exotic beauty, Lupe, like all the other women in his life, decided a little help was in order. Some benign, non-threatening situation was needed to break the ice between them and present him in a more positive light. She waited only long enough for Kavya and Anika to make themselves at home, then planned a second meeting – a casual family meal.

With the successful maneuvering of Derek and Kavya to seats next to one another, Lupe immediately began urging those gathered around the table to fill their plates after grace was spoken. Introducing a topic she knew to be of interest to Derek, she hoped he might show to better advantage.

"Derek, tell us a little about your volunteer firefighter training. That sounds very exciting." He had his mouth half open to respond when Lupe caught sight of her nephew taking her instructions a little too literally. "José, those enchiladas are not all for you! Put that serving spoon down and pass the dish to your uncle." Lupe then turned once more to Derek and smiled expectantly.

Thrown a little off balance by the interruption, Derek began a disjointed answer. "I've always admired firemen…" A smothered giggle on his right caused a slight stumble. "I mean I've always admired the idea of fire…fighting, that is," he added quickly as Kavya covered her mouth to stifle another snort of laughter. "What I mean is that I respect their service to the community, especially in smaller towns like Tinkers Well where they don't have a budget for a full-time fire department." Believing that he had finally acquitted himself well, Derek added with something of his usual cockiness, "Besides, who doesn't admire a man all suited up for battle?"

"Tío Carlos, may I have a little rice, please," Kavya said, pretending she had not heard Derek's comment. Lupe was a bit surprised and more than a little embarrassed by Kavya's rudeness. It was not like her. Kavya ignored the frown in Lupe's eyes and addressed her daughter instead. "Ani, eat your beans. Tia Lupe made them just for you."

With the timing of a seasoned veteran of the stage, little Anika twinkled engagingly at Derek and announced, "Fiahman! Wide fiah twuck, *pease?*"

Recognizing an ally, Derek grinned at Ani. Clueless about any protocol governing unofficial use of department equipment, he recklessly declared, "Baby girl, when old Derek finishes training, you'll be the first to have a ride." She clapped in delight as one who had just been promised a trip to the moon.

"Why would a man with a seemingly good job waste his time on a second job that pays absolutely nothing?" Kavya couldn't stop herself from being overtly rude to someone who had done her no harm. In the back of her mind, she had the sense to be grateful for his kind response to Ani, and to recognize that he was highly esteemed by the Aguilar family. She could not, however, forgive Derek for having acted like an idiot when they first met. Kavya believed a man of character must be in control of his emotions and thoughts at all times. Once before she had allowed herself to be fooled by a man who had exhibited a similar fatuous reaction upon meeting her. That memory wiped the tepid smile from Kavya's lips. She had trusted him with her heart, and he had deserted her in a moment of crisis. She would not make that mistake a second time. Accordingly, she waited in cold politeness for Derek's answer.

Derek's friends joked and teased each other all the time, except for those rare occasions when serious words were needed. Humorous sarcasm was their love language, and Derek spoke it fluently. During his army years, subordinate troops might have dared to speak to him disrespectfully – though never more than once. But he had rarely encountered open disdain. He might have allowed Kavya's inexplicable animosity to get under his skin had he not looked at those around him before responding to her loaded question. If the people who loved her were shocked by her words, Kavya's contempt might be masking something quite different. Derek was an expert at hiding one emotion behind another. For over a year after leaving the army, he had employed laughter to cover feelings of guilt and insecurity. Looking purposefully into her mocking eyes, Derek began to speculate as to what was really behind her scorn. Serious conversation was not his strong suit. He was willing to give it a try, though, if it meant helping Kavya.

Considering his words carefully, Derek said, "I'm really glad you asked. I owe a debt of gratitude to a lot of people who helped me through a very rough time. I can never repay that, but I can do something to help the community that gave me a new beginning."

His response both surprised Kavya and diffused any hostile comment on her part. She had expected some flippant remark about how firemen are all babe magnets, and he had shown her depth of character instead. She somehow felt cheated as if she had lost the upper hand. "Oh," was all she said.

To bridge the awkward moment, Lupe suggested Kavya share her news about a job prospect for the summer.

"I'm not sure why this would be of interest to everyone," Kavya said, and glanced sideways at Derek, who only displayed respectful attentiveness, "but one of the nurses at the clinic in Tinkers Well is going on maternity leave next week, so I've been hired part-time to fill in for her. At least it will help me save a little money before grad school starts at the end of August, though I don't know if someone with a bachelor's degree in microbiology is a great fit."

"Kavya is just being modest," Lupe explained to Derek. "She is also a registered nurse. Why, she alone nursed her dear mama, until… well, until she… died." Her voice grew softer and more hesitant as she saw Kavya's fingers close around her utensils like claws; the knuckles showed white through her brown skin. Realizing too late her mistake in mentioning the tragedy, Lupe mentally kicked herself for causing Kavya pain. She looked desperately at Derek for help. Like José, she was confident that he could handle anything.

Derek wasn't so sure. He was always the self-appointed life of any party and avoided heavy situations whenever possible. But he understood the lingering emotional pain of losing a parent, and Kavya had lost her sister as well. Now was clearly not the time to delve into that history, so Derek focused on the promising future instead. Praying that humor would not be misplaced, he plunged into the icy silence with all the confidence of someone exiting a plane at 25,000 feet without a parachute. Swallowing his fear, Derek said with his most engaging smile, "Prepare to be busy, Kavya. There's bound to be at least one of the Three Brothers crew paying you a visit every week. Right, little man?" José grinned and held up his bandaged right hand.

It was not a deeply intellectual comment. On the other hand, neither was it mocking nor dripping with unwelcome sympathy. Kavya watched in reluctant amusement as Derek pointed at José with a knowing grin. Relaxing a little, she responded in kind. "I'll be sure to sharpen all the needles," she said with the hint of an ironic smile.

Conversation during the rest of the meal stayed along conventional lines. With cool detachment, Kavya excused herself early to prepare Ani for bed. Derek would hardly have called it an auspicious beginning, but it was a beginning.

Sitting on the back porch in the growing dusk, Derek reflected on that evening and what he had learned about Kavya. Knowing what little he did about her mother's illness and death, as recounted by José, he had seen evidence of what he believed to be its continued hold over her heart. José had tried to warn him – Kavya was different than other women. In one respect, she was very much the same. Kavya had a rich depth of emotions, and they were capable of being hurt.

When he considered the plan for an impromptu BBQ, as laid out by Rose and Amy earlier that day, Derek was half grateful and half terrified. Any sane man would have gotten a taste of Kavya's armor-clad aloofness and executed a permanent about-face. An unusually tenacious determination, however, had taken hold of Derek's reason, and he refused to give up on her. Perhaps the experience of shared counseling with others who had lived through harrowing life events had given him a heightened sense of awareness. Perhaps it was recalling the devastation he had felt on losing his own father and the passage of time necessary to ease that pain. After all, Kavya had suffered compound loss. Perhaps he simply couldn't believe that anyone as beautiful and intelligent as Kavya would allow her heart to be so burdened with emotional scars as to render it unredeemable. Derek remembered how her voice had softened whenever she spoke to Ani. Tenderness still remained, no matter how deeply it had been buried.

While he would have preferred a little less public follow-on meeting with Kavya, Derek appreciated that she might feel more comfortable in a large gathering where she would be less likely to have too personal an interaction with anyone. He looked forward to the meeting even as he allowed self-doubt to creep in. Derek never tired of boasting about his prowess in romance to his friends. In solitude, he was more honest. *Could such a woman ever be attracted to me?* he wondered with a frown. A mosquito buzzing around his ear jerked him out of his melancholy; he found it difficult to brood when slapping himself on the head.

Shaking off his doubts, Derek stood and decided to take José's advice. "Have a little faith, brother, and believe in yourself."

With a jaunty smile, he entered the house murmuring, "You know *that's* right!"

CHAPTER 9

She should have a reputation for doing good: raising children, providing hospitality to strangers, ...helping those in distress, and dedicating herself to every kind of good thing.

1 Timothy 5:10 (CEB)

Thirteen for dinner. Rose frowned at the final guest list. Thirteen at Thanksgiving dinner the year before had resulted in a joyous holiday. She wasn't so sure about the thirteen scheduled to gather on Sunday afternoon. "This *could* be a success," Rose mused aloud. Contemplating the seating chart she had created to ensure Kavya was surrounded by the people she might feel most comfortable with and still be close to Derek, Rose had her doubts. One prediction had proven to be correct anyway. Jada Young had bowed out of the proceedings, leaving Rose to deal with the problematic number.

As expected, the remainder of the Three Brothers Crew showed up early to spend some time in the pool before the BBQ. After performing a running cannonball that thoroughly soaked those lounging around the deck, José beat a hasty retreat. He had seen Kavya's van pull up to the house. With Derek thundering behind him hurling threats, José reached the drive just as Rose and Angelica emerged from the house. The Aguilars greeted Angelica as an old friend and thanked Rose for her kind invitation. As they introduced their guests, Ani showed signs of being unusually shy. Her mother showed signs of being unusually sullen and withdrawn. Bewildered by her cold reception of such warm hospitality, José hurried into speech.

"Hey, cousin, you made it! Isn't this an awesome house?" Turning to the little girl, he said, "Miss Rose has a little pool just for you, *Changuita*. You wanna see it?" Ani's eyes glowed as she looked hopefully at her mother.

"I'm sorry, baby. Mama didn't bring anything for you to swim in," Kavya said.

Her softened tone surprised Rose. When Derek had described the young woman to her and Amy a week earlier, he had spoken of her natural reserve and of his desire to get past her defensive disposition, due no doubt to troubling circumstances in her past. With his self-confidence renewed, he was certain of his ability to charm her into a more mellow mood. Until Kavya spoke to her daughter, Rose doubted she had a disposition capable of being mellowed at all! Chastising herself for being too judgmental, Rose adjusted her own attitude accordingly.

"I apologize for not mentioning we would have a child's pool for Ani. I happen to have a little girl's bathing suit left here when friends came to visit a few weeks ago. They also left some swimmer diapers. You're welcome to them." It seemed to Rose that everyone waited for Kavya's response as if the success of the day depended on that one decision. Kavya hesitated, and everyone held their breath. It was little Ani who swayed the scales in favor of accepting the kind gesture. It would have taken a harder heart than Kavya's to resist the little girl's engaging smile. A collective sigh greeted her mother's cool acquiescence.

While Angelica helped Lupe and Carlos carry several dishes into the kitchen, Rose and Derek attempted to engage Kavya in conversation. They were aided in their efforts by Amy, who came around the corner from the front yard where she and Abe had been setting up tables and chairs in the shade of the old willow tree. Both women found conversing with Kavya an uphill battle, though they were set on doing their best to help Derek, who, for no apparent reason, was ignored by Kavya altogether. Amy hit on the idea of giving Kavya a tour of the house – who wouldn't enjoy that!

Momentarily discouraged by Kavya's cold shoulder, Derek headed back to the pool.

As they wandered through the rooms, Kavya made desultory comments about the décor and layout. She compared it with her family's residence in New Delhi and pointed out that it was only servants who lived on the top floor. "Our ayah alone was allowed a room on the floor of family bedrooms. She, of course, was expected to take care of my sister and me if we needed anything during the night."

If Rose's emotions had not been so softened by her pregnancy, she might have believed the other woman was being deliberately offensive. Amy had no trouble believing in such a theory. She bit back stinging replies for her friend's sake alone, knowing they would only embarrass Rose. Oddly enough, Rose was neither embarrassed nor hurt. She began to notice that Kavya spoke only of her life in India and said almost nothing about her home in California, where, presumably, she had spent the majority of her life. She mentioned Isabella and her ties to the Aguilar family, but never once did she talk about her parents, her sister, or Ani's father. Rose decided there was a great deal more to Kavya Jackson than she let on, and like it or not, the woman of the hour would not be allowed to isolate herself from those who cared enough to reach out to her, least of all Derek Warner.

J.T. Gaines and Jason Buchwald were dragged away from the pool only because they could smell meat sizzling on the grill and thought it best to take over as grill tenders. Tim had a reputation for presenting burnt offerings to his guests. Once everyone was gathered around two eight-foot tables, set end to end, Tim gave thanks for the day and the feast. Kavya graciously thanked Rose for providing a booster seat for Ani, though she managed to add a barb to her words with criticism of a faulty buckle. She could not hide her enjoyment of the comradery shared by the men, however, once the stories started flying. A few comments from Derek even surprised a laugh out of her. In turn, Kavya was obviously much admired by the single men present, though all were respectful, except José, of course, who pestered her into good humor whenever she showed signs of boredom or emotional withdrawal.

The one aspect of Derek's description of Kavya that rang true was that of her undeniable beauty – the kind of beauty men found intoxicating and women found irritating because it only served to highlight their own sort of ordinary prettiness. Amy, still inclined to be protective of Derek and therefore more apt to find fault with Kavya, decided that the other woman's eyes were set too far apart. Derek thought the effect added to their mysterious appeal. Only Rose seemed to notice the obvious flaw in Kavya's appearance. She had chosen to clad herself totally in black, as if in mourning. From her sleeveless top, tied at the hips, sarong style, to her legs wrapped in tight jeans, the only spot of color evident was found in the pale pink nail polish on her fingertips and toes. Such a woman, Rose thought, should be draped in bright reds and greens and blues, trimmed in gold and silver. Rose began to wonder if Kavya avoided such colors because they represented life and joy and serenity.

After the meal, Angelica suggested that Carlos and Lupe join her in watching Ani splash around in the pool provided for her pleasure. She too wanted to help Derek in his courtship, though she wasn't convinced he had set his heart on the right woman. Reminding herself that the outcome, one way or another, was in God's hands, she sought instead to know Kavya's adopted family better.

Conversation among the younger generation turned to sports, which led inevitably to college rivalries. Though Jason and J.T. could argue all day about the rival merits of Georgia universities, neither had attended anything but their football games. Kavya had never heard of the *American College of the Building Arts*,[10] though it made sense that Tim had chosen such a school. She respected his commitment to excellence in his field. When she

---

[10] American College of the Building Arts, 649 Meeting Street, Charleston, SC 29403. Used by permission.

heard that Abe had graduated from a prestigious College of Science and Technology in Virginia, she was duly impressed, until she learned that he intended to squander his education to follow a different path.

"Isn't it rather a waste," she asked, "to turn your back on guaranteed success? I mean, how much money can there be in saving people's souls?" On a bitter note, she added, "In my experience, it's just another lost cause." Kavya looked boldly at Abe, daring him to refute her.

"It is perhaps fortunate, then, that I do not believe there are any lost causes, only lost opportunities. Besides, it is not I who saves souls, it is Jesus alone. I am but his servant and the conduit of his words." Abe's polite forbearance threw Kavya out of her cynical stride and rebuked not only her, but, unknowingly, his wife as well. Amy gazed adoringly at her husband, ashamed of her previous unkind thoughts.

Embarrassed at having her own provocation thrown back in her face, however gently, Kavya looked to Derek for redress. She believed to have accurately taken his measure at their first meeting. And though he had shown himself to be a man of kindness and sympathy since then, she was certain that, with his unwitting assistance, she could once more gain the upper hand among those present.

Kavya had never been able to control her own destiny; she had had one tragic life event after another thrust upon her. With only a fragile spiritual grounding, such a history had gradually instilled in her a desire to command every situation, to be her own god. Anything less left her vulnerable and defeated. It didn't matter that she had been treated with generosity and friendship by all those she had met that day. It didn't matter that her daughter had received special favor or that her aunt and uncle were clearly enjoying a rare social outing. Those considerations meant little compared to her need for control.

"I suppose you are an honor graduate of some Ivy League university," she said, directing her "Mona Lisa" smile at Derek.

With a good-natured grin, he laughed and said, "Hardly. I went to a state school in Chicago. And – I am proud to say – I was the first person in my family to graduate with a four-year degree. Oh, yeah, just ask my mama. She'll brag on me all day long." The others at the table recognized and appreciated his cocky response as Derek just being Derek. Paper cups and plastic utensils were hurled in his direction while Tim reached around Rose to slap him on the head. Derek threw everything back, then looked politely at Kavya, and only at Kavya.

"Then I suppose you pursued some noble profession like…education, perhaps," Kavya asked. Her sly smile had turned, by infinitesimal degrees, into a smirk. Only her cousin recognized the warning sign and attempted to discourage her with a frown and a slight headshake. She employed willful blindness to ignore his efforts.

Like a lamb being led to the slaughter, Derek replied, "As a matter of fact, yes," pleased by her intuitive guess. José groaned inwardly.

"And with your obvious mental agility, I suppose it was *physical* education?"

A little too late, Derek detected the note of scorn in her voice. "Yes, I'm a qualified P.E. teacher," he said, "but I learned pretty early on that that wasn't for me, so I decided the Army could use my skills." *There,* he thought, *that will show her I'm not just some muscle-bound jock!*

Leaning forward, Kavya pointed out with relish, "So you went from teaching a bunch of impressionable young minds how to play games to teaching a bunch of impressionable young minds how to kill people. How noble. You must be so proud of yourself." Her mocking smile, devoid of mirth, dared him to answer. Various degrees of outrage, disbelief, and resentment rendered everyone mute. The only sounds that could be heard were that of Ani's distant laughter and the murmur of friends in conversation.

Wow! She must really be in a dark place! She doesn't have any idea how much she needs these people or how quickly she is alienating them. I have got to stop her! Derek thought, desperate for wisdom. He hesitated for a split second before speaking.

"I helped a bunch of impressionable young people understand that while violence is a last resort, if a war is thrust upon you, you'd sure as heck better be prepared to win it so you can go home to your loved ones. And yes, I was proud of that." Derek's words wiped the smirk from Kavya's lips. "I also saw one of those impressionable young people killed on my watch, and his death has haunted me ever since."

An unexpected emotion flitted across her face. Everyone but Derek assumed it was shame. He believed it to be compassion. "I'm… I'm so sorry… I didn't know…" Kavya stammered.

Derek's serious face, so seldom seen and, therefore, almost unrecognizable, was replaced by a more familiar relaxed amiability. "Don't worry about it. Everyone here knows." He looked around at those whose friendship meant the world to him. "These are some of the people who helped me deal with that nightmare. You should get to know them better."

Derek's gracious response allowed everyone to breathe easier. At the risk of being snubbed again, he even dared to introduce a little levity back into the day. He hoped it would help everyone forget what had gone before and inspire them to give Kavya a second chance.

"But there are a few things you need to know first," Derek said, as if imparting the wisdom of the ages to a proselyte. "Don't listen to Tim when he tries to convince you he's more handsome than me. I am obviously the best-looking man here." He ducked his head as cups and spoons were again hurled in his direction.

Despite every attempt to the contrary, Kavya couldn't stop a smile from breaking the solemn lines of her face.

"Now when Abe here tries to tell you he's smarter than I am," Derek said, winking at his friend across the table, "you should probably believe him."

Abe clutched at his chest. "Amy, love of my life, mark this day on the calendar. Such a declaration may never be heard again before witnesses."

Grateful to those surrounding him for following his lead, Derek grinned and declared as usual, "You know that's right!"

The others took up the mantle of conversation. Derek had impressed everyone – especially José – with his handling of a dicey situation; he deserved a break. Kavya gave short but courteous answers to any questions addressed to her and sat quietly observing those around her when not engaged.

She had waived the privilege of having any close friends in her youth. Driven by the thought that she must help her mother, she had allowed her spare time to be swallowed up by study so that she could graduate from high school early. The only respites she ever knew were the holidays spent in the Aguilar home where she was free to enjoy the comradery of family without the burden of responsibility. Watching those around her, Kavya experienced an unexpected surge of envy for what she had never really known. Even José, who was the closest thing she had ever had to a brother, was a part of this. With all the emotional baggage tied up in his PTSD, he had still found the courage to trust these people enough to work with them and to enjoy their company. For a dizzying few moments, Kavya allowed herself to imagine being a part of just such a circle of friends – sharing their laughter and sense of belonging. She glanced across the table at Derek and found herself unable to resist his irrepressible smile.

Then she heard Ani calling.

The child indicated no urgency or unhappiness, only the desire of a little girl to share a special day with her mother. Nevertheless, the spell was broken.

Recalled to the real world, Kavya shook her head, chiding herself for allowing even the thought of a different way of life. She had a child who depended on her for everything. And though Kavya loved the little girl dearly, almost fiercely, Ani was a living reminder of the life of solitude and service marked out for her. Glancing at Rose who glowed with the happiness of her first pregnancy, Kavya winced. She told herself that no woman married to a man who adored her and who shared in the joyful expectancy of two babies could possibly understand the weight of raising a child alone.

Convincing herself that she did not belong there among people who knew how to be happy in a way she never could, Kavya slammed the emotional shutters more firmly around her heart and stood abruptly to leave. Her expression had gone blank, and she explained, in a voice devoid of sentiment, that it was time to get Ani home. The inexplicable hardening of an attitude which had shown such tentative, yet hopeful promise caught everyone off guard. Rose recovered first.

"Of course you must see to Ani, but please don't feel that you need to hurry away. Abe and Amy had to leave to help our grandmothers and their friends down the road. We'd hate to see you leave early, too. Besides, Tim's parents will want to meet you. They were at Fern Cottage while we had our BBQ, but they planned to stop by here for a few minutes after the Yousefs showed up to take their place."

The plea might have worked had Kavya not caught Derek looking at her at just that moment. His expression compound of compassion and empathy shook her to her core. *He knows,* she thought, shocked that her emotional defenses could be so easily penetrated. *He knows! I will not let him take advantage of my weakness. I am strong. I can stand alone!* With barely a smile of farewell or a curt word of thanks, Kavya walked toward her aunt and uncle. She was quickly intercepted by her cousin.

José grabbed Kavya's arm and practically dragged her to the opposite side of the yard, chastising her severely in a strange mix of English and Spanish.

"You were kindly invited to join *mi amigos* so they could welcome you to Kansas. And what did you do? You insulted one of the best guys I ever knew. But did he make fun of you? Was he like, 'Hey, *Chika,* watch your mouth?' No. He was nice to you and showed everybody else they should treat you that way too, even if you di'n't deserve it. Then when it's like all okay again and everybody's happy, you jump up and leave. That is so messed up! I used to think you were smart and funny. Now you're just mean!"

Never had José been more ashamed of someone he had revered for years. Never had Kavya resented having her behavior called into question so thoroughly and so accurately. Tia Lupe, momentarily looking away from little Ani, was shocked to see the two coming toward her bristling with hostility. She could only guess at what had caused José to look so angry or Kavya to look so resentful. They had often exchanged friendly ribbing as teenagers, but there was nothing friendly about the frosty cloud of animosity that had settled between them.

Lupe was given no opportunity to discover the root of their obvious anger. Without a word, Kavya wrapped Ani in the towel provided by Rose and started toward the van. In between the little girl's protests, she tossed over her shoulder the information that "we are leaving – now." In dismay, Lupe watched Kavya disappear around the side of the house then turned to watch José walking back to the table. Not knowing what to do, she looked to Angelica for help.

"I have no idea what has happened," Lupe said. "José is obviously very upset, and there are dishes still on the table, and we cannot leave without thanking Rose and Tim for their wonderful hospitality, and…"

Angelica had her own theory about what must have passed between the cousins, based on things Derek had shared without realizing it. Her only thought was to calm Lupe.

"I don't know either, but I think it might be best if you just follow Kavya now." Both were surprised when they saw the van drive around the front of the house and wait for its other two passengers by the Spartan junipers lining one side of the driveway. "I'll explain to Rose, and I'll take care o' your dishes. I'm goin' back to the city tonight. I'll drop 'em off on my way." Seeing the tears of remorse in Lupe's eyes, she added, "Don't worry, my friend. I am certain i' t'will all be sorted out in time."

Angelica walked with them to the waiting van and watched until they passed the gate at the end of the drive. She was about to return to what was left of the party when she saw Miles and Marilyn strolling toward her from the direction of Aletha's house.

Though a slightly smaller crowd had gathered at *Fern Cottage*, all had been flattered to receive such a welcome invitation. Marilyn's suggestion for a potluck resulted in enough food to feed five times their number. Isaac and Deborah Rosenbaum were at first hesitant to venture from their forest retreat in light of the harsh sentiments expressed by a handful of ignorant anti-Semites in the local area. Aletha reminded them of their many true friends among the gentile community of Tinkers Well, making it impossible for them to refuse. They collected Irene Fields on their way. While Miles and Marilyn organized the food, the five friends – old and new – relived the glory of their crucial part in bringing a felon to justice months earlier. The pleasant dimming of any distasteful elements that might have occurred in the process inspired them to try to hit upon some other way of keeping their sleuthing skills sharp. They had just suggested forming a crime-busters club when they heard another car pull up to the house. Gertie Gunn suggested the others help the newcomers into the house while she and Aletha waited in the parlor.

"No sense in overwhelming the poor folks. They've got six legs between them!" Little did she know how weak some of those legs were.

Bobby Taylor, a widower and retired farmer, had recently invited his sister Eleanor and her husband to stay with him for an indeterminate period. Deteriorating health made it imperative that they no longer live alone, so Bobby offered to help them until they could settle on an alternative solution.

Eleanor June Taylor Stratton and her husband Herbert – Herbie to his friends – didn't often make the effort to go about socially. At 80, Ellie June, once the pillar of health, still bore the posture and broad shoulders of a swimmer, despite the evidence of worry over current unavoidable life changes. It took little nudging, however, for her to boast of her two Senior Olympic medals in swimming to anyone willing to listen. If her conversation seemed a little disjointed, flitting between her former triumph and present interest in abstract painting, those gathered to welcome her attributed the erratic utterances to an artist's temperament. After all, anyone whose head is crowned with hair tinted the color of lilacs in spring and whose thin, athletic figure sports a smock-like blouse in shades of pink over yellow bell-bottom pants cannot be expected to follow the conventional norms of conversation. In an aside to Gert and Deborah, Bobby shared the source of her befuddled state; the dreaded specter of dementia had gradually tightened its grip on her mind, finally necessitating around-the-clock supervision. Herbie, on the other hand, possessed a razor-sharp wit, but a crippling spine condition had left him totally dependent on a walker to get around. He could simply no longer physically keep up with his wife. Desperate to postpone the need to place her in a memory-care facility, Herbie had reached out to Bobby, who had agreed to take in the ailing pair.

With everyone present, Aletha insisted on giving a tour of her new addition – a gleaming master bath opening off her bedroom at the opposite end of the house from the dining room. It was built with a similar footprint and roofline as that of the gazebo just outside the kitchen. Her description of the building process was liberally interspersed with praise for her grandson's design, craftsmanship, and overall genius, forgetting to mention that Derek Warner had done much of the work. She saw each detail with the eyes of the heart as if they were clearly visible.

Three Brothers Construction, Inc. had truly outdone themselves, though Tim gave much credit to his wife for her design input. Double vessel sinks were mounted on a repurposed sideboard table, its shallow drawers having been remodeled to fit around the necessary plumbing. A low shelf mounted between the table legs contained a basket for towels and a chest for more unsightly, utilitarian amenities. Tim had incorporated a hanging stained-glass window over a casement window, thus allowing both privacy and access to fresh air. Geometrical floor tiles and a restored clawfoot tub recalled the Victorian era, while a modern shower stall added practicality. The work had only been completed the week before, so everyone was agog to take in such grandeur – everyone except Gert, who decided Miles and Marilyn needed her supervision in the kitchen.

With the tour completed, Aletha's guests made their way to the dining room, where intricately patterned wallpaper on a subdued scale allowed chintz curtains to surround the window with grand floral radiance. The floral motif was repeated in a muted watercolor painting hung in a place of honor above the buffet, while a crystal chandelier cast its twinkling brilliance over all. Once settled at the gleaming mahogany table, and with nothing left to admire but one another, everyone became less animated as if each suddenly realized they were a group of old people – with the exception of Ellie June.

She tilted her head to one side and studied the painting – a simple vase of cut flowers in pastel greens, pinks, and lavender on a light blue tablecloth. It might have been titled "Study in Serenity." Still staring at the picture, but with her head once more upright, Ellie declared, "I once painted a picture very like that – in cobalt blue and tangerine with great slashes of black and gray." While all eyes turned from her to the painting in astonishment, she smiled sweetly and murmured, "Yes, very like that…" Silence fell.

Gertie Gunn impatiently surveyed those around her and frowned. Her ever-ready opinion promptly surfaced. "Age may be no respecter of persons, but there's no sense in everybody sitting around feeling sorry for themselves." Her "whisper," directed at Reenie Fields on her right, was heard by nearly everyone at the table. "We might all be getting older, more infirm, and more dependent on others for daily support, but we still have plenty of good years left between us, even if some of us are blind or deaf as a post or riddled with diabetes, cholesterol, and gout. *That's* not who we are; it's only what we have to put up with!" Her opinion duly stated, Gert sat stewing for a few minutes. Suddenly, she slapped the tabletop and said, "What we need is a little life in this party!"

Into the collective hush that followed such a proclamation, Reenie smiled timidly and uttered in a true whisper, "I quite agree, Gertie!"

Apparently, the others did, too. Bobby began to tease Aletha over her uncanny luck at the Bingo table, which prompted Ellie June to proudly announce – as if for the first time – that she had won two Senior Olympic medals. And the Rosenbaums shared their pleasure in meeting with young Abraham Yousef each week to study the writings of the prophets.

"We don't agree with or fully understand all of his interpretations," Isaac said, "but he has such a fire in his voice when he speaks of the ancient texts, especially those from Isaiah."

Daring anyone to top her announcement of three great-grandchildren due before the end of the year, Gert folded her arms and beamed at her tablemates in a superior way. Since she shared in the expectation of two of those babies, Aletha felt justified in adding her other good news. It was information that all but the Strattons were already aware of, but it gave her such pleasure to repeat the glad tidings. Her beloved son Timothy Miles Hawthorne was engaged to Marilyn Ludlow, proving that one is never too old for a happy ending!

As if scripted, the couple in question entered the room bearing serving platters and dishes, which they placed around the table before Miles seated Marilyn and took his place next to his mother. While dessert was being passed around, the two middle-aged sweethearts looked at one another and smiled as if sharing a delectable secret. It didn't remain a secret very long and soon added another layer of unexpected excitement to Aletha's announcement. Eight voices were still talking at once when Abe and Amy showed up a half hour later to help with cleanup and any transportation needs. After a few moments of shock, their voices joined the clammer while Miles and Marilyn slipped quietly away.

Rose spotted three people walking toward them just as she was about to declare the afternoon a social disaster. She felt that she had somehow failed Derek. His serious face had taken possession of his features again, though the resulting expression looked more speculative than dejected. Still, blaming herself for her botched attempt at matchmaking, and without Amy present to remind her of her brilliant success in getting the Yousefs together, Rose experienced the letdown of a party that had lasted too long. If her greeting to her in-laws was less effusive than usual, it didn't matter. There was enough suppressed excitement emanating between them to fire up a funeral! Miles murmured something to Tim then demanded everyone's attention.

"Thank you for allowing us to come late to the party this afternoon, though it appears we may have arrived a little too late." Turning to José, who looked even more deflated than Rose, Miles said, "I hope you will pass on our regrets to your aunt and uncle. We were looking forward to seeing them again. Your cousin will no doubt also become a part of our community here, so we'll meet her another time."

José wasn't so sure. He was grateful that Miles apparently expected no reply.

"I'm sure you understand our desire to dine with my mother and her friends, but we also wanted to spend time with each of you. That being said, there is an item of special interest that Mari and I wish to share."

Rose looked at Tim accusingly as if he had kept a secret from her, but he was as much in the dark as she was. Angelica, who was Marilyn's closest friend, appeared to be as clueless as Tim, so Rose was left to wait impatiently for Miles to get to the point. Attempting to speculate as to what announcement could possibly require such a reveal, Rose decided it must be a settled wedding date, though a date on a calendar, months away, hardly deserved such a buildup. There was enough of Granny Gert in Rose, however, to make her want to know anything of interest before the bulk of her acquaintance did.

Taking Marilyn's hand, Miles announced to the assembly, "You are all cordially invited to attend our wedding two weeks from today at the *Prairie Gateway Hotel* in Kansas City. The service will be held in the same room used for our engagement party, so most of you are familiar with the location. Informal invitations with directions will be mailed tomorrow, but consider yourselves all invited."

It was the second time that day everyone was struck dumb.

Smiling in amusement, Miles looked at Marilyn. "It would appear that they don't believe us, my dear."

Returning his smile with a twinkle in her eyes, she said, "Perhaps you should have explained that we believe we've waited long enough to be a family again."

"And rather than bothering with all the bells and whistles of a formal affair, we prefer to enjoy a party with those closest to us after a simple exchange of vows," Miles added for the sake of clarity.

"You might also mention that if anyone wanted to, they could… say… go for a swim in the pool down the corridor from the venue."

"An excellent point," Miles said, with only a quiver of laughter in his voice.

Having sufficiently recovered his wits to form a clear sentence, Tim asked, looking from one parent to the other, "Are you *serious?!*"

"About going swimming?" his mother enquired politely.

Miles put his arm around Marilyn and answered his son with commendable aplomb, "I have never been more serious about anything in my life. Now, will you agree to be my best man or not?"

Unable to find any words adequate to express his feelings, Tim threw his arms around them both, only pulling away enough to allow Rose to join the family celebration. He finally stepped back and yelled to the treetops, "This is *awesome!*"

Much hugging and hand-wringing ensued. Between laughter and tears, Marilyn insisted Angelica be her matron of honor. "And don't say you might be working, because I've already secured Mr. Dawson's assurance that you will be free to dance at my wedding." Angelica wiped the tears from her beaming smile before Marilyn added with a wink, "Actually, he said you will be free to dance at my wedding *only* if you save a dance for him."

"For shame! How you do go on. I won't tell you to quit bein' foolish because I am so happy for you, my dear friend. But dance with Mr. Dawson? Ya must be jokin'!"

Rose talked endlessly of the wedding, the venue, and the incredibly short intervening two weeks for the rest of the day. She continued throwing out ideas and reimagining every detail until she heard Tim snoring softly. Then she called Amy, and the two girls started the process all over again.

It had taken all of Angelica's coaxing and kindness to convince the Aguilars that no ill will had resulted from their abrupt departure. When she stopped at their house to drop off their dishes on the way back to her temporary home in the city, she couldn't help but see how upset they were over the afternoon's events. When Angelica shared the news of a wedding, and that they were invited, she left them relieved and honored, though Lupe was bent on getting to the bottom of Kavya's strange behavior.

The drive to Kansas City gave Angelica ample time to consider all that had passed that day – the bad and the good. One of the positives she took away was Derek's response to Kavya's actions. He didn't shake it off with a laugh, nor did he allow anyone to make snide comments, particularly José. If anything, he seemed to be protecting Kavya. Angelica smiled knowingly and addressed the empty car, "I believe my son is finally becoming the man I always believed he would be!"

Later that evening, while cleaning the serving bowls she had taken to the picnic, she began to talk to the cat Bastet, who preened herself on the window seat next to the tiny café table in the kitchen. Angelica crooned to the self-absorbed feline, admitting that she had grown rather fond of her housemate. In truth, Bastet had become surprisingly good company, though not much of a conversationalist. An easy quiet fell between them while Angelica considered again Marilyn's great happiness. She smiled in deep contentment – until she remembered one absurd comment. The bowl she was drying slipped back into the sink with a soapy splash. Angelica looked once more at Bastet, who appeared only marginally interested, and said indignantly, "Dance with Mr. Dawson, indeed!"

Having voiced her opinion of such a ridiculous notion, Angelica finished cleaning the dishes then turned off the light and went into the living room in search of something to watch on TV that might distract her chaotic thoughts. Left in darkness, Bastet licked her paw a few more times and deigned to follow suit, though it was doubtful she had any thoughts other than those confirming her own perfection.

CHAPTER 10

"Behold, I waited for your words, I listened for your wise sayings,
while you searched out what to say."

Job 32:11 (RSV)

The mellow glow of lamplight provided the only illumination in the room Kavya shared with her daughter. Two twin beds took up most of the space with a small dresser between them, which doubled as a nightstand. Carlos had built a makeshift safety railing for Ani's bed – the bed once allotted to Anika. A picture of Mary and the Baby Jesus watched over her bed, and a crucifix hung over the other, each placed lovingly by Lupe. Kavya would have removed them, but such an act would have injured Lupe's kind heart, and Kavya loved her aunt too much to hurt her so callously. The images meant nothing to her anyway, so she left well enough alone and chose to regard the religious artwork as nothing more than wall décor. An exciting day, coupled with the happiness of seeing her new friend Derek again, left the little girl unable to stay awake.

Gazing with misty eyes at the sleeping child in her arms, Kavya experienced a pang of love so intense it pierced her like the sharp thrust of an arrow. She brushed her thumb across the soft, round cheek and kissed the dark, silky hair so like her own. With a tender smile, she contemplated the usually animated features now relaxed in innocent slumber. Imagining the little girl's playful nature and wit, Kavya's smile went momentarily awry. They reminded her daily of her sister, though the memory brought her more comfort now than pain. Kavya gently laid Ani in her bed, then went in search of Lupe. She had hidden behind the shield of maternal obligations long enough; an apology was in order.

Kavya found her aunt in the tiny living room doing her perpetual mending. Like all the rooms in the house, what it lacked in spaciousness, it more than made up for in hominess and the quality of being perpetually inviting. The richly hued terra-cotta rose walls reflected Lupe's love of color and served as fitting backdrops for family photos, a brightly patterned calendar, and miscellaneous artwork accumulated from local yard sales. Nothing went together, yet everything belonged. A sagging sofa, which had served as José's bed during their summer visits as teenagers, filled one wall adjacent to the fireplace, while her uncle's recliner was placed strategically to extend backwards across the front door. The place of honor in the corner next to the fireplace was reserved for Lupe's prized possession – an upholstered rocking chair.

Carlos had rescued the dilapidated piece one day from a pile of trash waiting for collection on the side of the road. He had strapped the broken-down chair into the bed of his truck and had hidden it in the barn, where he spent weeks restoring it to working form. A few scraps of wood mended the frame, making it functional again, and the exhausted old springs were given a reprieve by the addition of a new tufted seat cushion. Carlos patiently scrubbed the original faded fabric until it looked positively respectable. Any residual stains were hidden by the cushion. He presented the refurbished chair to his wife on her birthday years earlier, and she had been so thrilled she wouldn't have replaced the treasured gift if offered a hundred new chairs straight from the showroom floor. Lupe knew better than anyone that Carlos was a man of few words. He preferred to express his thoughts and emotions in more tangible ways. Every time she sat in the old swivel rocker, she imagined her husband singing a love song to her.

Kavya heard only soft guitar music issuing from a boom box on the mantle. A muted trumpet joined the musical mix, providing a soothing backdrop for a familiar scene; it was one Kavya remembered with nostalgia. Just so had she and Anika and José spent the evenings of their youth watching their aunt return a worn shirt to serviceable condition or give holey socks a breath of new life. Lupe had never considered herself poor. She had a fine, hardworking husband who loved her beyond words, a home to call her own – albeit a humble one – and a life of purpose. Only the presence of children had been denied her, and God had unexpectedly provided them in his own divine way.

When Lupe heard Kavya enter the room, she looked up and smiled, then bent once more over her work. "Come, child. See if you can remember how to repair the edges on that kitchen towel like I showed you." She watched Kavya out of the corner of her eye and was pleased to see the young woman measure out a length of thread and carefully insert it through the eye of a needle. Without thinking, Kavya knotted the strand and absent-mindedly began turning the frayed ends of the towel into a finished edge ready to be tacked into place. The two women sewed in companionable silence while the music strummed a rhythm of ease between them.

"It's good to see you enjoying the simple things of life again," Lupe said without looking up. "They will not bring you fame or prestige, but they can give you peace and satisfaction. For many years now, you have known little enough of either, have you? It is all right to let yourself be happy now, *mija*. Carlos and I hoped that coming back here might help you to remember the happy times you had with us in the past. Here your memories of Anika can be free of sadness."

Kavya said nothing as her aunt's words washed over her like healing rain.

"You may not know how deeply her death affected José. It happened only a month before he saw many of his friends killed by the explosion that crippled his mind and his heart. He came to us because he could not go back to California, knowing he would surely have visited his Tia Bella in your family home and been reminded of the young girl who had saved his life there. He punished himself for some time, thinking that Anika would have been ashamed of him, that all her efforts had been wasted."

Soft tears dropped from Kavya's eyelashes onto the towel in her hand. Lupe's gentle words cut through her conscience where accusation would only have met with rebuttal. She had been so caught up in her own despair that she had given little thought to anyone else's sense of loss. Isabella had hidden her emotions so that she could be strong for Kavya's sake and for the sake of a grieving employer who had forgotten how to process human emotion.

Lupe snipped a thread and reached for another sock from her mending basket. "He is much better now, thanks mostly to his work with the Three Brothers crew. And Derek Warner, especially, has been a gift from God. He has shown José how to laugh again, and how to trust again. He is a good man. But then, all his friends are good men. I'm sure you could see that at the party today."

"They were very… kind," Kavya admitted hesitantly.

"Oh, yes, very kind. Derek's mama, too. I don't know if José doesn't know or if he learned about it in their PTSD talking group and thought it too personal to share, but Derek lost his own papa when he was just a teenager."

Kavya looked up in surprise. Glancing at her niece, Lupe was encouraged by her reaction to that particular nugget of information. She bent her head once more and rambled on as if merely discussing her weekly shopping list. Little did Kavya suspect that each word was chosen intentionally.

"When Angelica told me that, I was amazed. How could a man be so full of the joy of life when he has known such loss, I asked myself." She shrugged her shoulders and shook her head, appearing perplexed. "All I know is, he is the second friend in José's life to give him hope and direction, and I am thankful to God for such a blessing." Crossing herself from the ritual habit of a lifetime, Lupe finished her task and looked at Kavya's handiwork, satisfied that the evening had not been wasted. No word of apology was necessary.

Between apprehending thieves, fostering her son's romantic aims, and assisting Marilyn to sort out the few details necessary to pull off a casual, intimate wedding with virtually no notice, Angelica had hit her stride. For someone who found her deepest calling in helping others, she sometimes wondered if she could keep up with it all.

To further the first aim, Mr. Dawson had moved her to "acting" head of housekeeping. This simply meant she was free to gather information – surreptitiously, of course – from the cleaning staff, and to "check" on their work, thus giving her legitimacy to enter certain rooms at will. Angelica often felt like she was living out a preposterous dream from which she would awaken to find herself back in Tinkers Well, taking food to a sick family. On such occasions she would give herself a mental shake and repeat aloud, "I made a commitment, and I mean to see it through – even if i' 'tis preposterous!" Invariably, she would leave a "suspicious" room only to run slap into Christopher Gordon, who was delivering room service or vacuuming the hallway. They exchanged common courtesies with no sign of recognition.

Angelica was still perplexed by his admonition to keep her knowledge of his role to herself. More than once, she had to bite back a comment about the head of hotel security when she turned a corner to discover Inspector Dulac emerging from any number of strange places. He had returned to Kansas City a week prior to the security conference and seemed to be everywhere at once. She caught him stealing out of the kitchen one day, where he paused only long enough to take her hand and kiss it gallantly before disappearing through another door. Thirty minutes later she saw him stepping warily into the hall beyond the event room. He closed the door slowly behind him – a door that gave stair access to the lower parking levels.

Twice he joined her in Mr. Dawson's office to share notes on Jamison's movements. The hotel manager made it clear in each instance that he didn't expect the Frenchman to tarry overlong. With Gaelic instinct, Dulac heard the meaning behind the words and excused himself gracefully, not wanting to appear *de trop*.

Reporting her daily findings to Mr. Dawson had turned into occasional visits to nearby restaurants for dinner or strolls through the botanical garden at dusk. It didn't seem to matter whether she had any pertinent information to share about Samuel Jamison or not. In fact, Angelica and Mr. Dawson were more likely to discuss their children, their hopes for the future, or their favorite forms of entertainment, valuing their time together like friends of long standing.

A few days before the Ludlow/Hawthorne wedding, while exploring a new path in the botanical garden, they came upon a group of musicians gathered for a lively jam session. The players on the covered bandstand displayed their virtuosity on an assortment of saxophones, horns, and woodwinds, accompanied by an upright bass. Drawn to the impromptu performance, Angelica and Dawson stopped to listen. When the music shifted gears to a smooth jazz medley, Dawson swept Angelica into his arms without warning and began to dance with her across the grass. Rigid with shock, she protested vehemently at first, but the music and the moment helped her to relax in his arms as his polished steps led hers with ease. When the musicians paused to confer over a tricky bridge section, Dawson explained that he merely thought it prudent to practice dancing before a more public performance at the wedding. Angelica believed such audacity deserved a sharp set-down. It was left unsaid, however, when her attention was distracted by an unexpected sight. Dawson still clasped her right hand while his other arm encircled her waist, but she hardly noticed. She was staring in disbelief at a group of men standing near the branch of another path.

A clump of hydrangea bushes loaded with blue and pink blooms partially blocked her view, but the faces were unmistakable. Angelica turned her hand in Dawson's clasp to drag him behind a row of adjacent butterfly bushes. Though not particularly dense shrubs, they at least provided enough cover for the two to get closer to their quarry undetected. What the quarry was, Dawson neither knew nor cared. He was enjoying himself too much to find out. With a twinkle in his eyes, he dared to ask where they were going but received only a firm "Shush!" in reply. They eventually came to a standstill where the butterfly bushes ended, and the hydrangeas began. By then little tufts of purple and white flowers stuck out at odd angles in Angelica's hair. She had chosen to wear a wide band around her head that morning rather than a scarf, leaving her hair to collect floral debris along the way. When a foraging hummingbird mistook a sprig of pink blossoms for a well of nectar, it was only by a superhuman effort that Dawson was able to contain the laughter welling up inside him. He even managed a commendably straight face when Angelica turned to roll her eyes with exaggerated intensity at three men ten feet away. At that distance, there was no mistaking them.

Samuel Jamison, Klaus Richter, and Christopher Gordon stood in close conversation. Though their voices were somewhat muted, the two observers watching and listening from the nearby shrubs were able to hear well enough, especially when Jamison spoke.

"I tell you, Herr Richter, this man can be trusted. In fact, he must be trusted for our plan to prosper."

"But I have seen him working in the hotel, and at several different jobs! I suppose you will tell me he is some kind of mole," Richter grumbled in distrust.

"I think it best that young Christopher explains himself," Jamison's voice rumbled. "I have worked with him on numerous successful enterprises, but I understand your hesitancy in trusting a stranger."

Richter merely glowered at Gordon, who took that as a sign to start explaining. If Angelica had not been staring directly at him, she would never have recognized the voice as his. The warm, cultured British accent she remembered from their meeting at church had become merely a cold device of communication almost devoid of human emotion. And had she not known who he was, she might have been tempted to believe the fantastic history he began to unveil.

"Life affords us many opportunities, Mr. Richter. We can follow the conventional path and lead a life of respectability, even affluence in some instances, or we can use those opportunities to live well beyond the scope of convention."

Richter made no comment, but his look of skepticism took on a speculative gleam.

"I began working in the security industry purely by accident. It was to prove the most fortunate accident of my life. I was recruited out of university to work for a technology company specializing in security systems. I found the work intriguing, and I quickly learned how to make myself indispensable, though I was careful to avoid assignment as team leader on any project. I did not want that kind of notoriety or responsibility. You see, in order to fly under the radar, as it were, I adopted the role of unambitious, subservient assistant. I volunteered to work on tedious project details, took verbal abuse without blinking or argument, and ensured the project leader always looked good to management. Few people ever bothered to learn my name. Such an unassuming fellow could move within a shroud of anonymity without raising any eyebrows.

"A strict company policy forbade anyone from taking work home with them. Our belongings were scanned and searched daily. But I had other plans. None of my coworkers saw me as anything but a reasonably intelligent, though hardly brilliant, technophile. I was pleased to foster that belief so that when I created a clandestine means of transmitting information, it went undetected. With that information I worked tirelessly at home and was finally able to create a backdoor into the system. It too went undetected simply because no one was looking for it. With my less-than-notable personality, I left that company after a few years without so much as an eyebrow raised. My résumé was unimpeachable, though, allowing me to repeat the same employment tactics at other security development companies. By the time I had had my fill of being dogsbody and general factotum to far lesser intellects than my own, I had created secure access to over twelve notable systems."

Despite being momentarily swept along by Gordon's narrative, Richter shook his head and stated emphatically, almost as if to convince himself, "*Nein! Es ist unmöglich!* Even the most creative thieves must learn to dance among laser beams or build decoder devices for random access code scramblers. And how does one capture someone's breath for a DNA breathalyzer scan? I tell you it is impossible! Yet you tell me you can hack unhackable systems, all of which will be in play at the security conference – the Baffington, the Fujita, the Vasiliev? Bah!"

"You are not listening, Mr. Richter. I have never had any desire to become an acrobat and, as you described it, 'dance among laser beams.' I am able to access each system with a sequence of keystrokes known only to me and simply immobilize them with no one the wiser."

Richter was clearly impressed. So was Angelica. She had all but forgotten Dawson's presence until he sneezed suddenly. She turned to glare at him holding a finger to her lips. He smiled meekly in apology, but she had already turned back to hear more of Gordon's fascinating story. Though Angelica knew it all to be a pack of lies, she was impressed by his ability to recount such lies so convincingly.

"I must admit, Gordon, that your knowledge of technology manipulation is most impressive, but why stay in the background when you would, no doubt, have been paid handsomely for such expertise?" Richter asked, still not convinced that he should trust the man.

Gordon's eyes burned with unsuspected passion. "Because, Mr. Richter, I don't want to live *very well* – I want to live *extravagantly!* I don't want a mere million-dollar home in Silicon Valley – I want a villa on the Riviera, a castle in Gstaad, and a Polynesian palace in Tahiti with my own private jet to fly about in. I want to live as the idle rich." Richter could hardly fault such a plan – it was precisely as he envisioned his own future. "I may have possessed the technical skills to steal anything guarded by a modern security system, but I lacked the means to move in the social circles where such wealth is amassed – not without some kind of *entrée.* After much research, including information gleaned from police files kept by investigators I assisted a few times as an expert witness, I came upon the name 'Samuel Jamison.' A renowned thief, yet one who had miraculously avoided capture, was the professional mentor I needed."

Jamison deemed it time to enter the discussion. "It was surely a collaboration written in the stars. The exponential rate of change in modern technology had outstripped my ability to keep up with it. I needed the help of someone with the expertise I lacked." He smiled indulgently at the younger man, almost as a father looking on a favored son.

Richter was no fool. When Jamison had contacted him the year before to be part of what would, undoubtedly, become one of the greatest heists in history, he had done his research. Among the upper crust of the criminal world, little was known of the young man who had aligned himself with a master of the profession. There had been rumors of select artwork collections and jewels gone missing. Months later the items were exhibited publicly as if to play down such tales. Everything had been authenticated, but who could be sure nowadays when nothing was as it seemed. Whether the stories were true or not, Richter was willing to take the risk. He was too old to join a band of youngsters who spent more time on their cell phones than on blueprints and rehearsed plans. Nor was he quite old enough to retire unless he had the wealth hinted at by Jamison. Ever the gambler, he was on the brink of taking a chance on the biggest gamble of his career, but something held him back.

Sensing Richter's inner struggle, Gordon produced several business cards from previous employment in the security industry and suggested the older man research his background and the technical measures he had boasted of mastering. "I will walk away now and leave this to you two gentlemen if you don't feel you can trust me. I cannot work with an unwilling partner, and it will take all three of us to pull off this job. Without trust, we will never succeed." It was an eerie echo of Jamison's words. Richter took the cards held out to him, agreeing to meet the next day as previously planned. Without another word, the three walked away in different directions. It never occurred to Angelica to wonder where that meeting might be or if she needed to keep a close eye on any, or all, of these targets.

"Well, I never!" Angelica breathed in disbelief. She allowed herself to be led out of hiding without thinking. After all she had heard, she could hardly think at all!

Dawson tucked her hand in the crook of his arm and led her back down the path unresisting. Before she had gathered her wits enough to process all she had overheard, and before she began to question how such a story could be corroborated, he reminded her gently, "It is more important now than ever that you do not show any indication of knowing Christopher Gordon."

Still a little dazed, Angelica answered truthfully, "I don't know what I would say to him even if I could!"

"That's my girl!" Dawson murmured under his breath.

I am no such thing! Angelica thought indignantly, though she judged it best to pretend she hadn't heard him. They wandered back to the car avoiding the topic of robbery altogether and speculated instead on what could possibly go amiss with events on Sunday. Angelica assured him that nothing is ever amiss at a wedding – the unexpected only makes for memorable moments. Dawson frowned slightly in the gathering darkness, hoping fervently that she was right.

An overstuffed cardboard box, two-foot square, landed with a shower of dislodged papers that had lost their tenuous hold amid the other random objects in the box. Invoices, estimates, and receipts eventually fluttered to a soft landing on Abe Yousef's desk. He looked on with dismay and groaned.

"Look what I found!" Derek declared triumphantly.

"No, no, *no!* Don't tell me these are the documents I asked you to look for when I first took over the mess you and Tim called bookkeeping." Abe groaned once more as he looked with despair at one piece of paper after another. "I'm afraid to ask where you found these."

"You're going to laugh…"

"I doubt it," Abe said with feeling as he glared at Derek and his irritating grin.

"They were under my bed all the time! Isn't that crazy?"

"*Crazy!* You mean all the time I was living in the room *next to you*, you never looked under your *bed?* You're going to drive *me* crazy!" Abe clutched at his hair in frustration. He had just been congratulating himself on tying up a lot of loose ends before turning his attention to a full-time seminary load. He could not leave *Three Brothers Construction, Inc.* without putting everything in order. It had taken him six months to dig through the paper mess he found upon joining Tim and Derek in their fledgling business. But before they hired the four additional crew members, the computers and tablets Abe had insisted on purchasing were sidelined so that he could learn to frame doors and hang drywall. It took all hands on deck to keep things going and meet deadlines in those early days. Now operating with a crew of seven, Abe was able to step back and do what he did best – organize and digitize. Billing, invoicing, and payment were now seamless, with paper trails a thing of the past – that is, until Derek turned up with a missing link to the stone age. While Abe considered the mess presented for his specialized attention, Derek disclosed his own personal conundrum.

"I've got to think of a way to justify showing up at the clinic where Kavya is working this summer, so I came to consult the genius. I figure it will look more convincing if I have a real injury." Abe only rolled his eyes and shook his head. "Man, I'm not kidding. What do you think would be the least painful?"

Abe had hoped to grab a few hours of study time before his Saturday seminar class the following day. He was in no mood to deal with one of Derek's half-baked ideas.

"Crack a rib?" Derek suggested doubtfully. "Though I don't exactly know how to do that. Maybe a gash in my leg that needs a few stitches?" Even as he spoke the words, Derek began to feel a little queasy.

"I think it would be less painful if you did not injure anything! Derek, do you honestly believe that pursuit of this woman requires that you physically *maim* yourself? And how will you manage your Thursday evening training cycles at the fire station if you are bandaged and unable to move?"

"Hmm. I hadn't thought of that…"

"I mean, is she really worth it?"

Not finding his friend's response very supportive, Derek countered with, "You told me once that you offered to cut off your other leg for Amy," then crossed his arms and waited for Abe to deny it.

"I was speaking figuratively. Surely, even you are familiar with the concept." Derek only glowered at Abe who continued undeterred. "As you are well aware, Amy and I were quite smitten with one another after our first date. As far as anyone can tell, Kavya doesn't even *like* you!"

"It's not that she doesn't like me – she just doesn't *know* me. She probably still thinks I'm the idiot who couldn't put two words together when we first met."

Abe looked up at that. "And you believe that getting yourself dismembered – or worse – will *change* that opinion?"

"Man, can't you see that I need an excuse to visit her at the clinic? That would at least look legit. I can't very well just happen to drop by the Aguilars' house unless I have José with me, and I don't think he wants to be roped into being a fifth wheel again." In an attitude of defeat, Derek sat on the end of the desk and frowned at nothing in particular.

Despite his earlier claim, there had been enough hiccups in his courtship of Amy Walker that Abe could empathize with Derek. And Derek had always been there for him. Now it was his turn. He leaned back in his chair and looked at his dejected friend. "I say this from the bottom of my heart. You are like a brother to me, and I want you to be happy. All your friends do. But are you certain that Kavya is the woman for you? What do you know of her background, her interests, her faith?" He added the last item gently though it carried the most weight. While he and Amy had very different backgrounds and family histories, they both shared a love for the Savior who had transformed their lives in ways they could never have imagined. That shared faith had only been possible because Derek had first shared his faith with Abe.

"Perhaps you should focus less on making Kavya fall in love with you and think more about ways you can minister to her. I give you full credit for being quite adept at that."

Derek didn't respond right away. A speculative expression lifted his eyebrows as he considered the possibilities. Presently, he nodded his head decisively and hopped off the desk. As he passed Abe's chair, Derek thumped his shoulder and said with a grin, "Thanks, brother. You really *are* a genius!"

Gingerly rubbing his shoulder, Abe looked after his friend and shook his head. "I don't know if I helped him or not, Father," he prayed, "but please give him wisdom and protect his heart – and his limbs!"

A siren could be heard in the distance. Lupe paid no attention. There were no emergencies at the Aguilar home unless one could consider the inadvertent uprooting of a stand of zinnias an emergency. Ani insisted on helping Tia Lupe with the weeding, which, in her generous little mind, meant pulling *every*thing out of the ground. As the sound grew louder, the child paused in her mission, much to Lupe's relief, and looked around for the source of such a commotion. When she spied a shiny red fire engine turn down the lane headed in her direction, she began shouting, pointing, and dancing around in circles all at once. A little worried, Kavya hurried outside only to be brought up short by the spectacle before her.

Three firemen in full gear jumped from the vehicle, while the driver expertly maneuvered it in the open space between the house and the barn until it was pointed back in the direction it had come. Temporarily overwhelmed into silence, Ani stood close to her mother, clutching her hand. When she recognized the fireman walking toward her, she suddenly let go and ran to greet the familiar form, screaming, "Dewek! Dewek!" He caught her and swung her up in his arms where she nearly choked him with an exuberant hug.

Kavya had been joined by Lupe, who mentally chided Carlos for choosing this time, above all others, to be out in the fields spreading manure! Derek approached the ladies with a sheepish grin and said, "Surprise! Since we were driving right by your place on our way to the county training facility, I asked the chief if we could make a slight detour. I told him he might find a potential firefighter here," he explained, placing a plastic toy replica of his helmet over Ani's riotous curls. "Besides, we're breaking in a new driver, and this is the perfect place to practice moving that beast around in a small space."

The chief walked up just then and essentially repeated Derek's explanation, beginning with "This young fool insisted…" He then invited the ladies to tour the engine and reached for Ani to lift her into the cab with the driver. Kavya was surprised when her daughter clung to Derek instead. She was even more surprised when Derek handed the child to her mother and climbed into the truck himself. When he reached for Ani, she stretched out her arms to him and sat happily on his lap while he pointed out all the interesting buttons and knobs. Finally feeling more secure in the strange new world of wonder surrounding her, Ani willingly moved to the chief's arms so that he could walk her around the engine. Lupe followed, eager to learn more about the fascinating machine called a "Quint," so named for its unique combination of pump, water tank, fire hose, aerial device, and ground ladders.

While the chief spoke in great detail about his favorite subject, Derek hung back a little, hoping to chat with Kavya. To his relief, she appeared to be relatively approachable that morning – her first words were not an insult, at least. He brushed aside her thanks for all the trouble he had gone to on Ani's behalf as nothing. In truth, it had taken a good deal of fast talking to convince the chief to deviate from the training schedule. Fortunately for Derek's aims, the chief had taken a great liking to the new recruit, recognizing what an asset he would be to the team. He allowed the exception, leaving Derek to make what he could of the moment.

"I expect I'll see you tomorrow at the wedding," Derek said with more hope than certainty.

"Oh, I hardly think so. My aunt and uncle plan to attend. They are so pleased to have been invited. But I've never even met the couple, so I would feel awkward and out of place."

"I say it's never too late to make new friends. And what better timing – what with free food and entertainment, and all? Besides, I happen to know they want you to come, and everyone you met at the picnic a few weeks ago will be there. I know they'll miss you if you're not there."

Kavya cringed a little, certain that *none* of the people she had snubbed and insulted would want her within a hundred miles of the wedding. But Derek could be very persuasive when he really wanted something.

Pretending not to notice her hesitation, Derek effectively put the lid on any more argument. "Have a heart. I hate to go by myself, and José refuses to be my 'plus 1.'" Taking Kavya's quickly stifled laughter as a positive sign, he pushed his point home. "Besides, I have a feeling that no one will have much time to socialize with the bride and groom, anyway. Tim thinks they'll be taking off right after the ceremony, which is expected to be pretty short. Then it's party time! Did I mention there would be *lots* of food? Did I mention the hotel has an awesome pool *and* kiddie pool where Ani can play until she's wrinkled and waterlogged?" Derek was encouraged by Kavya's spontaneous spurt of laughter. "Did I mention that I'll be dressed to kill?" he added with something of his usual swagger.

"You'll be wearing your fireproof jacket and rubber boots then?" she inquired with admirable composure.

The grin that had been hidden for a month spread across his face like a beacon of light. "Come and find out." Kavya couldn't help but respond to such a challenge with a smile, despite her determination to keep her emotional distance and refuse the invitation.

The tour ended all too soon when the chief rallied everyone back to the fire engine. After promising Ani another special treat on the following day, Derek swung himself up into the truck as if his heavy gear was suddenly weightless. The chief assumed the place of authority next to the driver, and they were off. Ani clapped in delight when the siren gave a short burst by way of a farewell, but her cheers soon dissolved into tears of disappointment as the fire engine drove away.

Lupe took the little girl inside to distract her with the promise of a new book to be read before lunch. Kavya stood looking down the lane long after the fire engine had disappeared. She had been shaken by two things: Derek's thoughtfulness in going to the trouble of bringing such joy to a little girl, and Ani's reaction to Derek. Kavya wasn't sure if her daughter was more distraught over the departure of the big, shiny truck or the departure of Derek. She refused to consider her own treacherous reaction to his presence.

CHAPTER 11

*Marriage is to be held in honor among all – that is, regarded as
something of great value…*

Hebrews 13:4a (AMP)

Those entering the *Plains Oasis* room as wedding guests of Miles
Hawthorne and Marilyn Ludlow experienced the odd feeling of
going backward through a time warp. Many had attended the
couple's engagement party in the same location only a month before. On
this second occasion, they were greeted by the same mix of familiar and
unknown faces gathered in groups throughout the space. And just as before,
guests sat in small groups or stood around high bar tables laden with enough
savories, crudités, and fresh fruit to please even the most finicky of palettes.
Further investigation, however, uncovered subtle differences. Random *hors
d' oeuvres* boasted toothpicks topped by tiny paper umbrellas – an
incongruity in an otherwise elegant display. Another small item added
credibility to the distinctive nature of the occasion; a modest, tiered cake,
nearly smothered with hibiscus blooms, stood on a rolling cart diligently
guarded by a member of the kitchen staff. And one corner of the room was
set with white, wooden folding chairs in neat rows.

A not-so-subtle change in the atmosphere of the room also declared this
to be a singular day. Rattan furniture, borrowed from the poolside deck, was
scattered in random groupings around the room. Cascading bougainvillea
draped the railing above the two-story waterfall and lay in artful disarray

across the lower level of the large planter, while potted palms, springing up throughout the room, completed the transformation of a western oasis into a tropical paradise. Shimmering strands of silver paper fell in torrents from a frame suspended below the three-story ceiling providing a rainforest feel.

Those who respected Miles and Marilyn for their taste and decorum might almost have described the décor as tacky. It was certainly something beyond the ordinary – a somewhat garish display that caught visitors by surprise. The whole effect was curiously somehow… off. Discerning critics wondered if the effect was purposeful, as if the intent was to draw the crowd's collective observation away from something else. Those with less discriminating taste found it delightfully gaudy. Whatever the reaction, most present assumed this to be a hint as to where the newlyweds would be spending their honeymoon. The destination had been kept a closely guarded secret. Only Miles' faithful secretary, Mrs. Castle, knew for sure, and she could be counted on to give nothing away.

The small wedding party had done a quick run through of the brief ceremony only a half hour before guests arrived, so Tim employed the intervening time in sampling the rival merits of cheesy stuffed mushrooms and smoked BBQ chicken on bruschetta. Between mouthfuls he asserted his refusal to pay off a bet with Rose as to where his parents would be headed after the ceremony.

"I'm telling you, it's not Hawaii or the Caribbean or any obvious place like that. I don't care what the decorations say to the contrary."

In response, Rose merely held out her hand and waited for the payoff. After all, a dollar bet is a dollar bet! With a devilish glint in his eye, Tim reached behind him then deposited a mini ham melt on her palm.

"Oooh, why you…!" Had it not been such a public place, or such a respectable affair, Rose might have considered thrusting the substitute offering into his charming smile. Commonsense, and the reminder that she was eating for three, overruled such waste. She popped the canapé in her mouth and reached for another.

The soft blur of tuning instruments could barely be heard over the festive sound of Calypso music floating throughout the room. Under its camouflage, Amy Yousef's violin and Abe's guitar glided almost effortlessly into pure consonance, while Mr. Dawson meekly adjusted their microphones at Angelica's insistence. Every now and then he glanced around at the gathered crowd and sighed in resignation. At this point, the day's proceedings were out of his hands.

Little Anika Jackson rested comfortably in Derek's arms while he walked her around the large space, pointing out things she might find interesting. Each gasp of surprise was followed by a look of wonder as she took in every detail, convinced that they had been provided expressly for her pleasure. Meanwhile, Kavya enjoyed watching her aunt and uncle's simple delight in being part of, what seemed to them, a very grand affair indeed.

It was left to Granny Gert and Aletha to perform the honors as dual hostesses. Both matriarchs wore varying shades of gray they considered appropriate for their age and positions. On Aletha, the dove-gray silk, coupled with her soft halo of white hair, created an ethereal quality. Tight iron-colored curls and battleship gray polyester gave Gert the appearance of a prison matron on lunch break. Their smiles were equally welcoming, however, as they greeted their friends who entered the room with exclamations of pleasure, awe, and random observations.

"I can't imagine why they put red bougainvillea next to a waterfall. Why, the color might run, and then where would we be with pink everywhere!" Ellie June Stratton commented vaguely before her brother settled her comfortably at a table reserved for seniors near the big windows overlooking the lush green space outdoors. The deep green of the grass reflected the tint of Ellie's fingernails as they plucked idly at her lilac hair. Isaac Rosenbaum helped Herbie to a comfortable chair, placing the much-needed walker within reach. Sensing Reenie Fields' hesitancy to be anything but a shrinking wallflower, Deborah Rosenbaum whisked her timid friend off to sample the delectable nibbles awaiting their enjoyment.

After everyone was comfortably installed, Gert and Aletha allowed themselves to be escorted to their seats of honor – the front row of folding chairs set up six feet behind a double kneeling bench. Scout led the way like a four-legged bridesmaid. Tim stood on one side of the kneeler while Angelica took her place opposite him. The background music began to fade, replaced by a gentle melody brought to life by Amy's expressive touch. Her violin was joined by the soft plucking of guitar strings signaling everyone to turn their attention to the main event in that corner of the room. They played through the song twice as the strains of Calypso music faded into silence, and a hush finally fell on the assembled crowd. All eyes looked at the performers. With a flourishing cadence, Amy led the music back to tonic. She lowered her bow and looked at her husband who nodded. With one breath they began a beautifully resonant duet of a moving folk ballad while Abe strummed his guitar.

> *The water is wide, I cannot cross o'er*
> *And neither have, I wings to fly*
> *Give me a boat, that can carry two*
> *And both shall row, my love and I*[11]

Everyone listened to the poignant performance, unaware of movement behind them. Gradually their focus shifted as a couple moved within the crowd to walk down the short aisle between the rows of chairs. The Yousefs continued to sing as Miles and Marilyn presented themselves at the makeshift altar as bride and groom. Those present who knew their history well were hard-pressed to keep tears from their eyes as the song continued. Love in the dawn of adulthood is a priceless gift full of romance and promise. Love rediscovered in the sober years of middle age is a priceless gift beyond measure or understanding.

---

[11] Cecil Sharp and Charles Marson, *The Water is Wide*, (Folk Songs from Somerset), Simpkin & Co., LTD, (London) 1906.

O, love is gentle, and love is kind
The sweetest rose, when first it's new
But as it twines, true beauty shines
Like diamonds sparkling with morning dew

Marilyn's fingers, nestled in Miles' clasp, moved to interlace themselves with his. Amy lifted her bow to play a tag of the verse before leading the music into its joyous final statement as Pastor Lindeman moved to stand before the bride and groom.

There is a ship, and she sails the sea
She's loaded deep, as the waves are high
But not as deep, as the joy we keep
Within our hearts, my love and I[12]

Tissues and handkerchiefs broke out everywhere. There was hardly a dry eye in the house. Though shining with tears, Rose's eyes managed to direct a triumphant look at her husband. Miles and Marilyn themselves bore out her belief in a tropical honeymoon more effectively than any potted plants. The respectable business suit of the rehearsal no longer showcased the groom. Instead, he wore loose-fitting white linen slacks with an open-collared shirt that exactly matched the floral pattern of Marilyn's dress in royal blue and white. The knee-length, one-shoulder dress, with shapely shirring at the waist, was accented by a spray of white orchids covering the single shoulder strap. The effect was extremely flattering and quite unlike her usual reserved style. Tim had to blink a few times to convince himself he was really looking at his mother. Miles had eyes for no one else.

Much the same could be said of the others present – with three exceptions. Catching the eye of Inspector Dulac, who stood near the entrance to the hall in what looked like some kind of service uniform, Mr. Dawson nodded almost imperceptibly. The Frenchman melted away

---

[12] Linda Edmister, altered verses 2 & 3, *"The Water is Wide,"* 2024.

behind the few guests standing in the rear of the room and disappeared. A third man, diligently guarding the cake, had followed Dawson's eyes. He pulled the top of his chef's *toque* to one side to better hide his features and lowered his head. When Dulac passed behind him in the hallway and entered the kitchen, Christopher Gordon waited two minutes and followed him.

Nervously smoking one cigarette after another, Klaus Richter waited impatiently near a support pillar at a spot predetermined by Gordon. The German's penchant for arriving at every meeting 15 minutes early only served to exacerbate his already highly strung nerves. When he finally heard a stealthy sound behind him, he whirled around with his hand in his pocket – a pocket that had taken on an oddly pointed shape.

"Herr Richter," Samuel Jamison said, "you must control yourself. There is no need for such a tool." Jamison nodded at the pistol now fully visible in the dim lighting of the parking garage beneath the hotel. His deep, rumbling voice seemed to soothe the other man's jitters. The pistol disappeared as Richter turned to Jamison's accomplice.

"I do not like to be kept waiting," he said, fully aware that the other two had arrived precisely at the designated time.

"And I do not appreciate having my word questioned. It is a waste of time to anticipate trouble. Now, let us begin." Gordon, who had exchanged his chef's garb for tight black pants, turtleneck, and a ski cap pulled down over his ears, stepped toward a nearby elevator. The lift provided access to the upper parking garage levels, the utility level of the hotel – where the laundry and mechanical rooms were located – and access to the main level hallway beyond the event room and lobby.

"But I just came from the lobby! Why are we returning? Again, we are wasting time!" As Richter's agitation and mistrust grew, Gordon retreated into stony silence. His unflinching stare unnerved the other man who barely bit back another string of foolish protests when the elevator door closed. With a light touch, Gordon pressed the upper panel of the elevator controls to disclose a hidden keypad. He punched in a few numbers and the elevator began to descend.

"*Nein!* It cannot be. We are going *down?*"

Gordon turned on Richter so quickly, the knife was at his throat before Richter saw it coming. "Many more outbursts like that, and you will no longer care in what direction we are moving." Still holding the knife to Richter's carotid artery, Gordon spoke through his teeth to Jamison, who had somehow managed to remain in the background. "You keep this fool quiet, or our deal is off. I will find a way to create my own diversion. I suddenly find that you are both expendable." Jamison nodded, a glint in his own eye. "And get rid of that ridiculous pistol. He's liable to discharge it if one of us sneezes!" Gordon replaced the knife in its sheath while Jamison deposited Richter's gun in his own jacket pocket.

The elevator doors opened after an agonizingly slow descent. A solid wall of darkness greeted them from a black void. Only the light from the elevator gave them guidance. It was all Gordon needed. Stepping forward with confidence, he waited for overhead lights to respond to his movement. He drew a small can of spray paint from his hip pocket and covered each of the rotating cameras lining the walls, then moved with purpose down a short hallway leading to three doors, one labeled "Restroom." The one on the left, he opened with a key and pulled two luggage carts from its darkened depths into the hallway.

"Do you mean to stand there like simpletons, or do we proceed with our plan?" he asked his henchmen, who hesitated just outside the elevator door. The two moved quickly, each grabbing one of the luggage trolleys. Gordon turned his attention to the adjacent heavy metal door. Withdrawing a small keypad from the tool bag he carried, he inserted an adapter into a tiny port almost hidden at the bottom of an electronic panel mounted on the wall. Just as he had promised, a few swift keystrokes later the door latch released.

"*Wunderbar!*" Richter exclaimed in satisfaction before doubt once again reared its ugly head. A familiar, belligerent look stole over his features as he shook his head in disbelief. "*Nein.* This is too easy! How did you know of the hidden panel in the elevator, and how could you possibly have known which of the security devices guarded the doorway? Jamison, give me my gun," he demanded with his gaze still leveled at Gordon.

"Perhaps I overrated your skill *and* your intelligence, Herr Richter. Can you truly be such a *Dummkopf?*" Jamison replied with disgust. While the two were glaring at one another, Gordon's knife came out of nowhere and pricked the skin on Richter's throat.

"This is the last time I will employ any restraint in dealing with your insecurities. One more question, and your lifeless body will not be found until conference attendees are brought down here tomorrow to view the equipment. Is that clear?" Richter only grunted. His nerves responded to Gordon's voice as those of helpless prey under the spell of a predator's stare. "I had knowledge of the lift because I ingratiated myself into employment at this hotel solely to gain access to this level. As the janitor tasked with cleaning this hallway, the utility room – where I hid the trolleys – and the small toilet behind the other door, I was granted that access. *Now, can we get on with it?*"

Without waiting for a reply, Gordon opened the metal door, which gave onto a room roughly 12 feet by 15 feet. Three doors opened off this space. Each was flanked by a unique electronic panel. He heard the other two men enter the room behind him, but he was already manipulating the panel for the first door. The door slid back with ease to display a laser grid moving across a smaller room at superhuman speed. Richter gasped but wisely refrained from commenting. Gordon dug in his tool kit and drew out a small screwdriver with a tip shaped like a three-sided key. He inserted the unique device into the side of the door panel, and a hidden connector appeared. It fit precisely into one side of his portable keyboard. Gordon deftly executed a few strokes, and the laser lines disappeared to reveal a glorious display of exquisite stones in ornate settings that could have rivaled the crown jewels of any country. Richter gasped again, but this time he was not alone. The three men, now in their element, began to work as a team. Each pulled a specially designed suitcase from one of the trolleys and reached for one priceless piece after another until the bags were full and the display shelves empty.

They carried the bags to the outer room where they were loaded on a trolley, then all turned their attention to the next door. Here Gordon released a tiny clasp on the top edge of the portable keyboard. Again, he worked his magic by drawing out a flexible chord affixed with tiny electrodes. Encircling the edge of the panel with the chord, he punched in a series of numbers on the keypad and waited while 8 digits continued to rotate randomly on the door panel.

"This you cannot open?" Richter asked. One swift look at Gordon's face and he clamped his lips together. He watched with growing interest as one digit at a time seemed to fall into place.

"If you must know, I have sent an override message to the device. Now, instead of allowing it to scramble random numbers in cycles, I am effectively teaching the scrambler a designated code." With a click the door opened inward. "It would seem the device is a faster learner than you are, Richter."

Stack upon stack of gold bullion and silver bars were revealed. Richter was inclined to stand and gape at the amazing sight that met his eyes, but Jamison and Gordon were more focused on the task at hand. Smaller, reinforced overnight bags were designated for the gold since its weight rendered larger containers impractical. The silver was thrown in wherever it fit.

The contents of the third room were only slightly more amazing than the technique used to gain entrance. Though seemingly impenetrable, the breathalyzer scan met its match in Gordon's genius. Richter was surprised to see the younger man breathe on the device, knowing the errant DNA would set off an alarm and keep them locked out. But Gordon had first placed a thin magnetized strip over the warning light then connected it to the ubiquitous keyboard. A few more keystrokes, and the thing was done. Sturdy leather garment bags were reserved for the Euros and US bills, which fit neatly inside the bags' narrow depth. The three men barely spoke. At that juncture, each knew that time was of the essence, and that gathering the treasure might prove to be easier than getting it out of the building.

As Tim had predicted, the ceremony was short, with only a brief message by Mark Lindeman about redemption and renewal. The guests looked on with varying degrees of satisfaction, curiosity, and indulgent affection. Kavya Jackson was somewhat disappointed. Compared to Indian weddings, the whole thing was quite tame! While the words by the pastor gave her pause, she was quite shocked when everyone was asked to join in a song that had nothing to do with a wedding at all. It didn't seem to matter; the words were a celebration and declaration in themselves.

> *What gift of grace is Jesus, my Redeemer*
> *There is no more for Heaven to release*
> *He is my joy, my righteousness, and freedom*
> *My steadfast love, my deep and boundless peace*
>
> *To this I hold, my hope is only Jesus*
> *For my life is wholly bound to His*
> *Oh, how strange and divine, I can sing, "All is mine"*
> *Yet not I, but through Christ in me*

Kavya listened to those around her and was strangely moved by their expressions of devotion, as if the song had been chosen for them rather than the bride and groom, though the words did speak of steadfast love. Kavya moved on from the idle thought to recall ideas Isabella had shared with her as a child – concepts such as joy and peace as being gifts from God even during times of sadness and uncertainty. And while she had discarded such ideas as meaningless after the death of her mother and sister, she now experienced a strange longing to know more.

No fate I dread, I know I am forgiven
The future's sure, the price, it has been paid
For Jesus bled and suffered for my pardon
And He was raised to overthrow the grave

To this I hold, my sin has been defeated
Jesus, now and ever is my plea
Oh, the chains are released, I can sing, "I am free"
Yet not I, but through Christ in me

With every breath, I long to follow Jesus
For He has said that He will bring me home
And day by day, I know He will renew me
Until I stand with joy before the throne

To this I hold, my hope is only Jesus
All the glory evermore to Him
When the race is complete, still my lips shall repeat
Yet not I, but through Christ in me[13]

The grave had *not* been overthrown – her mother and sister *had* died. But the words were so hopeful. They rang with assurance, especially as she heard Derek sing them beside her. When Kavya glanced at his face, she saw

---

[13] Michael Farren, Rich Thompson, Jonny Robinson, "*Yet Not I but Through Christ in Me*," © 2018 Farren Love And War Publishing, Integrity's Alleluia! Music, Cityalight Music. Used by permission.

unaccountable tears in his eyes which seemed at odds with his brilliant smile. She had almost resolved to ask him about their deeper meaning, but thought better of the plan, believing she would appear foolish. Having exposed herself on that score far too many times already, Kavya had no desire to add to her self-imposed humiliation.

As Miles and Marilyn repeated their wedding vows, Kavya thought of her father and Isabella finding happiness in the aftermath of sorrow. Here, again, was a middle-aged couple who had known despair and loss, yet they were able to love again.

Why can I not get past the sorrow and love again? she asked herself. *Are my emotions permanently damaged? Maybe I was right – I am meant to share my life only with Ani.*

On that thought, she looked at her daughter still resting in Derek's arms, perfectly content. Sensing her eyes on him, Derek looked at Kavya and smiled. She tried in vain to remain detached, smiling shyly in return. He nodded his head in unspoken accord, then turned back to follow the end of the service.

The baggage carts groaned with the weight of their treasure. Each hanging rod sagged slightly when the garment bags, with their reinforced hangers, were hauled, two men at a time, and hooked onto the cart. Gordon was closing the door handle of the third room when he turned to find Richter pointing a pistol in his face – the same pistol Jamison had confiscated an hour earlier. Gordon cast a furious glance at Jamison, who shrugged his massive shoulders.

"He pinched it after I took my jacket off during the loading process. What can I say? I am an old man, after all," said Jamison, spreading his hands in a gesture that rid himself of blame.

An evil, self-satisfied expression crept across Richter's face like spreading leprosy. All nervousness and insecurity were gone. "So, Herr Gordon. It seems we have come to a parting of the ways. I am sure you understand that a two-way split is far superior to a three-way split. And I really cannot afford to leave any witnesses behind, so if you would kindly turn the other way…"

"No!" Jamison shouted. The single word exploded in the small space. "I will not be a party to murder! This was *not* part of the arrangement, and don't try to threaten me into this madness. You cannot move all of this by yourself," Jamison said, waving at the enormity of riches loaded on the carts. "You know this to be true. Lock him in the room. He cannot go anywhere. The access panel is on the outside. He will be trapped, and we will be long gone before he is discovered."

Richter hesitated, but the sense of Jamison's words finally penetrated his greed-crazed mind. He merely motioned to Gordon with the gun, indicating that the younger man was to retreat into the room. Stepping backwards, Richter quickly closed the door and ensured it was properly locked before removing the magnetic strip and keypad.

"Now we come to your segment of the operation, my friend," Jamison said in anything but a friendly voice. "I only hope the elevator can carry both us and the two carts without getting stuck or setting off an alarm. But then, you have conveniently rid us of 180 pounds."

Richter only grunted and began pushing his cart the short distance to the waiting elevator. He was much the smaller man, but he refused to ask for help in getting the heavily weighted wheels over the grooved edge of the door. With his patience at the breaking point, Jamison shoved both Richter and his trolley into the limited space and maneuvered it to allow room for his own. Once loaded, the elevator groaned but obediently took the men to the main lobby level.

"Where is the van, Richter? You surely don't plan to take this haul out the front door?"

"The van is parked just outside the door at the end of this hallway. We will transfer the goods in two shifts. Was it not clever that I insist you wear that ridiculous bellhop suit?" Richter looked toward the event room. "We must hurry. The wedding is still in full swing, but if it wraps up before we can get the second trolley to the van, you must create the diversion as planned. Now, tape the 'Out of Order' sign over the call button. We must make haste."

The Hawthornes were pronounced husband and wife; they shared a kiss and were quickly surrounded by well-wishers. It was less a formal receiving line than a gaggle, but Miles and Marilyn managed to greet everyone, cut the cake, and bid Aletha farewell, before they were swept outside to depart on their honeymoon. A few stayed behind to feast on leftovers or to soak in the colorful, air-conditioned ambience. Derek suggested he and Kavya take Ani to the pool area during the lull. The older guests stayed inside to watch from the windows and avoid the heat and the crowd.

It had been a lovely day. Aletha and her friends relaxed in the relative quiet following all the clammer. They waved handkerchiefs and napkins from the comfort of deeply cushioned chairs by the windows and settled down to relive the day's events. The limo drove away, headed for the airport and beyond, wherever that was to be, and guests began to trickle back inside.

Angelica insisted Carlos and Lupe Aguilar stay and enjoy themselves. (She had been briefed by Derek to keep them occupied while he entertained the Jackson ladies.) They were walking to a table by the waterfall just as Samuel Jamison was giving the second trolley a tremendous shove down the hallway in the opposite direction. His partner in crime took advantage of the momentum to keep the cart rolling to the side door while Jamison turned to run toward the main entrance.

Alarmed by the commotion, Angelica looked across the room to see the impossible – Samuel Jamison running from the back hallway waving a small suitcase and shouting, "Wait! Mr. and Mrs. Hawthorne, your bag!" Instinct told her something was very wrong. Commonsense warned her to wait for Mr. Dawson. But the tiresome man was nowhere to be seen! There was nothing left to do but stop Jamison herself. Unfortunately, he was too far away. Her only recourse was a warning.

"Stop that man!" she shouted. "He is a thief!"

The peace of the afternoon was shattered.

With only one thwarted "caper" to their credit, the crime-busting bug had, nonetheless, bit the senior citizens of Tinkers Well with all the intensity of a cicada infestation. When Granny Gert heard Angelica's cry, she looked behind her to see a large black man rushing toward her. Spotting Herbie Stratton's walker, she grabbed it without thinking and threw it in the man's path. To her intense gratification, he tripped over the impediment, soared through the air and crashed into the table currently occupied by Ellie June and Aletha. The latter had just stood up in confusion and concern over all the fuss. Jamison bounced off the fragile figure and ended up spread-eagled with his face to the carpet. The suitcase flew from his hand, completed an impressive six-foot flight, and crashed into the remnants of the wedding cake, sending hibiscus blooms and buttercream icing flying everywhere.

Before Jamison could recover, Bobbie Taylor had thrown himself on one outstretched arm and yelled, "Isaac, grab the other one!"

Not to be outdone by the men, Deborah and Reenie lay down across his legs. Satisfied that all the appendages had been covered, Granny Gert walked over and calmly plopped herself down on Jamison's bottom, thus claiming her rightful position as amateur law enforcement mastermind. After watching Aletha crumble to the floor, Ellie June attempted to fathom the equally strange antics of her other new friends. Gazing around the room in bewilderment, she finally dropped to her knees and crawled over to sit cross-legged by Samuel Jamison's head.

"Hello," she said pleasantly, "I'm Eleanor. Don't bother to tell me your name; I won't remember it." She received only a grunt in reply. "Oh dear, I'm not much good at conversation anymore, but I'll try. Did I tell you about my two Senior Olympic medals in swimming?" Her husband looked on helplessly from the sidelines.

Just then, Mr. Dawson dashed from his office with Chief Inspector Ferguson close behind. This was no time for formalities. "Which way did he go, Angelica?" he demanded. Stupefied by such a foolish question, she could only stare at him and point to Jamison, imprisoned by his elderly jailers. "No, no, he's with us. It's Richter we want." Angelica's eyes almost doubled in size as she continued to stare in disbelief. Her confusion deepened when Christopher Gordon emerged cautiously from the stair door leading to the parking garage. At precisely the same moment, Richter slammed the door at the other end of the hallway and pushed the luggage trolleys against it from the outside.

"I've had all the exits blocked," Gordon yelled. "He won't get away!" With that, he dashed across the room, taking the wedding kneeler in stride like a high hurdle, and vanished around the corner on his way to the pool.

Dawson and Ferguson followed. But being a thoughtful man, Dawson called over his shoulder in parting, "Let Jamison go. He's not going anywhere."

Disappointment was hardly a strong enough word to describe the emotion paramount in her mind as Granny Gert was hauled from her errant seat of power over the assumed culprit. Tim and Pastor Lindeman, who had hurried inside when they became aware of the uproar, assisted the others to their feet as well and waited only long enough to learn that whatever the cause of the ruckus, its conclusion was to be found outside. They looked at one another, then ran after the other men.

Mark couldn't help grinning as he thought to himself, *This wedding has turned out to be even more exciting than the Ludlows' nuptials last year. What a family!*[14]

By that time, Angelica's mind had cleared enough to realize that her part in apprehending Samuel Jamison had not been all it seemed. She ran after Tim and Mark, itching to know more. Such a thrilling afternoon had

---

[14] *Intersecting Dreams*

never come within the scope of the Aguilars' unsophisticated orbit. They set off together, hot on Angelica's heels. Jamison, his sensibilities severely tried, followed with more dignity.

Catching sight of Dawson ahead of them, they all bypassed the pool and ran through a door to the small service parking lot opening onto a back street. Eight people surged through the door on the heels of Christopher Gordon and were stopped at the curb where they collided in a standing heap. A black panel van had just screeched to a halt when two unmarked police cars pulled across the parking lot entrance. Reversing with a skill and dexterity that would ordinarily have drawn praise from onlookers, the driver of the van shifted into gear and started down the ramp leading to the parking garage hoping to exit on the other side through its primary point of entry on the main street. He never made the first turn. Two more unmarked cars blocked that avenue of egress. He was trapped.

Responding to a demand from Gordon, the front doors were slowly opened. Upraised arms appeared as feet hit the ground. A soft gasp escaped Angelica's lips when the driver's face was revealed.

"*Mon ami!* Why did you not tell me that you too were working on this case? We might have caught the culprit sooner. But it is of little importance; we have done it, all the same,*"* Inspector Dulac said with his usual charm of manner as he approached Gordon with deliberate steps. He had reached the back of the vehicle. Richter stood at the other corner of the van, watching him through narrowed eyes. "Surely, I can lower my hands, no?" Dulac said with a jocular assurance that rang a little hollow. Without waiting for permission, he grabbed one of the handles and opened a back door to reveal the bags containing the stolen goods. "The treasure, it is safe, *n'est ce pas?*" After wrestling a small bag laden with gold from the van's contents, he turned and thrust it at Richter, crying out, "This is the fellow you want!"

Caught off guard, Richter staggered backward under the unexpected weight. He struggled to his feet, only to be captured by one of the police officers on the scene.

"He is not only a thief; he is a murderer," Dulac declared with a dramatic gesture quite in keeping with his histrionic style. "Why, he just boasted to me that he managed to dispatch Jamison inside the 'otel." Richter's face grew visibly redder as he bared his teeth. "He will no doubt try to pass off false details of their oh-so-clever plan – the plan which has failed!"

Goaded into rage, Richter released a string of invective quite unsuitable for print – even in German! He tore himself free from restraint and lunged at the other man. Dulac drew his weapon and fired. The German grabbed his abdomen and checked slightly, then kept moving. His hands encircled Dulac's throat like claws. Dulac attempted to fire again, but the bullet refused to advance in the chamber. While the breath was slowly choked out of him, all he could focus on was the impossible fact that Richter was still standing. The Frenchman could only think clearly again when the choking hands were torn from his neck and roughly handcuffed.

"A pity you failed to stop Richter's tongue before he could implicate you. Not only will *he* sing a telling tune – if he knows what's good for him – but Samuel Jamison, also, will oblige us on that score." Gordon spoke in the same dead cold voice Angelica had first heard in the botanical garden. It shocked her more now because it was no longer an affectation. At the sight of Jamison stepping purposely from the crowd, alive and well, the trademark charm that defined Dulac's character was suddenly replaced with the frantic fury of a wild animal at bay.

"Are you *mad?!*" he exclaimed as his eyes frantically sought some avenue of escape. "We both know they planned it together. You heard their conversation recorded last summer in Heidelberg. Why, it was *you,* my friend, who passed on this mission, leaving it in mine and that old fool Ferguson's hands."

Chief Inspector Ferguson stepped from behind the imposing figure of Samuel Jamison. "Och, furr a polis, you'rre farr too gullible, laddie."

In less than a nano second, Dulac whisked a small Glock® from a concealed ankle holster and held it to Gordon's temple, while he encircled his colleague's throat with his other arm. He dragged his prisoner along as he began backing to one of the cars blocking the street entrance.

"I am not above admitting defeat," Dulac panted in steely-edged fury. "Just let me take this vehicle without the nuisance of a chase, and I will let this gentleman go unharmed. Now, place your weapons carefully on the ground – all of you – and raise your hands. Perhaps I should mention that I am not above using his body as a shield if you have other ideas."

Ferguson told the others to do as directed. When the last man surrendered his gun, a slight hand signal from Gordon caused the older man to pull a pistol from his pocket and fire into a harmless bush growing on the curb near Dulac. Just as Gordon had counted on, Dulac reacted with the instinct of years of training. He moved the muzzle from Gordon's head and returned fire. No one moved or even reached for a weapon. Ferguson went so far as to pocket his pistol and cross his arms. In disbelief, the Frenchman attempted to fire again. And just as before, the gun malfunctioned. Throwing the useless weapon aside, he turned on Gordon – his final mistake. Anger and disgust, such as he had never known, flowed through Christopher Gordon, willing him to forget – just for a moment – that he was a policeman, urging him instead to take on the mantle of judge and jury.

One ringing blow to Dulac's jaw was enough to clear his vision. The charming mask of a well-respected detective was gone. Gordon saw clearly a ruthless criminal without conscience or feeling, a man who would destroy anyone or anything to get what he wanted. While the Frenchman was roughly seized and handcuffed, Gordon offered one brief explanation, though Dulac hardly deserved it.

"Early this morning, while you were sleeping off the effects of a strong narcotic, the live rounds were removed from both yours and Richter's weapons and replaced with blanks. We couldn't take any chances; we needed his testimony. You have both been under surveillance ever since." Turning to the arresting police officer, he said, "Take him away. I can't stand the sight of him."

Gordon followed Ferguson into one of the unmarked police cars. They drove off without a backward glance.

CHAPTER 12

Inside, the people were all shouting, some one thing and some another. Everything was in confusion.

Acts 19:32a (NLT)

Tears streamed down the faces of the newlyweds, though they were neither tears of joy nor tears of sorrow. Sitting in the sumptuous limo hired to deliver them to the airport in style, Miles and Marilyn Hawthorne dabbed helplessly at their eyes that seemed to fill from bottomless wells.

"Oh, Timothy, could you ever have imagined a more vulgar wedding for a staid, middle-aged couple? Just look at us! We look like extras from the film set of another *Hawaii Five-O*© reboot. There were chintzy paper umbrellas on the silver-plated *hors d' oeuvres* trays and *huge* umbrellas spread above those oversized deck chairs scattered throughout the hall. And the tacky "rain showers" glittering from the ceiling – what must people have been *thinking*!"

With barely a quiver to his lip, Miles replied, "They thought *you*, my darling Mari, were quite ravishing, and that you had taken pity on some beach bum off the street and agreed to marry him. Though I must say, I find these loose linen slacks rather comfortable. There is something to be said for the superiority of a drawstring over a tiresomely fitted waistband." His bride's infectious laughter erupted once more.

With great effort, Marilyn finally gained some control over the spontaneous gurgles surfacing at will. She wiped her eyes for the umpteenth time and managed to say, with something approaching command, "Oh, my goodness! Well, no one will be able to say our wedding was boring, even the people we didn't know!" She looked at Miles and said with a slight frown, "I still don't quite understand why we had to have *so* many people present or why they were exposed to such a… a spectacle."

"I think the best way to think of the whole exhibition is to see it as a cover. The bigger and louder and more ostentatious an event, the easier it is to hide or cover up something in its shadow. You remember that Mr. Dawson originally asked if we would be willing to hold a fake wedding just to give the criminals an excuse for choosing that particular time to carry out their plans, hoping to aid the police in apprehending them. It made sense, after all, since the big security conference is to be held tomorrow."

"Yes, I know all that, but were we mad to make the wedding real instead of a farce? There are moments when I feel like I've been caught up in some kind of enchantment in which nothing is as it seems, and my will is not my own. Am I to wake up tomorrow only to find I've dreamt it all even though I know it to be true?"

"Having second thoughts?" he asked teasingly.

"No," she answered with a decisive shake of the head, "Never again." After a brief pause, she sighed and added, "Though I must confess to a little disappointment."

Catching the twinkle in her eye, Miles said on a stricken note, "I knew it! Would that I were a better man…"

"I promise to disabuse your mind of such a ridiculous notion – later. For now, I'm just feeling a little let down. Why, we didn't meet a single criminal! Or if we did, I didn't know it. Nothing was stolen – not even our wedding rings, though I'd have put up a fight if anyone had tried!" She added a little wistfully, "I had hoped, at the very least, to have the opportunity of throwing the cake at a likely suspect. There it probably still sits, awash in hibiscus blooms like the centerpiece at a florists' convention. I can guarantee you that if Aletha or Gertie Gunn had had any idea there were villains possibly lurking about, they'd have done their level best to unmask them."

"Then thank the Lord they never found out! Can you imagine the possible carnage?" Miles replied with a shudder.

"Tell me our itinerary again," Marilyn said, having decided to put off frivolous disappointment in favor of contemplating the adventure awaiting them.

"Our flight to Vancouver leaves in an hour. Since we gain two hours flying west, we'll arrive in plenty of time for dinner. Then we leave on our rail tour across the Canadian Rockies on Tuesday. Do you think anyone has guessed our destination or was all that tropical nonsense enough of a blind?"

"I'm sure nobody has the least idea. And you can be sure that your Mrs. Castle will take that secret to the grave."

"*My* Mrs. Castle? Hardly. You are the only 'Mrs.' in my life now, my island temptress, and don't you forget it!" Miles spent the remainder of the short trip to the airport reminding her.

With everyone dashing off to who knew where, Granny Gert felt like she had missed the boat. First, the criminal so cleverly apprehended was released without an explanation, then she had to sort out the mayhem left behind. She gave little thought to any embarrassment attached to five elderly people tackling a complete stranger by mistake – the mistake was not theirs. She was a bit surprised, however, that Angelica, apparently, had also been misled. After dusting herself off, Gert counted heads and realized that Aletha had disappeared. Just before all the commotion, she had been sitting at a table with Eleanor Stratton.

"Ellie June, do you know where Letha is?" Gert received only a blank expression in answer. Ordinarily, she showed great patience and compassion for those she knew to be losing their cognitive ability, but she was worried about Aletha. "*Think,* Ellie June. Was she still here when you got up?"

Eleanor frowned in confusion. In the process, she dropped her eyes then suddenly smiled. "There's a dog under the table. And a lady, too!"

"*What?*" Sure enough, when Gert looked down, she saw a pair of petite size fives peeking out from under the tablecloth. "Letha, what are you doing down there?" she asked as she pulled the cloth onto the tabletop.

"I'm afraid I can't quite remember; it all happened so fast."

"Well, let's get you up." Gert said and backed away so Bobby and Isaac could get close enough to lift Aletha to her feet. But before either could take one of her arms, she tucked them close to her side.

"No!" she cried unexpectantly. "I think it would be best if I stayed here for now. Will someone please call for an ambulance?"

"An ambulance? What on earth do you need an ambulance for?" Gert demanded.

"Oh, Trudy. I feel so foolish. It's just that when whatever-it-was bumped me – that man I suppose – I fell so hard that I'm very much afraid I've broken my hip!"

Oblivious to the thrilling events exploding around him, Derek focused on his own plans. It wasn't until he emerged from the changing room that the full scope of the afternoon's activities came under consideration. While Kavya and Ani completed the transformation of bridal guests into pool-party girls, Derek walked aimlessly around the pool deck deep in thought. The process of working through every possible scenario for any given situation had never been his strong suit. His naturally positive attitude caused him to gloss over details. It was details, however, that brought him up short in his wandering. He stopped with his back to the wall of glass between the kiddie pool and the hallway just as Angelica and her oddly assorted entourage stormed past in pursuit of Christopher Gordon. A full marching band playing at maximum volume wouldn't have had any more impact on his situational awareness; he stood lost in preoccupation.

Despite his vanity over his outstanding muscular development, Derek was inherently modest about displaying those muscles – except to his coworkers, who just ignored him. On this occasion, he wore long swim trunks and a short-sleeved swim shirt. The only women he had seen in beachwear in recent years were Rose Ludlow and Amy Yousef, and they both adhered to the more is more theory – more coverage means more comfort and less self-consciousness or embarrassment. While he had wandered around the pool area, Derek couldn't help noticing the scantily clad girls who appeared to consider the notion of common decency a thing to be abhorred. He began to worry about spending several hours with Kavya in similar attire. He couldn't very well avoid looking at her all afternoon, but he would have fallen on his sword rather than let her think he viewed her as nothing more than an object of physical desire.

When he heard Ani calling to him from the door of the ladies' changing room, Derek turned toward her with something like dread. His eyes went first to Kavya. The sight of her loosely knitted white cover-up, knotted at mid-thigh, made him almost weak with relief. The outline of a high-waisted, fuchsia two-piece beneath was barely discernable, except where the top's square neckline showed above the slightly scooped cover-up. Her flawless skin glowed in the reflective glory of the vibrant color. Now more relaxed, Derek tore his eyes from Kavya to look at the little girl still demanding his attention. Ani would have looked adorable in a pull-up diaper and a burlap bag, but a ruffled swimsuit in light pink covered in black polka-dots, with a matching floppy hat, instantly declared her Princess for the Day.

Kavya, too, was pleasantly surprised. She hadn't been quite sure what to expect. But then, Derek continued to surprise her. With a degree of comfort neither had anticipated, they claimed two of the few deck chairs that had escaped appropriation for wedding décor and settled back to enjoy the afternoon. It was only then that they fully absorbed their surroundings, and they were worth taking in.

A retractable roof opened over the main pool to reveal a blazing blue sky with only random light fluffy clouds passing over from time to time. A stone wall lined the side of the pool next to the parking lot, blocking it from view entirely. Arborvitae gave life to the stone, ably assisted by a cascading waterfall midway along the wall, where water tumbled over roughly hewn boulders to disappear in the pool's depths. Though he had walked over it twice in his rambling, the narrow bridge across the face of the falls had barely registered.

The adjacent kiddie pool with its huge mushroom shower and "beach" area was under cover of the main building yet still bathed in light. Its graded surface was covered in gaily painted starfish and seashells and was sufficiently gritty enough to prevent little feet from slipping. No encouragement was needed for Anika to wade into the warm pool and run beneath the intermittent fall of water from a spreading mushroom dome. Squeals of laughter alternated with demands to marvel over her cleverness in filling and dumping buckets of water using the toys thoughtfully provided by Derek. Soon another family arrived. As young children often do, Anika and the brother and sister – only a year or two older than her – struck up a friendship without the necessity of names, backgrounds, or social standing. With her attention claimed, Derek and Kavya were granted the freedom to build on the shaky foundation of their own friendship.

It soon became apparent, however, that it was not only her swimwear Kavya sought to cover up. A veil had once again fallen over her emotions, leaving Derek to seek a means of penetrating the almost palpable divide. It was still a daunting task, but a month of effort on his part had shown him that it *could* be penetrated. He had learned to inspire laughter and expose her sharp wit, whether she was employing it to score superiority points over him or simply responding to friendly teasing. He had witnessed unconscious tenderness and kindness toward her daughter and her aunt and uncle. His friends sometimes marveled at Derek's tenacity in the face of constant rebuffs, though they gave him full points for his intuitive understanding of Kavya's nature in the way he approached her with patience and care. He recognized, as they could not, that she was akin to a wounded wild animal who trusted no one outside her fold and could only be won over by a love that would never disappoint or injure her again. He initiated a discussion of the wedding.

"I get that you don't know Miles or Marilyn, but wasn't that a great wedding? It just goes to show that even old people can find happiness if they have a little faith."

"*Old?*" She couldn't help laughing at his irrepressible grin. "They must be about the same age as your mother, and she's not old."

"I suppose you're right. I guess I'd like to see my mama marry again. She's been alone for a long time. Sometimes I think she's shut out the idea because of me, but then, I'd be hard to replace as a housemate. I mean, how many handsome, personable men is she likely to find who could compete with *moi?*"

"Not so fast, Mr. Warner. I seem to recall you telling me that your mother had moved to Kansas City and replaced you with a cat. I'd say she's managed quite well!" Having scored a point, Kavya turned her face to the sun with a triumphant smile that caused Derek's own to broaden.

"I guess I had that coming. So, moving on, what did you think of the music? I may give him a hard time, but I have to admit that Abe's guitar playing has improved, thanks to Amy. And her violin always sounds good. Their singing wasn't bad either, though I could have done better… naturally," Derek added with such smugness that Kavya was goaded into replying.

"*Seriously?*" I have never met anyone more full of himself! You obviously think you're God's gift from heaven to women, the fire department, and society as a whole." Derek wasn't a bit put out by her scathing observation. She'd had a hard time getting through it without laughing. "And don't even get me started on your... your hair!" The random addendum caught them both by surprise.

"*My hair?* What has my hair got to do with anything?"

Exposed by her own unguarded thoughts, Kavya stumbled over an explanation. "I will never understand why men... you know, men whose heads are naturally covered by *hair*... why they choose to shave it all off. I mean... you'll probably go bald soon enough. Why not let it grow... while it still can, that is. A little hair might – *might* – help you live up to the model of masculine perfection you obviously think you exemplify."

During his years in the army, a shaved head had simply provided easier management of hygiene in a field environment. It became a habit that followed him into civilian life. Derek rarely gave it a thought. But the realization that Kavya had given it a thought pleased him beyond words. His patent look of surprise was replaced by a slow grin, prompting Kavya to sit up and ask Ani if she'd like to jump into the big pool. Perfectly happy to comply with such a welcome diversion, Ani took her mother's hand but refused to walk toward the pool until Derek had taken her other hand.

The two adults stepped down into the pool after instructing the little girl to wait on the side until they were ready to catch her. They had barely made it into place before she launched herself into Derek's arms. He caught her and all three dipped under the surface. In that split second, the first blank round sounded from Inspector Dulac's gun. The three in the pool heard nothing. Kavya and Derek tossed Ani back and forth several times while she squealed with delight, then she cruised around the pool on Derek's back with her arms wrapped around his neck. When her mother decided it was time to return to the kiddie pool, Ani insisted on jumping from the deck one more time. Two more shots, fired split seconds apart, were masked again by the pool, aided by the roar of the waterfall. Their halcyon afternoon remained untouched by the drama unfolding just a few feet away.

Never had Angelica Warner known such betrayal. Without looking at anyone, she walked purposefully back into the building. If she had looked, she might have been surprised to see Mr. Dawson's usually jovial countenance overspread with guilt and anguish. He wanted desperately to follow her, to explain, but his responsibility was to oversee the recovery of the treasure and its replacement in the underground vault. Explanations would have to wait. He only hoped she would be willing to listen.

The other spectators were left with an inevitable sense of letdown; the sizzling excitement of a charged moment had dissipated quickly into the mundane. There were no sirens, no shouting, no more gunshots – as innocuous as they had been. Police routine took over, and anyone not of that fraternity was encouraged to move along.

On their way back to the wedding hall, the Aguilars stopped to peer at Kavya and Derek to see how that situation was progressing. Samuel Jamison retreated to the bar; he had put up with quite enough for one day.

Tim Ludlow and Mark Lindeman reached the *Prairie Oasis* room in tandem with two paramedics moving a rolling stretcher. It took Tim a few minutes to make heads or tails of the chaotic scene that met his startled gaze. Rose was attempting to rein in her grandmother, who had taken upon herself the role of commander-in-chief of operations, which only added to the challenge of the paramedics seeking to help their patient onto the gurney. Almost thankful for the turn of events that provided her with a distraction, Angelica hovered over Aletha like a ministering angel as several of the guests cleared a path to the door and the waiting ambulance.

"Will someone please explain what happened here?" Tim demanded. They all seemed to answer at once.

"The thief tripped over Herbie's walker – "

"But he wasn't really the thief – "

"Yes, but we didn't know that – "

" – so we tackled him, but you must know that because you helped us up."

Eleanor Stratton waved her hand and declared, "I found a dog and a lady under the table!"

Tim had just about given up any hope of getting at the truth when a piercing whistle split the roar of the verbal melee. Everyone fell silent and turned in amazement to see Carlos Aguilar with a finger on either side of his mouth. He might have been a man of few words, but he could get his wife's attention from five fields away on a foggy morning when the corn was taller than he was. Dropping his hand, he nodded politely at Tim who acknowledged the welcome intervention with an appreciative grin. Bobby Taylor quickly supplied the essential details. By then Aletha was secured to the gurney and headed to the door with Angelica on one side and Granny Gert on the other.

"Just a minute, please," Tim said to the paramedics. "This is my grandmother. I'd like to speak with her before you go." Taking her fragile hand in his, he said, "Aletha, I am so sorry this had to happen, today of all days! I'll call Miles and Mom. They probably haven't boarded their plane yet."

"You will do no such thing! Timothy James Ludlow, I want you to promise me right now – and any others of you who might have such a foolish notion – that you will on no account call your parents."

"But Aletha, he'll want to know! Besides, he'll have my head if I keep this from him. Surely, you must see that – well, you know what I mean."

"I do know what you mean, dear boy, but you are entirely mistaken. Would you have appreciated putting your honeymoon on hold for no good reason? Now, be honest."

"I'd hardly call this 'no good reason.' But that's not the point. He's your son."

Aletha placed her other hand over his and replied gently, "Yes, he's my son. Please, let me give him the gift of this time away with Marilyn. There is so little I *can* do for him anymore." Her eyes began to twinkle. "And unless he has somehow managed to complete a medical degree in the past few days, he won't be of much use to me in the hospital."

"Aletha is right, you know." Rose had moved to stand beside her husband. "She'll be well cared for, and I promise to take Granny Gert to see her every day," she said.

"You listen to your wife, sonny!" Gert said with spirit then turned to her friend and painted a somewhat daunting picture. "Why, I can read to you, Letha, and help you with your food, and tell those nurses just how you like things, and…"

"Now there's no need for you to be makin' that trip every day, Rose." Angelica thought it time to offer her services before Gertie Gunn threatened to "help" her way into alienating the entire hospital staff. "I won't be workin' here anymore, so I'll have plenty o' time." She reached out to gently rub the old woman's cheek. "Would that be alright, my friend?"

With the ghost of a smile, Aletha replied, "Well, at the risk of boring everyone to death, that would be lovely." A twinge of pain crossed her face. "I think perhaps I should be going now. Tim, will you make sure everyone finds a way home? And don't forget Scout. I think it would be best if only Angelica came with me now. Perhaps you can look in on me tomorrow," she added with a wan smile.

A chorus of objections broke out, but Tim took command of the situation, having finally accepted the wisdom of his grandmother's words – though he had no intention of letting her go to the hospital without discovering every treatment option and seeing her settled in himself. He kissed her forehead tenderly and stepped back to allow the paramedics to do their job. The crowd dissipated in relative silence.

Oblivious to the progress of her son's courting scheme, Angelica hurried to the parking garage elevator thinking only of her need to reach the hospital as soon as possible. Fortunately, she had remembered to grab Aletha's purse, containing all the pertinent information needed for admission. Her thoughts were all for her friend, so she was totally unprepared when the elevator door opened to reveal Mr. Dawson.

"Mrs. Warner! Angelica…," he began awkwardly as he stepped into the hall. From the beginning, there had been no uneasiness between them. Now he felt like a clumsy youth, unable to express himself with dignity or self-assurance. "I hoped to catch you before you left for the day…to explain…"

She could not – she *would* not – look at him. "Not for the day – for good. I quite see that my employment here was more of a charade than I imagined. I will be in tomorrow to collect any personal items I may have left here." She edged her way past him into the empty elevator. "I hope you and Mr. Gordon enjoyed watchin' me make a fool o' myself while I was watchin' Samuel Jamison and makin' all those silly, and apparently useless, reports on his activities." She sought to gain control of her voice. "And when I think of our dinners and walks in the park… I thought we were friends! How *could* you…?" She finally looked up with tears in her eyes.

But the elevator door had closed.

In the general course of events, Derek Warner would have insisted on being in the middle of all the excitement. On that day, however, blocking a grand larceny scheme, witnessing a pseudo shoot-out with police, unraveling the inadvertent capture of a not-so-criminal criminal by well-meaning but misguided senior citizens, and welcoming the arrival of an emergency medical team with fire truck backup were as nothing. Such singular occurrences paled in comparison with the precious hours he shared with Kavya Jackson.

It didn't take Derek long to learn that the surest way to draw her out was to set himself up as the butt of her stinging observations. Most men would have shied away from what some might equate to verbal abuse. He was shrewd enough to recognize it for what it truly was – a willingness to communicate in a way that allowed Kavya to protect her emotions and keep the world at arm's length. But with each of Derek's judicious comments, Kavya's responses began to reveal more of herself than she realized. After a while, her tone changed. Whether she finally regretted the severity of her words or simply grew more comfortable and secure in the face of Derek's non-threatening friendliness, Kavya began to open up.

While she watched Derek help Ani fill endless buckets of water, Kavya told him a little about her early life in India and its attendant wonders and uniqueness. When they each clasped one of Ani's insistent hands and walked with her countless times over the waterfall bridge and around the pool deck, Kavya shared the story of how Isabella came to join the Jackson family in Washington D.C. While they packed their things in preparation to go in search of her aunt and uncle, Kavya spoke of the years her mother lived in India while the rest of the family made a home in California, and of the stability Isabella had brought to their lives. And the more Derek listened, the more Kavya talked until she awoke to the novel awareness that he knew more about her than she knew about him!

Before Kavya could decide whether she was relieved or resentful, Ani demanded food – immediately. Her demands coincided with the appearance of Carlos Aguilar, who was assisting a hotel staff member to return the rattan furniture to its permanent home around the pool deck. He and his wife had kept their distance in the *Prairie Oasis* room until it was empty of people and party decorations. All the leftover *hors d 'oeuvres,* packed neatly in a box, had been presented to Lupe by a member of the kitchen staff with the chef's compliments. The movement of pool trappings was the excuse they needed to see if Kavya and Derek were still on speaking terms. The sight of them on evidently excellent terms, coupled with Ani's growing insistence on wanting something to eat, inspired Lupe to suggest they have dinner at the poolside grill. Derek seconded the suggestion with the caveat that he be allowed to pick up the check.

"I'll just go find my mama so she can join us."

Anticipating a lengthy explanation, Lupe simply told him that Angelica had already departed and that the Aguilars had promised to give Derek a ride home. She then shooed him and Kavya away to change out of their wet things before dinner. After digging out a banana for Ani from a large handbag, Lupe settled the little girl into a booster seat and awaited events in casual luxury.

Their table, located on the east side of the grill and covered by a striped awning, welcomed the warmth of early evening without the intensity of the sun glowing in the western sky. The seats were deeply cushioned, the service was fast and friendly, and the food was excellent. To say that the dinner was a success was an understatement. Carlos even went so far as to add his commentary to Lupe's colorful yet succinct account of the afternoon as experienced by seemingly everyone but Derek and Kavya. They asked so many questions, they had to be reminded to eat.

With a suspicious, teasing smile, Derek asked Lupe, "Are you *sure* you're not making this up?"

Lupe's responsive laughter set off a string of spurious observations by Derek, which grew more absurd with each rebuttal.

"There must have been at *least* three armored cars… What? *None?*… It sounds like the entire Kansas City police department showed up… Don't you mess with me, Lupe Aguilar. You left out the four international spies, right…? Now, if you'd told me a gang of jewel thieves were held at gunpoint by Granny Gert, who threatened to blow off their kneecaps if any of them moved… *that* I could believe!"

Listening to Derek's ridiculous comments, watching people she loved laughing and enjoying themselves, Kavya experienced a sense of contentment and well-being almost foreign to her. For that shining moment, she was at peace. It was to be short-lived. Derek had moved on to speculation about the details surrounding the emergency vehicles.

"I suppose there was a ladder truck to get a cat down from one of those five-foot palm trees?" His grin faded when Lupe frowned and reached out to pat his hand.

"That is the real reason your mama is not here. She went with Mrs. Mason to the hospital. It looks like that kind lady may have broken her hip."

"*Aletha?* Oh, no!" He looked from Lupe to Carlos. "Has anyone called Miles? I'll bet Tim –"

"No, Mrs. Mason would not allow it. She made everyone promise to leave the Hawthornes to their honeymoon. That means you, too, Derek," she added and patted his hand again. "Your friends Tim and Rose also went to the hospital to make sure she is settled comfortably for the night. She will be fine. Now finish your steak. I think it's time to get this little one home."

Ani had grown very quiet, and her eyes were glazed over, making Kavya thankful she had thought to pack the little girl's pajamas amongst the swim gear. Lupe took Ani off to prepare her for the night, knowing she would fall asleep in the van on the drive home, while Carlos headed for the parking garage. Derek and Kavya were left alone to gather their things. They might as well have been standing in the middle of Times Square on New Year's Eve a minute before the ball drop; Derek was again oblivious to his surroundings. Kavya had to remind him twice that it was time to leave.

"What?" he said absentmindedly, then picked up their totes without waiting for an answer and started walking toward the entrance with an uncharacteristic, preoccupied frown. It was a side of Derek she had not seen before.

As maddening as she found his ridiculously arrogant attitude, Kavya discovered that she actually missed the "Derek Norm." She was moved to ask in genuine concern, "Are you okay?"

He shook his head and smiled ruefully. "I'm sorry. I guess I'm still thinking about Aletha and my mom and the whole hospital thing. But," he added on a suddenly lighter note, "it sounds like they got it all sorted out despite being deprived of my superior input."

Kavya gave an involuntary snort of laughter and rolled her eyes. The "old" Derek was back.

"Hey, I'm really glad you and Ani came today. It was nice," he said and nudged her shoulder in a friendly way. Before any embarrassment could set in, Derek added, "Even if we *did* miss all the excitement…"

"… though you really don't believe it actually happened."

"Exactly!"

Kavya laughed in spite of herself and said with a hint of Derek's playful arrogance, "And you thought I was just another pretty face."

The laughter in his eyes deepened into warmth and – Kavya could have sworn – tenderness. She looked away with an effort, not entirely sure she was glad they had reached the van parked under the porte-cochère at the hotel's entrance. Derek climbed into the back row of seats and turned to watch Kavya settle Ani for the trip home, not realizing she was also trying to settle her own chaotic thoughts. Taking her daughter's hand, Kavya began to sing softly while she stroked the little girl's riotous curls until Ani's sleepy eyes closed and her head lolled against the cushioned car seat. Derek felt something stir and twist in his gut. Under his breath, he murmured, "No, definitely not just another pretty face."

CHAPTER 13

*But as for me, this secret has not been revealed to me because I have
more wisdom than anyone living, but for our sakes…and that you may
know the thoughts of your heart.*

Daniel 2:30 (NKJV)

The ursine qualities usually associated with Mr. Dawson had
devolved overnight from jolly teddy bear to disgruntled predator
awakened prematurely from hibernation. After leaving messages at
every conceivable place within the hotel that Angelica Warner might have
touched in her undercover roles, Dawson retreated to his comfortable, well-
appointed office and began pacing. The room soon became a claustrophobic
cave. The fact that he had arrived at the hotel two hours earlier than usual
that morning did nothing to soften his mood. By the time word reached
him at 8:15 that she was spotted in the housekeeping staff room cleaning
out her locker, he had nearly worn a hole in the plush carpet.

Fifteen minutes later, he opened the door to a hesitant Angelica, and his
face immediately softened into humble contrition. Any strain between them
was temporarily forgotten, however, when her attention was caught by the
sound of a deep-throated cough. She glanced behind Dawson, and her
expression of anxiety gave way to patent disbelief. An unlikely group of men
rose at her entrance. Angelica allowed herself to be led to a chair where she
awaited an explanation in something of a daze.

Christopher Gordon and Chief Inspector Ferguson, who managed to
sound blustery without saying a word simply by blowing out his cheeks and

clearing his throat several times, remained standing after she was seated. The fact that Gordon was dressed in all black, as he had been the day before, registered only as an afterthought. A third man provided a portrait of elegant negligence – a reprobate with a sense of style. Samuel Jamison chose to lounge on the couch, seemingly without a care in the world. The odd trio provided a sufficient enough diversion to block any thoughts of resentment or hurt toward Dawson. In fact, they blocked any rational thought at all!

As if by unspoken agreement, Gordon took charge of the proceedings. He began by handing Angelica a small leather case, much like a wallet. She opened it to find a shield displaying two mythical looking creatures on either side of a gate topped by a crown. She had never seen the image before and handed it back, not knowing quite what to say.

"Mrs. Warner, you mustn't blame Mr. Dawson for his silence regarding the full scope of our joint venture. Indeed, it took a lot of convincing before he would promise to keep certain… details from you. The first is that I am *not* the head of security for this property. I am, in fact," he said, and waved the leather case before returning it to his pocket, "an agent with the NCA. You've probably never heard of it. Most people think Scotland Yard is the last word in policing in England, but they are now the metropolitan police force for London. Crime on a national level is investigated by the National Crime Agency, with whom I am employed."

Angelica's confusion settled in like a thick fog bank, growing more impenetrable by the moment, while Gordon, perched on the edge of Dawson's desk with his arms folded, frowned into the past.

"For several years now, I have investigated certain crimes related to art theft, jewel heists, and the robbery of large quantities of currency from private individuals. While I was wrestling with larceny in England, a close friend of mine was making a name for himself in other circles. He and I first became friends when we were trainee constables at the National Police Academy of Jamaica." Gordon grinned when a soft gasp escaped Angelica's lips. "Oh, yes. I am a native son of Jamaica," he said, slipping into a naturally warm, lilting accent. "I cultivated a formal British accent because it suited my work."

She smiled at the welcome sound, but Gordon quickly reverted to his more familiar form of speech.

"My friend was from a small island once part of the French Antilles. We both had delusions of grandeur and a desire to prove to the world that top-notch police officers could just as easily come from the Caribbean as from Europe or America. In his case, he seemed born to it. We both completed our courses with honors. It was his exceptional ability to solve complex situational problems, however, that showed real brilliance. After only a few years as a constable in the islands, he transferred to the *Sûreté* in Paris. There he made miraculous promotions through the ranks because of his ability to break cases wide open when more senior detectives were stumped – sort of a latter-day *Hercules Poirot*[15]. He was assigned to homicide as a junior officer – quite an accomplishment. But he was still sought out as a special advisor by other divisions. When not grappling with murder, he assisted in exposing graft, money laundering, drug trafficking – you name it." Gordon spread his hands and shook them as if he couldn't believe his own story. "I tell you; the man had a *genius* for crime. I admired him more than anyone because we shared a similar background. I wanted to be like him, to follow him right to the top." He smiled ruefully at Angelica who sat mesmerized.

"Alas, I was not so talented. It took many years of sweat and determination before I could make the move to England and the NCA. I dragged my sainted wife and our, then, two children – we now have four – from her sunny Jamaican homeland to the fog and the rain and the cold. An assignment to white-collar crime might have appeared a tame substitute for the world of high-profile cases, but I dug in all the same. I wanted to excel just as my friend had. Besides, it suited a secondary, long-term goal.

---

[15] Hercules Poirot, Belgian detective created by author Agatha Christie.

"Thanks to a very patient, supportive supervisor, I too experienced professional success. And the more adept I became in my allotted field of expertise, the more I wanted to know. I read every page of every file the agency had, going back decades, and became an encyclopedia of the white-collar crime world. The further back I went, the more one name surfaced – that of Samuel Jamison, particularly in files from 15 years ago and before. As far as the British Commonwealth was concerned, he was untouchable, and because word of any exploits in England grew more sporadic after that 15-year mark, the powers that be didn't much care. I, however, wasn't about to admit that *any* thief was untouchable. That's when I turned to Interpol."

Gordon suddenly rose and, with his hands thrust in his pockets, began to cover the same stretch of worn carpet Dawson had flattened earlier that morning. His pleasant features clouded over, and he shook his head slightly as if to rid himself of a distasteful thought.

"Sometimes, when we look too deeply into a subject, we unearth things we wished we had never found out. All that I had learned of Jamison's personal history was that he had family ties to France, so I started there. I felt like a bloodhound that had suddenly picked up a hidden scent. Jamison's name was connected to a string of thefts over the intervening period, but none of the cases had been solved, and the valuables remained missing. To anyone acquainted with his legendary career, such a record of success was hardly surprising – anyone except me. You see, the truly amazing fact I uncovered in my studies was that at least three robberies a year, during the last 12 years or so, were investigated by a special team augmented by the darling of the *Sûreté*. Can you guess his name?"

So bewildered was Angelica, she would have been hard pressed to guess her *own* name! Once again, she had been drawn into a fantastic tale and had gotten lost in the storyline. Gordon proved to be almost as riveting a storyteller as Inspector Dulac. On that thought, she suddenly remembered the incredible events of the previous day and gasped. The pieces were falling into place. She stared at Gordon and whispered, "You can't mean… *Inspector Dulac?*"

Gordon merely raised his eyebrows as if expecting more, his fixed gaze never wavering.

"But *he* can't be… *your friend?*"

"I'm afraid so," Gordon replied on a grim note. "As I mentioned earlier, he was a master at solving crimes, and apparently, he *continued* to be successful in his work. And because he was so successful – bringing high-profile murderers to account, breaking up counterfeit rings, exposing corruption – these anomalies of unsolved thefts went unnoticed. After all, no one is perfect. The other, more egregious cases – from a societal standpoint – held more weight in the blind eyes of justice. But I considered each robbery on its own merit and couldn't help thinking that the culprits *should* have been apprehended. An errant lead, a misunderstood address, arrival on the scene an hour after the loot and the thieves were gone – the pattern didn't make sense if Dulac was in any way involved. While it is true that no one is perfect, neither is anyone so *consistently wrong,* especially someone with such intelligence. Nevertheless, I could not get any of my superiors to give credence to the results of my research. So, I set out on a personal quest to destroy the credibility and honor… of a friend. It became almost an obsession for me. I believed a fellow officer of the law to have gone bad, and I could not let him get away with it. The reputation of our agencies and the honor of policemen everywhere were at stake.

"It was a terrible calling; each revelation caused me exponentially more guilt and pain. It took me five years, but I finally gathered the evidence I needed, though I couldn't have done it without help from an unexpected quarter."

Samuel Jamison took his queue. With a grace uncommon in such a large man, he rose to his feet. So commanding was his presence that each piece of artwork and grouping of books on the shelves behind him seemed to perform a dress-right-dress maneuver as if awaiting inspection. All eyes turned toward him, and Chief Inspector Ferguson took a step back, yielding Jamison the floor. The deep, vibrant voice gave the narrative a musical quality like that of an operatic recitative, holding all listeners spellbound.

"Young Gordon and I were working toward the same end, yet with very different goals. But one must be prepared to adjust to life's changes," Jamison said, with a slight shrug. "As Gordon surmised, correctly, Dulac was something of a genius. I managed to illude capture twice through my brother's intervention, but Dulac found me and the jewels I had so carefully… gathered, shall we say. He was in a position to arrest me legitimately *and* claim the jewels. But he chose not to. Instead, he suggested an… arrangement. In exchange for allowing me to carry on my professional practices, I would pay him a percentage of whatever I… acquired.

"Initially, I looked at the proposition as an insurance policy. And it turned out to be an effective one. I also found that we – Dulac and I – were kindred spirits, in a way. I admired his drive and intelligence, and he respected my previous success. In some ways, he reminded me of myself as a young man. He was also from my homeland – a sentimental vulnerability I developed late in life. As someone who has essentially always worked alone, other than any assistance I received from my brothers, I rather enjoyed the relationship, a relationship that may well have been rooted in some familial tie, with both of us claiming the same small island as home. The only people I had ever trusted were the members of my family. I looked on Dulac as a member of my family. Against my better judgment, I carelessly revealed my full personal history to him."

"Then *that's* how …" Angelica spoke under her breath. It had never occurred to her to question how the police came to know so much about a man who had never been apprehended.

"Guid leddy, di' ye no' wonder-r how we nyoo so much aboot his er-r-rly life?" Angelica jumped in her chair when Chief Inspector Ferguson thrust himself without warning into the conversation.

"Well… I…"

"For the first time since I'd known him, Dulac took a misstep and gave himself away," said Gordon. "His ego turned out to be his Achilles heel."

"Och, the ar-r-rogance o' the man!"

"That information gave him the leverage he needed." Jamison had once more claimed center stage. "Without batting an eye, Dulac began to demand more and more, holding over me the threat that not only I, but my brothers – particularly my brother, Judge Max Dugal – could be brought down with me. With his brilliant professional record, Dulac was above reproach. If it came to a case of his word against mine, I had no hope of winning, so I went along. First it was 10 percent, then 15, then 25. And in addition to a percentage of my profits, he began to demand that I share any select information I might pick up about prominent members of the criminal classes. I wasn't sure if he wanted the information merely to add a feather to his cap in the arena of successful criminal apprehension, or if he planned to try the extortion game with a rougher crowd. It mattered little to me. I only knew he had to be stopped."

"That's where I came in." Gordon said, picking up the threads of the story. "Though I had never arrested Jamison, he knew of my record. He 'arranged' a heist where only I would be present so that he could be apprehended. I'll spare you the details. Suffice it to say, we set up a sting operation involving Jamison and Richter, believing Dulac to be in league with the other gentleman already. You see, Interpol was most helpful with information about larceny in Germany as well. Besides, Richter knew Jamison, at least by reputation, and the prize was big enough to tempt all the players. By that time, I had convinced the powers-that-be to listen to me. They aided me with the necessary contacts in order to cook up this security conference.

"The marketing campaign for the conference was quite genuine. Those registered to attend were all legitimate names in the security industry. This hotel was chosen for its relative anonymity and lack of any history or employees of longstanding. Every facet of this operation had to be authentic.

Dulac would have smelled a sham from 5,000 miles away. But, as I have said, he is a very clever man. Could we catch him? Would all the smoke and mirrors truly convince him? Then a miracle happened. And that miracle, Mrs. Warner, was you."

"*Me?!?*" Angelica stared, unbelieving, at Christopher Gordon. "But I was the biggest sham o' them all! Just a foolish woman chasin' shadows."

"*But François Dulac did not know that!*" Gordon moved to take her hands in a reassuring clasp. "Your perfectly timed arrival on the scene was positively providential!" Angelica was no nearer to understanding any part of the past few weeks than she had been when she entered the room. If anything, her mental fog began to take on the qualities of a fortified structure. Her agitation finally seemed to break through the young man's enthusiasm.

"I do apologize, Mrs. Warner. I seem to have gotten ahead of myself. It's just that everything went exactly to plan, thanks largely to you. But let me back up." He moved to sit on the desktop again, where he surveyed the room, and nodded toward Samuel Jamison.

"The success of the mission hinged on Dulac believing that *Jamison* was the target – that and not suspecting that I was at all involved. *That* is the reason your silence about me, where Dulac was concerned, was so crucial. The security staff here at the hotel had all been thoroughly vetted by Mr. Dawson. Those he had known for less than ten years were either given the weekend off or tasked with projects that would keep them clear of our operating base."

"Operatin' base? And who *is* the Director of Security? Does he even exist?"

"Fair questions. We have been working together closely for months. I'll let Mr. Dawson answer any questions you might have about his credentials later, but for now, let me provide a bit more background about this particular mission.

"Almost a year ago we had two agents following Jamison round the clock. Every meeting between him and his known associates was recorded. It was by sheer luck that I had taken my family to Germany on holiday, and we were staying in Heidelberg when Richter was spotted with Jamison. The assigned agent followed him and captured their conversation. I was waiting outside the pub when Jamison emerged. From that moment we began to plan in earnest."

Stealing a glance at Mr. Dawson, whose eyes had never left Angelica's face, she caught the glimmer of a smile. Without thinking, she smiled back, and he knew himself to be forgiven. But she was not yet ready to leave the story of the other men behind. Frowning a little, she asked, "I quite see that you had your reasons for keeping this to yourselves. What I *don't* really see is why… why Samuel Jamison agreed to help you. Surely, by allowin' himself to be captured by you, Mr. Gordon, he will be imprisoned." Angelica's frown deepened as she looked between the two men.

As was the case every time Chief Inspector Ferguson opened his mouth unexpectedly, he startled Angelica, who, again, jumped in her chair. "Stachoot 'o Limitetions, 'o cour-r-rse!"

A broad grin broke out on Christopher Gordon's face. "What the chief inspector means is that Jamison's crimes, seven years before he contacted me, are exempt from prosecution under the Statute of Limitations."

"Oh, aye," Ferguson confirmed with a grunt.

"As to anything stolen after that, Jamison agreed to provide information about the goods in exchange for leniency. His cooperation in apprehending Dulac will go a long way toward avoiding prison time. And as you can see," Gordon said, as he hopped off the desk and walked over to Jamison, again seated leisurely on the couch, "he has been fitted with an electronic ankle bracelet." Jamison rolled his eyes and lifted his right pant leg a fraction to expose a wide band encircling his ankle. A blinking light declared the device's effectiveness. "He will be released at a destination of his choosing when we leave here. He knows to choose wisely. If he moves beyond a radius of 50 miles from that spot… well, let's just say… unpleasant events will ensue."

Turning his attention to Chief Inspector Ferguson, Gordon said, "Sir, will you escort this gentleman to the van waiting to take us all to the airport. I have a few more things I wish to share with Mrs. Warner."

With rare and unexpected gallantry, the Scotsman took Angelica's hand and kissed it in farewell. A soft giggle escaped her at the touch of his bushy moustache. He closed the door after marching Jamison through the portal.

"I'm surprised you have not commented on my unusual attire – the same costume I wore yesterday." Angelica looked at Gordon, as if seeing him for the first time.

"I was to play the role of silent accomplice. Richter had never met me, and when he did – "

" – that day in the park!" For no good reason, Mr. Dawson smiled, pleased at Angelica's perceptive guess.

"Why yes, but how did you…"

"Never you mind. Just go on with your story." Gordon smiled and obeyed.

"When we met in the park, and I gave him that ration of nonsense about my professional experience, he swallowed it without blinking – the greedy sod. The business cards were real enough, and the detailed background history well-established by NCA, if he had bothered to check. He didn't.

"Now, back to my clothing, stocking cap included. It served two purposes: one, to present me as a seasoned thief, and two, to hide the earpiece that kept me connected to the actual hotel security office – their role was crucial in pulling off a convincing heist. Jamison was *not* provided with any details on how to access the vaults – I wanted his surprise to be as genuine as possible. That, and because I didn't fully trust him.

"When we stepped off the elevator, I quickly painted over the 'security' cameras in the hallway. They were fakes that had been installed a few days earlier. And because there were no more cameras in the vault rooms, Richter, and possibly Jamison (though I'm inclined to think he's more intelligent than that) made the leap of thinking we were then working completely unobserved. I won't tell you where the real cameras are concealed – it's a burden you don't need to carry. Just know that we were followed throughout the process. The video footage was so damning, Richter was inspired to sing like a canary when we got him to the police station." Gordon smiled and surprised Angelica when he extended his arm to Mr. Dawson, who moved around the desk to sit in the chair on her right.

"Mrs. Warner… Angelica… did I ever tell you about my childhood desire to be a magician?" She couldn't help laughing at such a ridiculous question in the middle of a discussion about international intrigue.

"A *magician*? What in heaven's name are you talkin' about?"

With a heavy sigh, belied by the twinkle in his eye, Dawson said, "I probably never mentioned it because I was so bad at it." Angelica crossed her arms and tilted her head to one side, giving him such a pointed look, he felt compelled to go on. "Yes, I gave up on the idea by the time I was ten and had quite forgotten it until I met a fellow at church a few years ago who owned an electronics shop." Between Dawson's nonsensical reflections and Gordon's grinning acceptance of such ridiculous commentary, Angelica wondered if they had all fallen down a rabbit hole like the characters in *Alice in Wonderland*!

Taking her hand and patting it comfortingly, the "teddy bear" said, "We're all quite sane, I assure you."

Eyeing both men suspiciously, Angelica said, "The both o' you best be tellin' me somethin' sensible."

With a carefree laugh, Dawson complied. "When young Christopher here contacted me last summer and proposed this perilous venture, I couldn't help adding a few of my own suggestions to the plan. I really do have a friend – Henry – who owns an electronics shop. I think you may have met him when you came to church that Sunday. No matter. While there is a very effective security system in place at the *Prairie Gateway*, I thought a little 'sleight of hand' might add some color and impress Richter, at least. I think Henry had as much fun creating these smokescreen devices as Gordon had in manipulating them. I'm certain he got many of his ideas from video games and spy thrillers – they were quite ingenious. When Gordon approached each electronic panel, the security office – watching on camera and listening through his earpiece – unlocked each door. After going through the motions of overriding whatever electronic security measure was in place, he simply opened the door!"

"Smoke and mirrors…" Angelica breathed softly.

"My personal favorite," Gordon explained, "was the laser grid I 'disabled.' After fiddling with a portable keyboard, I punched a button and said 'There!' While Jamison and Richter were focused on the grid, I simply flipped a wall switch, and the laser beams were gone. If Richter had only known how hopeless I am with anything 'techy'; I have to ask my nine-year-old son how to adjust the ring tone on my cell phone!"

"Well, I'm not sure I fully understand the whole thing, but I am *very* impressed by your cleverness," Angelica said. She frowned for a few minutes, as if working something out in her mind. "But why were you not in the elevator with the other men when it opened on the main level?"

"Because Richter had locked me in one of the rooms. It was his way of eliminating members of the 'team.' He got rid of Jamison by having him create a diversion, thinking he and Dulac would get away with the entire haul." His voice grew momentarily serious. "I'm fully convinced that Dulac would have rid himself of Richter – permanently – had the two gotten away with everything." He shook himself and was once again a storyteller immersed in his tale. "As soon as Richter and Jamison went up in the elevator, security released me from the vault room, and I followed the other two by using the emergency stairs. I had told them earlier that the door accessing the stairs only led to a restroom. I suppose the sign on the door to that effect was enough evidence for Richter. He never checked.

"That about ties it all up in a neat ribbon. You saw everything that happened outside. It couldn't have worked out better. No one was hurt, the goods were recovered, and I discovered a new recruiting source for the police forces of the world." When Angelica looked a question at him, Gordon grinned. "Though I only caught a glimpse of some of your stalwart senior citizens pinning down Samuel Jamison after they brilliantly tackled him, I may suggest to my professional colleagues that they consider adding an undercover unit of elderly crime stoppers to their respective forces."

"Don't you dare! That group, invariably led by someone like Gertie Gunn, would drive the local police crazy!"

Angelica assumed everything had been explained. She was wrong. Gordon abruptly switched his attention to a framed photo of the Dawson family displayed on a shelf adjacent to Mr. Dawson's desk. He began speaking again, while still studying the photo.

"I know there are times when you have been puzzled by a phrase, a gesture, a vocal inflection… the feeling that we had met before." He replaced the picture frame on the shelf and looked at Angelica. "I believe you first attributed it to the fact that you had seen me around the hotel, which would have been before we met formally at church that Sunday." Angelica could only nod in agreement. "Then you heard me speak o' bein' from Jamaica." The brief return of his native accent inspired a smile. "I'm told that I favor my mother a good deal, though I know it's more difficult to see those similarities between a mother and son. I think Sabryna would be pleased that you remember her so well." He waited for the words to sink in.

"*Sabryna?*" The single word was barely audible. Angelica's facial features, her hands, her very posture worked in tandem to put together the answer hinted at by the young man's words. With a quick intake of breath, she asked, "Are you tellin' me… is it possible… you are *Sabryna's boy?*"

Gordon pulled up a chair to sit on Angelica's left and took her agitated hands in his. "I am her *eldest* son, and you alone – other than my father, Joseph – know what that means." Another soft gasp.

"You are *Samuel Jamison's* son?" She looked into a past that had suddenly become very present. "Does he *know*?"

"No," Gordon replied softly. "Nor will he ever know. My true father is Joseph Clarke. It was Joseph who taught me to be an honorable man. It was Joseph who gave me his faith, and Joseph who believed in me when I decided to move my family to England to follow my dreams."

Finally, reality broke through the miraculous travel through time. "But you call yourself 'Gordon.'"

A rakish grin flashed across the young man's face. "Only on this job. I was christened 'Joseph Christopher Clarke.' And to Chris Clarke I will now return." The grin faded to be replaced by a pensive look. "You see, I've been on a quest to find my biological father and bring him to justice. Not just for what he did to my mother, but for all the people whose lives he toyed with for his own amusement and gain. I think you'll agree it's ironic that his downfall began at the hands of François Dulac. The relationship they shared was closer than either imagined. They, too… are father and son."

"Ya must be *jokin*!"

"Interpol made the connection through DNA samples."

"But that means that you and Inspector Dulac are…"

"Half-brothers, yes. When I told you earlier that sometimes, if we look too deeply into a subject, we unearth things we wished we had never found out, I meant it. I believe François inherited not only Jamison's genius, but also his weak character and code of ethics. He was easily swayed to exchange his great success as a policeman for the promise of riches and power. Sadly, he was not blessed with a Joseph Clarke in his life."

"What an extraordinary story!" Angelica and young Clarke had forgotten Mr. Dawson's presence.

Chris stood to take his leave. "I don't think I need to tell either of you not to breathe a word of what I've just told you." He looked pointedly at Angelica. "Not even to my mother. Please, Angelica." She stood to hug him in farewell.

"I don't imagine I'll see your mother soon, but I promise. 'Tis a blessing to have met you, Chris."

"And I you. Now," he said, shaking Dawson's hand, "I leave you to get back to England and help my wife with the packing." In answer to Angelica's raised eyebrows, he said, "I've had enough adventure on the big stage. It's time I took my family back to Jamaica so my children can know their grandparents, their cousins, and their homeland. I submitted my resignation to the NCA this morning. I don't know what comes next, but I know God has a plan. Thanks to both of you for your help. We couldn't have pulled this off without you."

Though nearly everything had been cleared up and brought out into the open, the conversation Dawson and Angelica had avoided for an hour was now inescapable. He chose to skip it altogether.

"Angelica, what do you say to a stroll through the park, before it gets any hotter, followed by a leisurely breakfast. I wasn't in a mood to eat this morning, but now, I could eat a… a house!" His teddy bear smile beamed without reservation.

"As far as I can remember, I've never eaten a house before, but I'm willin' to try anythin' once, provided you answer one more question." He knew as much as she did about the intrigue of the past six weeks. He couldn't imagine what more he could tell her. "Since we seem to be on a first-name basis now, which makes perfect sense, you still have the advantage o' me. The hotel website, your signature, and the sign on your office door all say A.B.C. Dawson. What is the big mystery behind *your* name?"

Dawson threw his head back and laughed. Then he bowed suddenly and said with a flourish, "Aloysius Baptiste Chevalier Dawson, at your service, madam." Angelica couldn't help laughing.

"Oh, my! Tha 'tis quite a name." He had taken her hand and tucked it in his arm.

"My maternal grandmother was a Cajun Frenchwoman who insisted on saddling me with that ridiculous mouthful. As a kid, my friends called me Albie, but that never sounded dignified enough when I began working in management positions," he explained, "so I just stuck with Dawson. I hope you will now consider the alternative."

"Let's be goin', then, Albie," said Angelica, walking with him to the door. "Though I think it might be best if we just shared a stack o' pancakes…"

CHAPTER 14

Therefore, dear friends, as you look forward to these things, make every effort to be found in peace, spotless and blameless in his sight.
2 Peter 3:14 (EHV)

The epicenter of life-changing events that had brought so many together, pulling them into a veritable maelstrom and spinning them around before sending them soaring in myriad directions, showed no evidence of impact on the catalyst itself. The *Prairie Gateway* stood as welcoming and unruffled on Monday as it had on Sunday after all the excitement had died down. For those who had entered its portals, however, any number of words might describe their altered physical and emotional states – shaken, surprised, hopeful, or content.

Following the thorough explanation provided by Christopher "Gordon" Clarke, Angelica Warner resumed her duties at the hotel on the following day, though limiting her role to working part-time at the front desk for the time being. She wanted the freedom to minister to Aletha, to help her friend where she could. Convincing Gertie Gunn to allow anyone but herself the privilege of helping Aletha was the real challenge.

Emergency evaluation of Aletha Mason's injuries revealed the need for a full hip replacement to remedy the damage done by her unfortunate collision with Samuel Jamison at her son's wedding. Only hours after she had waved goodbye to Miles and Marilyn upon their departure for their honeymoon, a new hip joint replaced the broken one, thanks to the expert efforts of the on-call orthopedic surgeon and OR associates at UMKC. That was perhaps the easiest step on the journey which now confronted her. Already blind, aged, and frail, Aletha faced the daunting task of learning to walk confidently with a new titanium hip joint. These factors led to the decision to transfer her to the Overland Prairie Rehabilitation Center, a modest inpatient hospital in Kansas City where her safety and medical progress could be best assured.

With the help of her granddaughter's daily "Lift" service, Gertie Gunn, with Scout at her heels, attempted to see to her friend's every need – whether she wanted that assistance or not. Gert insisted on reading from Aletha's favorite murder mystery just as that gentle soul was feeling inclined to sleep and tagged along, uninvited, to every occupational and physical therapy session. Scout was a welcome participant in these activities. Gert was not. So, she focused instead on supervising the change of bed linens with such demanding precision that a student nurse once left the room in tears.

"Granny Gert, she was just trying to learn how to do her job," Rose said, hoping her grandmother would take the hint. She didn't.

"Rosie, you can't have proper hospital corners with the sheet and blanket stuffed under the bed all willy-nilly. Why, I could have done it better myself in half the time! Hmm… maybe I should suggest that to the charge nurse. She seems a sensible enough person, though we didn't quite see eye to eye over that business about how to properly place Letha's pillows…"

Panic gripped Rose's heart. She had no trouble in believing that Nurse Kowalski would show them both the door if her grandmother continued to boss everyone from food service personnel to the janitorial staff. Their expulsion from the hospital must certainly include Scout, needlessly causing Aletha as much pain as it would her grandmother, so Rose continued to run interference until she hit on an inspired idea. On the drive home Wednesday afternoon, she said with a sigh, "I'm so glad we're able to spend time with Aletha every day, especially since you'll be leaving in less than two weeks." She sighed again.

Gert looked a little surprised as if the established fact was a novel revelation. "I guess I will at that. It's been such a busy summer, I plum forgot I'll be going back to Kentucky soon." Rose glanced at her grandmother to see a promising frown forming before artlessly continuing with her theme.

"You know I wouldn't take one minute away from your time with Aletha, but I can't help wishing you and I had had more time together, especially since I found out I was pregnant. I know I talked about decorating one of the bedrooms as a nursery, but I have such a hard time picking one fabric pattern over another or even choosing a color for the walls. But you're always full of good ideas." Another carefully gauged sigh preceded her final suggestion. "If only there were a few other people who could visit Aletha, you know, on sort of a rotating schedule. I would even take Scout to their homes, if need be."

Rose almost laughed out loud when her grandmother snapped her fingers and sat up straighter in her seat. "Now why didn't I think of that?" She had previously scorned the idea that anyone could better manage Aletha's needs than herself, despite offers of help from the Rosenbaums, Angelica, and others. Gert quickly dug a small notebook and pen from the remote depths of what some might describe as an oversized carry-on bag and began scribbling. Soon she had compiled a list to cover the visitation needs of a dozen invalids. Gentle comments and suggestions by Rose helped guide the project to manageable numbers.

"From what I understand, Miss Fields has a car she can drive now, but I overheard her once telling Aletha she didn't feel comfortable driving in city traffic. Can you think of anyone who might be able to drive her to the rehab center?"

"Easiest problem in the world. I'll just ask Bobby Taylor to take her. Did I tell you I think he's a little sweet on Reenie? I guess he'll have to take his sister Ellie June, too, but the outing might do her good." Gert considered the rest of the list on the drive home, taking into account work schedules, Jewish Sabbath, Sunday commitments, and Bingo. By the time they reached *Willow Walk* (Rose had insisted her grandmother move in with the Ludlows while Aletha was recovering from surgery) only a few days were left open to spend together, which was just as well. Rose had chosen the accent fabric for the walls and nursery curtains about an hour after she learned of her pregnancy.

When Tim and Rose greeted his parents at the airport a week later, the news of Aletha's plight brought a flash of anger to Miles' eyes, as expected, but he listened to Tim's explanation with admirable calm. Marilyn's influence was already obvious. Aletha further acquitted her grandson of any negligence and dug her heals in when Miles announced that she would, of course, move in with him and his bride after her hospital discharge.

"For an intelligent man, you sometimes say the silliest things! There will be no 'of course' about it. I refuse to be a gooseberry in a home occupied by newlyweds. Besides, the whole purpose of my rehabilitation is to allow me to live in my own home again." Her stubborn streak was no match for her son's; they settled on a compromise.

Knowing Gertie Gunn would be departing for Kentucky the day before Aletha was to be discharged, Miles insisted on employing a woman to stay with his mother as a companion. A word with Aletha's doctor earlier had impressed upon him the necessity for regular exercise, healthy food, and the prevention of any more falls. Despite her brave front, Aletha was relieved not to be facing a solitary existence just now. Though Scout was always by her side, there were limits to what he could do. For the present, Miles would be nearby to check on her regularly. The Hawthornes had decided to live in Marilyn's current home until they made a long-term decision about a new domicile.

Of all the participants in that July afternoon's drama, perhaps the two least directly affected, yet the most profoundly changed, were Derek Warner and Kavya Jackson. Those hours spent together – talking, laughing, playing with Ani – opened doors that both had feared might be shut forever. Though Derek had set his heart on Kavya at their first meeting, her subsequent aloof behavior had kept him at arm's length. Kavya had resolved to keep her emotions so controlled that she would never again allow herself to be hurt or betrayed. But the power of celebration, abundant sunshine, and Derek's smile, which would not quit despite her best efforts to check its inevitable penetration of her emotional armor, forced Kavya to admit that she had enjoyed a rare day free of care and the burden of unhappy memories. She was also forced to admit that the unexpected outcome was due to Derek and his ability to make her feel valued and safe.

Still only friends, a mutual affection grounded in respect grew and deepened between them. While the presence of little Ani reminded him that Kavya had once shared the most intimate essence of her nature with another man, he honored her for choosing to love and raise the child who had resulted from that broken union. Derek, like everyone, had his fair share of mistakes and regrets; he would not judge hers.

Another subtle change showed Kavya that Derek had taken one unguarded critique to heart. Within a week, his bald head was covered in stubble. In a month, it was fully transformed by a covering of thick black hair trimmed in a neat taper fade. Though unaware of the motivation behind the new look, all his friends were quick to praise the change. It not only made him appear taller, it seemed to add an aura of sophistication hitherto undetected.

A closely trimmed moustache and soul patch added the final touch, inspiring Abe to remark, in a charitable moment, "I cannot believe I am saying this, but you actually appear passably good-looking. I did not know you had it in you, my friend."

"*Really?* Was that so hard to admit?" Derek demanded.

"Maybe a little." Abe's mocking grin widened.

"Well, I may not be *tall,* dark, and handsome like you, but I'll settle for dark and handsome."

Afraid to openly praise Derek too much and give herself away, Kavya merely commented that he looked nice. He might have been offended by such a tepid reaction. His response to her criticism of his personal style had drawn wild applause from everyone else. But once, when looking up unexpectedly, he caught her gazing at him with open admiration, and his cup overflowed. Derek was so lost in the throes of love, whatever Kavya said or did held a magical quality. He wouldn't have changed a single thing about her – almost.

One facet of their relationship gave him pause. Derek was naturally transparent about everything. Helped by an extroverted nature and his desire to lighten anyone's burden, he shared the reality of Jesus in his life with as little self-consciousness as he might have felt in discussing the weather or a football game. In rare moments of honest reflection, Derek was compelled to admit his disappointment in Kavya's continued refusal to acknowledge his assertions about God and how the King of Kings had always guided his life. He had been blessed in unexpected ways, even during difficult times, and he knew, beyond doubt, that God would do the same for her. And though Kavya had at least gotten past the desire to answer such comments with scorn, it was obvious that she had well and truly shut off that part of her mind and spirit. Every time Derek attempted to share his faith with her, she listened politely, then abruptly changed the subject. He never gave up hope. He merely filed Kavya's consistent reaction in the "don't worry about it" corner of his mind and trusted blindly in the future.

They never discussed the ultimate direction of this obvious season of courtship – obvious to Derek, anyway. They were content, in the moment, to spend time together without fear of rejection or prejudice.

Swearing an oath to follow all of Granny Gert's directives regarding oversight of Aletha's needs, after her friend's release into the care of "that woman," Rose relinquished the responsibility for her grandmother's safety to the airline personnel at the departure gate. Rose was far more worried about Granny Gert changing planes in Covington than she was about Aletha's future well-being. As far as Nancy Simmons was concerned, Rose had no worries at all.

The retired med-surg nurse had taken to home healthcare as more of a remedy for loneliness and boredom than any need for income. As a spinster, her family had always been her coworkers and patients. She came highly recommended and cheerfully faced the daunting task of meeting her future charge and the Hawthorne/Ludlow family shortly before Gert's departure. Though her brisk, professional manner impressed them all, it was her kindness and sense of humor shining through the efficient façade that put the final stamp of approval on Miles' choice. Despite her excellent qualifications, however, Nurse Simmons managed to put Gert's nose out of joint over some trivial matter. She was mercifully spared knowledge of Gert's disapproval when that opinionated lady, in an almost unprecedented display of reticence, chose to save her choicest comments for her granddaughter. During her final drive back to Tinkers Well – on that visit, at least – she gave vent to her emotions. Rose cringed and told herself that her grandmother's words only reflected concern for Aletha. Tim grinned silently in the driver's seat, wondering just how much of Granny Gert's feisty nature Rose had inherited.

It took little time for Abraham Yousef to stand out in his classes at *Mid-American Theological Seminary.* His intelligence, articulate speech, and thirst for biblical knowledge made him a favorite of professors and fellow seminarians alike. Never loathe to jump into any discussion, Abe could also be counted on to listen and learn from his classmates. He had never felt more at peace with his decision to pursue a Master of Divinity degree and a future marked out for him and Amy in ministry. Three years seemed a long time, though he realized the preparation was critical for his success. This was where he belonged.

It was the custom of the school for all new students to share their personal faith stories during their first semester of classes. When it was Abe's turn, he held his audience enthralled, moved by all he had sacrificed to follow his Savior. Knowing people connect best to visual images, Abe had prepared a photo slideshow that first took those present to Lebanon, the land of his birth, an alien world unknown to all but himself. Pictures of his family during his childhood; images of his fellow soldiers in the barren hills of Afghanistan; the medical staff at Bethesda – all had a place in his improbable journey from Muslim boy to American soldier to Christian seminary student. Another slide showed him and Derek Warner, clad in dusty ACUs, standing outside a tent. The sun, setting behind a craggy ridge in the distance, provided poor light, but both men exuded a joy that lit their faces. Abe held a small, tattered Bible clasped between his long fingers. It was the moment that had changed his pathway forever.

Though Derek had been unable to join Abe in class that day, Amy was there. She slipped into the back of the room unnoticed during Abe's dialogue. He concluded by describing the final confrontation between himself and his father, and the resulting decision to attend seminary.

"I have known great loss, yes, but I have also been richly blessed. Five months after I left my parents' home for good, I married the love of life. She is my biggest inspiration and my most energetic cheerleader." As a proud smile dawned, everyone turned to see Amy walking toward him. Taking her hand, Abe flipped to the last slide. "Her wedding surprise for me was the truly impossible attendance of my mother and youngest sister and brother. I know you will be delighted, as I was, that my mother became a Christian that day."

As everyone stood and applauded, a speculative gleam lit the eyes of a professor unknown to Abe. He sat apart from the others in the back of the room. He had been labeled curmudgeonly, grumpy, and quarrelsome – upon first meeting. Those who knew him better were able to penetrate his rough exterior, recognizing it for what it was – an unintentional, deceptive veneer. Behind the perpetual frown lines, woven into the thread of every terse conversation, and hidden beneath the misshapen, threadbare sweater, beat a heart of humility burdened for the lost.

The professor grunted and nodded his head while something very like a smile accented the deep grooves on either side of his mouth. "I did not see that coming today," he muttered. "Thank You, Lord."

More than a few eyebrows were raised when Angelica Warner took a seat beside Derek at Community Church. Two months had passed since the Hawthorne wedding. Aletha Mason, settled once more in her beloved *Fern Cottage,* was thriving under the diligent eye of Nurse Simmons. Her family and friends took turns staying with her to afford her excellent caregiver some time off.

Insisting she be granted a place in this partnership, Angelica stayed with her old friend one weekend a month. It was all she was allowed to contribute to the patient's well-being. The Hawthornes, Ludlows, and others filled in the remainder of coverage, leaving Angelica with no excuse to limit her work schedule at the *Prairie Gateway.* The longer she worked there, however, the less she wanted to limit her work time. A growing sense of satisfaction with her new life could be attributed to two sources. Her natural warmth and generosity touched the lives of both the guests she served and the hotel staff with whom she interacted. She was born to minister to others, and she found opportunities to fulfill that calling every day in a job she would never have considered even six months earlier. The other source of satisfaction could be traced directly to the person of Mr. A. B. C. Dawson.

The walks and dinners begun during Angelica's "undercover" employment period became occasional weekend outings and home-cooked meals at her temporary home in the city. She had also repeated her visit to Dawson's church and Sunday School. Derek's failure to convince Kavya to have anything to do with the religious side of his life meant Sundays were the only days he allowed his mind to focus on anything but her. And when he did, he couldn't help noticing his mother's absence from time to time. Never one to keep a lid on his curiosity, Derek demanded an excuse for her truancy, followed by a demand to know when this Mr. Dawson was going to come to church with her. The question was answered on a cool Sunday at the end of September.

After Introducing Dawson to her son, who greeted that genial gentleman with a friendly enough smile despite his suspicions, Angelica took her seat, aware of curious eyes focused on their pew. Blithely oblivious of having caused a sensation, Dawson admired the stained-glass windows and the wooden support arches overhead, pleased by what he saw.

"Albie, you seem to have made quite an impression on the Community Church family," Angelica murmured.

"That's only because I'm sitting next to the most attractive woman in the room."

His angelically innocent smile goaded her to say, "I'll have none o' your nonsense. Remember, we are in church!"

"Then I'll repeat my observations *after* church," he replied meekly. Angelica struggled to hide a betraying smile.

Derek, who had overheard the conversation, wondered if there wasn't a good deal more than nonsense going on between them.

Critically studying her reflection in her bedroom mirror, Rose Ludlow grimaced. Her skin glowed, and her hair shone in glossy waves, appearing thicker and straighter than usual. But all she could see was her belly – her great big, enormous belly. She was convinced that she looked like she had swallowed the giant inflatable turkey from the Thanksgiving Day parade. Huge was not a strong enough word – and her pregnancy had almost three months to go! The novelty of new maternity clothes had already worn off; even they had begun to feel tight. Her grimace quickly turned into a smile of wonder, however, when she felt a tiny foot poking at the side of her abdomen. Soon another appendage kicked the other side. Fascinated by the evidence of an internal soccer match, Rose missed the sound of her husband taking the stairs in bounds to land with a thud outside the door. Leaning on the door frame, he gazed at his wife and was reminded for the thousandth time that he was the luckiest man in the world.

"I have never seen you look more gorgeous," he said, finally capturing her attention.

Rose looked up at his reflection in the mirror. "*Gorgeous?* Tim, I look like a beached whale!" Her eyes dropped again to continue critical examination of her very rounded figure.

He moved to stand behind her, wrapping his arms so that his hands could rest on her abdomen. "Yes, but a very *beautiful* beached whale." A gurgle of laughter escaped her lips, bringing out Tim's lopsided grin. "That must be the weirdest sensation in the world – to have two little people jostling for position inside you. Feels like the warm-up to a wrestling match to me, so they are clearly boys."

"Not so fast, big man. They are obviously practicing ballet positions, so they must be girls."

"Well, whatever they are, we agreed to wait until they make an appearance to find out. And since that date appears to be getting sooner by the minute, you'll be happy to know I finally finished the secret project I've been working on in my shop."

Rose spun around to look eagerly at her husband. "Does this mean I finally get to see… whatever it is?" For the past six weeks she had been forbidden entrance to Tim's workshop at the end of the garage. Hardly a patient person, Rose had, nevertheless, respected his dire warning about not crossing the threshold without permission. He had explained that he was working on a surprise that he would reveal in his own time. That time had apparently arrived. She grabbed his hand and practically dragged him back down the stairs.

The garage was a detached building designed to mirror the Victorian architecture of the main house, complete with a small roof turret and weather vane. It had originally been built to serve as a carriage house, but as horses and carriages gave way to automobiles in the early 20th century, the large structure had been repurposed as a garage. Built on generous lines, it could accommodate both their vehicles and Tim's boat. A large storage room on the end had also been repurposed and claimed by Tim, who declared that every carpenter needs his own workshop. Rose had no idea what his latest project was. She had presented him with a long "Honey Do" list soon after the wedding, so the possibilities were endless. When he opened the door and told her she could open her eyes, they immediately filled with tears.

Two perfectly matching cradles stood side by side. The wood was unfinished – the craftsmanship, unmistakable. The Early American design relied on the use of round and square pegs for construction rather than nails. Scrolled wooden appliques linked them to their Victorian surroundings. Tim demonstrated how a wooden ball affixed to a second peg on the end of each cradle could be pulled out, allowing the cradle to rock supported by the other structural pegs on either end. He described every detail – why he had chosen open, railed sides rather than solid ones, and how each bed could be easily taken apart and moved in pieces. Rose remained silent while the tears welled up and trickled down her cheeks. Tim became a little worried, wondering if he had overstepped in not asking for her design input, or even if she wanted cradles. They had already picked out cribs for the nursery.

"I know you've been worried about having the babies on a different level of the house at night. Initially, I thought of moving the baby beds into our room, but that would really fill up the space, so I came up with cradles as a solution. They're smaller and can fit on either side of our bed more easily, but they should be big enough to hold the babies for several months." Rose's lips trembled as she reached out to rub the smooth walnut finish. Tim wasn't sure whether he detected a smile or a frown.

"I even looked up the specifications for standard-sized cradles online so we can order mattresses and sheets." Still not a word. "Sweetheart, I… I know I messed up… *really* messed up when you told me about your… I mean *our* pregnancy – though you're doing all the heavy lifting. Then we found out we were having twins, and I didn't handle that well. I know you forgave me for being an idiot, but I just wanted to… well, to show you how excited I am about our little family." He was almost afraid to stop talking. "I didn't put a finish on the wood because I wanted you to choose that. I can stain them or paint them or…" He finally ground to a halt and just stood there helplessly. "Did I screw up again?"

Standing on tiptoe, Rose kissed him tenderly and attempted to put her arms around him – a process that had become increasingly difficult. "You have never *un*-messed up more perfectly." A giggle into his shoulder sealed his relief. With an impish smile, she looked into his eyes. "Maybe I should have made you sweat a little longer, but honestly, I am so, *so* pleased. These cradles are works of art. And you've solved the problem of how to fit the babies in our room while they're so little. I had thought of using the Pack-N-Go beds for that, but they don't hold a candle to the Tim Ludlow level of excellence."

"Phew! You had me going there for a while." He kissed the top of her head and released her. "Now just stand there and continue to marvel at my genius while I clean up this mess." It was time to restore order to the creative chaos.

Tim had been so anxious to show Rose his handiwork, she was allowed to see his workshop in an unusual state of clutter and mess. Despite Tim's repeated pleas to take it easy, Rose was not one to stand around when there was something she could help with. Unearthing a hand whisk and push broom, she went to work on the sawdust. She liked the earthy aroma of fresh wood shavings. It recalled the companionable hours spent in her father's workshop when she was a girl. While she swept the wood residue from workbench and floor, Tim cleaned an array of tools and returned them to their allotted places.

"We could paint the cradles the same color as the cribs – gray frame with white rungs," she said. Before he could respond, Rose had thrown that suggestion out. "No, that might look a little contrived." One white and one gray seemed equally unimaginative. Pulling an accent color from the nursery curtains and wall wainscotting was quickly discarded when Tim reminded her that the cradles would be in their bedroom for several months, not the nursery.

She was still pondering the question as Tim locked the shop behind them. "What if, instead of painting them, we stain them." It was the solution he had fervently hoped she would land on, though he'd have painted his handiwork chartreuse if Rose had set her heart on it. As far as he was concerned, fine wood should *never* be covered in paint. It would be like defacing a delicate oil landscape with diagonal stripes. Stain allowed the grain of the wood and the craftsmanship of the joinery to shine through. Though he wanted to shout his approval, he simply commended her decision and suggested they look at some stain options on the computer.

"We do make a pretty good team, don't we Mr. Ludlow?"

"The best, Mrs. Ludlow." Taking his wife in his arms, Tim sealed the deal with a thoroughly satisfying kiss before they walked back to the house, hand in hand.

Life during that glowing autumn was filled with promise, just as it was ablaze with natural beauty. Any and everything seemed possible. The scent of hope in the brisk air was as prevalent as that of burning leaves. The inhabitants of Tinkers Well seemed to move in tandem toward a collective, certain future. Each evolving relationship and career path reflected the serenity of a mountain lake. There were no choppy waves or disturbing ripples whipped up by an unwelcome wind; a placid, peaceful surface prevailed.

Beneath the surface, reality wielded greater influence. Undercurrents began to stir.

CHAPTER 15

The professor's office appeared more like a museum of anthropology *cum* lending library than an administrative retreat. Still pondering the summons that had directed him to this location at precisely this appointed time, Abe Yousef poked his head through the open doorway. He knocked and called out but received no answer. Afraid to assume the meeting had been cancelled, he stepped cautiously over the threshold and began perusing the various books scattered on shelves or in stacks around the room. Intermingled with intellectual treatises were colorful wall hangings and cultural artifacts. Most were accompanied by a plaque or contained writing in some unknown language. He recognized the Cyrillic alphabet of Eastern Europe, the strange lines and circles of Korean Hangul, and the Devanagari Script of Hindi, in which the characters all seemed to contain some variant of a "T" combined with a curved figure. He had no idea what they said, though he guessed they might be a paraphrase of the one scroll he did understand. As a former son of Lebanon, Abe could read and write Arabic fluently. The graceful curls and dots of his native tongue spoke clearly to him.

"Thank you for sharing with us the priceless gift of the Savior, Jesus. May God's richest blessings be with you always."

"That was a gift from the new believers of a small town in Jordan. Lovely people. I only wish I could have communicated directly with them rather than through an interpreter. And that is precisely why you are here, young man."

Abe spun around in surprise when a gruff voice spoke out of thin air; he never heard the other man enter the room. He was waved to a seat without any apparent expectation of a response.

"Mr. Yousef, we've never met. You have no classes with me this semester. You've probably never even heard of me yet." Abe didn't know what to say, so he remained silent, which seemed to suit his host. "We may never have met, but I know you. I know all about you. I've been around this institution so long they made me the chairman of the admissions board a few years back. And when your application floated across my desk, I was cautiously optimistic. I've been waiting for a student like you for a long time, a very long time."

A humble man, Abe could not fathom why he had been singled out among hundreds of other men with far more knowledge of Christianity and its practice. He had already determined that he was handicapped by his limited faith background, his age (most of the other seminarians were in their 20s), and an undergraduate degree that hardly seemed best suited for someone desiring to study theology. He was a computer geek with a whopping two-plus years of experience as a Christian. Unless he was expected to re-engineer the school's digital network, Abe couldn't imagine why he was there.

"I know you, but you don't know me. Let me change that." The other man was clad in a tweed jacket with worn elbow patches. He held out his hand, saying, "The name is Gundersen, Dr. Richard Gundersen, Professor of Global Outreach and Missions." Abe had already studied the course catalog thoroughly. Dr. Gundersen's classes were reserved for third-year students and doctoral candidates. Instead of shedding light, the professor's words only served to confuse Abe more. The unintentional obfuscation of his message was lost on the older man. He followed his own, clear train of thought. "I was present when you shared your life story and extremely effective testimony. I knew your background, of course, from your seminary application, which is why I was there. What I couldn't have known was that you would be the answer to a prayer I have been praying for years. I never gave up, and God, in his graciousness and perfect timing, delivered you at my door."

"Sir, I don't know… that is, I'm not quite sure…"

"You are new to the Christian faith but, judging by everything you have made known about your character, I'll warrant you have read every word of Scripture."

"I have read through the Bible several times, yes, but I have much to learn –"

"Of course, you do." Dr. Gundersen scowled at Abe under heavy brows. "But you no doubt know that Esther is the only book in the Bible without any direct mention of God."

"Well, yes. But I…"

"It's the story of a mere slip of girl, albeit blessed with beauty and brains, who finds herself in a position of royal influence that she neither sought nor wanted. She was humble, uncertain, and downright scared to death when confronted by her uncle –"

"Mordecai –"

"Yes, that's right. Good man. Her uncle instructed her to go to the king without being summoned, and to plead for her people, the Jewish people, knowing it might mean her death. But Mordecai assured her, 'Who knows, perhaps you have come to your royal position for such a time as this?'"[16] Gundersen stopped abruptly, and his stern, craggy features broke into an unexpectedly charming smile. "You do see, don't you?" Abe saw nothing. The professor might as well have been speaking in Mandarin.

---

[16]Esther 4:14b, *Holman Christian Standard Bible* (HCSB).

"You want me to speak on behalf of the nation of Israel?" It was Abe's best guess.

"No, no. Well, then again, yes." Looking at Abe, the professor was confronted by a polite, but blank expression. "My wife always tells me I get ahead of myself. Let me start from the beginning." Abe tried not to look too relieved. Shifting a pile of dusty, leather-bound commentaries from an equally dusty, leather chair, Professor Gundersen sat down and finally got to the heart of the matter.

"My passion has always been focused on spreading the gospel. And I have been privileged to travel most of the globe in pursuit of that passion as evidenced by all these little mementos I've collected over time. But in the past 10 – 15 years, that focus has shifted to our own country. As generations of Americans have walked away from the faith of their fathers, a growing segment of society – overseas immigrants – have brought with them the faith of *their* fathers, and these beliefs are *not* rooted in the Judeo-Christian traditions upon which our country was founded." He was pleased to see that he had finally caught Abe's attention. "You understand this better than most. The older generations of these immigrants are difficult to reach. They live, work, and worship within tight-knit communities, as you are well aware. But the younger generations, particularly those of college age, are more accessible. This is especially true of students who attend school away from that family enclave." Abe immediately thought of his brother, Husam. "When you presented your personal testimony last month, I knew my prayer had finally been answered. God brought you to this seminary, in this part of the country, for 'such a time as this.'" Abe's pulse quickened, and he found himself holding his breath.

"Mr. Yousef, I don't know what you had envisioned for your life after completing seminary – probably seeking a position in an urban area somewhere where you might shepherd a moderately sized flock or serve as an associate pastor."

"Is it wrong to belief that God could use me such a way?"

"Not at all. But I want you to think bigger, to have faith like Esther and Mordecai. Did you know, there are an estimated 35,000 Muslims living in the Kansas City area, alone. That means there are *thousands* of Muslim young people who will be educated in colleges and universities across the Midwest. But who can reach them with the gospel? Your friend – I believe his name is Derek – helped you to a saving knowledge of Jesus Christ at a time when you were far from home and the influences of Islam and Muslim culture. I believe that with your heritage, your background, your knowledge and fluency in Arabic, your extreme life experiences, and your obvious intelligence and sincerity, you can reach these young people in ways an old, white, rumpled professor never could. You have walked the road they're walking. You know what it is to be cut off from your family because of your newfound Christian faith. You can be a voice crying in a wilderness where few others can be heard."

"I… I don't quite know what to say. Of course, I want – more than anything – to share the knowledge of Jesus' forgiveness and loving justice with American Muslims. But you must understand that these young Muslims on college campuses are not only accessible for the truth of the gospel; they are also prime targets for the worst kinds of radicalization and anti-Semitic brainwashing. And then there is the systemic philosophy of atheism so pervasive in higher education. I lived at home and attended the family mosque when I was a university student, so I had a buffer around me. My father had his own vision of spreading Islam, which did *not* include forced allegiance — at least not outwardly – though it is just as chilling and something I did not fully understand until after my injury. Perhaps we may speak of it another time.

"Please understand that I am not saying this ministry is in any way hopeless or that there are any lives God cannot touch, but if we want to effectively spread the truth of the gospel – and you must believe that this is the calling of my heart – we must recognize the lies of the enemy and how best to refute them. I do, to a certain degree, possess this knowledge where

Muslims are concerned, but I am not trained in evangelism. Besides, it will be three years before I complete my seminary degree. Even then, I will have no experience in a pastoral role. I don't quite understand what you are suggesting."

Dr. Gundersen crossed his arms and contemplated the young man sitting before him. "We don't need a trained evangelist. We need a disciple who is also a *discipler* – one, moreover, who can identify with his mission field. I am suggesting you begin that ministry next semester." Abe's facial features adopted a look of incredulity. "Now, there's no need to feel agitated. Some fellow colleagues and I have been laying the groundwork for such an endeavor for some time. We have arranged access to meeting places on three different campuses and have canvased student-life professionals for speaking opportunities at these institutions. Then we waited for the right man to come along. I believe he has."

While Abe sat in stunned silence, Dr. Gundersen outlined his plan of campaign and his expectations regarding Abe's role. Initially, he would be assisted – mentored – by an older man, also a former Muslim. From the outset, however, Abe would take the lead on personal interactions with students. Gundersen further explained that the demands of such a ministry would make it necessary for Abe to limit his class load with a goal of completing his studies in five or six years rather than three. If this outreach proved to be successful, as he believed it would, Abe could expect to travel several days a week within a 100-mile radius. The long-term goal was to have him speak regularly with an established, national college ministry. The implications of such an undertaking were staggering. He would receive a regular stipend, though a limited one. The professor concluded by praying with Abe and giving thanks to God for answered prayer. He told Abe to discuss this unique opportunity with his wife, because her life would be impacted, too.

On the drive back to Tinkers Well, and a reality he could grasp, Abe fought panic, insecurity, and fear. He prayed "without ceasing" all the way home. He had never contemplated such a future, and he was filled with doubt, but the more he thought about it, the more he heard Jesus telling him to "Feed my lambs." He screeched to a stop by the back door and hurried inside to find his wife. Amy was sitting at the dining room table studying a new musical score for her band students. When she heard the back door slam, she looked up and immediately knew something extraordinary had happened to her husband. Without a word, Amy walked into his outstretched arms. They closed so tightly around her she could hardly breathe. She felt the thudding of his heart. With a gentle touch, she stroked his hair and murmured words of assurance until she heard his breathing grow steadier and felt his heartbeat normalize.

"I don't know what changed for you today," she said, gazing into eyes hungry for assurance, "but whatever it is, I believe in you, and I support you."

Abe immediately experienced the sensation of being totally invincible and wholly unequal to the task at the same time. But if Amy believed in him, and Professor Gundersen believed in him, who was he to question the calling of a sovereign God whose will would be done through the vessel of his choosing? Returning her tender smile, Abe kissed his wife and drew strength and certainty from her enthusiastic response. With a sudden surge of confidence, his legendary appetite returned. Promising to fill her in on all the details of his miraculous news, Abe pulled Amy into the kitchen and began scouring the refrigerator for a fortifying snack before dinner. He hadn't eaten in three hours.

The return of Albie Dawson's daughter from her temporary, five-month assignment in Ecuador set into motion a chain of events no one could have foreseen. In addition to reclaiming the apartment Angelica Warner had been occupying during her absence, Ronnie Dawson also had to reclaim her cat. Bastet's fickle allegiance had gradually been transferred to her substitute housemate, who finally understood just how Bastet liked things. The cat initially greeted Ronnie with suspicion and disdain until she, too, honored "Her Majesty" with the same level of reverence exhibited by Angelica.

There had been next to no warning of Ronnie's arrival, so Angelica, like Bastet, had to make a few speedy adjustments. She returned to her home in Tinkers Well after a quick meeting with Albie and his daughter, promising to come back on the weekend to gather her things. Ronnie would have agreed to any reason that brought Angelica and her father together again. She had detected in mere minutes that her months away had allowed that association to flourish, and she couldn't have been happier. Besides, she had her own revelation, and the more people present, the better. She even begged Angelica to bring Derek along, insisting that a BBQ is best enjoyed with a crowd.

Accordingly, mother and son arrived in Kansas City late Saturday afternoon with enough boxes to move a family of four. Derek had only agreed to make himself available because he was not on call at the fire station that weekend, and more importantly, because Kavya was slammed with a term project for her most difficult class. She refused to see him or even talk to him until it was completed, proofed, and submitted, a process that would probably require every waking minute until late Sunday night. Angelica was not offended at being relegated to second best. She loved her son and wanted him to know the same happiness she had known with his father, though she still had misgivings about the woman Derek had set his heart on. As always, she left that issue to prayer and looked forward to an enjoyable evening unalloyed by concern for a future that might well never evolve. Derek, loaded with boxes, turned to follow his mother into the building and ran smack into another man headed in the same direction.

"Jamal Young! What are you doing here, brother? This isn't where you and Jada live."

The other young black man did not appear as surprised by Derek's presence. His perpetually serious expression broke momentarily into a gentle smile directed at both the Warners as he bent to retrieve one of the boxes dropped during the collision. With a nervous gesture, he straightened his tortoiseshell glasses and greeted Angelica with polite diffidence. A little taller than Derek, he was built on slim lines and managed to look well-dressed in simple light gray chinos and untucked, white button-down shirt under a casual linen jacket. He was nothing like his sister Jada, who was short, unsophisticated, and loaded with attitude. During her year with *Three Brothers Construction, Inc.,* she had proven herself to be a respectable carpenter. But it was Jamal, with his brilliant mind and education, who stood out as the consummate professional of the two.

"It's nice to see you again, Mrs. Warner. Derek, I almost didn't recognize you with all that hair!"

"I know, I'm even more awesome now. But don't be jealous. You still look like you just walked off the cover of GQ®."

Jamal was no more proof against Derek's grin than anyone else. His own smile widened. "That's good to know. I have my reasons for wanting to present myself well tonight."

"I guess that means one of us knows why you're here, and it's not me! Start talking."

Holding the door for Angelica and Derek, Jamal explained that he was the guest of Ronnie Dawson, whom he got to know better while in Ecuador. "You see, we are both employed by the same engineering firm and worked as partners on the bridge project near Cuenco in the southern part of the country."

The door to Ronnie's apartment opened before anyone could knock. Her eyes swept past Angelica and Derek to settle on Jamal waiting respectfully in the rear. They softened and glowed and told the Warners everything Jamal had left unsaid. Quickly recovering her manners, Ronnie invited them all inside on a wave of welcome and barely contained excitement.

"Is that the Warners?" a male voice called from the kitchen. "Ask Angelica to come help me with this confounded cheesecake." He waited expectantly for a saucy reply. He was not disappointed.

"Mr. A.B.C. Dawson, you can just come out here and ask me yourself!"

Their various children exchanged glances fraught with questions whose answers were left to speculation. Upon entering the living room, Dawson saw Jamal first. He paused for a split second before squeezing Angelica's hand and shaking Derek's. "Now, who might this young man be, Veronica?" Though the words were for his daughter, his eyes never left Jamal's face. His voice was not unkind, but there is always an element of tension inherent in a daughter introducing a love interest to her father.

"Daddy, this is my work friend I told you about. Jamal, this is my father Albie."

In addition to intelligence, Jamal possessed wisdom. He shook the hand extended to him and spoke in a clear, assured voice. "It's a pleasure to meet you, Mr. Dawson. Thank you for making me feel so welcome." Dawson gripped Jamal's hand a little harder before releasing it and nodding his approval. Derek watched the exchange critically, making mental notes for future reference. Ronnie looked from one to the other and beamed.

All Angelica knew of the Dawson family she had gleaned from a hundred casual conversations. She had seen the framed photos in Albie's office and knew Ronnie to closely resemble her mother. Her narrow face was heightened by hair cut short over the ears with loose, wavy curls on top. Warm oval eyes softened her features, and her luminous smile gave evidence of years of successful orthodontia. She was as loving as she was intelligent and had the sense to realize she would always be her father's darling, despite being a successful, independent professional woman. There are some aspects of the parent-child relationship one never outgrows. But no one in the room was left in doubt about the "working relationship" between Veronica Dawson and Jamal Young.

By the time the tie between Jamal and the Warners was sorted out, it was time for dinner, and packing was put on hold. The meal and company were everything Ronnie hoped they would be. She glanced nervously at her father a few times, but Jamal seemed to have passed muster. Angelica noticed too. What Albie could not know was the very real possibility of pushback from Jamal's sister. Angelica wondered how much Ronnie understood of that bond. She knew very little herself, other than her experience of witnessing an emotionally dependent relationship, at least on Jada's part, into which few others would be welcome. It was not her business, but she liked both Ronnie and Jamal and hoped their future would be a success. At least they provided something else to focus on besides Derek and the shaky future he seemed determined to pursue.

After dinner, Angelica set to work packing the personal items she had accumulated in the bedroom and bathroom. She left the living room to Derek after pointing out a shelf of books and the row of framed photos above them. Jamal had been shooed out of the kitchen, so he idly glanced at the picture frames as Derek wrapped each with an old towel. He reached for the last one and suddenly stood stock still. His usual poise utterly deserted him, and the hands holding the frame began to shake uncontrollably. He spoke with great agitation.

"Why does your mother have this picture of Sarge?" It was only then Derek glanced at Jamal and was amazed by the change in him.

"Brother, are you *okay*? You look like somebody just walked over your grave. And who the heck is Sarge?"

Jamal's knees buckled; he landed on the couch. His eyes devoured the face in the photo while he touched the features almost reverently. As if speaking to himself, he said, "This is the man who saved my life when I was a kid in Chicago."

Sitting next to him, Derek gently took the picture from Jamal and looked at it for the first time. His senses began to swim. All the habitual humor was wiped from his face, and he called out sharply, "Mama, you need to come out here. Now!" The urgency in the words was not only detected by Angelica; it also drew the Dawsons from the kitchen.

"This man you call 'Sarge' was my father, Lt. Isaiah Warner. He was a cop in Chicago, and he died in the line of duty when I was just 16."

"This is *impossible!*" Jamal shook his head in disbelief. "You've worked with my sister almost *every* day for a year, but I swear to you, neither of us knew who you were in relation to our past." Retrieving the picture from Derek's numb fingers, Jamal gazed at the smiling face with a nostalgic sweetness. "You have no idea how much I envied you. He never told us your name, but he talked about his son all the time. I used to pray that I could have a dad like him. But I wasn't so lucky." Jamal's voice was suddenly burdened by the grim reality of his childhood.

The Warner family had never been told the name of the boy whose life Isaiah Warner had saved during confrontation with a local gang. The youth was a minor, so his identity had been protected. Likewise, the family name of the boy's rescuer was kept from him. When Warner began to work with kids from one of Chicago's rougher neighborhoods, he was still a sergeant. He told the kids to simply call him "Sarge," and that was the only name by which they ever knew him. The passage of a few years brought about a promotion; Warner remained Sarge.

Derek had idolized his dad. Though always active in his son's life, the elder Warner felt called to provide a positive male role model for kids who, for the most part, never knew their fathers and were headed for bleak futures. A younger Derek saw only the father he loved choosing to spend time with other kids rather than with his own son. He resented that time away and asked repeatedly to go with his dad, to be included in that part of his life. But Isaiah was just as determined to keep Derek separated from that world, protected and nurtured.

"I might have lived my whole life and never guessed you were the guy I've wondered about all these years," Derek said. "Jada has never mentioned her early life to any of the Three Brothers crew *or* their wives. She just talks smack about being a marine and brags about you. I mean, look at you! You're smart, educated, and successful. How could you have come from the south side of Chicago? I still can't believe it!"

"I am all those things because your father, and others like him, believed in me. He gave me a chance, and I've spent my whole life trying to honor that gift. I wanted so desperately to make my life worth his sacrifice."

When the news of his father's death burst on his world, Derek's youthful jealousy grew into bitter resentment. Though time and maturity had helped that wound heal, a lingering emptiness never quite left his heart. Now Derek sat next to the boy whose life had been saved when his father's life had been taken, and the emptiness immediately left him to be replaced by compassion. Angelica saw a young man who had carried an unbearable burden for far too long. She knelt before Jamal and gently covered his hands still holding the picture frame.

"Jamal, I don't understand how this miracle has happened. But I would like to know the whole story, if you are willin' to share i' 'twith us."

Jamal stared at her, mystified by her kindness. "Do you know what you're asking?"

"It's time we know the truth so we can finally bury our dead. I believe everyone here has a right to know." She looked from Ronnie, who had taken the place vacated by Derek, to Dawson, who nodded gravely from a nearby chair. Angelica moved to a chair facing Jamal while Derek leaned on the armrest. Before he began, Jamal turned first to Ronnie, who was obviously mystified by the unexpected turn of events.

"Ronnie, I told you I had a sister, but there is so much I did *not* say. Mrs. Warner is right. I owe her – and Derek – the truth. And," Jamal continued, looking at her father, "I want our relationship to be one of honesty and transparency.

"My sister, Jada, and I were raised by our grandmother – Mama June Young. She was a good woman, tough but fair. Our mother – Lashonda was her name – couldn't take care of us. She was only 15 when I was born, and

Jada was born two years later. Hers was a sad but not unfamiliar tale. She was born wild. Mama June used to say she should have named her Gomer, like Hosea's wife in the Bible. She never finished school but continued to live in our home until Mama June finally kicked her out; she had found out how easy it was to make a lot of money by selling what men were willing to pay for instead of just giving it away. Her handler got her hooked on drugs so she would continue to 'work' to pay for her habit. It was her downfall that gave Jada and me a fighting chance.

"It took two jobs to support us – Mama June refused to take any handouts. If she worked hard, we worked just as hard. We never had a TV or internet, and since we weren't allowed outside to play when she wasn't home to watch us, we found other ways to entertain ourselves. I became a voracious reader. I thought I'd been given the keys to the kingdom when I got my first public library card. Jada had no such academic bent, but she was fascinated by watching the building super when he came to fix things around the apartment, and she began tagging along with him on his rounds. He was a young guy, but he was unusually patient with her. In hindsight, I think he may have been her father. We definitely had a different mix of genes. I never knew who my father was. For me and Jada that didn't really matter – we were brother and sister, and nothing would ever change that.

"When I was 14, Sarge started the neighborhood program for kids. Mama June insisted we participate, though I was kind of an outsider. I was looked down on because I was a good student. The program helped me to avoid those attracted to gang involvement, and Sarge looked out for me. He encouraged me to study diligently. Oddly enough, he was very adept at mathematics and took the time to help me understand a subject most kids barely passed."

"He had to pound it into me, too," Derek interjected. "I'm glad I wasn't the only kid who had to suffer through that!"

The power of positive memories infused excitement into Jamal's narrative. "Yes, but it wasn't a chore for me. I loved it! Sarge helped me explore the complexity and creativity of the equations. He showed me how to think in terms of numbers. It opened a vista before me I had never imagined. Thanks to the community youth program, and guys like your dad, I felt like I had a real future. Then Mama June got sick, and everything changed." Jamal frowned and was silent for a few minutes before going on.

"It was something to do with her lungs. She had to drag an oxygen tank around and couldn't do much of anything. She didn't even have the strength to fight my mother when she moved back in. In my fear and ignorance, I never told Sarge about the situation. I was afraid Social Services would be called in and that Jada and I would be separated and sent to foster homes. I thought I could take care of things myself. But any money I could earn doing odd jobs was stolen by LaShonda to support her habit. I caught her once trying to sell the services of her own daughter! Jada sent that 'client' home with a busted lip and an uncomfortable gait. I knew LaShonda wouldn't give up, though. I had to do something to protect my sister and provide for the family." The desperation of the boy still rang true in the voice of the man.

"As much as I tried to distance myself from gang activities, I eventually approached a member of a local gang to let me participate in the robbery of a convenience store I had overheard him bragging about. I convinced him that I could get close to the counter without raising an alarm because I was so obviously *not* a gang member. He agreed, but when push came to shove, I couldn't go through with it. I was thrust aside, and the store was robbed anyway. I heard a gunshot just after the store alarm went off, but I was so scared I couldn't move. Two guys grabbed me and drug me down the street into an alley." Jamal had forgotten he was sitting in a gracious modern apartment surrounded by people who admired and respected him. He was once again a terrified boy facing a death that would come all too soon. His voice trembled with emotion as he forced himself to talk about a horror he thought to have buried long ago.

"One of the gang members had a gun pointed at me. I was shaking so badly I couldn't tell who it was. It didn't help any that I had lost my glasses. I finally just closed my eyes and waited. It was so surreal. I heard the gun go off, and I waited to feel pain from the bullet's impact. Instead, a body came out of nowhere, knocking me off my feet. In a whisper I could barely hear, I was told to stay still. A siren started blaring, and everybody scattered like roaches in a floodlight." Jamal had begun to shake again. He looked helplessly at Angelica, and the anguish in his voice pierced her heart. "It was Sarge. He pushed me aside, and the bullet hit him instead. If I hadn't gotten mixed up in that mess, if I had just trusted him, he wouldn't have died. It was all my fault! I am *so, so sorry.*"

Angelica took his trembling hands between hers and spoke gently to a frightened child, as indeed, in that moment, he was. "Jamal, listen to me. I' 'twas *not* your fault. He was respondin' to a call. I *know* this to be true. I don't believe he had any idea you would be there. He was after the others and might very well have been shot anyway. Don't you understand what this means? His death is no longer meaningless. He laid down his life for someone he believed in, someone he cared about."

They all watched a lifetime of guilt and doubt melt away. The weight was gone, and Jamal experienced a peace such as he had never known. Nor was there anything left for Derek to resent or forgive. He realized in that moment, as he never had before, what a rare man he had known in his father and felt proud and humbled by that knowledge.

"You have given me something I never thought to find – answers," Jamal said. Relief made his voice almost lighthearted. "Now, may I explain to you the connection that brought all of us together at last?" The unanimous affirmative was hardly needed. Once begun, he had to complete his story.

"I was exonerated of any culpability in the crime. But after all that happened, I confessed to my part in the plan. I was so devastated by Sarge's death, I felt I had to somehow make amends. That took the form of a part-time job arranged by one of his fellow officers. It was work I could do after school and on weekends. The deli was several blocks away, so I had to take a bus. He made it sound like a condition of parole to report into the nearest policeman when I got back to my neighborhood every night. It didn't take me long to figure out that they were making sure I got home without any trouble. From the very first day, I took Jada with me. I couldn't leave her where LaShonda could get to her. The deli manager was a decent guy, so he agreed, and she was soon keeping all the shopping carts oiled and the shelving repaired while I was working in the stockroom or kitchen. We survived. As soon as I turned 18, we moved out for good. Mama June had passed by then. We lived in a dingy studio apartment with a couch for Jada and an air mattress for me, but at least it was our own. One of Sarge's friends helped me apply for scholarships to a community college. I took every class there I could, but I couldn't afford to pay for tuition to a university. That's about the time Jada graduated from high school and enlisted in the Marine Corps. She requested an MOS with a large enlistment bonus –"

"Which is why she ended up in EOD.[17] *Now* that makes sense." Derek was putting the pieces together.

"Exactly. I wasn't crazy about the idea, but she insisted. She said I had protected and supported the two of us for long enough. Now it was her turn. So, while she was off doing her military thing, I finished a degree in Civil Engineering. During that process I received a scholarship to their five-year program, enabling me to earn a master's degree. I moved to Kansas City to work for –"

"Brickhouse Associates." This time, it was Ronnie who filled in the gap.

"– just about the time Jada was injured. She came here after rehabilitation. I promise to tell you more about Jada, Ronnie, because there are significant details you need to know, but at least everyone is caught up on the rest of the story now."

---

[17] EOD – Explosive Ordnance Disposal

"Amazing. Simply amazing." Albie Dawson had come out of the verbal shadows. "Jamal, I don't know one man in a million who could have begun as you did and made something of his life, not to mention protecting your sister and affording her the same opportunity. I salute you." Turning to Angelica, he added, "And I don't know one woman in a million who would react with such compassion and kindness. You are truly a gem." Derek watched the interchange with critical interest. The tribute reserved for him only confused the issue further. "Derek, any father would be proud to call you son. I know I would."

The evening's disclosures left everyone with much food for thought.

CHAPTER 16

A pleasant season of cool breezes, accompanied by abundant sunshine, played a devious trick on Derek Warner. It so closely followed the tenor and ease of his blossoming relationship with Kavya Jackson, he was wooed into the belief that success was inevitable. He should have known better. He had once heard Abe Yousef, who was always spouting annoyingly wise "Abeisms," describe courtship as an uphill climb – a challenge worth conquering. Such a comparison fell short by epic miscalculation as far as Derek Warner's pursuit of Kavya Jackson was concerned. It began to more closely resemble a slog up the frozen slopes of Mt. Everest on a broken leg, while battling a blizzard. Just as he believed himself to be making real headway, Derek was hit by an unexpected avalanche or forced to circumvent an enormous boulder blocking his path. The fact that these obstacles came not from Kavya, but from those closest to him, caused him to feel equally resentful and more determined than ever to succeed.

First, his mother cautioned him not to rush into a permanent relationship in which both parties carried such disparate philosophical views. It didn't help Derek any that her words echoed those of Abe, whose judgment he honored more than he cared to admit. Angelica had broached the subject on the way to Ronnie Lawson's apartment the day before. The incredible revelations each encountered there pushed everything else to the back of their minds. Those discoveries continued to consume Derek's thoughts until he emerged from his mental fog to hear the pastor's words during the sermon the following day.

In an overview of Second Corinthians, Pastor Lindeman walked the congregation through topics previously studied. He spoke of forgiveness within the body of believers, and of the call to provide a witness as "a pleasing aroma of Christ." After reminding everyone of Paul's contrast between the veil covering the eyes of the heart of all those still bound by the old covenant, with the unveiled glory of Christ reflected in the faces of the redeemed, the pastor quoted from chapter 4. *"For God, who said, "Light shall shine out of darkness," is the One who has shone in our hearts to give the Light of the knowledge of the glory of God in the face of Christ."* Pastor Lindeman further explained, "References to light and darkness are found throughout the Bible. Light penetrates darkness. Jesus described himself as 'the light of the world.' In Chapter 9, one of the more familiar passages of Isaiah regarding the Messiah, the prophet proclaims, *'The people who walk in darkness will see a great light.'*[18] We all understand that to reach the lost, we must let our light shine among them."

That's what I'm talking about! Derek said to himself. *I want Kavya to see the light. Why can't anybody understand that?*

"Today we reach Paul's teaching regarding our most significant relationships. We must not underrate this critically important truth. In this passage, Paul flips the intersections of light and darkness." The pastor went on to expound on 2 Corinthians 6:14-18. As he spoke about the need for all who walk in the light to separate themselves from the darkness, and as he pointed out the lack of harmony between a believer and an unbeliever, Derek allowed indignation to influence his reaction to the message. Though

---

[18] Scripture text taken from *New American Standard Bible* (NASB).

not directly mentioning marriage, the implication was clear: what relationship between two people could be closer than that of husband and wife? He took no pleasure in comparing himself and Kavya to oxen harnessed together unequally and therefore rendered incompatible and unproductive.

Derek wanted to argue against the wisdom of the text and the sermon. He wanted to shout his denial of the logical tenets contained in Paul's admonition. He could not, so he left the church during the closing song before anyone could say "I told you so."

The physical rehabilitation of Aletha Mason was the stuff of medical journals. She flourished under Nancy Simmons' care, and grew stronger each day, determined not to let "this little setback" define her life going forward. By early September, her walker was an unregretted thing of the past, and she moved around the familiar layout of *Fern Cottage* with ease. In truth, Aletha could have dispensed with Nurse Simmons' assistance within a month of returning home. She chose not to; caregiver and patient had become friends.

When strong enough, daily walks to the main driveway, and eventually up and down its length, had provided the two with ample opportunities to become better acquainted. With the justification of promoting Aletha's integration back into the daily life of the community, Nancy frequently drove her charge into Tinkers Well where they might be spotted on any day of the week collecting groceries at the market or sampling new fall fashions at the boutique on the square. Nancy was welcomed by the Thursday night Bingo crowd and happily remained as a guest after driving Aletha to the Rosenbaums' forest retreat or to Bobby Taylor's house, where they were sure to find a pleasant mix of friends. Though wholly content to continue in her present position, Nancy began to feel she was taking advantage of Aletha's generosity. Aletha knew it but shrank from any change in a situation she found imminently satisfactory. As long as Nancy remained, under the pretense of providing skilled care, Aletha could postpone the prospect of eventually living alone again.

Still determined not to make herself a nuisance in Miles' and Marilyn's lives, Aletha saw no other alternative than a solitary existence, with Scout as her sole companion should Nancy's services be terminated. And knowing "Trudy" Gunn would return in December for the birth of their shared great-grandchildren, Aletha decided to allow things to continue as they were until that time. Alas, she was not given a choice in the matter. Nurse Simmons received a summons from her sister, insisting she come at once to their mother's bedside. It seemed she was on the brink of death and required round-the-clock attention. Aletha bid Nancy fond farewell early on a November Sunday morning and faced a life of solitude, at least for the present, with more resignation than optimism.

On that same Sunday, while Derek was speeding away on his own quest, Miles and Marilyn were preparing to leave church accompanied by Aletha. She would join them for lunch at their house before being returned to her own home. The interlude provided a buffer for the loss of her housemate. And any time spent with her son and his bride brought her great joy; their happiness helped bolster her flagging spirits. Aletha couldn't help noticing, however, that Miles acted somewhat preoccupied that afternoon. He was a bit vague in his conversation, and she could hear him fiddling with his silverware – a habit that had carried over from childhood. He must have come to a decision somewhere between the beef stew and the promised homemade lemon bars. While Marilyn was clearing the lunch dishes, he seated his mother on the couch and came directly to the point.

"Mother, I know you are well and truly mended, and I'm grateful that Nancy Simmons was able to stay with you during your recovery and beyond." He stopped and gently took Aletha's hand. "I won't beat around the bush; I am not comfortable with the idea of you living alone now that she's gone."

Aletha released a heartfelt sigh. "I am *so re –*"

"*–* Now, don't be resentful. *Please.* You *must* know that I respect your desire for independence, but I worry about leaving you with no one to be there if something should happen."

"That seems quite sens –"

"*– Senseless?* Mother, nothing about your safety is senseless."

Aletha began to show signs of agitation. "Timothy Miles Hawthorne, I did not raise you to act like a ninny! If you would just *listen –*"

Watching from the kitchen, Marilyn thought it time to intervene before mother and son found themselves hopelessly tangled in a fruitless yet entertaining exchange of mixed messages. She sat next to her husband and completely disarmed him by kissing his lean cheek. Miles looked at her in surprise, only to catch a mischievous smile on her lips. His stern features melted into bewilderment. Before he and Aletha could begin speaking at cross purposes again, Marilyn calmly explained everything as clearly as a UN translator disarming a heated argument between quarreling principalities.

"Aletha, you will be happy to know that Miles has found another companion for you." He was shocked to see his mother relax before his eyes. "She is not a registered nurse, as was Nancy, but she has an LPN license and has worked for several respected home-care agencies. Her name is Sheila Singleton. She is a widow, aged 49, and she has agreed to live in only as long as you have need of her, meaning she understands that her services may end when Gertie Gunn arrives in December. Sheila won't be available until Wednesday, so Timothy and I would be so pleased if you would be our guest until then. As you know, Angelica has moved back into her home in Tinkers Well, and she asked for the privilege of your company tomorrow while I am at school. Isaac and Deborah will collect you on Tuesday morning, along with Reenie Fields, to spend the day sampling delicious kosher recipes. And that takes us to Wednesday when Sheila will arrive at *Fern Cottage.*"

"You did that so well, my dear. Now why can't men be as perceptive as women. Timothy," Aletha said, addressing her astonished son. "If you had only let me speak, I would have told you that I was *relieved* by your suggestion, that I thought it quite *sensible,* and that your inability to grasp the obvious borders on idiocy!" She concluded on such an unusually tart note, Miles blinked and sat up straighter. Marilyn couldn't help laughing. A frail, elderly, woman had put her devastatingly attractive, self-assured, professional negotiator of a son in his place with a few pithy comments.

"Come with me, my clueless darling, and help me with the lemon bars. I'll explain everything," Marilyn promised. Miles followed obediently, still trying to figure out what had just happened.

Derek drove to Bailey Crossroads in a trance. Conscious thought would have reminded him that Kavya was working on an important research project due the following day. Memory would have told him she had no time for him. Reason would have highlighted the fact that she would not be alone; Ani would be at home, too. None of those tiresome mental processes impeded his mission. Born of an instinctive need to see Kavya, to hear her voice, to know that all the dissenting opinions were wrong, Derek raced blindly toward the woman whose image intruded on his every thought. When he finally reached the Aguilar home, Derek was surprised to find Kavya not only alone, but apparently happy to see him.

After practically pulling him into the house (a familiar paralysis had set in at the mere sight of her), she explained that the research project was miraculously completed early, and that she felt like celebrating. When he asked about Ani, she told him that the little girl had been attending St. Isidore Catholic Church with the Aguilars for several weeks and that they had not yet returned. He was so cheered by the news that Kavya had consented to let her daughter cross the threshold of *any* church, he allowed his emotions to dominate what little sound judgment he had left. On impulse, he suggested they go for a drive. Her answering smile sent his senses reeling.

"Grab a few of those old quilts in the basket by the door while I change my shoes."

Without asking why they needed blankets for a drive, Derek complied with her command. He had just thrown the quilts in the bed of his truck, after hastily emptying a month's worth of construction debris, when he turned to see an angel floating toward him. It never occurred to him to wonder how a simple change of shoes had changed everything. Her luxurious dark hair had escaped its perpetual ponytail and lay in cascading, silken strands on her shoulders. He knew nothing of make-up; he only knew her mysterious, amber eyes glowed behind their veiling lashes. The angel illusion was provided by a shimmering gold top worn with flowing cream-colored pants. Her gold, open-toed flats were hardly suitable for a brisk November day; Derek saw nothing but flirtatious, pink-tipped toes. He was glad she merely carried a black wool jacket. Donning it would have spoiled the whole effect.

Kavya *was* happy to see Derek. Over the course of five months, and against her will, she had been drawn to him more than to any other man she had ever known. Her futile attempts to throw barriers between them had been decimated by his smile, his kindness, and her own reluctant admission that she had come to trust him implicitly. In brutally honest moments of self-reflection, she admitted to herself that she did, in fact, love Derek Warner. The desire to spend time with him had driven her to complete her project early, and his unsolicited presence at her front door confirmed her suspicion that their hearts truly communicated as one. In her pleasure at discovering that everything had turned out just as she had hoped, Kavya chatted easily during the drive, providing Derek with intermittent directions to an unknown destination.

During a long stretch between turns, she waited for him to start bragging about something in what she had come to think of as his "smiling voice," but he remained strangely uncommunicative. She asked pointed questions to which he returned only monosyllabic answers. A cocky, self-assured Derek she knew how to deal with. The serious, taciturn man sitting next to her was an enigma. Not knowing how to reach him, Kavya settled for steering them to a clump of trees along a winding road. She had discovered the spot on one of her drives of discovery soon after her arrival in Kansas and had visited it several times whenever she needed the respite of solitude. Little did she know, it was the same spot an unsuspecting Rose Thompson had been lured to the year before.[19] That episode had almost been the other young woman's undoing. It was as well that Kavya was unaware of its ignoble history.

They spread the blankets on a bed of soft pine needles. Kavya half-sat, half-laid on her side and patted the spot next to her, inviting Derek to join her. He chose to remain standing as he wrestled with the weight of his thoughts. A cold dread began to creep over her heart at his refusal to lie next to her. When he finally spoke, she experienced, instead, such an upsurge of joy she felt weak.

"Kavya, there is something I have to say. I should have said it months ago, but I was afraid; afraid I would push you away; afraid that you could never feel the same way I do. Kavya Jackson, I love you. I love you so much it feels like a knife turning in my gut every time I think of you. I love your mind, I love your spirit, I love your beauty, I love the way you care for your aunt and uncle, and for the patience you show toward José and his struggles. But most of all, I love the way you love Ani. It takes an incredible woman to bring a life into the world alone; to raise a child whose wuss of a father rejected both you and her when you needed him most." Derek stopped speaking abruptly. He couldn't go on until Kavya said something, one way or another. Her response was the last thing he expected.

---

[19] Intersecting Lives

Suddenly covered in shame, Kavya looked away from Derek as she stood to answer him. "I, too, should have told you something months ago. But I was afraid. I thought if you knew the truth, you might not… I wasn't sure I could trust you to…" Forcing herself to look at him, Kavya finally said, on a defiant note, "I am not ashamed of making Ani my daughter." Derek found her choice of words curiously suggestive. "It wasn't easy at first. I didn't want the responsibility. I had spent most of my youth shouldered with the burden of duty to family. But when Tia Lupe came to Anika's funeral, she taught me how to love the baby; how to be a mother." Kavya could not bear to see the disillusionment and confusion in Derek's eyes. She lowered her own and spoke quietly. "Ani is not my child." Hearing Derek's quick intake of breath, she rushed on.

"After my sister's car accident, she was kept on life support until her baby could be safely delivered. Her boyfriend was also badly injured and in no condition to take on the care of an infant. Lupe's gentle spirit and selfless devotion to Anika's child saved us all. My love for Ani grew each day. Finally, I realized she was meant to be mine. She was my sister's parting gift to me. My devoted fiancé," she added, with a sardonic curl of the lip, "bolted as soon as he got a whiff of my plans.

"I legally adopted Ani. She is my daughter as surely as if I had given birth to her. I didn't tell you because I was afraid you might bolt, too. And by the time I knew you to be a man of honor and integrity, I didn't know how to tell you." She looked helplessly at Derek. Without a word, he pulled her into his arms and held her gently. Tears of relief fell from her eyes, and she clung to him, savoring his strength and understanding.

"Didn't you know?" Derek murmured, "I love Ani, too." Kavya rested in his arms until her tears stopped, and she could raise eyes glowing with love and gratitude to look into his.

"Didn't you know?" she said softly, "I love *you*, too." Her gently mocking smile invited the kiss they had both been longing for.

Gazing into eyes that sparkled with remnant teardrops, Derek believed himself to have been transported to heaven. But as he cupped Kavya's face with his hands, before tasting the nectar of her generous lips, Derek heard a single word repeated in his head. Heaven – the kingdom of a holy God who ordains his children to live as he wills, the promise of a loving God who directs the paths of his followers, enabling them to remain rooted in him rather than in the world that calls them from his righteous ways.

It's just a kiss, Derek told himself, desperately. *My love for Kavya won't change me.* In anguish, he heard the words of the morning Scripture reading echoing in his brain, *"What does light have in common with darkness?"* With a supreme effort, Derek dropped his arms and stepped away.

"I can't," he said in a strangled voice.

"You can't… what?" Kavya had proclaimed her love to the one man she dared to believe in, and he had stepped away. She felt as if she had turned to stone.

"Kavya, I meant every word I said. I love you, and I love Ani. But what future do we have if we can't share a knowledge and love for the God who orders our lives? I have tried to help you see that, to share my faith with you, to show you what it means to follow Jesus. You've carried such a heavy burden needlessly. Won't you let him take if from you?"

"Isn't it enough that I tolerate your insistence on religion? Can't you practice your precious faith without dragging me into it?" Kavya's voice took on a tinge of anger. "Tia Lupe understands. I let her take Ani to church, to let her be exposed to religion, just as I was as a child. I chose to live life as I see fit and not let anyone or anything dictate to me. She will be free to make her own decision, too. You ask me to respect your God? Why can't you respect my decision to be my own life guide?"

Derek couldn't believe what he was hearing. "Don't you *get* it? I am who I am *because* I followed the call of the only just and righteous God." Before he could stop himself, he gave her an impossible ultimatum. "If you truly loved me, you would embrace the Savior who calls me to be the man I am."

"And if you truly loved me, you would accept me for the woman *I am* without imposing your rigid dictates on me."

Clasping his hands on his head, Derek bent double. "Oh, God, what have I done?" he cried, rocking back and forth in a fit of anguish. Nothing had gone as he had hoped. His words of heartfelt devotion had somehow turned into unintentional accusation. He looked into Kavya's face, searching for any sign of softening. "Kavya, I never meant to hurt you. I have only ever wanted to love you, to share my life with you and Ani. I know you're angry now, but I'm begging you, don't shut me out. Can't we at least continue to see each other as friends?" As the words left his lips, Derek knew that such a relationship would only torment them both.

"*Friends?*" Kavya's anger, fueled by a bitter feeling of rejection, burned red hot. "I would gladly have given myself to you, body and soul, right here on this blanket – something I was never stupid enough to offer any other man – but you made it clear that I wasn't good enough for you." Hating herself for every cruel, unfeeling word she said, Kavya nevertheless continued to lash out at Derek as a twisted balm for her own pain. "*Friends?* You can take your sanctimonious religiosity and get out of my life. I don't need any friends. Ani and I will get along just fine without you."

Struggling to maintain the upper hand, Kavya threw the quilts into a heap and drug them toward the truck. Too late, she realized she was dependent on Derek for transportation. In her present state of injured fury, that would never do. Instead, she tossed the quilts into the truck bed and headed for the road on foot. Within seconds, she felt an iron clasp on her arm and was ruthlessly spun around to face Derek, who was now seething with his own combination of anger, resentment, and self-loathing.

"Get in the truck," he said through clenched teeth.

Kavya yanked her arm free. "I can get home by myself!"

"The hell you can," Derek muttered under his breath and dragged her, adamantly resisting, toward the driver's door. Wrenching it open, he demanded she take the seat. Furious that she had no recourse but to comply with his command, Kavya strapped the seatbelt around herself, intentionally avoiding his eyes.

"The keys are in the ignition. Now stop acting like a spoiled brat, and drive. I can walk to Tim's house from here. He can take me to retrieve my truck later."

"Ugh!!!" was all Kavya said as she ground the truck into gear and drove off in a cloud of dust.

A profound hunger was awakened in Lupe Aguilar. During her nephew's tenure as Derek Warner's housemate, José Nuñez had far surpassed her in the knowledge of Scripture and biblical teachings. Her understanding of God's Word had been largely spoon-fed over the years through references to various texts during weekly homilies by her local parish priest. Such teaching honored the sanctity and sacrifice of the Holy Trinity, and the many saints and apostles who had spread the gospel around the world. Lupe had been content to nibble at such spiritual crumbs until José made her aware of a veritable smorgasbord of biblical truths just waiting to be sampled.

Under Derek's leadership and tutelage, José had gradually learned his way around the Bible and developed a working knowledge of its structure, purpose, and cohesiveness from the Old Testament through the New. His heightened understanding inspired a desire to attend church more regularly with his aunt and uncle, and to discuss each day's lesson afterward. Carlos, who rarely said anything unless solicited, was content to listen to Lupe and José trading ideas. She soon realized she was falling behind. Despite a deeply ingrained understanding and love for Catholic history and tradition, Lupe was disappointed at her inability to tie such teachings directly to God's

Word. José did not have the time – or the patience – to help her, and in truth, such an endeavor would have been akin to the blind leading the blind.

When he mentioned Lupe's quandary to his buddy a month earlier, Derek put a bug in his mother's ear, suggesting she invite Lupe to attend the ladies' Bible study at Community Church. Angelica arranged her schedule accordingly, and the weekly venture became something she and Lupe anticipated jointly. After the very dramatic falling out between Derek and Kavya, the older ladies prayed together for some kind of resolution. Knowing the separation was in Derek's best interest in the long run, it nevertheless pained Angelica to see her son so unhappy. Lupe, too, had been disappointed in the breakup, but she still believed Derek to be the man for Kavya. Without knowing it, both ladies prayed for Kavya's heart to be opened to the message of Jesus, recognizing his divine grace to be the only solution.

Until that event occurred, they continued to study and pray. The latter presented no limiting parameters, but the former required that they gather at Community Church every Tuesday morning. Since Lupe took care of Ani whenever Kavya attended classes or worked in the research lab, she took the little girl with her. Though Kavya was none too pleased to be told her daughter would be playing in a church nursery while her aunt was otherwise occupied, she was in no position to argue. Following her falling out with Derek, she had insisted Ani stay home with her on Sundays, thus limiting her exposure to what she believed to be censorious Christian teachings. Kavya's emotional blinders distorted her perception of such beliefs. She would never allow herself to admit the truth of Derek's claim that he was the man she loved *because* of God's elevated prominence in his life, *not* in spite of it.

The Tuesday before Thanksgiving saw the usual gathering of women in the room designated for ladies' Bible studies and social events. The space doubled as the Bride's Room for weddings because of its convenient location off the main foyer of the church. A hallway connected the foyer to the education wing of the church, which also contained the church nursery. Six weeks of visits to the nursery had made Ani a regular, and she ran into the room eagerly when Lupe dropped her off. It was the only day of the week she had the opportunity to play with other children, and she made the most of it. Without a backward glance, Lupe returned to her class, knowing her little niece to be happy and well cared for.

On the Tuesday before Thanksgiving, the university would ordinarily be closed for the holiday. The lab was open to students, though, and Kavya took advantage of the time and relatively empty workspace to get a jumpstart on completing a semester project ahead of schedule. The plan failed, however, because her thoughts kept drifting to her final conversation with Derek, when they should have been focused on procedural protocols. After restarting one series of tests three times, she gave up in frustration. Kavya knew her aunt would be in Tinkers Well for her weekly Bible study, so she decided to meet her and Ani at the church and suggest they go out for lunch together. Aware that her attitude of late had been unpleasant at best, Kavya's conscience compelled her to at least make peace with her family. She stubbornly refused to admit her longing to make peace with Derek. Nor would she give credence to the idea that Derek's absence was the direct link to a persistent emptiness she could not fill. Kavya blinked away unwelcome tears and kept driving.

On that Tuesday before Thanksgiving, the Community Church kitchen hummed with activity preparatory to the Wednesday evening feast offered to those in the greater Tinkers Well area who would not otherwise be able to enjoy such a celebration. The halls of the church were redolent with the tantalizing aroma of roast turkey and stuffing prepared early for quick reheating before serving. One of the favorite tastes associated with the meal was Edith Hitchins' homemade turkey gravy. She expertly seasoned the flour for thickening and drew drippings from the cooking pans in the oven, heaping layer upon layer of delicious flavor into every drop. She had just completed preparation of a large batch and put it in a ceramic dish to cool. Counter space in the busy kitchen was limited, so she sat the dish on an unused stove burner. Edith was sure the gas burner was unlit, but since she couldn't see any flame under the oversized dish, she conscientiously made sure the burner switch was in, what she believed to be, the off position. The rich aroma of cooking rose to the floor above where children in the nursery became aware of something yummy in the air, though it was doubtful whether they could identify the source. The smell teased their noses enough that they requested their snacks early.

At eleven o'clock on that Tuesday before Thanksgiving, Derek stopped at the church between scheduled jobs in the hope of seeing Ani. He had followed the practice for the past three weeks, knowing Kavya would have resented his appearance at the Aguilar home on any pretext. The truth was that he felt the absence of little Ani in his life. While his entire being ached for her mother, he also missed spending time with the little girl and savoring her mischievous smile. He longed to hear her silly chatter and to receive one of her warm, impetuous hugs. So, he parked in a far corner of the parking lot and waited.

Because there were many prayer requests that morning, Angelica was late ending the closing prayer with her soft-spoken "Amen." All was well until…

The peace of the moment disintegrated into pandemonium when someone pulled the fire alarm in the education building. A few minutes later, the piercing wail of the town's emergency siren blotted out everything but unspecified fear. Still sitting in his truck, Derek looked up from his phone to see smoke issuing from a basement window just as his pager began buzzing incessantly. He jumped out of his truck and climbed into the bed where he kept his fire gear in a utility box. Donning it quickly, he ran toward the fire as he heard the scream of a siren approaching.

Cooks, along with the event set-up crew, ran out the basement doors between the kitchen and Fellowship Hall, while the ladies of the Bible study streamed out the front entrance, followed by frightened children evacuated from the nursery. Mothers, along with Angelica and Lupe, hurried to comfort the little ones who were terrified by all the noise and commotion. The nursery workers frantically counted heads to make sure all had made it out of the building safely. Kavya Jackson pulled into the parking lot in the wake of the city's fire engine and desperately sought a glimpse of her daughter. When she jumped out of her car, she almost collided with a fireman, hauling a hose toward a hydrant.

"Ma'am, the kids should have been evacuated through the emergency exit on the end of this building, but no one has come out that way. We think the fire started in the kitchen," he told her, while he worked. "They must have taken the kids out the front of the building." Nodding toward the sanctuary, he suggested, "Go around that end of the church and I'm sure you'll find her." That was all he had time for. When he looked up after connecting the hose to the hydrant, she was gone.

Rounding the front corner of the church on wings of panic, Kavya caught sight of Lupe talking to someone. She looked scared to death, which only increased Kavya's own fears. When she reached her aunt, Kavya heard the other woman say, "We've counted three times, and we keep coming up one short. We can't find Ani. She must still be *in the nursery!*"

Kavya's first instinct was to run headlong into the building. She would have faced Dante's *Inferno* to save her daughter. Her second instinct was more productive. She raced back to the parking lot in search of help. Derek must be there by now, she thought. He would know what to do. But when she got to the fire engine, he was nowhere in sight. Two firefighters were manning the hose, and she could see two others investigating the emergency exit. When they reached the open door, a wall of flames greeted them. They slammed it quickly and ran back to the truck.

Despite a growing sense of desperation, Kavya fought to keep her emotions in check. Hysteria would not help her daughter. Approaching the man who seemed to be in charge, Kavya explained the situation. The fire chief was kind, but firm. "Look, I know you're worried, but you'll have to stay back and let us find her. Thanks to you, we know where to search." Kavya took little solace from his words. If only Derek had been there, she told herself. But when she needed him most, he was conspicuously absent. Without realizing what she was doing, Kavya began to pray. She didn't even know who she was praying to, but it's what Derek would have done. The more discouraged she became, the harder she prayed until she found herself on her knees with her face to the ground.

A fifth firefighter had been unstrapping a ladder from the truck when Kavya was talking to the chief. After receiving approval from his superior, he grabbed a partner, and they headed to the far side of the education wing with the ladder. One braced the ladder against the building, while the other man climbed up to the second story and broke a window to gain entrance. There was little sign of the fire in the room other than smoke billowing outside the windows. He moved quickly to a corner of the room where he went to work with an axe to break through the floor, then the ceiling of the room below. Through the opening, he could see toys and walls covered in colorful murals. The room showed evidence of a hasty departure with spilled glasses of milk and plates of crackers strewn across the surface of a short table. He let himself down into the nursery while keeping a steadying hand on the rope secured around his waist. His partner held the other end, waiting for a signal to initiate retrieval.

The fireman made a swift but methodical search of the room. There were few places to conceal a small child, but he had been trained to look everywhere, knowing children often hide when frightened. All the lower cabinets contained nothing but what might be expected in a nursery: diapers, paper, crayons, and plastic cups and plates. He checked the small restroom between the toddler and infant rooms without success. A sense of urgency such as he had never known gripped his heart. He could feel the heat intensify in the floor under his boots and knew it was only a matter of minutes before the fire would consume the room. Already flames were forcing their way up through the floor and the air was growing thick with smoke. In desperation, he closed his eyes and listened. A terrified whimper, punctuated by harsh coughing, could be heard coming from a corner where a storage cabinet was built flush with the wall. A simple changing table had been rolled away from the cabinet about eight inches, and the door was slightly ajar. Clearing the table out of the way, he yanked the cabinet open to find a little girl huddled between piles of sheets and towels.

It was against protocol, but he didn't care. This little girl was special. He ripped off his mask and placed it over her nose and mouth. "Breathe, baby, *breathe*. Now take a deep breath and hold it." When he saw her hold her breath, he took the mask from her, filled his lungs, then strapped the mask around her head. Wrapping her inside his jacket, he ran for the hole he had cut through the ceiling. He began tugging on the rope as he ran and could feel the answering lift when he reached the ceiling opening. It was none too soon. The floor beneath his feet gave way as he hung precariously between heaven and hell. The rope continued to tow him while hands reached down to pull him to safety. Opening his jacket, he lifted up his priceless cargo and yelled, "Get her some O_2!" before retrieving his mask, but not before inhaling more of the suffocating smoke. He'd have sworn his boots were melting off his feet by the time he made it to the upper floor, and his lungs burned unbearably.

Once on the ground, paramedics stripped him of his gear and attempted to administer oxygen while he sat on the tailgate of an ambulance. He would have none of it until he was assured that his efforts had been successful. "Did I get to her in time?" he asked in a raspy voice, laboring to breathe. "Will my Ani be alright?"

"Thanks to you, she'll be fine. She's in the other ambulance with her mother. And I might add, she's a better patient than you are. Now, shut up and start breathing!" Suddenly weary to the bone, Derek Warner leaned against the door of the ambulance and gulped in the life-giving oxygen.

When word reached the occupants of the second ambulance that Ani's rescuer was safe, a grateful mother insisted on being allowed to express her gratitude to the man who had saved her child. Kavya Jackson approached the other vehicle with great humility, unsure of how to adequately thank him for his heroic actions. But before reaching the back of the ambulance, she stopped. She could hear someone being ruthlessly berated.

"You young *idiot!*" Kavya recognized the voice of the chief now furious with pent-up anger. "Do you know how many rules you ignored? You put your life in danger, which means someone else might have had to risk his own to go after you! I've never met anyone with less respect for his training, the badge, or his brothers! I *should* put you on suspension…" In a grudging tone, he added. "The medics tell me that little girl might not have made it without your air… good job, son."

Kavya hurried to the back of the ambulance and stared in disbelief at the miracle that met her astonished gaze. *"You!"* was the only word she uttered. Every nerve in her body began to vibrate like a bow string before she collapsed on the ground in a dead faint.

CHAPTER 17

– to bestow on them a crown of beauty instead of ashes, the oil of joy instead of mourning, and a garment of praise instead of a spirit of despair.

Isaiah 61:3(NIV)

When the smoke cleared and the ash settled, the education building of Community Church was a hollow, charred ghost, devoid of life. Miraculously, the fire was contained within that structure alone, sparing the sanctuary and the fellowship hall below thanks to the arrival of a second fire engine and crew from a neighboring county.

Investigation traced the fire's source to the ceramic bowl filled with gravy – gravy containing fat from the turkey drippings. When Edith Hitchins placed the bowl on the burner and turned the dial to "off," she mistakenly turned it on. Any markings on or around the worn knob had been rubbed off years ago. And her inability to see the flames, hidden by the large container, left her secure in her actions. She moved on to sautéing celery and onions for the stuffing and never so much as glanced at the gravy. The heat from the mistakenly activated burner eventually shattered the ceramic bowl, sending boiling hot, fat-infused gravy onto neighboring burners.

The exploding gravy shocked everyone, and the room was thrown into a tizzy, while ladies rushed to and fro trying to snuff out the fire. One remembered to smother a fire, so she dumped the hot vegetables from the frying pan into the sink and inverted it over one burner. The residual cooking oil only caused the fire to flare up. Another remembered, incorrectly, to throw flour on a fire. Before anyone could stop her and remind her it was baking soda, not flour, that was needed, she had grabbed the flour canister next to the stove and attempted to empty its contents onto the blaze. The canister exploded. A spontaneous fireball erupted and filled the room with smoke, thus obscuring the location of the fire extinguisher, and sending all the cooks running from the room in terror. Hours earlier, a conscientious staff member had propped open the emergency door for the fire exit mistakenly thinking the aroma of cooking might not be appreciated on the upper floors. (The 30-year-old vent hood had vented its last fumes the year before.) That portal to fresh air drew the fire like a magnet. The kitchen workers ran instead to the basement entrance shared with the Fellowship Hall and slammed the door behind them. By then, the fire had taken on a life of its own. Those who watched helplessly from afar were devastated. But in the midst of devastation there was rejoicing; a precious life had been spared.

During the initial moments following Ani's rescue, only those immediately concerned were aware of the ensuing drama. When Derek saw Kavya collapse, he wanted to race to her aid, but his strength was used up, and one of the paramedics had her in hand almost instantaneously. Lying on her back, with her feet elevated, Kavya came around within minutes. She immediately looked for Derek, but his ambulance was already on its way to the hospital in Kansas City. She was helped to Ani's side – her knees were still a little wobbly – and their ambulance soon followed.

Both patients were admitted for overnight observation. When Kavya could see Ani's breathing normalize, with only intermittent coughing, she sang softly to her until the little girl fell into the slumber of exhaustion. Knowing Ani would sleep for some time, Kavya sought out Derek in the ER, where he was resting until a ward bed became available. News of his heroic efforts spread almost as quickly as the fire had. When the ER staff learned that Kavya was the mother of the child he had rescued, they couldn't do enough for her. One nurse kindly escorted her to his cubicle, while another found a chair for her to sit on. Derek, too, appeared to be asleep, so they left them in peace and pulled the drape closed, allowing for a modicum of privacy.

As soon as Kavya saw him lying there, his nose and mouth covered by an oxygen mask and an IV line taped to his hand, she was overcome by the reality of all that she might have lost if not for his courage. Her legs grew unsteady again and she sat down abruptly on the chair next to his bed. She was desperate to let him know she was there and that she loved him. Afraid to even hold his hand for fear of jarring his IV needle, she laid her head next to his leg and poured out her heart to a sleeping man.

"Derek, I was so wrong. I was wrong about everything – about you, about us, about God. I don't fully understand who he is, but with everything that has happened in the past few hours, I was finally able to rid myself of all my prejudices and misconceptions, and I could see, really see for the first time, that he has been orchestrating my life since I was a child. He used Isabella to teach me simple truths I should have been able to understand, but I was stubborn, even then. I wanted to believe in a God who would make my life easy and guard me from pain. So, when my mother got sick, I got angry. I never told you this – I never told *anyone* – but I actually prayed for her; not to her Hindu statues, but to the God I wanted so badly to believe was listening. Somehow, I think she heard me and was praying *with* me. Toward the end, when she should have been more distressed with declining function, she seemed more peaceful and relaxed. I swear, she died with a smile on her face. The hospice nurse told me it was just an involuntary muscle contraction. I never said anything because I didn't want to appear foolish. I *hate* to appear foolish. You of all people know that, but you've never mocked me, even though I've been so mean-spirited and unfair to you." Kavya's voice was momentarily suspended by tears. She brushed them away and went on.

"Still, I couldn't see her death as a release, I could only see it as a punishment... for me, because I had doubted. Then Anika died, and I was left with a baby to raise. You know about my struggle to embrace motherhood and how much I came to love Ani, but all I could feel when my fiancé walked out on me was more of God's punishment. If I had only had the faith that you have, I might have seen that departure as God's way of leaving the door open for you to walk into my life. But I had developed such a cynical, distrustful attitude about men, Jesus could have shown up in person and presented you to me, and I would have argued with him. I did argue – with Lupe, with you, with myself."

Kavya's voice, again, grew thick with emotion. "And then I thought of Ani trapped in the fire, and I prayed for a miracle. I didn't know how that was possible since you weren't there, because I knew as sure as I'm sitting here, that only you could get to her in time. But I kept praying. When I saw her carried down the ladder by a fireman, I was sure it must be you. But it wasn't. I went with her to the ambulance, so I didn't see you come down. And then, when I went to thank whoever was responsible, I couldn't believe it was you all the time." With her throat constricted from weeping, Kavya whispered, "Derek Warner, you are... and always will be... my miracle."

Far from being asleep, Derek had been very much awake and aware of every word Kavya had spoken. With each syllable, he felt his body suffused with life and energy... and hope. The sound of her sobbing into his blanket nearly brought him to his feet until he realized they were cleansing tears, washing away years of self-imposed, emotional isolation.

The sound of her distress carried to a doctor passing by who pulled the curtain back to investigate. "Mr. Warner, is ev..." He didn't complete the question. Inasmuch as it is possible for someone to glare with one eye shut, Derek Warner did. The last person he wanted there at that moment was a doctor. His left eye remained closed; let Kavya think he was asleep. With the other eye, he communicated effectively, "Brother, you need to *leave –*

immediately – and close the curtain behind you, thank you very much!" The doctor grinned and complied… without a sound.

When her emotion was spent, Kavya stood and gazed at Derek with a tenderness that would have melted his heart into a puddle of mush – had he been aware of it. Finally deciding it was time to join the conversation openly, Derek stretched and twitched a little. The signs of impending consciousness sent Kavya into a panic. She was suddenly covered in confusion, wondering if he had heard any of her unguarded declaration. Confession was one thing. Deeply meaningful dialogue was another. She kissed his forehead and ran blindly from the intimate space. The two nurses, who had taken her to see Derek, looked at one another and went to investigate. They found the patient no longer wearing a mask and lying with his free hand under his head. His smile, displayed in unabashed splendor, was bright enough to illuminate an entire hospital during a power outage. His pulse was strong and steady, perhaps even a little fast, but he appeared to be recovering nicely.

From the beginning, Aletha Mason had misgivings about her new housemate. Without any obvious shortcoming she could sink her teeth into, Aletha was sure the newcomer was untrustworthy. Sheila Singleton was respectful and pleasant enough in her speech. But, to Aletha, she seemed a little too… nice – shades of the Big Bad Wolf in grandmother's clothing. Nancy had been crisp and professional, and Aletha had instinctively known her to be a sympathetic spirit. When Nurse Singleton arrived (Aletha felt she simply could not call her Sheila), she appeared to have a clear understanding of what was expected of her and proved to Miles' satisfaction that she could make a decent cup of tea. After graciously waving farewell to him as he drove off, leaving his mother alone with her new caregiver, a different Singleton emerged. Retreating into *Fern Cottage,* she immediately set about telling Aletha how things were to be run. It was all done in such a subtle, honey-coated way that anyone not possessing Aletha's keen powers of perception might have been taken in. The old woman decided there and then to catch the creature in some dubious undertaking. Far from imagining herself in any kind of danger, Aletha embraced the situation. She would not run to Miles and Marilyn without concrete evidence, and gathering such evidence would add a little excitement to what had become a somewhat tedious existence.

Two weeks passed without any significant incident to which Aletha could pin her growing unease. She still saw her son and his wife once a week or so, but they were both so busy trying to manage various facets of *Veritas Academy,* she felt a little guilty about placing added demands on their time. Singleton assured Aletha that many of her friends had stopped by for impromptu visits ("Most inconsiderate, in my opinion," she would say), but Aletha never recalled hearing a car drive up or the sound of the doorbell. She was told, "Oh, you know how you tend to doze off," though it had *never* been her habit to doze off at all hours of the day. Still, she found herself waking up later and later each morning, often with a headache. Aletha thought of these as trifling matters and kept them to herself. Then she began to develop a slight wheezing cough, which seemed nonsensical, given the fact that she rarely went out of doors since the weather had turned colder, and Singleton was not inclined to exercise. She decided to get her own exercise by walking laps throughout the house with Scout as company.

During these seemingly aimless rounds, she began to take inventory. Though now profoundly blind, Aletha had moved into *Fern Cottage* while she still had limited sight and before her husband Martin died. Together, they chose each piece of furniture, wall hanging, and *objet d'art* displayed throughout the house. And she knew the pieces, and their placement, better than any sighted person.

While sauntering slowly by the large hall stand next to the front door, Aletha reached out for an umbrella with a silver handle. She had given the elegant gift to Martin on their 25th anniversary, and he had carried it with pride. It was missing. Waiting until she knew Singleton to be in the bathroom, Aletha made a quick check of the buffet in the dining room. The sterling silver flatware and tea service had vanished. Before she went to Miles with her discoveries, she decided to share her news with Trudy. Her friend could always be depended upon to know how to deal with the criminal element. When she reached in her pocket for her cellphone… it was gone. She was searching her room when Singleton emerged from the hall bath.

"Now, what on earth can you be looking for?" she asked innocently, though her eyes took on a steely glint. Aletha might not have seen the calculated look, but she sensed something amiss.

"I cannot find my cell phone. It wasn't in my pocket when I reached for it, and I *know* I picked it up this morning after I got dressed."

"I'm sure it's right where you left it, dearie. Let's have a look around. We wouldn't want people thinking you were growing forgetful, now would we." Aletha resented the patronizing tone as much as she despised the implication of Singleton's words. "Why, here it is on the nightstand still attached to the charging cable."

Aletha felt her first premonition of danger, though it wasn't directed at Singleton. She began to wonder if she was experiencing the onset of dementia. Not one to jump to conclusions, she decided to have a cup of tea to steady her nerves while she listened to one of her favorite books on CD. Settling herself in the library, she gratefully accepted the tea prepared by Singleton. It was hot and strong, though a trifle over-sweetened. The narrator of the story droned on as Aletha's eyes grew heavy. She awoke to the smell of lunch being prepared in the kitchen and hurried into her new master bath, where she might find some privacy. Before calling Trudy, she washed her hands and reached for the hand towel by the sink. Instead of a towel, she felt the handle of an umbrella hanging there – Martin's umbrella. With shaking hands, she lifted the umbrella and confronted Singleton with the discovery.

"Why, however did that come to be in your bathroom, dearie?" the creature exclaimed in typical gushing fashion. "I saw it on the hall stand just this morning. I wondered where it had got to." Aletha remained silent, while she frantically attempted to process the woman's words. "I wouldn't worry too much. We all forget things from time to time. Dinner will be ready soon. Just you sit here at the kitchen table while I finish getting it ready."

Dinner? Aletha shouted in her head. *I never ate lunch! Or did I? Am I losing my mind?* When she heard the chair being pulled out for her, she sat dutifully and gave up on any idea of calling Trudy. What would she say? Until she had sorted out the increasing number of strange, unexplained events, she dared not speak of them. After dinner, while Singleton cleaned the kitchen, Aletha stealthily returned to the dining room and once again checked the items in the buffet. All the sterling silver was in its place.

So many families had been eager to enroll their children in *Veritas Academy,* that the decision was made to open its doors, at least figuratively speaking, before the campus itself was completed. Thanks to the willingness of Community Church to support the enterprise, the school year began in the education wing of the church.

During the entire month of October, Miles had been working overtime to move up the completion date of December 31st, knowing two of the church's busiest seasons to be Advent and Christmas. The loss of meeting space on weekdays would pose a bigger problem for many ministries during that period, so he had been pushing for a move-in date of the Monday following the Thanksgiving weekend. Calling on every connection and favor owed him within the property development world, the impossible was accomplished. The deadline was met on the Tuesday before Thanksgiving – at least for the K-5 classes, which were all Community Church had been able to accommodate. Since staffing for the more complex educational demands of a middle school was still incomplete, with several teachers committing to the following school year, the site developer agreed to pour his resources into finishing the first phase, allowing more focus for the other later in the spring and summer. The early completion turned out to be more fortuitous than imagined.

In another miraculous turn of events, the school was not in session for the entire week of Thanksgiving, and believing an early move to the new facility would be possible after all, any books, posters, and other educational supplies were removed the week before. Not a student or administrator was present during the fire. But they were all aware of its aftermath. Without hesitation, the new school leadership returned the generosity of Community Church by opening their doors for Sunday school indefinitely. And, until the church had been thoroughly inspected for any hidden structural damage and the possible harmful effects of residual smoke, Sunday services would be held in the school lunchroom, which doubled as the auditorium.

Their preoccupation with building completion had impacted the frequency with which Miles and Marilyn had been able to visit Aletha, though they called her regularly. If she sounded unusually reserved, they attributed the change to the challenge of learning to live with a new caregiver. She attended church with them twice. On the Saturday before Thanksgiving, Miles received a call from Sheila Singleton, reporting that Aletha was a little under the weather and should spend a few days in bed without visitors. Sending her their love, Miles hung up and shared the news with his wife.

On the following day, after the Sunday service, they were accosted by several of Aletha's church friends, who were concerned that she was no longer taking any calls and that they were refused admittance to her house when they dropped by unannounced. In the church parking lot, Miles was approached by the Rosenbaums. They had driven into town for the express purpose of making Aletha's son aware of their disquiet over her strange reticence to see them, and of her absence from regular events like Thursday night Bingo. Checking with Tim and Rose, Miles was told much the same thing. Concern for his mother began to break through the haze of final construction details. The Ludlows were a little surprised that he sought information from them. Miles had proven himself to be quite assiduous to his mother's needs since re-entering her life. But then, they had their own preoccupation; the twins were due in just over five weeks, and their impending arrival took precedence over everything else. Rose was shocked, therefore, when she received a call out of the blue from Granny Gert on Monday telling her that she needed to be picked up at the airport the next day.

"I don't understand what has happened to Letha. Or why no one has been to see her. I couldn't get anything out of that Singleton woman when I called at the house, so I decided somebody needed to find out what in heaven's name is going on. I know I wasn't supposed to come until next month with your mother, but that might be too late." Gert continued in the same vein all the way from the airport to Tinker's Well. Later that day, news of the devastating fire took an immediate backseat to more pressing concerns. Calls were made that night and a plan of action formulated. At exactly 9:00 the following morning it was implemented.

A team of Special Forces soldiers decked out in full camouflage and armed to the teeth would have struck less fear in the heart of Sheila Singleton than the formidable group demanding admittance to *Fern Cottage.* She grudgingly opened the door to Miles' peremptory knock and was effectively sidelined when he entered with Marilyn, Tim, Angelica Warner, Bobby Taylor, and Isaac and Deborah Rosenbaum in his wake. Gert crossed the threshold last. Leveling her piercing gaze at Singleton, who had shrunk into the background, she said, "You don't know me, but I guarantee you won't forget me! Now where is Letha?"

"She's not well this morning," Singleton answered in her most ingratiating tone, attempting to regain mastery of the situation. "I'm sure you understand the importance of not overwhelming the poor soul." It was impossible for her to push everyone outside; they had already breached her meager barricade and stood with grim expectation in the parlor. She quickly recalculated her options and began to sidle toward the hall. "If you'll just wait here, I'll go and see if she is up to receiving company."

Before Singleton could break free of the imposing crowd, Gert moved to block her path and started barking orders like a ship's boatswain coming into port. "Isaac, you and Bobby keep her here. Don't let her out of your sight, and don't let her get away. Tackle her if you have to; I know you can. Tim, block the back door. Sonny (as Gert liked to address any man she felt needed to be put in his place), call the police. I think they might want to have a little chat with *Ms.* Singleton."

"While I appreciate your excellent stage management, Mrs. Gunn," Miles said, with a touch of humor in his voice, "don't you feel summoning the police might be a bit premature."

Without batting an eyelid, she answered, "If that woman hasn't loaded her suitcases and car with loot, I'll eat my hat! You ladies come with me."

The smile was wiped from Miles' face in an instant as he contemplated the implications of Gert's words. He looked around and was shocked to find ornate picture frames missing from the walls and priceless trinkets absent from their places of honor. An intricately woven tapestry in the living room had also disappeared. He looked up to see his son exiting through the sliding door off the new family room addition. "Tim," he called sharply, "what is it?"

"I heard Scout – outside. He's been tied up, and the poor guy looks like he hasn't eaten in days!"

While the men rescued Scout and carried out their orders to the letter, the ladies entered Aletha's room with trepidation. They were almost knocked over by the stench. Angelica went quickly to the bed and reached under the bedclothes to discover the sheets were wet and soiled. Gertie and Marilyn had to shake Aletha awake, and when she came around, she began spouting nonsense about secret agents taking her hostage, and the need to free the other prisoners. She asserted the bizarre claims between paroxysms of uncontrolled wheezing. The source of the latter was made apparent when they heard Deborah's cry of dismay and saw her closing both windows, left open at the bottom. It was only then they noticed the chill in the room.

"Sonny!" Gert called in a voice of undisguised urgency. Miles appeared as if by magic. "We need to move Letha to another room and get her warmed up – fast!" She turned to see Angelica wrapping Aletha in several blankets after having stripped away her wet nightgown and underwear. Miles lifted her effortlessly and carried her to the parlor, where he laid her on the couch. Deborah and Marilyn rubbed her vigorously from head to toe until they felt warmth creeping back into her frozen limbs. By the time the ambulance arrived, Angelica had packed an overnight bag with her toiletries, clean nightgowns, and slippers. In the interim, Scout had been restored with food and affection and was ready to ride with his mistress to the hospital.

Miles and Marilyn followed quickly, promising to pass along any updates. They left Isaac and Bobby faithfully keeping a close watch on their prisoner until the police arrived to collect her. Agreeing to lock up after the officers had completed a preliminary search of the property, Tim stood alone with Granny Gert on the porch to see everyone off. He put his arm around her drooping shoulders and thanked her for being such a faithful friend to his grandmother. She astonished them both when she leaned against his substantial shoulder and promptly burst into tears.

Four days passed following the fire without a word from Derek. Kavya didn't know what to make of his silence. He had evidently not heard a word of her monologue in the hospital and was probably still angry over their previous encounter. He would be unaware that her crisis of faith had been resolved in a life-changing personal revelation. After her harsh disavowal of his insistence that it was Jesus who had shaped him into the man she loved, and having left him with the mistaken understanding that she still openly disdained any expression of faith, Kavya feared he might never forgive her.

She doubted he would even believe her. She was left in the uncomfortable position of wondering what she should do. Her misguided belief in God's irrational punishment threatened to surface again, but she firmly put it behind her, trusting instead in the faithful God who was slowly revealing himself to her.

Tia Lupe had done her best to lighten the mood – to help everyone forget the danger that was past and to celebrate the joy that remained. With the help of little Ani, who rarely left her mother's side, Lupe covered the windows with colorful, stick-on plastic leaves and made paper chains to drape across all the doorways. Despite her efforts, Thanksgiving in the Aguilar home was a little flat that year. José spent the weekend with the family, providing a sweet memory of times past, but one conspicuous absence left Kavya feeling restless and worried.

Of course, she told herself, *Derek has his own family and friends. He'll be spending the holiday with them.* But she couldn't help thinking – after all he had done for Ani – that he should at *least* stop by and check on *her*. Then Kavya recalled the startling news they had heard about Aletha Mason, and how distraught her friends were – including Derek's mother – and she was ashamed of her selfish thoughts.

While listlessly setting the table for dinner Saturday night, she heard the doorbell ring. In her frenzied attempt to reach the door before the last echo faded away, Kavya dropped two plates, tripped over a chair, and collided with Tio Carlos, who was already ushering several unexpected guests into the house. Inexplicably, Kavya suddenly shied away. Ani was not so afflicted. She flew past her mother, yelling, "Dewek! Dewek,!" and hugged her hero tightly when he lifted her in his arms and swung her around in circles. "I miss you," she said sternly. "Why you dinin' come see me?"

Rubbing her button nose with his thumb, he softly reminded her, "I came to see you on Tuesday. You were so brave, and I was *so* proud of you!" The little girl glowed and hugged him tighter. "Now you need to let me go so I can talk to your mama." José received Ani and lifted her to his shoulders so she could see better. She had more at stake from the outcome of the next few minutes than anybody else. While everyone's eyes were on Derek, Angelica moved into the room and stood next to Lupe. Only Kavya appeared astounded when Dwayne and Isabella Jackson joined the crowd.

With a look that made her knees go wobbly again, Derek advanced on Kavya and claimed her hands before she could argue or start demanding answers. In the back of her mind, she couldn't help thinking that his customary swagger had been transformed into something far more lethal for a woman in her precarious emotional state – an unshakable assurance in himself and his mission. She waited a little breathlessly for him to say something. When he did, it was at a level calculated for her ears only.

"I heard every word you said in the hospital. Every. Single. Word. I wanted to jump off the bed and start dancing! But I had my reasons for not saying anything… then. I'm going to talk now… and *you* are going to listen." At that moment, Kavya couldn't have put two coherent words together with the aid of cue cards. Tearing his eyes away from the image that had both taunted and inspired him for so long, Derek looked around the room and addressed the large group filling the tiny home almost to fire-code occupancy limits.

"I have something to say to Kavya, and I wanted you all here as witnesses. You are the people who have put up with the two of us the longest, so you have a right to hear this." He could feel Kavya trembling. Gripping her hands more tightly, he held them against his chest. "Kavya, you and I are getting married as soon as we can settle on a date and a place." When she gasped and opened her mouth to speak, he quickly squashed any retort. "*Girl*, did you not just hear me say *I* am going to do all the talking now? As you would probably point out if I let you – and I won't – I didn't ask you if you *would* marry me. I am *telling* you that you *will*, because I'm not about to give you a chance to say no." Something between a sob and a spurt of laughter escaped Kavya's lips and tears began to spill over her tremulous smile. "When I called your dad on Wednesday – Lupe helped me with that – he agreed that the element of surprise was the best plan of attack. As you can see, he also agreed to fly out here with Isabella to meet the guy who dared to think he was good enough for you. One more thing – I plan to adopt Ani and claim her as my own. If she's going to be a big sister someday – and I sincerely hope she is, several times over – I want her to be a Warner like the rest of us." Before Kavya could say anything, he turned to Ani and asked, "I want to be your Daddy, baby girl. Would that be okay with you?" She answered by bobbing up and down on José's shoulders and slapping his head in delight.

Kavya attempted to appear indignant despite a shining smile; she couldn't let Derek think he would *always* get away with such high-handed tactics! "Oh, so you *ask* Ani, but you *tell* me."

"Absolutely. *Ani* is smart enough to know a good thing when she sees it."

"Oh, for the love of God, Kavya," Dwayne Jackson said, moved to interject some rare fatherly advice, "live as argumentatively as you like for the rest of your lives; just marry the man!"

Pleased with his future father-in-law's timely recommendation, Derek once more spoke to those gathered expressly for the occasion. "Unless anyone, other than my fiancée, has an objection, do I hear an 'Amen?'"

The room burst into shouts of "Amen!" and various forms of "Thank Goodness!" and "*Finally!*"

Under cover of the resulting commotion, Derek lowered his voice and murmured in Kavya's ear, "Let me make this clear right now; no matter how much we may *want* to, there will be no giving of any *body* to any *other* body until we are married. Agreed?" He felt her responsive shiver. Addressing the room once more, Derek made his final declaration. "Now, if you all will excuse us, we're going to step outside for a few minutes." He turned such an intense gaze on Kavya, *every* joint in her body went wobbly. "If I don't kiss you within the next 30 seconds, my *head* is going to explode!"

Carlos grinned and held the door wide, while Lupe threw a coat over her niece's shoulders. Kavya Jackson, who had always felt the need to control every situation, meekly submitted to the tug of Derek's hand. The two lovers exited in haste and didn't make an appearance again until dinner time, some 45 minutes later.

CHAPTER 18

When her time came to give birth, there were indeed twins in her womb.
Genesis 25:24(HCSB)

The year marched relentlessly to a close, while new beginnings continued to crop up everywhere. Unusually fine 60-degree weather made move-in day at *Veritas Academy,* on the first Monday of December, easier and better attended than had been hoped for. Older students and parents of children from all grades were ready to work when furniture and supplies arrived. Teachers supervised disposition of classroom assets between decorating and touch-up cleaning. Little of the latter was needed. *Veritas Academy* gleamed in the late autumn sunshine.

When Marilyn Hawthorne walked through the front doors, a lump rose in her throat. This modern center for learning was not only a gift to Harrington and surrounding counties; it was a daily reminder of Miles' sacrifice of time, money, and professional prominence all because of his love for her. Just as he had imagined, the school's motto, emblazoned in gold lettering, was displayed prominently on the wall opposite the entry doors.

You will know the truth, and the truth will set you free.
John 8:32

When the entire school body arrived the following day, decked out in appropriate uniforms complete with a sweater for each student embossed with the school crest, an air of excitement and hope filled the air. The feeling was infectious – infectious, that is, for everyone except the academy's visionary founder. Miles Hawthorne came by to see the polished fruits of his labor, the first phase anyway. He had great faith in a summer completion for the second. But, for the present, his heart was elsewhere.

Since his mother's rescue the week before – he could think of the concerted operation in no other terms – Miles had been haunted by the memory of her condition. It took four days before the beneficial effects of powerful IV antibiotics brought an end to Aletha's ravings. It took a full week before the infection had cleared up enough to enable her to tell her story. Miles visited her every day. His guilt at missing the signs of elder abuse caused him to sink into such gloom, it took all of Marilyn's persuasive words to convince him he was not alone in his guilt and regret. *Everyone* closest to Aletha had missed the signs.

Marilyn's excuse, like Miles', was that of tunnel vision focused on the new school. Angelica had been preoccupied with the revelations regarding her late husband's death. Those revelations, as they were connected, indirectly, with Albie Dawson and his daughter, served to entwine the Dawson and Warner families more than ever. And Angelica had had the added distraction of the drama surrounding Derek and Kavya. Tim and Rose were completely taken up with preparations for the arrival of two babies.

"At some point, we all become consumed by some urgency of the moment, and we simply can't see anything else. In a bizarre coincidence of timing, those distracting claims on everyone's attention seemed to occur almost simultaneously. We *all* missed the obvious," Marilyn told him gently. "Maybe it was Gertie Gunn's detachment from everything happening in Tinkers Well that allowed her to see what we could not."

"Thank God for that," Miles said, "and thank God for you, my darling. I don't know what I'd do without you."

Albie Dawson had no wish to find out what he would do without the woman who had opened his heart to love again, either. Despite his inability to pinpoint exactly when it happened, Angelica Warner had become a part of the Dawson family. She and Albie found both companionship in their relationship and the blessing of trusted confidants, especially where their adult children were concerned. And just as Angelica had foreseen, the romance between Ronnie Dawson and Jamal Young met with opposition from Jamal's sister, Jada. She and Jamal were more than brother and sister; they were a tightly knit team that had suffered together and survived together. Jamal had found an identity and a life beyond that relationship. Jada had not.

She had never witnessed a healthy relationship between a man and a woman, and though protected in childhood, first by her grandmother and then by Jamal, Jada was left on her own to figure out the process of becoming a woman. The Marine Corps taught her to be tough and strong – so much so that Jada identified more with men than with women. She was more comfortable around men and worked in a man's world. When Jamal returned from Ecuador, Jada saw Ronnie only as an interloper, someone usurping her place as Jamal's best friend. Her hostility left Ronnie at a loss. It was Angelica who stepped in to do what only a mother could do. She took Jada under her wing and began to show the troubled young woman a different way of looking at her roles as sister and coworker. It didn't take Angelica long to realize the process would be a protracted and delicate one.

When Aletha's nightmare was uncovered, Angelica was torn between her allegiance to the Dawson family and her love for a dear friend. Albie recognized her struggle and gave her the freedom to put everything else on hold when the time came to leave the *Prairie Gateway* for the sake of another. He was a patient and a generous man, recognizing that rare treasures are worth waiting for. He would wait for Angelica until she was ready to return to her work at the hotel, to the Dawson family, to him. In the meantime, Albie set out to be a better role model for his own children, while helping Jamal and Jada understand how to relate to a father figure as God intended.

When Aletha was finally able to talk about the horror she had lived through, Angelica was by her side with Miles and Marilyn. Aletha's admission of her error in keeping the situation from Miles helped him to better understand how it had happened. "At first, I thought it was a lark," she confessed. "I foolishly thought I could outsmart Singleton. It didn't take long to figure out that she was stealing. But before I could report the theft to anyone, she began to make me question my own sanity. Never in a million years would I have believed that I could be the victim of gaslighting, but so it was. She cleverly cut me off from my family and friends by controlling the phone, the front door, and me. When I awoke to the knowledge that I was being drugged, it was too late. She must have done most of her work at night, knowing I would be out for hours. My inability to get out of bed in my doped state left me prey to a vicious UTI, and exposure to the night air exacerbated this wretched asthma I thought I had under control."

The lengthy speech exhausted Aletha, sending her into a coughing fit. Everyone was sent home when she resumed oxygen therapy after resorting to use of her inhaler. No other visitors were to be permitted until her symptoms improved and she was able to build up a little strength.

The upshot of the whole horrible episode was the exposure of as clever and ruthless a criminal as the prosecuted and imprisoned Inspector Dulac. A thorough search of Singleton's car and belongings unearthed a veritable treasure trove including silver, jewelry, oil paintings, and a rare coin collection belonging to the late Martin Mason. A police investigation revealed that Sheila Singleton, under several aliases, had been operating in multiple states for the past five years. Because it is often difficult to keep live-in employees for home healthcare agencies, background checks by numerous employers had been less than thorough. Local and state records set off no alarms because Singleton moved around regularly. She had always been careful to accept only wealthy, elderly patients who could be easily controlled, and whose incidental deaths could be attributed to natural causes, if such an event occurred during her tenure. When she agreed to take on Aletha Mason, she reckoned without Gertie Gunn. She would never be given the opportunity to make that mistake again.

While Aletha's condition continued to improve, with hope for a full recovery, Rose Ludlow showed signs of exploding with health. Her abdomen had grown so large and unwieldy, walking a straight line without waddling from side to side was a near impossibility. She had gained almost 40 pounds and began to wonder if she would ever feel human again. With four weeks to go before her due date, Rose had resorted to sitting and sleeping in Tim's worn-out recliner in the family room. It alone accommodated her bulk and offered relief from back pain.

Tim set up the family room with everything she needed to save her from unnecessary trips up and down the stairs. He was more worried about her than he let on. Despite recognizing that thousands of twins were born every year in the US, they weren't born to Rose, the person he loved above all others. Until he could hold those two tiny lives in his arms and know that she was safe, he insisted on her limiting any unnecessary activity. And until they could return to their attic retreat together, he would sleep on the couch in the family room next to the old chair.

The management of *Willow Walk* was effectively seized by Granny Gert, leaving Rose with little to do but make gentle suggestions. She asked her grandmother to go easy on seasoning (everything Gert cooked tasted too salty or spicy), and to wash clothes on a cooler setting (most of Tim's tee-shirts had shrunk a full size). When Rose asked to keep the front parlor curtains open, in direct opposition to her grandmother's insistence on drawing them closed an hour before dark, her request was met with a derisive snort.

"You know people have no business looking into other people's homes, young lady!"

Willow Walk was visible from the bypass in winter, and Rose liked to think passersby might be cheered by the sight of the house lit up for the season. Though the decorations were toned down quite a bit from the previous year, the house looked welcoming, all the same.

"Besides," Rose called after her grandmother as she left to do just as she pleased, "we hardly need to worry about privacy. Our closest neighbor lives half a mile away!" Then Rose thought of *Fern Cottage* on the other side of their driveway, standing alone in the darkness, and she was attacked by one of the mood swings common to pregnant women. She was still wiping her eyes when Granny Gert returned to close the blinds covering the wall of windows in what had been referred to as the Conservatory in grander times. Rose began a half-hearted explanation of the evidence of tears.

"No need to explain, Rosie. I'm worried about Letha, too. But she's a fighter. You just focus on bringing those young'uns into the world so they're ready to greet her when she's feeling better."

Concern for Aletha was only half the story. Rose was worried that her mother would not arrive in time for the delivery. Beth Thompson was in high demand at the moment. Rose's sister, Lily, was still expecting her first baby three days after her due date, but that little miss was slow to make an appearance. Beth promised Rose she would be on the first plane to Kansas City as soon as Lily and baby were settled at home. Knowing her emotionally demanding sister well, Rose was afraid that that level of comfort and security might not be achieved until Lily's daughter started kindergarten! Rose might have indulged in a pity party, but Tim walked through the kitchen door with her favorite Chinese takeout before despair could get a foothold. That was the day *Veritas Academy* opened its doors.

A week later, Aletha was settling once more into the life of *Fern Cottage.* She was free of infection, and her lungs were functioning well. She should have been pleased with the way she had bounced back from considerable trauma. She should have been relieved to be back in familiar surroundings with people she trusted and loved. She should have been energized by the sound of Scout happily sniffing around every corner and under every chair. But something had changed.

Miles seated her in her favorite chair and offered to fetch a cup of tea from the kitchen where Angelica could be heard puttering around, moving everything back to the locations Aletha was familiar with. The glaring reminder of the cruelty perpetrated against her gentle friend caused a cloud to pass over Angelica's usually sunny expression. She shook it off and had the tea ready when Miles rounded the corner to collect it.

The mistress of *Fern Cottage* was experiencing far more comfort than the mistress of *Willow Walk.* On that same Tuesday, Rose was given clearance by Dr. Hardesty to "sit back and let things happen." She had made it through the all-important 37th week of pregnancy with healthy blood pressure, little edema in the feet and ankles, and good strong heartbeats from both babies. "My, my, aren't you the exemplary patient. Why, you were born to have twins! Now remember, though the onset of labor is usually slow with a first pregnancy, it can go faster with twins. So, if you feel even the hint of a contraction, I want you to go straight to the hospital. And if by some miracle these two are still stubbornly refusing to join us by next Monday, I'll see you back in my office, and we'll decide what's best to be done." At Rose's look of dismay, Dr. Hardesty patted her hand and added, "There, there. No need to worry. I haven't lost a twin or a mother yet."

With Tim's help, Rose waddled to the truck after her appointment, wondering if she would be pregnant for the rest of her life.

Between them, the Hawthornes and Angelica set up a schedule of care so that Aletha would not be alone until a reliable, long-term solution could be reached. Her lack of energy concerned them all, though the doctor had warned that her body might recover more readily than her mind from the ordeal she had survived. He advised patience and love; they would reap far greater rewards than any modern medicine. Angelica stayed with her during the day and Miles and Marilyn came directly from work and spent the night. Friends stopped by, bringing gifts of flowers and reports of all Aletha had missed out on during her isolation. Gertie Gunn often joined them when she was sure Tim would be home with Rose. But despite their combined efforts, Aletha grew increasingly listless and withdrawn, requiring great coaxing by Angelica to even get out of bed each morning. It was almost as if she had given up on life.

Within days of her homecoming, Aletha received a visit from her attorney. When Angelica opened the door to him on Friday morning, she was surprised to learn that he had been summoned the day before. Aletha agreed to join him in the parlor after Angelica and Gertie convinced her that she would feel better for getting out of bed. They succeeded in getting Aletha out of her bedroom, but not out of her nightgown. Wrapping a warm robe around her, Angelica helped her to her chair while Gert fussed about her and settled her feet on a footstool. They would have left Aletha alone with her guest, but she stopped them, insisting they had a part to play in the visit.

"Trudy, you are one of my oldest and dearest friends, and Angelica, you have been an angel to me since Martin died. It is only right that you be the witnesses to my new will. I wanted to make a few changes to the existing one, so I called Mr. Roland yesterday, and he kindly consented to bring the updated document today. If you would just give us a few minutes to go over things, he'll call you when we're ready for the signing."

Fifteen minutes later, Angelica and Gertie Gunn entered the parlor with heavy hearts and dragging feet. They watched Aletha sign her name with the aid of a signature guide held in place by her attorney. Angelica blinked away a few tears and dutifully signed on the line over her printed name. With her lips pressed tightly together to hide her emotion, Gert followed suit on the line above "Gertrude 'Trudy' Gunn." With the completion of that grim task, she glanced at Aletha and was shocked to see the change in her friend. Aletha's expression showed traces of peace, though that peace was heavily overshadowed by exhaustion, and she somehow seemed to shrink into herself. Before she could stop it, a gasp escaped Gert's lips. Angelica quickly ushered the lawyer to the door and came back to help Aletha back to her bed. Worry over her friend's condition caused all thoughts of Rose, alone at *Willow Walk,* to be temporarily forgotten by her grandmother.

Tim had dropped Granny Gert at *Fern Cottage* on his way to the airport to collect Beth Thompson. An unexpected early snowstorm was already wreaking havoc in Harrington County. It downed a nearby power line, plunging Aletha's house into darkness. Tim was thankful to be onsite at the time so that he could ensure the upgraded generator, installed earlier that year, adequately maintained light and heat. He called Rose to confirm that backup power at *Willow Walk* had also kicked on automatically and asked her for the tenth time if she was okay. It was a miserable day with visibility dicey at best. He had almost decided to arrange a "Lift" ride for his mother-in-law, but Rose had assured him that she felt fine, and that she would rest easier knowing her mother to be in good hands with road conditions so poor.

Still not content with leaving her alone, Tim called to ask Derek if he would come over and wait with Rose until he returned from the airport with her mother. Though Derek would rather have spent a rare day off with Kavya than doing almost anything else, he agreed. He and Kavya had just been served a late breakfast at Milly's Diner.

"I know we were going back to your place after breakfast to help Lupe and Ani make Christmas cookies, but I think Tim is really worried about Rose, so I'm worried, too." Kavya tried to hide her disappointment, but after six months of intense study, Derek knew her too well to be fooled. "We'll just stay with her until he gets back from the airport. And there's no hurry. I'm not going anywhere until I eat breakfast."

"I don't know," Kavya said with uncertainty, "maybe you should just take me home first. I hardly know Rose, and I haven't exactly been an ideal guest on the few occasions we've met."

"Trust me. She'll be happy to see you." When Kavya still looked doubtful, he added "You should know that it was partly because of Rose and Amy Yousef that we got together in the first place." That got her attention. "Besides, Rose is crazy about me. I'm like the favorite older brother she never had. You'll see."

They were finishing a leisurely meal when Milly announced that the diner was closing early. "The storm is much worse than expected and I want to make sure my staff, and all of you, can get home safely."

When Derek and Kavya stepped out into the driving snow, his customary smile was tinged with uneasiness. Instead of moving quickly through the area, as predicted, the storm seemed to have stalled over Harrington County and points east, thanks to a secondary front from Canada dropping down to intercept it. He was glad they had left his truck at the Aguilar home and had driven Kavya's van into town. The added traction would come in handy. While he was peering into the blinding white veil, Kavya pulled up the weather map on her phone. Unfortunately, the blizzard was already impacting the cell signal. Before it scrambled completely, she caught a flash of the temperature. It had risen enough that the snow was now mixed with ice. It began to build up on the windshield as they drove, and Derek could hear the crunch under the tires. He only had a few miles to drive, but by the time he turned in through the gate to the Ludlows' driveway, he could barely see ten yards in front of him.

They were met at the kitchen door by Rose, clutching her belly. "Derek!" she said on a sob. "I've never been so glad to see anyone." Derek looked behind him to grin smugly at Kavya. The grin disappeared abruptly when Rose added, "I think the babies are coming, and I'm here all alone!" Kavya saw a terrified young woman, and any thoughts of embarrassment fled. She hurried indoors behind Derek. If anything, Rose seemed even more relieved to see her. Quickly removing her outer gear, Kavya sought to calm the young mother. Once more in the big recliner, Rose found some temporary relief.

"I swear I didn't feel *anything* this morning when Tim left. Nothing. And then about 30 minutes later, contractions started. By the time I admitted to myself that I was really in labor, I couldn't get through to him. I can't get in touch with Dr. Hardesty's office either, and this storm just keeps getting worse." Derek knelt beside her chair. Another contraction hit Rose, and she reached out in fear and desperation to clutch Derek's collar. "Derek, you're a fireman. *You have to deliver these babies!*"

His eyes grew to golf ball size as the blood seemed to drain from his rich, brown skin, leaving it pasty and clammy. "Rose, I love you like a sister, but I do *NOT* want to know you that well! Besides, I'm not an EMT. I don't *do* babies!" Rose started crying uncontrollably. "Calm down now, missy, calm down. We'll figure this out." When her pain subsided, Derek loosened the death grip on his collar and moved quickly out of reach. He considered their options while both women watched him, hoping for a miracle. His frown cleared as he snapped his fingers. "The phones may be out, but I've got a radio in my tr…" he began, then realized his truck was parked 15 miles away.

"Aren't you glad I grabbed it before we left?" Kavya said. "You're always telling me how important it is to have multiple lines of communication in case of a fire, though I don't see a fire making much headway in this weather…"

"I knew there was *some* reason I loved you," he said before running for the back door. He was speaking with 911 when he came back, liberally sprinkled with snow. "What do you mean all ambulances have been deployed in *four* counties? Over." He listened attentively while the groove between his eyes deepened. "Okay, I get it. But here's the situation." As succinctly and accurately as he could, he explained the emergency. He listened for a few seconds and shook his head, then looked at Rose. "Where is the contact information for your doctor's office?" While Kavya retrieved Rose's phone, Derek went on. "They can't get an ambulance here. Apparently, people are sliding off the roads everywhere, and accidents are piling up like dirty laundry." Rose looked up the number and handed it to Derek, who relayed the info to 911 along with his call sign. "Roger, I'll stand by."

Before he could explain what had transpired, another contraction seized Rose, and she was convulsed with pain. As soon as it passed, Kavya helped her to lie down on her left side on the couch. If he hadn't been so worried about Rose, Derek would have been bursting with pride over how Kavya was handling the situation. Her serenity in the face of hysteria helped Rose to relax and gave him the assurance he needed to hold everything together.

"Yes, I'm still here, 911, over." Derek listened for a few more minutes. "Roger, out." He looked gravely at Rose and forced a smile. "Now don't look like it's the end of the world. Thankfully, the 911 operator got through to your doctor's office. When she explained that you couldn't get to her, Dr. Hardesty started working on another option. There's a midwife who lives about 16 miles south of here near Pitkin Ford. It only got hit by the edge of the storm, so the roads should be passable. Her name is Anna Blaine, and she's on her way."

Tears of relief streamed from Rose's eyes until she recalled some of her research on twin births. "But it's not recommended that twins be delivered by a midwife. Not at home, anyway. There are too many possible complications." The tears started surging. "What are we going to do?" she wailed. Derek had been told much the same thing by the 911 operator.

With all his training in emergency situations, he felt powerless to help Rose. But he no longer had to carry the weight of leadership alone; God had given him a partner. Kavya went about quietly tidying the room and making Rose more comfortable by strategically placing pillows behind her back and between her knees. She found a tablet and began scribbling notes in columns. "The midwife will need to know how far apart the contractions are, and how long they last," Kavya said prosaically, as if discussing the proper planting of annuals in a flower bed. "Rose, do you have a waterproof pad? No? How about latex gloves?"

"I think Tim has some in his workshop in the garage."

"Derek," Kavya said, "You'll have to go find them and look for some large trash bags, too."

"If I go out there again, I'll come back looking like a *white* man!" Two sets of eyes glared at him. He obeyed without another word and before Rose could ask him when he thought Tim would get home. The operator had told him that all roads leading in and out of Kansas City to the west were a tangled mess. Derek knew Tim kept a radio in his truck, so he tried reaching him while out of range of Rose's ears.

Once inside Tim's shop, it took Derek three attempts, but he finally got through. "Oh, thank God!" Tim answered. "I've been worried sick about Rose. I know she was feeling okay this morning before I left, but the cell signal is non-existent, and I've been going through every worst-case scenario in my head. Derek, please tell me I'm an overanxious, first-time father who is letting all the snow and ice and crazy detours get to me. Please tell me she's sitting in my recliner, watching a Jane Austen movie for the tenth time. Over."

Derek only hesitated for a moment, but it was long enough. The gap told Tim everything Derek wanted to keep from him. One more panicked person would not help Rose. Before he could respond, Tim took a nosedive down a dark hole. "What's wrong? Derek, for God's sake, tell me *what's wrong!*"

"Buddy, *chill!* Rose is okay. Kavya is with her, timing her contractions. There's a midwife on the way, and I'm working on getting some incubators here in case the babies need to be transported. Don't ask me how – I don't even know myself. Do you have Rose's mom with you? Over."

"Yes. She was on the last plane that landed before the airport was closed. They can't keep up with the de-icing. But she made it, thank God. We're on our way back, but it's taking forever because we keep getting rerouted. Over."

"Good to know. Now standby. In a few minutes, I'm leaving your workshop which, by the way, is *freakishly* neat and clean, and I'm walking back to the house. I'll let you talk to Rose for a few minutes, but if you upset her any more than she already is, we're going to have a 'Come to Jesus' talk later. Over."

"I'll stand by. Over." True to his word, Derek made it back to the house and stomped to dislodge as much snow and ice from his boots as possible before turning the radio over to Rose. Tim was the essence of calm, promising to get there as soon as possible with Beth Thompson at his side. They might have spoken longer, but a contraction cut short their conversation. It was just as well. Derek's next call was to the fire chief.

A crew-cab pick-up truck made sluggish progress toward the Ludlow residence. Its bright red exterior put some heart into the driver. His wife, watching the road anxiously from the passenger's seat, was less assured. Fifteen or even ten years earlier, they might have faced the prospect of chasing a blizzard with the excitement of anticipated adventure. But they were no longer in their late twenties; they were approaching middle age with the wisdom to recognize the gravity of the situation rather than any inherent romance. A young, frightened mother needed Anna's help in what might prove to be a ticklish undertaking. Anna Blaine had been assisting with home deliveries for 12 years, but she understood the unique risks of this particular delivery better than most.

She and her husband, Mike, had left Pitkin Ford 20 minutes earlier with every expectation of reaching the Ludlow home in good time. They made it just three miles from their own driveway before the full force of the storm hit them squarely across their windshield. They pressed on. With only two miles left to their destination, the truck hit a slick spot and skidded sideways. Mike made a skillful recovery, but he wasn't about to count on surviving many more near misses. He couldn't see much of anything, but he knew precisely where he was.

"Anna, do you remember P.J. Murphy? He's the old guy who only comes to mass on Christmas and Easter since his wife died." One glance at her bewildered face, and he hurried on. "He lives just around the next bend." Approaching the curve carefully, he continued with extreme caution and eventually turned into a gravel driveway. "He doesn't know it, but he's about to be a fairy godfather."

Anna Blaine remained in the truck with the motor running while her husband disappeared into a small brick home crouched behind a row of barren poplar trees. Minutes later, Mike Blaine emerged from the house followed by a stooped old man wearing a plaid wool jacket with a trapper hat pulled over his ears. His muck boots made erratic progress through the deep snow on his way to a dilapidated barn a hundred yards behind the house. It took the combined efforts of both men to open the heavy barn door against the force of the wind. Mike held it open while P. J. carried a lantern into the barn's depths to reappear moments later driving a shiny green tractor that looked like it had just been purchased at a farm machinery show. Mike closed the barn door and followed the tractor on foot. When he reached the truck, he jumped inside and turned to his wife.

"Honey, I think the most important thing right now is to get you to your patient. That tractor can go places this truck can't. P.J. told me the house is just over half a mile due west across country. You can sit on the side seat he had installed for his grandkids. He'll be able to get you there faster than I will. Strap your essentials bag across you, and I'll follow with the bigger stuff. Okay?" He wasn't crazy about the idea, but Anna understood the need to get there as quickly as possible. She could improvise equipment setup, if necessary. Her husband wrapped her scarf tightly over her head and helped her on to the seat. He prayed as he saw them set off, then hurried back to the truck.

Tim caught a glimpse of writhing hands from the tiny corner of his right eye not focused directly in front of him. Beth Thompson, sitting silently beside him, peered through the icy windshield, following an irregular line of poles marking the edge of the narrow road. They had given up on conversation; they hadn't heard a thing from Derek – or Rose – in two hours. The tedious journey from Kansas City was almost at an end. One last turning would take them back onto the bypass. Beth almost cried out in relief when Tim pointed toward the intersection ahead. He didn't dare slacken speed before turning onto the larger surface because the feeder road accessed the junction from an incline. He prayed there were no other fools out in this weather, held his breath, and kept the truck steady through the turn. Almost there. He straightened the wheel and drove a quarter of a mile before he started tapping the brakes. Two cars had slid sideways and blocked both westbound lanes. Tim wanted to curse in frustration. The presence of his mother-in-law kept his tongue in check, coupled with the realization that losing his cool at this point could prove to be disastrous.

A bright spot appeared when he scrambled out of the truck to assess the situation. He had been able to keep the windshield fairly clear between the defroster and wiper blades working overtime. His peripheral view, however, had been obscured. Once free to look around, he saw that the blockage occurred just past a crossover accessing the eastbound lanes. Neither vehicle appeared to be occupied, and when he looked closer, he saw multiple sets of footprints headed toward a house set back from the road to the north. That gave him an idea. Without a word to Beth, he jumped back into the truck, reversed a little, turned onto the crossover, and pulled into what he knew to be the remnant of a driveway leading to the ruins of an ancient homestead.

"I'm afraid this is as far we can go in the truck," he said to Beth, who was beginning to show signs of panic. "I keep rubber boots for both Rose and me in the back. Do you feel up to walking the rest of the way?" It would be the worst mile he had ever walked in his life, but he had to get to Rose.

In a supremely courageous decision that would have amazed her daughter, Beth clamped her lips tightly together and nodded in the affirmative. She had seen desperation in Tim's eyes, and she would not add to his burden.

They had just walked back to the bypass when they heard a siren coming from the direction of Tinkers Well proper. A big, beautiful, blaring fire truck came down the wrong side of the highway like it owned the road. Tim flagged down the driver. A red pickup truck on his tail stopped too.

The engine operator lowered the window and yelled, "By any miraculous chance, are you Tim Ludlow?" When Tim grinned and saluted, the driver said to Beth, "Then you must be Rose's mother." Feeling as if she had just been asked to believe "six impossible things before breakfast,"[20] she laughed and curtsied.

The opposite door opened, and someone came around the big truck, directing Beth to climb up into the seat. Addressing the men in the backseat, he said, "You two get out and ride on the tailboard. Mr. Ludlow, you can help me steady these incubators. Derek Warner tells me you're about to have a very full house." Once underway, the chief asked, "How did you get past the barrier we dropped back at the entry to the bypass?" When Tim

---

[20] Lewis Carroll, *Alice's Adventures in Wonderland* (1865).

explained the detour, the chief replied, "Well, I'm glad GPS is updating quickly, at any rate."

It was quite a procession that announced the arrival of the expectant father and grandmother. At the sound of a siren, Derek put down the radio receiver with great relief and moved toward the family room door. Rose and Kavya helped him to understand that he would be allowed to leave only under penalty of dismemberment – or worse. Reluctantly resuming his post, he looked out the window to see two of his buddies unload an incubator and carry it toward the house. Tim and the chief followed with a second.

Presently a voice rang out. "Did somebody here call for the jaws of life?" Before he could stop himself, Derek acknowledged the warped first-responder humor with a shout of laughter. Rose was not amused.

"The jaws of life!" she shrieked in the middle of a particularly strong contraction.

With something like a Vulcan death stare leveled at him by Kavya, Derek asked, " *What?*" He gave up on expecting any rational response from the women. Advising the person on the other end of the radio communication to "stand by," he ran from the room to greet the cavalry. "Send me into a burning building any time you like, but don't *ever* ask me to do this baby thing again," Derek told Tim with feeling. "I've seen and heard more in the past three hours than I *ever* wanted to know. We're connected to Dr. Hardesty's office on a landline, thanks to a ham radio operator, so you can take over that, too."

"Derek, I don't know how to thank you…"

"You can thank me later," Derek said, pushing Tim toward the family room. "This is your baby now – literally. I think I'll just hang out here with the guys and drink coffee."

Tim's face expressed everything that needed to be said. He turned to Beth and gestured for her to proceed him.

"No, Tim. This time is for you and Rose. I'll be here if you need me." She kissed his cheek and sent him off, thankful for the man her daughter had married.

When faced with the decision to await another emergency call at the fire station or to accept the hospitality offered in the warm kitchen, Derek's fellow first responders opted for the latter. Once cleared for childbirth earlier in the week, Rose had started baking like crazy, so there were plates of cookies, granola bars, and blueberry-orange bread spread across the island countertop. Beth started a fresh pot of coffee after putting a pan of cocoa on the stove to heat. The impromptu gathering couldn't have been more successful if it had been planned. Derek gladly welcomed the predominantly male camaraderie, and Mike Blaine happily resigned himself to waiting for his wife until her job was done. With no reason to hurry back to an empty house devoid of heat, and knowing his prized tractor was settled snugly in the garage, Patrick Joseph Murphy made himself at home. He hadn't enjoyed himself so much in years! Beth began to work on sleeping arrangements for the suddenly augmented household.

Finally freed from his other duties, Derek soon made a dash to *Fern Cottage* with an overnight bag for Granny Gert and the news that Miles and Marilyn were advised by Tim to stay at home. There was little to report on the baby front; Rose was still in labor. By five o'clock, the wind ceased its howling, and much lighter flurries added the final touches to a blanket of white such as Eastern Kansas and neighboring Missouri had not seen in years. It was during the serene quiet of the silent snowfall that a fragile bleating cry heralded a new arrival.

If it is possible to have a perfect delivery, the birth of the Ludlow twins came close. None of the dreaded complications occurred. Dr. Hardesty listened in and provided direction as needed, but it was Anna Blaine who orchestrated the proceedings with confidence and professionalism. Kavya, working in the background, followed the process with awe. Her deft response to Anna's instructions proved to be invaluable and created a bond between herself and Rose that came as a surprise to them both.

In as privileged a position as any man ever holds, Tim witnessed the sacred ritual reserved for women since the dawn of time. He was humbled by the strength, stamina, and determination demanded of every mother who dares to bring a new life into a world at once alien and frightening. An innate, visceral love blocks the memory of pain, allowing her to instinctively cradle that life, protecting it from fear and want. Though he knew men to be the stronger sex physically, he couldn't imagine a man alive –himself included – who could endure what Rose had just gone through and arrive on the other side even more tender and loving than when the struggle began. And she had to do it twice.

One tiny baby girl made an appearance and nestled close to her mother, followed 20 minutes later by a little boy who was cradled against his daddy's chest, calmed by the steady beat of his heart. Though theirs was not a silent night, it was a holy night, set apart in time to honor the fulfillment of creation's mandate. They had been fruitful and multiplied, and they were richly blessed.

See, children are a gift from the Lord. The children born to us are our special reward.

Psalm 127:3 (NLV)

CHAPTER 19

"Go in peace! The two of us have vowed friendship in God's name, saying, 'God will be the bond between me and you, and between my children and your children forever!'"

1 Samuel 20:42 (MSG)

Cellphone service was soon restored after the wind abated, and the world was once more connected. Photo images flew between the Ludlows, anxious grandparents, and the inhabitants of *Fern Cottage.* Baby Boy and Baby Girl Ludlow weighed in at 5 pounds, 6 ounces and 5 pounds, 7ounces, respectively and passed all their newborn tests with flying colors. Anna Blaine spent the night in the family room with the babies and the parents to provide some medical oversight in the unusual situation. She couldn't have left the Ludlow home any earlier if she had wanted to. Snowplows and salt trucks worked around the clock for two days to clear at least one lane each way on four-lane state and federal highways, including the bypass into Tinkers Well. But secondary roads remained mostly impassable for almost a week.

As is often the case in the aftermath of an unusually early, exceptionally severe snowstorm, conditions normalized, temperatures returned to the 40s and 50s, and all evidence of the mother of all blizzards melted away into a soggy, sodden mess. Those who had gathered in the shelter of *Willow Walk* to assist in the arrival of its two newest inhabitants, found their various ways home with the help of tire chains and white-knuckle driving. There remained the family nucleus, who poured the energy of every waking moment (which seemed to take up the majority of every 24-hour period) into making the two tiniest Ludlows feel at home.

Each day passed in a surreal dichotomy of focus. Tim and Rose saw the future broaden exponentially before them. Those who sought to provide comfort and care for Aletha saw the future slipping away. When Beth Thompson returned to Kentucky a few days before Christmas, Miles told Tim that he and Rose should visit Aletha soon because there might not be many opportunities left to do so. Gert echoed the sentiment to her granddaughter, so Rose reluctantly left her sleeping babies in the care of their Hawthorne grandparents and set off with Tim on the short walk to *Fern Cottage.* Marilyn promised faithfully not to pick up either child unless she was wearing a mask. And Miles swore he would leave the thermostat at 72° with two humidifiers working overtime, making the family room of *Willow Walk* feel a bit like a tropical rainforest. Whether they followed the strict dictates or not, the nervous parents never knew. Those matters became less critical when the Ludlows were confronted with the image of Aletha lying in bed, a shell of the woman they remembered from just a few short weeks before.

Rose was immediately smitten by a sense of guilt for giving so little thought to anything but her own tiny family. She saw tears in Tim's eyes and knew he must be thinking the same thing. Those attendant on Aletha had intentionally spared the young parents any details about her condition. Let them revel in the joy of the moment; hard truths would confront them soon enough. When they saw Aletha, each wondered if she would ever leave her bed again. The change in her overall condition was shocking. Pronounced cheekbones made her flesh appear to be tautly pulled across her face. Her breathing, though steady, was shallow, and her voice was weak. The only color in her skin was reflected from the brightly colored throw laid across the bed. The essence of the room was that of a memorial chapel. Low lamplight created a subdued feeling of reverence, leaving the distant corners in shadow. Not a gleam was reflected in the heavy, ornate Victorian furniture, once the focal point of the room.

"Is that you, Tim? Rose?" Aletha's voice had always been gentle and soft, but it had resonated with life. Now it sounded thin and breathy.

Tim pulled a chair up to her bed and took her frail hand in his. "Of course it's me. Were you expecting some other handsome devil? I suppose you have a slew of men dashing in and out of here at all hours." His attempt at levity met with marginal success.

Aletha smiled wanly and replied with a hint of her former self, "You sound just like your grandfather. You never knew him, but he used to tease me all the time." She fell silent for a few minutes, then spoke softly, as if to herself. "He was a good man, and he would have been so proud to know you." It was almost a benediction. Tim looked at Rose, who had taken Aletha's other hand. Silent tears ran down her cheeks. He wasn't ready for this. Not now, not when there was so much to celebrate.

"I'd like to think he would have approved of his great-grandchildren, too." Despite knowing how terrified Rose was of exposing the twins to any germs beyond the confines of their new home, Tim, nevertheless, wanted them to be connected to their ancestry, to somehow receive the blessing of Aletha's generation while they still could. He glanced at his wife and was surprised to see her nodding and smiling through her tears. "Aletha, we think it's high time you got to know your great-grandchildren. You can't let Granny Gert have all the fun." He was encouraged by her gentle smile. "Would it suit your busy social schedule if we brought the babies by tomorrow?"

"Now, there's the ticket!" Gert said from the doorway. "I'd say that's an excellent idea. Maybe we'll finally get to learn the names of those young'uns. I told you, Letha, these two have been keeping that information under wraps like it was a state secret."

"What a lovely surprise. I would be quite pleased to receive them," Aletha said formally, with the shadow of a twinkle in her eye. The Ludlows soon took their leave, promising to return with their offspring.

As soon as they left the cottage, Rose went full "mama bear" mode and started worrying about exposing the babies' lungs to the cold outside air and wondering whether their frail immune systems were up to a new environment. Finding both babies still sleeping soundly side-by-side, while their grandparents sat reading nearby, calmed some of her fears. When the time came to make the short trip to *Fern Cottage* the next day, Tim warmed up their new van to sauna level before he and Miles each carried a baby outside in their respective car seats, covered with a blanket to keep out any cold air.

When they pulled up to Aletha's house, Tim and Rose were a little surprised to see an unfamiliar car parked next to Angelica's. Miles didn't appear surprised at all. The babies took the short journey in stride until they were lifted out of the snug security of their car seats. Two plaintive cries announced their arrival. While the anxious parents tried to calm their children, Marilyn came into the parlor to advise them that Dr. Benson, a member of Community Church and a good friend, had stopped by to check on Aletha and to wish her a Merry Christmas. They were all grateful for his kindness, though they realized that the latter hope was unlikely.

The babies were still fussing when they entered Aletha's room, but the sound was like the song of an angel choir to the shrunken old woman lying in a welter of blankets. She smiled sweetly and took a deep breath when instructed by Dr. Benson. He listened to her lungs, then checked her pulse before laying her hand to rest atop the other. Looking at Miles, he gave a barely perceptible shake of the head and retreated to a corner, allowing the others to draw closer.

A little unsure of himself, Tim instinctively walked to the bed and moved his grandmother's arm so that he could lay the whimpering baby next to her side. "Aletha, I'd like you to meet Peter… Miles… Ludlow." He heard a sharp intake of breath from the foot of the bed and turned to see Miles nodding his head in delight, while his lips trembled with suppressed emotion. Aletha repeated the name softly and touched the little boy's head, making soothing sounds of comfort. He nestled into the curve of her arm. Her gentle fingers found evidence of the Hawthorne family legacy in his tiny cleft chin.

Rose placed the baby girl on Aletha's other side. "And this little lady is Trudy… Beth… Ludlow." Granny Gert could not contain a chortle of glee even as she mopped tears from her cheeks.

"A perfect name. The world needs more Trudys," Aletha said and spoke softly to the tiny baby. As if by magic, little Trudy also grew quiet and lay perfectly content at Aletha's side.

"I am so blessed to know these two. Thank you, Tim and Rose, for granting me this privilege. And now, while you're all here, I want you to know of some special bequests I wish to leave." Any pall that might have fallen over the room was forestalled by the sight of both fragile stages of life drawing comfort from one another, holding any gloom at bay. Most of the bequests were known or expected. One was not. Angelica was puzzled when Aletha asked her to come nearer.

"My friend, you musn't think there's anything I expect from you but your friendship," Angelica said, troubled that Aletha would think otherwise.

"Don't worry yourself, Angelica. I know you to be the most selfless of women. You have watched over me for years, asking nothing in return. Now I am asking you to do one more thing for me, as my friend. Would you help me to dispose of this house? I have accepted the fact that I will not live here much longer, and *someone* must have it."

"Aletha, you know I would do anything for you, but how can you ask me to take *Fern Cottage* from you… Besides, I know nothin' of real estate."

Aletha's features adopted a familiar mischievous look. "You won't be taking it from me. I have already signed the title over to Timothy, but he has promised to *sell* it for the exact amount of one dollar… to you. I don't want you saddled with inheritance taxes." She was pleased to hear Angelica gasp. "Yes, my friend, I want you to have *Fern Cottage.* It should be yours. And before you tell me you don't *need* a house, I'll remind you of a certain young man who will soon be getting married. *He* will need a home for his new family. I'll let the two of you sort that out." Too overwhelmed to speak, Angelica kissed Aletha's cheek and moved to stand by Marilyn, her head in a whirl.

Other than a generous gift to Abraham Yousef's college ministry, the rest of the bequests were much as they had been. Having discharged her burden, Aletha closed her eyes and appeared to doze off. Tim and Rose reclaimed their babies, allowing Dr. Benson to again assess Aletha's condition. An uncertain frown clouded his face. He listened once more to her breathing, then quickly checked her pulse, and his frown deepened. He looked up and motioned the others to leave the room. But Granny Gert tarried. After everyone departed, she sat on the edge of Aletha's bed and took her hand.

"Letha, you've got be strong, do you hear me? You can't just give up, not when there's so much to live for! I can't teach those babies everything they need to know by myself. Who will help me tell them about the old days when we didn't have cellphones, or satellites, or microwaves? Who will help me explain rotary-dial phones and TV sets with only three channels? How will they learn that board games are more fun than video games or understand what writing letters is all about?" Tears of despair began to fall. "And who will show them what it means to have a friendship that lasts a lifetime? And then there are their parents – they're bound to get into a kerfuffle again and need sorting out. *They* need you, Letha. *I* need you," Gert pleaded. "*Please* don't go. Please don't leave me…"

She wept softly, certain that only God could hear her now.

Winter settled in with its customary cold and damp. Barren trees stretched their crooked fingers toward a leaden sky. Another snowstorm would have alleviated the desolate ugliness of dormant fields, but instead, a driving, relentless rain fell, leaving the landscape dotted with muddy puddles. There was little to recommend the season other than the necessity of staying at home, close to a warm hearth.

No such luxury was afforded an elderly woman making her way to the front of Community Church on a bleak January day that might have been fashioned expressly for a funeral. Overcast skies allowed very little natural light through the stained-glass windows, and gaudy, hothouse flowers looked out of place sprawled across a simple casket. Soft organ music could be heard in the background. At best, the old woman tolerated organ music, but she hated the use of what Aletha Mason had once explained to her as the *vibrato* stop. Gertie Gunn preferred to think of it as the "wa wa wa," and she fervently wished it *would* stop. The undulating sound reminded her of baseball parks and the roller-skating rinks of her youth. Upon reaching the casket, she touched the lid – the only link to a life now gone. Presently, she was joined by another woman seated in a wheelchair. An obliging usher had kindly guided her to the front of the line of mourners.

"Maybe it's wrong to say so, but I think this was a blessed release for her."

The woman in the wheelchair nodded in agreement. "I believe you're right. Poor Eleanor, I'm not sure she even knew who she was in the end," she said, followed by something that sounded like "Stk, stk, stk."

Gertie Gunn considered the face before her, so serene and carefree in death. "Oh, I don't know. I think, in her mind, she became the girl she once was. I remember her telling me once, when she was randomly hopping from topic to topic – you know how she did – that she loved to make snow angels.

She probably looked outside during the night after the big storm and saw fields of white just asking to be 'snow-angeled.'"

"Very likely, I should think," agreed her companion. "Bobby Taylor was amazed that she found the key for the front door and manipulated the dead bolt with such ease. I suppose that was due to one of those flashes of memory when her brain functioned quite lucidly."

"*Lucidly?*" Gert snorted. "The woman went outside in the dead of night wearing only her pajamas, then proceeded to make snow angels all over the front yard. She wasn't even wearing shoes!"

"That's true. But in her befuddled state, the process probably made perfect sense to her. It may have been the cold that finally confused her so, and that's why they found her down the road, laying in the snow half frozen."

"I suppose we'll never know. It's a miracle she lived as long as she did, what with pneumonia, overexposure, and the like." Gert touched the casket one last time in farewell. "I'm glad Herbie and Bobby had her laid out with her swimming medals. That's one memory that stayed with her to the end."

Gert took the handles of the wheelchair and began pushing it toward the foyer, where the elevator stood ready to take them to the fellowship hall in the basement. The much-needed lift had mercifully survived the fire in good working order.

"If anyone had asked me a few weeks ago whose funeral I'd be attending now, I'd have said yours. I truly thought you had slipped away while I was sitting there, blubbering like a silly fool. How was I supposed to know you were just sleeping? Doctors should never be allowed to frown like that! I thought Bill Benson shooed everyone out the door to tell them the worst — not that you'd had a sudden turnaround after holding those blessed babies or that your pulse was strong and steady."

"But Trudy," Aletha Mason protested, "you must have known I would never leave you without saying goodbye. Besides, *I was tired.* It was the end of a *very* hectic year!"

"Well, I'll grant you that, but what was all the business with your will and bequests and such?"

Once more the mischievous look appeared. "I simply wanted Angelica to know that Derek would have a home for his family. He did most of the work on the additions last summer, almost as if he was preparing for a future he was – at the time – unaware of." She paused, and the twinkle in her eye became more pronounced. "It was rather a good scene, wasn't it?"

"Letha, you scamp!"

They entered the fellowship hall to be greeted by as unique and faithful a circle of friends as anyone could hope for. Farmers, a retired investment banker, a wealthy widow, a poor spinster, a rabbi's daughter, Christians and Jews. All had found a home and a place in the community of Tinkers Well, Kansas. They parted after the wake for Eleanor Stratton with plans for future gatherings. Gertrude "Trudy" Gunn, who had added such life and meaning to those who were privileged enough to claim her friendship, promised to return to celebrate the first birthday of Little Trudy and Peter in eleven months, if not sooner. They all rather hoped it would be sooner.

EPILOGUE

Muted light glimmered through the windows of *Willow Walk,* shedding its soft radiance across the front porch, where fading daylight cast friendly shadows beyond the railing. The shadows deepened and crept across the garden, setting the central fountain and surrounding trees and shrubs into ghostly silhouette, though the stark outline of branches was already blurred by the eruption of spring foliage. The receding glow gave way to fairy lights dancing in the evening breeze, their solar-powered bulbs providing an ethereal quality to a landscape emerging from winter sleep. In early April, no crickets broke the silence of the evening, only nesting birds settling down for the night.

Another Resurrection Day had been honored and celebrated, and Tim and Rose Ludlow sat on the porch swing to enjoy a rare moment of peace and quiet, left alone after the last of their guests had departed. Not content with merely holding his wife's hand, Tim pulled her legs across his lap so that she could nestle into his embrace, with her head against his accommodating shoulder. His sweater smelled of baby food and diaper wipes. Rose thought the combination irresistibly sexy. Her husband was never more attractive to her than when she watched him playing on the floor with his children or rocking them to sleep, crooning silly, made-up songs. A sweet smile played about her lips, and without thinking, she began moving her hand across her swollen abdomen. The gentle circular motion had become as natural to her as breathing.

Tim covered her hand with his own and murmured into the silky softness of her hair, "Are we ready for this again?"

Her smile broadened. "I think we have to be. This little man will be with us in two months. But think how much easier it will be this time. Keeping one infant happy, fed, and cuddled will feel like a walk in the park after doing the same for two. And Trudy and Peter are blessedly sleeping through the night now."

"Thanks to my brilliant pre-bedtime routine."

"You mean getting them so stirred up they run endless laps around the first floor until they're so tired they fall asleep while you're carrying them upstairs?"

"Can *I* help it if you married a genius?" Rose's answering giggle warmed Tim's heart in a way nothing else could. "After all the excitement today, they ought to sleep till *noon* tomorrow!"

"I'll bet Ani Warner will too. She's always happy to play 'big sister' to the twins…"

"…egged on by 'Daddy Derek'…"

"… which will serve as good practice for them both. Kavya's baby will be here before they know it; September isn't that far away." Rose couldn't help laughing as she recalled Derek's dismay at being a part of her own birthing experience. "I hope he toughens up a little by then. Kavya won't let him off the hook when it's their turn to go through labor and childbirth!"

"Well, he's got five months to get used to the idea." Tim grinned into the darkness. "He told me Kavya is already making him watch videos of delivery techniques."

Rose laughed at that. "I know. I can almost hear him saying 'Oh! *That* can't be right!'" She felt the answering rumble of laughter deep in Tim's chest. They swung in silence for a while, perfectly content. Presently she commented, "Isn't it amazing?"

"Mmm?" As often happened, when Tim shared a golden moment with his wife on the front porch, he was inspired, by her inviting proximity, to begin systematically nibbling her ear lobe and neck.

"Tim, are you listening?" Just as often, Rose found it challenging to follow her train of thought while he pursued a very different one.

"I'm listening," he mumbled while his deliberate movement found its way to her shoulder. "Despite what women say to the contrary, men *can* multitask. We just need sufficient motivation."

Since she could find no real fault with such rationale, Rose continued to ponder aloud. "I believe it was the chaos and uncertainty of that wild winter night 16 months ago that led Kavya to change her education plans. Now, instead of pursuing cold, impersonal science, she wants to be a nurse practitioner, and in a rural setting, no less. I think I've seen more of a change in Kavya than in anyone I've ever known. I remember when we first met. Amy and I wondered what Derek could possibly see in her. In fact, we had a hard time believing we would ever be Kavya's friends. And now the three of us have such a close bond, we feel like sisters, especially since we're all sharing motherhood, or at least, almost. I was a little worried about Amy after her miscarriage last winter, but she and little Miss Yousef appear to be a model team. With their first baby on the way, I think Amy would like to… Tim, are you still listening?"

"Model team," he whispered in her ear, sending a shiver down her spine.

"As I was trying to add," Rose managed with some difficulty, "I think Amy would like to change her work schedule to allow more time at home. She has often mentioned the desire to focus on private music lessons in her home studio. I honestly think that was tied to the idea of having kids. That way, she would only need a babysitter for four or five hours a week. And since Abe started receiving that generous increase to his ministry stipend, I believe they'll manage it. I wonder if that 'bequest' Aletha mentioned wasn't at least partially earmarked for that, to be administered *before* her death.

What do you think? Tim?" When she received no answer, she turned to look at him. "Tim, I am trying to get your attention!"

A little indignantly, he responded, "Well, *I'm* trying to get *yours!* The kids are asleep, the house is empty of visitors, and the night is young. We should 'make hay while the sun shines,' as they say."

Rose giggled again and patted his hand still resting on her belly. "I might point out," she said, with a hint of irony, "that there doesn't appear to be a shortage of 'hay' in the Ludlow home." Tim's grin shone in the half-light.

"Point taken," he said and carefully shifted her legs off his lap. When she looked indignant, he explained politely, "I'm sorry, but you distract me." He turned his head to look straight ahead as if standing at attention. "Okay, I'm all ears. What other theory have you to postulate, my darling wife?"

"*Postulate a theory* – very impressive."

"Did you like that? I thought it sounded rather erudite. Spending time with Miles has broadened my vocabulary substantially. I can almost keep up with Abe now." He chuckled softly. "Did you know that he 'reads' the Bible to the baby every night? She'll probably be born reciting all 150 Psalms. Moving on, what secret have you winkled out of Derek and Kavya? (That expression is courtesy of Aletha.)"

"Tim Ludlow, I do not *winkle!* I don't have to – I simply listen and learn. For instance, did you hear that Albie Dawson is taking the whole family – his kids, their families, and Derek, Kavya, and Ani – to Jamaica in June as a belated wedding gift to Angelica?"

Tim snorted derisively. "How could I *not* hear? Derek reminded me five times today." Narrowing his eyes thoughtfully, he mused, "I wonder if I could convince Miles to make such a grand gesture…"

"Well, not any time soon." Rose reminded him, rubbing her belly again. "We're going to be very busy for a while. And Granny Gert is coming back in June to help me with the baby, though I suspect she and Aletha are already plotting some hair-raising scheme." The twinkle faded from her eyes as she frowned into the shadows. "I probably shouldn't say things like that. Every time I see Granny Gert, she looks a little older and moves a little slower. I know I can say the same of Aletha, but we see her nearly every week, so the changes are more subtle. I do believe her move to the new retirement-slash-assisted living residence last year was a blessing. I know she's a little self-conscious about the name Miles chose for the facility, but *Mason Manor* does have a nice ring to it. And he honored the legacy of the Cooper family by incorporating architectural elements of the old farmhouse into the new building. Or I should say, you did."

"I did, though that wasn't the original plan. He wanted the farmhouse to be the center of the two wings, but it would have been impossible to tie that old building into a modern one and have any hope of meeting code. It did turn out pretty well, though, if I do say so myself, and I think Miles agrees."

Rose laughed. "You *think?* He brags about your work to everyone – as he should. I'm just glad your folks live so close to Aletha now. I have a feeling Miles reserved the nicest house in the new subdivision surrounding the school for him and Marilyn. With the field behind them still empty, their place has the feel of living in the country while still being close to town – lucky for them!"

"Lucky, my foot!" Tim declared. "He planned that all along – and broke ground on the school – months before Mom agreed to marry him. My father is no fool, and he's no coward either. He would have pursued her as long as it took. He planned every detail down to where they would live, and the need to purchase the empty field along that border. I'm just glad it was sooner rather than later and that they've finally found lasting happiness together."

"Me too. I'm also glad that Three Brothers is doing so well. With the town growing like it is, I can't imagine that will ever change." Rose had once again snuggled close to her husband, contemplating the future with great satisfaction. Tim saw things from a slightly different perspective.

"Hmm," he said and frowned. "You're right, of course. Tinkers Well *is* growing, but the 'Three Brothers' we know has already lost one brother, though I can hardly grudge Abe his life choices. The man is on *fire!* Between ministering to Muslim students and digging into biblical history and theology, he'll probably have his own podcast before long. And next month, he'll be throwing the title of Father into the mix."

"You know, I think the wildest aspect of his testimony," said Rose, "is the way a young, former Muslim man has opened the minds of an elderly Jewish couple, challenging them to consider a different understanding of Messiah. Amy told me the Rosenbaums agreed to join them in attending a Messianic Jewish Synagogue in Kansas City for their next Sabbath. I can't wait to hear how *that* turns out."

Tim laughed. "I am no longer surprised at what Abe has accomplished. He is an amazing man and a good friend." After a pause, he added, "And then there's Derek."

Rose sat up, attempting to read Tim's face in the waxing moonlight. "What about Derek?"

"With Tinkers Well growing like it is, I think we'll eventually need a full-time fire department, or at least a partial full-time crew. And I know how much Derek loves that work. I suspect he may want to make that his long-term career. And if I'm completely honest, I can't think of anyone better suited to it."

Leaning against her husband once more, with his arm around her, Rose reflected, "Well, at least they'll all still be living in Tinkers Well."

Absently playing with Rose's curls, Tim commented, "True. If we must have change – and I know that's the essence of life – at least we have our family of friends around us. God is good."

"All the time," Rose responded. It was as peaceful a moment as anyone could hope for. Then, without warning, the peace was broken by an insistent poking at her side. A gurgle of laughter escaped her smiling lips as a thought struck her.

"And what is so funny?" her husband asked suspiciously.

Rose stood suddenly and pulled Tim to his feet. "I was thinking that even if you get down to *one* brother, the business will always be *Three Brothers Construction Inc.* to honor its foundation in friendship. And, who knows, *one day* you may have three *Ludlow* brothers working for you."

"I like where you're going with this…"

"So, *maybe,* "Rose said, twining her arms around Tim's neck, "we should practice a little of that 'hay making,' as you suggested."

Tim brushed a stray curl from her cheek and gently stroked each flawless feature of her beloved face. "Have I told you recently," he said tenderly, "that the day you barged into my life on this very porch, when the roof was falling in and you nearly stepped through a rotten spot in the floor, that was the day I finally understood what it meant to fall in love."

Rose ruffled his hair and traced the cleft in his chin. "As a matter of fact, no, you haven't," she replied, in a way that set his heart pounding "But I'll remind you the next time I do something that drives you nuts." Tim lowered his head in answer to his wife's inviting smile, when…

First one, then another fussy cry could be heard clearly through the baby monitor sitting on the porch rail.

Tim dropped his head onto her shoulder, muttering, "You have *got* to be kidding me…"

Laughing, Rose kissed his cheek and reached for the monitor. "Hold that thought, Daddy." He did. Thirty minutes later, after peace had been restored to the nursery, she followed her husband to their attic retreat, where he expanded on his original thought, arguing strongly in favor of total surrender. Though she put up a teasing show of protest, she quickly agreed to his very persuasive suggestions with alacrity.

Reflecting on all the miracles that had brought them together, planned and executed by their sovereign God and Savior, Tim and Rose Ludlow, and their many friends in and around Tinkers Well, looked to the future with confident expectation. Their assurance lay not in the belief that life would be without struggle or pain. Rather, each stood on the promise that, no matter what lay ahead, God's steadfast love and direction would go before them and walk beside them always.

And while they did not live "happily ever after" – that is the myth of fairy tales – they *did* live joyfully and faithfully… and abundantly!

ABOUT THE AUTHOR

Linda Edmister is a self-proclaimed lifelong vagabond. She has lived on four continents and made a home for her Army husband and their two children in 13 different residences over 45 years of globe-trotting. She is a former US Army Major, State Department Community Liaison Officer, and Church Music Director, and holds a Bachelor of Arts degree and a Master of Music degree. Her favorite authors are Agatha Christie and Georgette Heyer. When not teaching piano lessons or volunteering in her church library, Linda enjoys gardening, travel, and Bible study.